# H M S  MARATHON

For the first time Thurston was afraid. *She's going to turn over.* He grasped the stanchion with both hands, pulled and then pushed to get his legs clear, got one foot on to the thing, bounced off the topmost rail, kicked the other foot away and toppled backwards into the sea. He gulped in air, then found he was breathing water. With a roaring in his ears the ship turned over on top of him; he struck out with his arms but *Connaught* was more powerful than he; she was taking him down. Pain in the ears, crushing pain in the chest, terror; this was what it was like to drown.

# H M S  MARATHON

## A. E. Langsford

*Trail all your pikes, dispirit every drum,*
*March in slow procession from afar,*
*Be still the hautboie and the flute be dumb,*
*Be silent, ye dejected men of war!*
*Display no more, in vain, the lofty banners,*
*For see! where on the bier before ye lies,*
*The pale, the fall'n, the untimely sacrifice,*
*To your mistaken shrine, to your false idol, Honour.*

*The Soldier's Death* by Anne Finch,
Countess of Winchilsea

**ARROW BOOKS**

Arrow Books Limited
20 Vauxhall Bridge Road, London SW1V 2SA

An imprint of the Random Century Group

London Melbourne Sydney Auckland
Johannesburg and agencies throughout
the world

First published in Great Britain in 1989
by Barrie & Jenkins Ltd
Arrow edition 1990
© A. E. Langsford 1989

Phototypeset by Input Typesetting Ltd, London.

Printed and bound in Great Britain by
Cox & Wyman Ltd, Reading

ISBN 0 09 968290 7

*To Mary*

## Acknowledgements

The author particularly wishes to thank Dr J. S. Munro, Mr B. T. Dodd and Mrs M. E. Lyon for their help with the medical aspects researched for this novel.

# — Prologue —

## HMS *Connaught*, November 1940

'I'm going below, Mr Galbraith. Call me as usual.'

'Aye aye, sir. Goodnight.'

Thurston took a last look around the bridge as he made for the ladder. The Officer of the Watch saying something to the Sub-Lieutenant who was seconding him preparatory to standing a watch himself, the Sub listening carefully and nodding, his round boyish face pale against the dark blue of his greatcoat collar. Galbraith was an RNR lieutenant; it always surprised Thurston that he was actually older than himself, and had commanded his own ship until the war made him a junior watchkeeper in a light cruiser.

He descended the ladder to his sea cabin, pulled off his boots, stretched out on his bunk. With any luck he could sleep undisturbed until Dawn Action Stations. Five days from now he would be on leave, the ship would be in dockyard hands for the first time since the war began. *Connaught* was an old ship, first commissioned in 1917 and good only for convoy and blockade work in this war. Fourteen months of sheer grinding hard work, with barely a sniff of the enemy to break the monotony. But the signal had finally reached her at Gibraltar, ordering her return. Thurston thought with pleasurable anticipation of the leave to come, fourteen lovely days.

He never knew what brought him awake, but he found himself instantly, terribly aware that something was wrong. The readings on the course and speed indicators on the bulkhead were as they should be, the gyro emitted its regular ticking, a sudden gust wailed through the ventilator, but the unease remained. He squinted at the luminous dial of his watch: 2341; he had been below precisely half an hour. *This is bloody ridiculous.* But he got up, distrustingly, and started for the bridge. He would see the change of watches, satisfy himself that all was well, then resume his interrupted sleep.

The impact came when Thurston was halfway up the ladder. For a moment he retained his balance on one foot, body swinging outwards from one arm, then found himself falling, and landing in a heap of limbs against the bulkhead. His first thought was that *Connaught* had collided with something, but she was not in company, and this was not a convoy route. A moment later the ship heeled again; there was the muffled sound of an explosion. *We've been torpedoed*, he thought, unexpectedly calmly. The ladder was no longer vertical. He grasped the handrail, pulled himself up, slipped on the heeling deck and hung on. The ship lurched again, the other way. She was settling very fast, his seaboots slipped on the rungs, one hip hurt where he had landed on it, the heaving pulled at his shoulder sockets as he worked his way up the ladder, finally grasped the edges of the hatchway.

Galbraith shouted in his ear. 'The stern's gone,' the usual courtesies forgotten. Thurston turned his head aft over the bridge screen, saw with the same unreal calmness that beyond the after funnel there was nothing save a few shreds of twisted metal, silhouetted grotesquely against the palely starred horizon.

'Pipe Abandon Ship.' Then to the Sub, 'Muster the confidential books and ditch them.' This was the final acknowledgement that *Connaught* was lost, the jetti-soning of her codes and ciphers.

Automatically Galbraith flipped open the engine-room voicepipe to give the order. The sound which met their ears was compounded of screams and hammering, frantic shouts as men fought one another aside in their efforts to escape the rising water. 'Stop your shoving and let go! I was here first!' The voice reached a child-ish wail, changed abruptly to a scream, and was then lost in the rush of water.

Around Thurston men were moving towards the rails. There seemed very few of them. But the world shrank to his immediate vicinity. He found himself taking out his penknife and hacking with it at the lash-ings of a Carley float, without knowing how he came to be there. The knife broke, the blade spinning upwards, narrowly missing the eyes of the seaman alongside him, then falling with a clatter to the deck. Thurston found to his surprise that he felt no fear; it was all too sudden, too unreal. The seaman was still at work on the lash-ings, cursing richly and fluently. There was another lurch, the beginnings of a roll to starboard. The Carley broke free and Thurston jumped aside to avoid it as it toppled from its mounting.

'Off you go.'

The man made for the rails, sliding rather than walking. Small red lights from life belts were beginning to dot the water.

'She's going,' someone shouted.

He found himself skidding towards the rails as the remains of the ship heeled; pain flashed from his groin as he was brought up short with one leg crooked around the stanchion and the other hanging over the side. The water was very cold, waves sloshing as far as his thighs. For the first time Thurston was afraid. *She's going to turn over*. He grasped the stanchion with both hands, pulled and then pushed to get his legs clear, got one foot on to the thing, bounced off the topmost rail, kicked the other foot away and toppled backwards into the sea. He gulped in air, then found he was breathing water. With a roaring in his ears the ship turned over on top of him; he struck out with his arms but *Con-naught* was more powerful than he; she was taking him down. Pain in the ears, crushing pain in the chest, terror; this was what it was like to drown.

Then he was on the surface, without knowing how, thinking stupidly that heaven could not possibly be as cold and wet as this, gasping out quantities of water. His arm met something solid, he got hold of it, dragged himself across the providential piece of broken hatch cover, clinging on until the paroxysms ceased, gulping in great lungfuls of gloriously sweet night air. Training took over once more; he mumbled words of thanks to the God he wasn't sure he believed in, kicked off his seaboots, got rid of duffel coat and jacket, fumbled for an age with his lifebelt before he got it inflated. He started to swim, counting heads, here and there towing a man to a Carley. He found Galbraith, floating upright in his lifebelt, shook him when he did not reply. Galbraith's head lolled forward over his chest, his neck broken.

On the rafts they were singing, the same song, again and again.

*Underneath the arches, I dream my dreams away,*
*Underneath the arches, on cobblestones I lay . . .*

'Bloody cold, innit?'

At first he welcomed the numbing of the pain in his groin and hip, but it was the cold which killed. One by one men died; first the men in the water, then men on the rafts, all through the long night, quietly for the most part. By dawn there were thirty-two left.

*Underneath the arches, I dream my dreams away . . .*

Once it was daylight they paddled to the other raft, which had drifted a full half-mile away, looked at each other in dull horror, each seeing himself in the fuel-coated wraith opposite, got the rafts lashed together.

Thurston organised guessing games with vigorous forfeits, examined each man orally for his next rate, had them each choose a subject and lecture the rest on it, with questions to follow. He set lookouts, paired the men off to watch each other, keep each other awake. He inspected feet twice daily, started quizzes, singing, went through all the poetry he could remember, anything to fight the easy apathy which meant death. Life and death were no longer a matter of the body, but became a thing of the mind. One of the first to die had been a PTI who was a former naval heavyweight champion. Some men found hidden reserves. Someone raised the day's first laugh by complaining loudly that he had 'fucking lost my false fucking teeth, the only ones that ever fucking fitted'. One man started to teach the rest French, a band corporal lectured on harmony and counterpoint. Someone imitated all the characters of ITMA, another told dirty jokes hour by hour.

*The paybob went to market, and bought a side of beef, a crate of beer, a house in the country, a silk ensign, two hundred ticklers . . .*

Feet. White, swollen bladders like lumps of lard, robbed of all feeling. No pain, only numbness now, a creeping lassitude.

*The paybob went to market and bought a side of beef, a crate of beer, a house in the country, a silk ensign, two hundred ticklers, a packet of three, a pound of Stilton, twelve dancing girls, a cathouse in Soho . . .*

On the first day the men had been quite cheerful, could be pushed into activity without too much difficulty; expected to be picked up before long. Thurston kept to himself the facts that there had not been time to get off a distress signal, they were seven hundred miles south-west of Bantry Bay, off a regular convoy route, and the drift was taking them further out into the Atlantic. The Sub-Lieutenant died on the third day. Nineteen years old, his stiffened body tipped off into the grey water like others before. Morgan lay wedged against the coaming, muttering to himself in Welsh.

11

*Je vais, Tu vas, Il va, Elle va, Nous allons . . .*

The lectures had grown more esoteric; one man explained how to repair a lavatory cistern, another about pruning roses.

*Pardon, monsieur, où se trouve le consul Britannique?*

A man went mad, screamed at him in incoherent fury, stood up, almost overturning the raft, leapt into the sea and was gone before anyone could get to him.

By the fourth night there were twenty-three left. Horizons had shrunk, they had split into tight little huddles, mostly just one man and his chosen mucker. Thurston and Jeffries, the band corporal, teamed up, rubbed each other's legs by turns, talked of happier times. Jeffries had run away from a Manchester slum at fourteen to be a band boy in the Royal Marines, and ten years on had played his clarinet around the world. At some point, sensing that Jeffries was weakening, Thurston put an arm around him, stripped of all awareness or rank, talked to him about his family and the good days before the war. Towards morning, in the darkest and coldest hour before dawn, Jeffries went quiet. It hurt to put him over the side; he held him against his chest for long minutes after he was dead. Not much longer now, few of them would last another night.

They could hardly speak now, huddled together for some illusory warmth and the primeval comfort of another living body. They were too exhausted, too empty, even to be seasick any more. Morgan, white and tear-streaked, and gone quiet. Thurston tried to think of his wife, his son and daughter, but he could not summon up their faces any longer.

'Captain, sir. There's something out there.' It was said quietly, flatly, without a trace of emotion, by an eighteen-year-old signalman who four months earlier had been behind the counter of a Taunton bank.

It was a corvette, searching for a straggler from

her convoy. Twenty minutes after sunset; another few minutes and she would never have seen them. A long moment, and she altered course towards them. They watched numbly as she closed, slumped in cold and exhaustion, unable to comprehend. The corvette stopped engines, put down a scrambling net, someone shouted at them to look snappy in case of U-boats.

Thurston had a dim memory of climbing the net hand over hand with some reserve of strength, spurning offers of aid, of slumping in a heap on the wet steel deck and being violently sick after someone poured hot rum down his throat. The crew of *Hyacinth* gave up their bunks and hammocks, rubbed the survivors down with great care and powerful-smelling liniment, forced rum and hot drinks into them, bullied them into life and tended them through the agonies of returning circulation. They clothed them in a motley assortment of garments from their own lockers and kitbags, brought round cocoa and soup and more rum and a rough kind of tenderness. 'Wrong time of year to go swimming, chum. Want your feet rubbed again? Hey, Taff, this one talks like a fucking officer!' But two men died just after being picked up, another the next day.

*The Board of Admiralty regrets to announce the loss of the cruiser HMS* Connaught, *Captain R. H. M. Thurston, RN. There were some casualties. Next of kin have been informed.*

# — Chapter One —

## Alexandria, December 1942

'We're going to keep you in for a few days, for a complete rest. You're overtired and a bit run-down, and you've obviously had a hard time recently. Peace, quiet and no worry.'

But there was something more, some black canker of the soul which had descended on him. The hospital expected him to stay in bed and do nothing. When he insisted, and demonstrated, that he was quite capable of getting himself to and from the beds, or told the sister who came to give him a blanket bath that it would save a great deal of time and trouble if he simply got up and had a bath, it was always, 'Sorry, sir, doctor's orders,' and, 'What are you doing out of bed?' over and over again. At first they wouldn't even let him have books, and when they did he found he could not concentrate to read any more; he would start to write a letter home but not get beyond the address. What could he tell Kate anyway? The nights were a welter of dreams and fragments of dreams, despite the sleeping pills they were feeding him.

The old horror of Jutland, York's dead eyes accusing. A Carley float, alone on an empty sea, men staring vacantly around them, because they had no eyes and their faces became naked skulls. At other times he was shouting orders which no one heeded. He would wake out of it, sweating, shouting, on the edge of vomiting. 'No . . . No. Leave me alone!' At these moments he missed Spencer, but he was in Cairo on leave, and in any case he could never face Spencer again. He would get up and start pacing the corridors, searching for some relief in physical effort, and sooner or later run into a brisk night sister young enough to be his daughter, 'Aren't you supposed to be in bed?' She would insist on making him Horlicks and asking if there was 'anything you want to talk about'. 'Why don't you just lie back and enjoy being pampered for a few days?'

But he didn't want sympathy; he was lying idly in bed while his men were suffering and dying. They wouldn't let him get up to see the men who were still in hospital, or go to Garrard's funeral. 'You're supposed to be resting. You'll only upset yourself. You may be very important aboard your ship, but here you're a patient.'

Garrard was dead, after lingering on without legs for six days. Gibbons was dead, Barnett, Norris, Krasnowicz, Sloan, Wilmott, the Padre. His men, and the hospital could not understand. The ship was in dry dock, the ship's company on leave in Cairo, the rest of the squadron out on a sweep. There was an emptiness in his life now that it was all over. The ship would go to America for a full refit and pay-off, the ship's company of two years' standing would be scattered. Another doctor came and kept asking what the trouble was. An emptiness at the heart of things, a yawning void, the days passed slowly, drearily, the hours differenced by meals to be picked over, pills to be swallowed, doctors on their rounds, nothing to distract him from the blackness at the core.

They let him up after a week, wearing a uniform that felt strange and didn't fit any more, hedged when he asked why they were keeping him in. 'Just another few days' rest and some tests. You've had a hard time recently. Nothing to worry about.' The dreams came, the weight of guilt and misery bore down.

The squadron returned from the sweep. Philip Woodruffe and Charles Dowding brought him books

15

and the news of Dowding's seven-pound, two-ounce daughter and tried to cheer him up. The Admiral came. 'Dammit, Bob, what the devil's the matter with you? You can't let losses get you down. You've got to buck your ideas up and get out of this.' He seemed to have used up the last of his resistance. The doctor came, prodded and pummelled him, sent him for X-rays and blood tests and suggested he see someone more expert. Yes, to be frank, a psychiatrist, but he had been under a lot of strain recently and it should help to bring things out into the open.

*I should not be here. I should be dead with the rest.*

Because he was a post captain they had put him in a side ward by himself. He seemed to spend more and more time there, staring at the wall, unable to face any more the chance of bumping into one of his men. Someone brought him lunch. No, he didn't want anything. The sister lectured, as if he was a small boy being difficult, tried to coax him to eat it. He told her to go to blazes. They weren't going to let him out of here, they would take his ship away. There was nothing left but the descent into madness, to finish up like Morgan on the raft, mad, stark staring mad, with some psychiatrist telling him that it was all because he had a secret desire to sleep with his mother! Someone aboard *Hyacinth* had told him that they had worked on him for an hour before he began to revive. Why had they bothered? Why hadn't they just left him to die?

*I should not be here. I should be dead with the rest.*

Mortimer, in his confidential report when he left *Ostorius*, had described him as a *capable, enthusiastic, and most promising young officer*, 'And stop looking surprised! I wouldn't have written it if it wasn't true!' Mortimer was wrong. They were all wrong. Damn you, Thurston, you're a complete bloody fraud. Post captain, VC, DSO and a parchment for lifesaving from the Royal Humane Society, and look at you now. Damn you, damn you to hell!'

His razor lay on the windowsill, stropped and sharp. Sharp enough. He put it in his pocket, went through to the bathroom, into the far cubicle, pushed the bolt home. He took off his jacket, spread it on his knees and began to cut the stitching which held the red ribbon. It was more awkward than he expected; it was several minutes before the last piece of thread came away. He looked at the ribbon for a moment, with its miniature bronze cross in the centre. He had done nothing to earn it and now he had forfeited any right to it. He stood up, took off his watch, rolled his sleeves up in immaculate two-inch turns. He tested the edge with his thumb, watched for a moment the play of the light on the bright steel, the blue tracery of veins which was to be destroyed for ever. Better the revolver, a clean bullet through the brain, but this would serve.

Better this way, to atone for what he had done, and failed to do. He should have died long ago, in the wreckage of the forrard turret with York and Booth and the rest. His negligence had killed all but seventeen of the four hundred men in *Connaught*, and sentenced the seventeen to death in life on the raft. This was what he deserved. He took a deep breath and very deliberately dug the blade into the untanned strip left by his watch, as far as it would go, then drew it across. For an instant there was nothing, then a white shriek of pain all the way up his arm and a bright jet of blood struck him squarely between the eyes. He heard footsteps in the corridor, tried to get the razor into that hand, but he found the fingers wouldn't grip. They were coming for him. He tried again; the razor dropped from his hand, clattered on the tiles. Kate, forgive me. The floor came up, the side of his head struck the hard enamel edge of the bath.

Someone pulled his tie off, rapid jerky breathing close by. 'Oh God, don't die on me!' Something tightened round his arm, high up, biting deep into the muscle. Running feet, with steel-tipped heels, a man's voice. 'What the fuck did you do that for!' He struck out blindly, felt his fist connect. The man swore, dropped on top of him. Struggle, instinctive, primeval, slippery blood all around, but he was too weak, almost unconscious again. One man sat on his chest, pinning his right arm to the floor, others on each leg. 'Are you going to be sensible?' His left arm was up in the air, a reddening towel wrapped around it, the hand swelling, engorged, pulsating pain.

'Made a proper bloody job of it. Gone through the bloody radial artery.'

'I was just coming to see if he'd eaten any lunch.'

'Who the fuck left him with a razor anyway?'

'Commander Lloyd said he wasn't suicidal!'

'Well, Commander Lloyd is going to look *very* silly' . . .

There was a grey blanket over him, rough against his flesh. Straps secured him to a stretcher. Someone was holding his arm up, slackening the torniquet so more blood spurted out, a change in the quality of the pain before the thing twisted tight again.

He lifted his head, a woman's face a foot from his, her voice: 'No, you can't have a drink. You're going into theatre in a minute and you've caused enough trouble already.'

A man's voice further off, 'Wonder what he did it for? And a VC too.' The woman was issuing instructions. Blood, duty surgeon, have to get these tied off, get hold of . . .

Bright lights, an authoritative voice complaining about being called out of his lunch. 'Just going to stitch that for you.' The mask came down over his face, ether and rubber in his nostrils, finger pressure on the back of his hand, a different, more detached voice persuading him to count. 'One, two,' struggle against the anaesthetic, the mask pressed down harder, suffocating, 'three, four, five,' the world turning sickeningly green. 'Good, just going under nicely,' 'six, sev . . .'

18

'All right, Sister, you can take him away.'

In the adjacent room the surgeon peeled off his gloves and began to scrub his hands anew. 'I daresay he'll be sitting up and taking nourishment in a couple of days,' he remarked to the anaesthetist. 'Though whether we've done him any favours is another matter.' He shook his hands, reached for the towel and continued, more to himself, 'We never really know why these chaps do it. I don't suppose he could tell us himself.'

# — Chapter Two —

## HMS *Marathon*, Alexandria, November 1942

Thurston woke up screaming. He was in his bunk, or half out of it, the blankets flung off, his body slick with sweat. Again the nightmare had come; the faces of the turret's crew dissolved in front of him; charred and burning hands lunged out of the yellow fire. *Flood the magazine or she'll go up!* But his feet were caught up; he could not move. His hands were blistering, the flames coming closer. A dead face in front, the eyes boring into his, accusing. He was shouting at the rest but none heard him. Once more he tried to move, but his legs were hopelessly jammed. Heat licked his face, and one of the flailing obscene talons reached to his shoulder. That was the point where he always woke up. He switched on the light, noticed that the telephone handset behind his head was dangling at the full extent of its cable. he replaced it on the bracket. Immediately the telephone buzzed.

'Captain, sir. Switchboard. Have you been trying to get through?'

No, I haven't.' That was all he needed, an alert switchboard operator.

'I saw your extension light on, sir, and I thought . . .'

He cut him short. 'Thank you. I must have dislodged it getting up just now.' He managed to keep his voice steady.

'Aye aye, sir. Sorry to disturb you.' The operator rang off.

'Sir, are you okay?' Spencer was standing in the

doorway, arms coloured with fading tattoos, vest bulging over the waistband of the uniform trousers he was wearing. He went through to the bathroom, came back with a glass of water. Thurston sipped it and felt better.

'Sorry to wake you.'

'Do you some cocoa, sir?'

His breathing had steadied, the sweat was drying stickily. 'No thank you, Spencer.'

'Sure, sir? It'd only take a minute.' Spencer was all concern. 'Or 'ow about somethin' stronger?'

'Quite sure. Goodnight, Spencer.'

Spencer went back to his hammock. After a moment Thurston got up, pulled his greatcoat on over his pyjamas and went out on deck. The marine sentry presented arms, his face impassive. Thurston began to pace briskly over the quarterdeck, ignoring the rain gusting in from the sea.

*You're finished if you go sick*. It was logical enough. To go sick, to back out at such a time, was a betrayal of trust, a retreat from responsibility, virtually an act of cowardice. But he couldn't go on like this.

*Was* he going mad? The dream came every night now. Spencer would come in and cluck over him, and then he would come out here and walk the deck. Thank God Spencer knew when to keep his mouth shut. But how much had the switchboard operator heard tonight, and the cabin sentry? It would probably be all over the ship by the forenoon stand-easy. He was getting thoroughly – what was the word? – paranoid. Up and down, up and down, legs thumping out the mileage, shoes sending up little spurts of water from the planking, the rain soaking his hair and running down his neck.

*When I consider how my light is spent,*
*Ere half my days, in this dark world and wide,*
*And that one talent which is death to hide . . .*

He had commanded *Marathon* for two years; if he

21

backed out now he would never get another ship. Turn beneath the twin muzzles of Y turret, into the wind, the fierce Mediterranean rain lashing his face, chilled through now, but caring little.

Turn at the stern rails, sense the ship worrying at her moorings, the wires tautening almost imperceptibly and then easing as the strain came off. Two years. He had come to her, a brand-new ship, at a few hours' notice, to replace a predecessor who had been carried ashore with peritonitis a week before her acceptance trials. He couldn't give up, but still he couldn't go on like this.

He used to enjoy shiphandling, for instance; there was an art and a personal pride in bringing a big ship alongside or on to a buoy at speed, plenty of way on and then a nicely calculated burst of full astern at the last moment. But not any more, somewhere his judgement had gone with his peace of mind. A month ago the rudder had jammed hard a-starboard coming in from a sweep. Something had happened to him then; he had been in a hurry to complete the manoeuvre, to get it over with. He had gone into the turn a little too fast and a little too late, had to put on full helm and it jammed. For a moment it had looked as though they were going to collide with the flagship; he had managed to counter the swing with engines and then it took a nerve-stretching half-hour to extricate the ship from an awkward position and pick up moorings using emergency steering. He could have waited for a tug, should have waited for a tug, and not long ago he would have laughed it off, as one of those things; but no, he had to get on, get it over with, and prove something to himself.

Afterwards, below in the bathroom, he threw up and Spencer was anxious. 'Sure you're okay, sir? Somethin' you ate?' No something more, something had happened to him in the last few months.

*I should not be here. I should be dead with the rest of them.*

Morning. Thurston was shaken by the Midshipman of the Watch after he had read himself back into uneasy sleep. He went through a circuit which included press-ups, sit-ups, squat-thrusts and running on the spot, interspersed with doubling around the upper deck, then shaved, sluiced down and dressed in uniform. Back to the quarterdeck, to walk in solitary eminence until breakfast, telescope under arm, cap in hand.

The rain had ceased and a fitful sun created a myriad of colours on the oily harbour waters. The Mediterranean Fleet was in harbour, swabbing parties on decks, midshipmen at PT, knots of officers pacing up and down and making desultory conversation, captains pacing the weather side in solitude. Four cruisers, each five hundred and twelve feet long, displacing 5,500 tons. Three had ten 5.25-inch guns in twin turrets; *Marathon* had eight, owing to a temporary shortage at the time of her completion; six 21-inch torpedo tubes, five hundred and thirty officers and men and a designed speed of thirty-three knots. Four cruisers and eleven destroyers. There had been many more; *Barham, Neptune, Naiad, Galatea, Kandahar*, all had lain here in the stillness of the morning.

'Sir, you've 'ardly touched your breakfast.' Spencer rattled the plates. 'I'll do you some fresh toast. That stuff must be cold by now.'

'Spencer, would you mind your own business and clear away a bit more quietly!'

'Aye, aye, sir.' With a final clatter, Spencer disappeared. He didn't know what had got into the Old Man lately, but he didn't like it.

Spencer had been with him in his last ship and followed him to *Marathon* at his own request, a squat three-badger of nineteen years' service, once more an able seaman after another fracas ashore. The captain of a cruiser was entitled to a petty officer steward, rather than an AB, but Spencer suited him and showed no desire to lose a cushy number.

Thurston was further entitled to as much space as a couple of dozen ratings, a boy seaman as his messenger, motorboat and crew, so many picture hooks on which to hang his photographs of his Dartmouth term, his first destroyer command, the ship's rugby team, prints of hunting scenes and the English countryside, and the weather side of the quarterdeck for his morning exercise. This cabin differed from the last one in little beyond the absence of a large oil of the heavily moustached features of Field Marshal His Royal Highness the Duke of Connaught and Strathearn; furnishings as laid down by some Admiralty committee, desk, dining table with eight chairs, wine-red carpet, a couple of easy chairs, portrait photograph of the King in uniform as an Admiral of the Fleet. Thurston could have had something done about the pale green paint and the chair covers, but they could be lived with. He had contented himself with having one of the ship's carpenters add three inches to each of his bunks, here and in his sea cabin, stowing his books in the bookcase and hanging some sketches.

After Divisions Thurston got down to the paperwork which always accumulated in harbour; all the business of ammunitioning and stores and men due for advancement, or courses, or punishment, and a steady trickle of compassionate cases. There were also the things which paymaster Sub-Lieutenant Jenner, his secretary, seemed to take a delight in dredging up, and the Admiralty Fleet Orders which drew his attention to KR & AI Number such-and-such prohibiting the wearing of shoes by ratings, or to the anti-malaria regulations. A long discussion with the Paymaster Commander about a consignment of suspect beef, another with the Gunnery Officer about two-pounder ammunition.

The Midshipman of the Watch brought a signal.

'Mr Pearson, your collar stud is showing.'

'Yes, sir.' Pearson fumbled uncertainly with his tie. He had only joined the ship a couple of days ago; tallish, fair-headed, almost a pretty boy.

Thurston appended his initial to the signal, passed it back. 'Thank you, Mr Pearson. How are you shaking down?'

'It's all a bit strange, sir, but I'm getting used to it.'

'Good. Carry on.'

'Very good, sir.'

'It's not "Very good, sir", it's "Aye aye, sir"! Didn't they teach you anything at *King Alfred*?'

'Nossir, I mean yessir!'

Oh God, there was no excuse for that. Remembered snatches of conversation from the bridge voicepipe. 'Starboard leg of the zig-zag, twelve knots and the Old Man's in one of his moods, so watch out for fireworks.' '. . . Nearly put the cable party in the water. James French was not amused.'

He was aware of Pearson still standing before him. 'Carry on, Mr Pearson, and get your hair cut.'

Pearson fled. *Face it, Thurston.* He rang the bell for his messenger.

'Give the Surgeon Commander my compliments and ask him to come up at his convenience.' The Boy Seaman looked surprised. 'McCormick, get on with it!'

Surgeon Commander Savage, *Marathon*'s Principal Medical Officer, came up twenty minutes later.

'Now what can I do for you, sir?'

'I can't sleep.'

'Do you mean that you have difficulty in getting to sleep in the first place, or that you keep waking up?'

'Both.'

Savage did not sound unduly surprised. 'How long has this been going on?'

'About a month.'

'Been taking anything for it?'

'Whisky.'

'Much?'

'No. It doesn't seem to have much effect.'

'Not surprising,' Savage said briskly. 'Whisky is an excellent drink but its properties as an anaesthetic have been greatly exaggerated. Strip off and I'll have a look at you.'

'Is this really necessary?'

'Yes,' Savage said simply. 'I don't believe in simply doling out sleeping pills. Much better to find and deal with the cause of your insomnia than to try to push you under artificially.'

Savage was going to be thorough. Thurston picked up the telephone and issued orders that he was not to be disturbed, then unbuttoned his jacket, his eyes avoiding the red ribbon which silently mocked him. He had inspected himself critically in the shaving mirror that morning, searching for some clue. A lean square-jawed face, weathered brown and red and scored with fine lines around the eyes, a dominant high-bridged nose which had been broken and diverted from the centre line. The old white scar, which cut through the right eyebrow and ran on upwards across his forehead at a shallow angle. Another scar, pink and twenty-five years more recent, on the left side of the jaw. Dark hair, beginning to go grey at the sides. The eyes were grey too, deep-set, with a steadiness he did not feel any more.

'. . . Stomach all right . . . ? Bowels . . . ? Head-aches . . . ? Any dizzy spells?' Savage fired questions at him, the shouts of one of the Gunnery Instructors coming through the scuttle, the slightly antiseptic smell of the Surgeon Commander's hair oil as he listened to his chest. 'Cough . . . Again . . . That shoulder bother you much?'

'Only when the *gregale* blows.'

'Inevitable. Let's see your feet . . . Look a bit messy, don't they? I'll give you something for that. Make sure they get plenty of fresh air . . . All right, get dressed.'

Savage settled himself in a chair. He was a rather

fleshy man of about Thurston's own age, with a voice that somehow reminded Thurston of treacle flowing over a sponge pudding. He had his fingertips together and was contemplating the nails, an habitual gesture of his, waiting for Thurston to finish dressing and seat himself at his desk.

*Get on with it, Doc.*

'Well, sir,' Savage said at last. 'Basically you're a disgustingly healthy specimen. The footrot is a minor nuisance and it's controllable.'

*Trust Savage to start at the feet.*

'Blood pressure's up a bit, but nothing untoward. Within the normal range. But . . .'

*Here it comes.*

'I'll be blunt. That fact is, you've had enough. You're showing all the usual signs. Not sleeping, loss of appetite, loss of weight, irritability.' Savage laid a slight stress on the irritability. 'That much is obvious. The question is where do we go from here? When were you last on leave?'

'July.'

'Bottom-scraping in Massawa, the most charming spot in the Red Sea. That hardly counts. Time you had a proper break.'

'I can't go on leave now.'

'I'm sorry, sir. If you'd come to me earlier . . . It's gone beyond a simple matter of a week's leave here or ten days there. You'd be all right for a couple of months and then it'd start again.' Savage paused for a moment. 'And before you start thinking about cowardice and all that tommy-rot, it's got nothing at all to do with that. You're manifesting a very normal reaction to prolonged stress. The human mind can only take so much at one go. You've simply used up all your reserves.'

'So what are you suggesting?'

'Two or three months' leave at home; to recharge the batteries, so to speak. That should break the vicious circle you've obviously got into. Fretting about your operational efficiency only makes things worse.'

'I can't do that.'

'Why not?' Savage was playing the old family doctor. His eyes were a surprisingly bright blue over the arch of his hands. 'You've been at sea since this lot started. You've had a sinking and a serious wound. It can hardly be said that you haven't done your bit. Three months' leave now and there's no earthly reason why you shouldn't go into another command after that.' He gave a wry smile. 'And what have we been doing for the last couple of months? Shore bombardments, odd trips to Haifa and everlasting bloody sweeps. Nothing very startling but it's all strain on you and it all builds up. Of course it hardly helps that you Dartmouth chaps all think that unless you're on the bridge twenty-four hours a day you're not doing your job properly. In fact, I'd go so far as to say that from a psychological point of view Dartmouth has a lot to answer for.'

This was one of Savage's hobby-horses. 'Don't start on that.'

Savage's hands were back in his lap. 'I'm sorry, sir. You asked for my professional opinion and I really think you should ask for a relief and take that leave. I know it goes against the grain, but you've done your share already, maybe more than your share in some ways. Time to forget all the rubbish that was dinned into you about duty and honour and all the rest of it. Take the leave now and you'll feel like a spring lamb in a few weeks.'

'Boat ahoy?'

'*Marathon!*'

To Thurston, hunched moodily in the cabin of the Captain's galley, it seemed the worst moment of his life. It would be the last time that Petty Officer Stephenson gave that heart-searching answer, the last time that they would pipe him aboard the flagship, indeed any ship. Or not, but only until his relief took over. He had been in the Navy since he was twelve, he had joined his first ship as a midshipman six weeks before his fifteenth birthday. A long road, and it was all to end like his.

He had known what Savage would say, which was the reason he had put off seeing him. He had argued with him for another ten minutes but the doctor was adamant. 'I could give you sedatives, but that would hardly help your efficiency and it's only papering over the cracks.' He could have put it in writing: Sir, I have the honour to request, etcetera, and that he had the honour to remain, Sir, your obedient servant, but he had shifted into his best uniform, sword and medals; Spencer had gone over him with a clothes brush, saying nothing, but knowing. The Commander, Ted Bradshaw, had simply said, 'Yes sir, I'm sorry, sir,' no more. He was grateful for that. His boat's crew, picked men, must know that something was happening: Stephenson, Able Seaman MacLeod who came from South Uist and spoke the almost musical English of the Outer Hebrides, Able Seaman Mills, Stoker Grant and the rest. He was going to miss them. The boat reached the gangway.

'Wait here, Stephenson. I shan't be long.'

Up the accommodation ladder, holding the sword up out of the way.

'Man the side . . . Pipe!'

Salute at the top, turn aft, exchange a few words with the Flag Captain who had appeared on the quarterdeck.

*Thou hast been weighed in the balance and found wanting.*

Rear Admiral Reginald Beecham was grey-haired and heavy, a noted rugby player in his younger days and his nose and ears showed it. He listened in silence. Thurston was sitting up very straight, his hands resting

29

on the pommel of his sword, staring at the Admiral's cap lying on his desk.

'Obviously I would prefer not to, but my PMO is advising it.' Save your face. Blame the doctor.

Beecham pushed a cigarette box towards him. He ignored it.

'Well, old chap, it's up to you. I think that sawbones of yours has a point. Yon Thurston hath a lean and hungry look. He thinks too much . . . But, to be frank, it's come at a damned awkward time. "Stonehenge" will be coming off any day.'

Stonehenge was the next Malta convoy; it had been postponed and rescheduled at least twice in the past month.

The Admiral went on. 'It's your decision, *Marathon*. I can't give you an order either way. If you really don't feel you're up to it, I'll relieve you. Bradshaw's quite capable of taking over for a day or two, isn't he? Quite frankly I couldn't attach any blame to you if you did, not with a record like yours. Your decision, old boy.'

Beecham sat back, waiting for his answer. Thurston stared straight ahead for a moment, met the Admiral's eyes, then looked over his head at a photograph of a younger Beecham with the Combined Services XV of 1921. His hands tightened on the sword. On the one hand the words of Savage, the possibility that his nerve could go in an emergency, perhaps even his reason. On the other . . . dammit, there wasn't any choice.

'I'll carry on, sir.'

'Good man. You're about due for a boiler clean, aren't you?'

'Yes. One of the condensers is still giving trouble.'

'I don't pretend to understand boilers. We'll get that done once Stonehenge is out of the way. That'll give you a week. Find yourself a good woman.'

'He what, sir?' demanded Savage. 'My God, the man's

30

a bigger fool than I thought and so are you. I'll signal the Admiral and give him a piece of my mind!'

'You'll do no such thing.'

'You forget that I'm responsible for the health of every man aboard this ship, without any exceptions. There's a world of difference between proper reluctance to make a fuss and blind refusal to see reason. Can't you get it into your thick Dartmouth skull that because your mind and body are crying "Enough!" that doesn't make you a coward, or whatever else you've decided. Good God, haven't we moved on since Admiral Byng! I'm putting you on the sick list for your own good.'

'You will not.'

'It's for your own good.'

'Oh don't give me that.'

Savage clicked his tongue. 'All right, Captain, sir. If you're determined I shan't interfere. But I think you're a bloody fool. If you really want a nervous breakdown, you're going the right way to get one, but you won't be told.'

Savage could never understand that he had to go through with this. He was pacing a few feet of carpet, hands jammed into his side pockets. 'Get out, damn you!'

Savage, all sail set, swept out. Thurston took out his cigarette case, studied the design engraved on it. The case had come from his grandfather on his twenty-first birthday and had survived *Connaught* in his trouser pocket. He looked again at the motto, then put it away.

Spencer came in. 'Are you ready for your lunch now, sir?'

After lunch, back to his desk. He saw Able Seaman Craig about his recommendation for a commission, the Commander (E) about the condenser.

'That same lot of tubes has gone again. All we can do is strip that section down and hope we find the leak.'

31

'How long will it take?'

'Depends how much there is. We're doing it a bit at a time so we can put it back together if we need to raise steam.'

'You know what you're doing, Chief.'

Ted Bradshaw arrived next. 'The Military Police in Cairo have just been on to us. They picked up two of our stokers last night. Brown and Wallace.'

'They've been adrift about two weeks, haven't they?'

'Just about. I'm sending an escort for them and they should be back on board by midnight. Just in time for your Defaulters tomorrow.'

'Where did they get them?'

'Usual story. They were in a club when it was raided, tried to get out the back way and landed straight into the arms of the MPs.'


'Goin' ashore tonight, sir?'

'Doubt it.'

Tradition ordained that ships' captains were distanced from their officers; they messed separately and entered the wardroom only as guests. It was a hoary old chestnut that a commander served six years of hard labour and a captain twelve years of solitary confinement. He and Ted Bradshaw got on well enough but rarely went ashore in company; he used Bradshaw's Christian name in private but the Commander could not reciprocate. A post captain in command was expected to restrict his friendships to his brother captains and keep all others at arm's length. Anything else bred favouritism and affected decision-making adversely.

Ashore in Alexandria he could ride, walk or swim, play golf, squash or tennis, take Turkish baths, or drink, after first running the gauntlet of the small boys pimping at the dock entrance: 'Captain, you want girl? My sister – very good, very clean, very cheap, all pink inside like English lady,' or, more rarely, 'Captain, you want boy?' Or he could stay aboard and drink in the solitary splendour of his cabin, and wish his wife was not three thousand miles away. He could attend cocktail parties given by the British residents, most of whom loudly proclaimed that they would be in uniform themselves, were it not that they had a business to run/got a whiff of gas last time/malaria you know. The majority had precipitously left in July and August, when it was feared that Rommel would reach the Delta, and had now somewhat shamefacedly returned. There were certain of the ladies, it was known, who would oblige a lonely sailor in the afternoons while their husbands were hard at work making money out of the war; and, for some, the more gold lace the better. But that was not the important thing; it was company that really mattered, an opportunity to talk something other than shop, with someone who didn't yes-sir and no-sir you all the time.

The Chief Telegraphist refolded the letter which had been burning a hole in the pocket of Telegraphist Meadows since 1100. 'All the same, women, aren't they? Good thing you came to see me instead of jumping over the side or going on a runner. The Navy's got a way of dealing with everything. Tomorrow you go up on Captain's Requestmen and request to see the Captain in private. Officially all that means is that the Jaunty and all the rest gets out of the way and it's just you and him across the table. But in practice, with this captain anyway, he'll see you in his cabin afterwards. And you show him that and tell him what you've just told me. Don't expect to be on the next plane home but he'll do what he can to sort things out. Got that?'

'Yes, Chief. Er. Thank you, Chief.'

'Don't thank me, son. It happened to me once.'

# — Chapter Three —

In the Dog Watches the Captain went ashore and lost heavily at squash to the First Lieutenant. The ship's concert party held its second rehearsal for the Christmas show. *What the Hell Next*? Able Seaman Spencer got on with a pile of interrupted washing. Surgeon Commander Savage played nine holes of golf with his opposite number from *Bellerophon*. Men under punishment doubled around the upper deck in full kit with rifles over their heads. Midshipman Pearson sat on the gunroom settee and contemplated the virgin pages of his Midshipman's Journal.

The journal was a record of events, of work done, of what happened to the ship. 'Put in all the football matches, concerts, changes of personnel – officers that is. Anything that's the slightest bit out of the ordinary.' But everything was out of the ordinary at the moment, everything new and strange. This gunroom to start with. It was a long narrow compartment, with scuttles spread along one bulkhead (mustn't call them portholes now), a dining table at one end, where the stewards were laying eleven places for dinner, serving hatch beyond it. At this end the narrow leather settee, some easy chairs for the use of sub-lieutenants and senior midshipmen only, a gramophone and a battle-scarred piano. Through the door was the chest flat, where the midshipmen slept in hammocks which were not to be slung before 2200 hours when in harbour, a draughty open space with constant through traffic, sea chests arranged along the bulkheads, racks of chained .303

Lee-Enfields, no scuttles, blue police lights constantly burning.

*16 November 1942. Kept Forenoon Watch under Lieut. Harker, understudying Mid. Angus.*

Should he put in that he had finished going through the Squadron Standing Orders (by Rear Admiral R. B. Beecham OBE), the ship's Standing Orders (by Captain R. H. M. Thurston VC DSO), the Gunroom Standing Orders (by Sub-Lieutenant D. G. Hastings) and the Training Programme for Midshipmen (by Lieutenant-Commander J. St J. ffrench DSC)? Better put it in. *Completed study of Standing Orders. Produced sketches of ship as requested by First Lieutenant.*

*Marathon* had looked much smaller than he expected, when he first saw her from the motor cutter taking him across, hardly big enough to have sunk the *Seydlitz* last year. He could hardly believe it: he, David Pearson, posted to a famous ship like that. He never expected anything like that, when he joined the Navy five months earlier.

He had lived in Enfield all his life. His father worked in an office in the City, going in to London on the same train every day for twenty-odd years, ever since he had come out of the army in 1919. Pearson had gone to a local grammar school, passed his School Certificate and enrolled on a three-year course at a local art college. He liked drawing and it was his best subject at school, and he had no desire to be like his father. The war began that September. At first it was all going to blow over; the British Expeditionary Force sat around the Maginot Line, the RAF dropped bundles of leaflets over Germany, a few ships were sunk. Life in Enfield continued as usual, except for some shortages, and the bother of fixing the blackout every night. Gradually the war came closer. A cousin in the Territorials was taken prisoner at Dunkirk; rationing was imposed; Enfield was bombed. His father joined the ARP. He began to think that the war would go on, he would

35

have to go, be called up, fight. Some of his friends were going, mostly into the army, a few into the RAF; one had declared himself a conscientious objector and been sent to do farm work in Suffolk.

He went on with art college, took to going for long walks and pondering what he should do. He would be eighteen on 1st March 1942; the course ended in July and he could expect to be called up a matter of weeks after that. He didn't have the convictions to be an objector, but he supposed there were parts of the army in which you didn't have to fight. After all, his father had spent the last war in the Pay Corps and never got nearer the trenches than Rouen. But in a vague way he felt this wasn't the answer. Not the army: square-bashing, spud-peeling and being shouted at by sergeant-majors. And that awful battledress. He wondered about the RAF, but flying didn't really attract him.

Time went on. Japan came into the war, sank *Prince of Wales* and *Repulse*. Singapore fell. Art began to seem less important as his eighteenth birthday approached. He came to realise that he had only started the course to fill in the time while he worked out what he was going to do with his life. He pondered much while walking the cinder path beside the railway line. In the end he took the plunge and applied to join the Royal Navy Volunteer Reserve; the Navy had a certain style.

The machine took him in, and disgorged him three months later as a midshipman RNVR with maroon patches on his collar, put him on a troopship and sent him round the Cape to join *Marathon*.

A good ship, everybody had told him. But it was nothing like he had expected; there was so much that *King Alfred* had not taught him, so much to think about, so many things to remember. To start with, how would he ever find his way around that rabbit warren of compartments below decks?

When he arrived, two long days ago ('Midshipman Pearson, come aboard to join, sir'), the First Lieutenant-Commander J. St J. ffrench DSC, had met him and said a few words, introduced him to Captain R. H. M. Thurston VC DSO, who had shaken his hand and said a few words; then he had been handed over to Sub Lieutenant Hastings, president of the Gunroom Mess, who in turn passed him on to Midshipman Nairne RN, who would show him the ropes.

He had quickly learned that Nairne's father was a retired admiral, now serving as a commodore of convoys, that Nairne had been a cadet captain at Dartmouth and had every intention of becoming an admiral himself. He was led through compartment after compartment, up and down endless ladders for what seemed like hours, until his head was reeling from engine room, boiler room, chain locker, magazine, handling room, transmitting station, submerged flats and all the information that Nairne was anxious to impart.

'You've joined the best ship in the Med Fleet, which means the best ship anywhere. *Marathon*'s been in lots of scraps, the *Bismarck* chase, the Malta runs. And we sank the *Seydlitz*.'

'I read about that in all the papers. What was it like?'

'Well, actually that was before I joined, but it was really something. The Old Man got the VC, the Commander got the DSO; Guns and Number One both got gongs. It's because of the *Seydlitz* that there's so much fruit salad aboard this ship. And that's not all. We've really been in the thick of things since. We were part of Force K in Malta until last April, had the Wops on the run.

'The Midshipman of the Watch makes the officers' cocoa – the bridge messenger does it for the ratings – runs messages and generally gets chased about. The officers will all shout at you, but it doesn't mean anything. When you write up the log you've got to use your best handwriting and a propelling pencil, *not* an ordinary one, so it's sharp. The fair copy is done in ink later, and you sign with initials and surname only, not Christian names. We don't use Christian names on duty either, and especially not in front of ratings. So you call me Mr Nairne and I call you Mr Pearson. When you keep the Morning Watch in harbour you have to shake the Captain and Commander. Don't forget to check up on the met because they always expect you to know it. The Old Man's usually awake but the Commander's a bit deaf one side – gunnery specialist – and you have to shout, but don't lay a finger on either of them, because technically that's assault and you'll get a dozen.'

'A dozen what?'

'Cuts,' Nairne said simply. 'Any time you step out of line or make a balls of something or forget to do anything the Sub'll give you a dozen, or half a dozen if he's in a forgiving mood.' He saw Pearson's worried look. 'Better than extra watches or having your leave stopped. Hastings is all right. He doesn't beat just for the fun of it. Most of the officers are okay. The Old Man's really good. The First Lieutenant – you've already met him 'cos he's Snotties' Nurse – is Lieutenant Commander ffrench, spelt with two little ffs. Don't ask me why. The only thing you've got to watch with him is that he likes to see a well-kept journal, lots of pretty pictures. You can't get away with writing it up in five minutes just before you hand it in. Your journal's got to be written up every day and the First Lieutenant and the Captain see it every week. Who else is important? The Navigator is Lieutenant The Honourable Henry Hart,' Nairne's voice acquired an extra plum. 'He's good for a laugh, you should see his hair. Guns is okay. Shouts a bit, that's all. The only one you've got to look out for is Torps – Lieutenant Taylor. He keeps you on the run with all kinds of useless errands. First he wants his greatcoat, then he doesn't, and you've got to remember that he always drinks tea, never cocoa, and he's very particular about it. Hastings is Sub of the gunroom. There are three other subs but he's the one that counts. The others are Cowper-Coles, Buchan, the Engineer-Sub, and Jenner who's a paybob and the Captain's secretary. There are eight snotties including you. Four seniors, that's me, Angus, Krawnowicz and Zurakowski, who are both Polish and got flown out of Poland by Zurakowski's brother or something. The other warts are Norris, who's RNR and came from some banana boat, Graham and Watson, but Watson's in dry dock at the moment. Jaundice.'

'What's a wart?'

'You are! A junior snotty.' He opened a door. 'This is the gunroom, which is our mess. One of the Marines will sling your hammock and do your shoes and stuff, and might even do your dhobi. You pay your mess bill by the seventh of every month and if your wine bill goes over fifteen bob you get a dozen and a lecture on the sins of over-indulgence from f-f-ffrench. If it happens again he'll stop your wine bill for a couple of months. No spirits until you're a sub, but you can smoke if you're over eighteen and you don't carry cigarettes in a packet. Any questions so far?'

'Er, no.'

'You won't get a boat to start with but you might get some other job. Norris is Navigator's tanky – that's Navigator's assistant – at the moment, but there's a reshuffle due pretty shortly so you might get it. It's not a bad job, you get loads of charts to correct, but you can pick up quite a lot. The only snag is that the Old Man's a navigator and likes to take an interest, which is fine if your maths are up to scratch but could be a bit dodgy if they aren't. By the way, Pearson, what did you do ashore?'

'I was at art school.'

Nairne had looked at him pityingly. 'Then you should be good at correcting charts. I suppose you write poetry as well.'

'A bit.'

'Better keep quiet about that. Krasnowicz plays the violin and that's all the culture we need.'

The journal to be written up daily, watches and instruction, and a mass of regulations both written and unwritten. He wondered how long it would be before he got 'cuts'. PT on the quarterdeck at 0600 hours, in the dark and cold. 'Put some effort into it, Mr Krasnowicz! You're not in Paderewski's orchestra now!'

The Captain had been drinking steadily since dinner, trying to blot things out, and it wasn't working. Well down the second bottle, he poured another glass, held it up to the light.

One more convoy. One more Malta convoy. But nothing had got through from this end, the 'men's end', for eight months. In June two convoys had set out simultaneously from Alexandria and Gibraltar, and neither had made it. The four cruisers and a dozen destroyers left to the Mediterranean Fleet had been augmented for the occasion by an aircraft carrier detached from the East Indies and by the old battleship *Centurion*, lately a target ship for the Fleet Air Arm and now mocked up as the new battleship *Duke of York*. By day *Marathon*'s steel decks absorbed the sun's rays; the ship remained at Action Stations with watertight doors dividing her into a honeycomb of separate compartments, interconnecting by means of tortuous passages, dog-legging from port to starboard and back again, Marines with fixed bayonets positioned at key points. All fans were shut down, temperatures below reached a hundred and thirty degrees, one stoker almost died from heatstroke. The quartermaster was relieved every thirty minutes, to lie gasping on the deck, sodden with sweat. It was possible to fry an egg on the turret roofs; someone tried it in a spirit of scientific curiosity. At night the steel threw back the heat; fans, if in use, barely stirred the overheated air. Prickly heat became a scourge; when conditions allowed the officers rushed to take cold baths, the men drew buckets of seawater and doused each other with them. And there was Beecham. *Ariadne* was under repair in Alexandria and Beecham shifted his flag to *Marathon* at the last moment. There was a mad rush to embark him, his Flag Lieutenant, secretary, Staff Officer (Operations) and a personal staff comprising a petty officer cook, two stewards and four marine orderlies ('Who looks after you, Bob?' 'One seaman, sir.'), an upheaval to find accommodation for them all, the uneasy transition from private ship to flagship. Beecham had only taken over the squadron about a month before; it was his first big 'do'; he had come from a desk ashore and was itching to make a reputation. The Honourable Henry Hart summed up *Marathon*'s opinion of him. 'Beecham?' he mused. 'As in pills?'

But it was not a time for reputations. The convoy was heavily mauled, and eventually, only hours short of Malta, was ordered to withdraw, being harried by aircraft and U-boats all the way back. The August convoy from Gib had been reduced from fourteen merchant ships to five, despite being escorted by most of the Home Fleet; the old carrier *Eagle* and several other escorts had been sunk with them. The tanker *Ohio* had been abandoned by her crew and reboarded, to come into Grand Harbour with her upperworks awash, lashed between two destroyers, to sink as soon as the cargo was pumped out of her.

He drank some of the whisky. It befitted a man of taste and discrimination to drink himself senseless on single malt. *Marathon* had had five months there as part of Force K – two cruisers and two destroyers, bombed all day in harbour, sallying forth by night against Axis supply convoys between Italy and North

Africa. One night *Marathon* had blown an escorting destroyer out of the water with a single salvo, must have touched off a magazine; the rest fled for Taranto leaving their charges to their fate. Force K sank all twelve of them in half an hour of slaughter. *Marathon* picked up a couple of hundred survivors afterwards, reinforcements for the Afrika Korps. And you found, when you saw shocked and exhausted German soldiers on your mess decks and a very correct, very Prussian colonel thanked you, a little diffidently and in halting English, for saving his men, that they weren't so very different. Apart from half a dozen who defiantly began to sing the Horst Wessel song and were forthwith frog-marched below and put in the cells, they were like any other survivors. In other circumstances he and Colonel von Tempelhoff could have been friends, but it was no good thinking about that. You had to treat them as targets, think of the U-boats which sank our ships, not about the men aboard them, about enemy sightings and asdic contacts.

It had been April when Force K pulled out of Malta, after sinking three destroyers and twenty-six merchant ships, for the loss of one cruiser and one destroyer when a temporarily enlarged force blundered into a minefield off Tobruk. *Persephone* had been damaged by a bomb and the Malta dockyard pulled out all the stops to get her seaworthy again, her guns still firing from the drydock. The submarines in Marsamuscetto spent the daylight hours on the bottom of the harbour. The last three weeks an outbreak of Malta Dog affected nearly half *Marathon*'s ship's company; dozens of men spent the days laid out on mattresses in stinking air-raid shelters ashore and stood watches at sea each night, because there was nobody to replace them. The medics instituted the strictest hygiene precautions and put the invalids on a foul-tasting mixture of sugar, salt and twice-boiled water. Thurston had had the Dog for the last ten days, so had the Commander, the Gunnery

Officer, the First Lieutenant, the commander (E) and most of the midshipmen. 'This gives a totally new meaning to the term Dog Watches,' said ffrench during one sortie, after his tenth dash to the heads in a couple of hours.

Thurston drained the glass, reached for the bottle once more. Malta. A lively place before the war, horses at the Marsa, swimming at Tigne or Kalafrana, a café near the bottom of the Strada Reale where he and Kate occasionally took George and Helen for magnificent multi-coloured ice creams as a special treat. Summer, with the sun lighting up the great bastions of honey-coloured limestone and the blue waters of Grand Harbour, deep shadow in the narrow stepped streets leading down from the spine of Valletta. Battleships with spread awnings and light grey paint, destroyers going stern-first and with invincible swagger into Sliema Creek, *dghaisas* painted bright red and blue and green, a single eye painted on the prow to ward off evil. Now Valletta was said to be the most bombed place on earth, the people becoming troglodytes, emerging between raids to forage for food and, devout Catholics, to pray.

His hand wobbled as he poured the whisky again, the liquid slopping on to the polished table top. He could still marvel at the change wrought by a week at Gib and real food, and then the relative holiday of escorting a fast troop convoy around the Cape. The Dog disappeared as if by magic, the men filled out and the drained, exhausted look vanished from their faces. Routine was relaxed a little. Those off watch were permitted to sunbathe on the upper deck, though orders had to be hastily issued that shorts must be worn at all times after complaints from the matron of a party of nursing sisters aboard one of the troopships. The Bandmaster, with some gentle prodding, declared the bandsmen to be a little rusty and instituted daily practices on the quarterdeck in the Dog Watches, which rapidly became impromptu concerts when requests began to be semaphored from the troopships. 'If I hear "There'll Always Be an England" or "The White Cliffs of Dover" again I shall scream!' A concert was held at which hair was thoroughly let down and all the officers taken off without mercy: the Gunnery Officer's walk; the Navigator's wavy fair hair, which was never cut till it draped his collar, if he could get away with it; the Commander's inability to pronounce the word 'meteorological'. At Durban there were twenty-seven men on Captain's Defaulters after a monumental fight with seamen from another ship who made the mistake of saying that the Mediterranean Fleet had it soft.

One more convoy and then? *The trouble with you, Thurston, is that you've a yellow streak a mile wide*. That was what was wrong with him, however Savage tried to dress it up; he was afraid, afraid of responsibility, afraid of the next convoy, afraid of everything now, even afraid of facing up to what he was. He stood up, walked unsteadily to the sleeping cabin. The medal lay in its velvet-lined box. He took the cross in his hand, the others hanging suspended from the bar. *For Valour*, made from bronze from one of the Russian guns taken at Sebastopol, his own name on the back. Oh you gutless bastard. He was slumped in the chair again, glass in one hand, cross in the other; buttons undone, tie at half-mast, drunk and sorry for himself. That citation was a load of tosh, 'most conspicuous gallantry and devotion to duty', 'in the highest traditions of the Royal Navy'. A load of balls. Another convoy and then a shore job somewhere out of the way, a fitting end for a man whose nerve had gone. There was a revolver in the bottom drawer of his desk, and twelve rounds of solid lead unjacketed .455 ball ammunition. He knew someone who had done it in Shanghai years ago, after being found in bed ashore with a boy seaman. Muzzle to the temple, squeeze the trigger, as simple as that. At that range the bullet had

44

blown half his head off, blood and brains splattering the bulkhead.

He started to pour another glass. Bloody waste of good whisky. It would look good if they suddenly got sailing orders. 'If you've learned nothing else from me, remember one thing. If anything goes wrong and you've had anything stronger than coffee in the last twelve hours, they'll break you.' Lieutenant-Commander Mortimer, in his first destroyer when he was bright-eyed and bushy-tailed and eighteen years old. What had happened to Sub-Lieutenant Thurston, aged eighteen, to make him Captain Thurston, aged forty-three? *For Valour*. He didn't deserve it, had done nothing to earn it. He should be dead with the rest. Or a passed-over two-and-a-half in a shore job, or in some clapped-out old ship like Berry in *Connaught*, resentful of the bright boy from the Staff College who had taken her over when she came out of reserve. Berry had gone down with her along with three hundred and eighty-two men out of four hundred.

The door opened. He heard Spencer's tuneless whistling. 'Evening, Spencer,' he said thickly.

Spencer had been ashore, a few beers in the Fleet Club or some bar in the back streets. For a moment Thurston almost envied him; all he had to do was get on with his job, no bloody responsibility. Spencer began to clear away. 'Time you was getting your head down, sir.' He took the medals from his hand, quite gently. 'These could do with a clean. I'll do 'em in the morning.'

'Goodnight, Spencer.'

He stood up, walked three paces before his legs gave way. His stomach heaved, ejected its contents on to the carpet. A fitting end, he thought drearily, face down in his own vomit.

He felt Spencer take him by the armpits and hoist him upright. 'Come on, sir. You're goin' to feel awful in the morning. Glad I won't be on your Defaulters.'

An arm went round his shoulders. 'S'pose I'd better put you to bed.'

Spencer let the Captain down on to the bunk and started to undress him. 'You poor old bugger. Ought to get ashore and fuck a few women.' The first turn of the screw mendeth all broken hearts. The Old Man was a red-blooded fellow and it didn't do no good to abstain in a hot climate. 'There you are, sir. Sweet dreams, you old bugger.'

The Captain's eyes opened. 'Spencer, I heard that.'

'Goodnight, sir. Sleep tight.'

Spencer finished clearing up, swabbed the carpet down with disinfectant and made for the pantry, pulling his jumper over his head. Not like the Old Man to get drunk. And talk about this morning. You'd have thought he was going to knock the doctor into next week.

*If there's anything you feel is important . . .*

Was this important? And even if it was, should he go behind the Captain's back? Anyway, the doctor 'ud be ashore or have his head down by now. It'd have to wait until tomorrow anyway. He took down his lashed hammock and began to sling it with the ease of years of practice.

He had been in the bathroom, in the middle of a pile of dhobi, when the pipe had come. *Able Seaman Spencer to the sick bay, Able Seaman Spencer to the sick bay.* What did they want him for? He never went near the sick bay. He went of course; a pipe was a pipe. The sick bay PO said something about his jabs being out of date and he'd have to see the PMO. Bloody silly, why didn't old Sellars just give him the jab and get it over with? He could see this was going to take all day, and he'd left the Captain's bath full of dhobi and the way the Old Man was at the moment . . .

'Sit down, Spencer,' the doctor said. 'Smoke if you want to.'

Bloody funny. Usually with that lot it was strip off, what's wrong with you? Take a Number Nine and don't waste my time again. But Dr Savage wasn't like the rest of them at all. Bit smooth, but he was all right. Bemused, Spencer dug out his tobacco tin and expertly rolled a cigarette.

'You may be wondering why I've asked to see you, Spencer.'

'Sir.'

'Your typhoid inoculation is a month out of date, but that's really an excuse to get you in here.'

'Sir.'

'Relax, Spencer. This is entirely off the record. Just a chat.' He leant forward slightly. 'You're very fond of the Captain, aren't you?'

'Sir, I'd die for 'im.'

'Let's hope you won't have to,' the Surgeon Commander said briskly. 'I've asked to see you to talk about the Captain. Obviously it's highly irregular, but I believe it to be necessary and nothing we say will go beyond this consulting room.' He settled himself more deeply into his chair, elbows on the arms, immaculately white-coated, stethoscope peeping out of one pocket.

'Sir, I don't understand.'

'Spencer, I think you do. The Captain's not been himself recently, has he?'

'What's that got to do with me?' Spencer said defensively.

'You're the Captain's steward. You see more of him than does anyone else aboard.'

'Sir, I don't spy on the Captain!'

'Of course you don't. I'm not asking you to. What I'm interested in are the things you see in the normal course of your work. I know you feel this smacks of disloyalty, but you could help him by helping me.'

'Yes, sir,' Spencer said to buy time.

'Spencer, loyalty doesn't necessarily mean keeping your mouth shut. There are times, not very often, when it's better to say something, even if it means going behind the person's back. The Captain's a sick man, Spencer. You know what I mean.'

'Well, sir.' He hesitated, took a pull at his cigarette, stubbed it out in the ashtray at his elbow. 'He 'as been a bit funny lately.'

'In what way?'

'I don't like talkin' about 'im behind 'is back, sir. It's not right.'

'Of course you don't. But you're helping him by talking to me, by giving me another perspective on the problem.' The doctor brought out a cigarette case. 'Have one of these.'

Spencer lit up and inhaled deeply. Good ones these.

'There's no hurry, Spencer. Just take your time.'

Yeah. Take your boots off, lie down on the couch and tell Uncle Savage all about it. There couldn't be much doing in the sick bay if the PMO was prepared to sit down and yatter at him like this.

He told him in the end, all the business about the Old Man waking up shouting and shaking like he was having one of his goes of malaria. Made your blood run cold, it did, the poor bugger. How long had this been going on? Difficult to say, hard to remember, like, but it started about the time we went to Port Said, just the odd night, but it'd got really bad the last few weeks. Just about every night, 'I can 'ear 'im shouting, sir, and I go in.' And the rest. 'Part of the time 'e's all right, same as 'e's always been, but 'alf the time I can't do nothin' right. First the bacon's too crisp, then it's not crisp enough, or the toast's not done enough and then 'e leaves 'alf of it anyway. Right off 'is food, sir. I've been with 'im in two ships now and I'll admit 'e 'as 'is moments same as anybody, but 'e's never been like this before.'

48

'And how do you feel about this, in yourself?'

Well, he had to admit it was getting him down a bit. It wasn't much fun for him and he didn't think it could be much fun for the Old Man either. 'Wish I knew what was eatin' 'im, sir.'

'Trouble at home possibly?'

'Don't think so, sir. Gets 'is mail regular, and Mrs Thurston's a real nice lady. A proper lady, but a smasher all the same.'

The doctor wasn't half nosy. Wanted to know how often the Captain went ashore and what he did. Well, he was always back on board to sleep and didn't come back with lipstick on his collar or nothing like that. He played squash with Jimmy ffrench or the Gunnery Officer quite a bit and he was pretty thick with a couple of the other captains, but he hadn't been going ashore much lately, come to think of it. And did the Captain drink much? ('Have another cigarette, Spencer.') 'Well, sir. Usually the Captain's a man that's very moderate with 'is drink. Don't touch a drop at sea. Never 'as. Don't drink at lunchtime either. 'E 'as a glass of wine with 'is dinner and maybe the odd drink after, but that's all.'

And all this had started about the time we went to Port Said, which is about four months ago; that was when he, Spencer, had started to notice things?

'Yes. sir.'

'Thank you, Spencer. You've been very helpful.'

'What'll 'appen to the Captain, sir?' If he really was off his trolley . . .

'Now leave that side of things to me. He's not mad in the clinical sense, don't worry about that. Ever served in submarines?'

'No, sir.'

'But you have a rough idea of how their propulsion systems work?'

'Yes, sir.' Spencer was puzzled.

'Submerged, a submarine runs on electric motors and there is a continuous drain on the batteries, which can only be recharged on the surface, when the diesels are running. Going at full speed, a lot of manoeuvring and so on, create a heavier drain on the batteries and so he can't stay submerged for as long as he would running more economically.'

'Yes, sir.' What the hell had this got to do with the Old Man?

'In some ways the human mind is not dissimilar to the submarine's batteries. Operational service causes a drain of guts, bottle or whatever you like to call it. Going on leave or into a shore job can be taken as the equivalent of surfacing to recharge, but, just as the submarine may be compelled to submerge again before his batteries are fully charged, so going on leave may not always be enough. And as time goes on and the reserves get more and more depleted, it takes longer and longer to recharge and in some cases the battery will no longer hold a full charge. Do you follow me so far?'

'Yes, sir.'

'In the case of the Captain the batteries are pretty flat and it means that the system isn't functioning properly. And as human beings are a bit more complicated than submarines it means he's been a bit funny lately, to use your words. He's tired and overdue for a spell ashore. He doesn't like the idea but it's got to come.'

'Yes, sir.'

'Remember, it's pretty unpleasant for him, so try to humour him a bit. You're doing a darn good job. But if there's anything you feel is important, come and see me. Anything at all, don't hesitate. And now we'd better sort out your jabs.' The doctor opened the door. 'Petty Officer Sellars, Able Seaman Spencer for typhoid and paratyphoid.'

So one of the sick bay pansies stuck the needle in him and that was that. But he wasn't all that sure he'd done the right thing, whatever the doctor said. He finished folding his Number One suit away and swung himself up into his hammock. He wouldn't say nothing about tonight, a man was entitled to the odd bender.

# — Chapter Four —

'All you've got to say, ' Nairne had said, 'is "Are you awake, sir?" even if he's snoring his head off, and keep on saying it until he is and then you trot out the met.'

It was still dark as Pearson hurried across the quarterdeck, the wind gusting. South-westerly, Force Five, he remembered. Why was waking senior officers one of the duties of the Midshipman of the Watch? And why did it have to be at such an ungodly hour? If he was a captain or commander he certainly wouldn't get up at six a.m. Oh no, he'd have breakfast in bed at nine at the earliest. Barometric pressure twenty-nine point six. Cloud cover seven-tenths. Was there anything else?

'The captain of my last ship was mad on yoga and when you went in he was usually standing on his head bollock naked!' Nairne remarked cheerfully.

What could he expect? At least he had got his hair cut. 'Better get it done,' Nairne advised. 'All senior officers have to have something to get steamed up about. With the Captain it's hair and with the Commander it's boot heels.' He prayed he would pass muster with both.

Three minutes to six. Better not barge straight in, especially if this captain was a yoga enthusiast. Someone who voluntarily did PT on the quarterdeck at crack of dawn was capable of anything. He took the opportunity to have a proper look at the Captain's pictures, a welcome change from the bare paint of the gunroom. There were a couple of sketches he had noticed yesterday, before he was bawled out. A village church beneath a hillside, an old stone bridge crossing a stream, a bicycle leaning carelessly against it; *St Cuthbert's, Langdon, Sept. 1941*. A narrow cobbled street, with areas of deep shadow between the buildings, patches of bright sunlight silhouetting the overhanging balconies, a sense of deepness and permanence; *Mdina, March 1942*.

A rating appeared from the pantry, bustled about. 'Like that, sir?'

Pearson was embarrassed. 'Yes, I do.'

'The Old Man did it. Nice, innit?'

What was the man's name? The point had been stressed at *King Alfred* that an officer should address his men by name at all times, but he had barely learned any names yet and he had never seen this man before. And it was time he faced the Captain.

'I'm Spencer, sir. Captain's steward.' He cocked a glance at the door of the sleeping cabin. 'I'd leave it for this morning. Touch of malaria in the night. Sleepin' it off now. I'll shake the Captain meself presently.'

After all that! But there was still the Commander (Commander E.G. Bradshaw DSO), who required to be woken at 0630 and was a bit deaf one side.

'Are you awake, sir?' The ritual question, stabbing through the pain-filled fog behind his eyes. 'Are you awake, sir?' He opened his eyes, and quickly shut them again.

'Mornin', sir.' Spencer was standing over him, holding a glass of some brown liquid instead of the usual cup of tea. 'Get on the outside of that.'

There were yellow viscous lumps in it. 'What is it?'

'A Spencer Special, sir.'

'A what?'

'Hangover cure, sir. Better stick to beer in future. Use it meself. Never fails.'

'What's in it?' Thurston said dubiously. He hadn't

been as bad as this since the morning of his wedding. Oh God, last night.

'Tell you when you've drunk it, sir.'

He risked it. It could hardly make things worse.

'Two eggs, double tot of Worcester Sauce, a good dose of black pepper, and a leetle pinch of gunpowder, sir.'

'Are you trying to finish me off?'

'It works, sir.'

'On the kill or cure principle.' He glanced at the clock. 0700 hours.

Spencer gave one of his conspiratorial looks and said impassively, 'Thought you could do with some extra kip, sir. I told young Mr Pearson you'd 'ad a go of malaria in the night.'

'Thank you.' Discretion. Good for Spencer.

'Breakfast, sir. Double fried?'

'Good God, no.' He couldn't face any more eggs this morning.

'Do you some toast, sir.'

Thurston ran for the heads.

Paymaster Sub-Lieutenant James Jenner removed the completed sheet from the typewriter and lit a cigarette. He'd joined the Navy to fight, not to push paper from 'In' tray to 'Out' tray and be a bloody shorthand typist! Jenner had had a number of civilian jobs, none of them lasting very long, and it had been his increasing disillusionment with selling life assurance which had led him to volunteer for the Navy in the summer of 1941, that and the knowledge that he was in any case due to be called up shortly and there was a certain kudos in being a volunteer. His success in the School Certificate qualified him for a commission, but his medical had revealed an inability to distinguish certain shades of green from certain shades of blue, and it was goodbye to any dreams of glory he might have harboured. They would take him in the Paymaster branch, or he could try one of the other services. Jenner had no great desire to be an infantryman and the RAF would take the same attitude towards his colour vision as the Navy, so he had accepted, and here he was pen-pushing aboard a bloody spit-and-polish cruiser in the bloody Mediterranean Fleet. Once the Navy had seemed exciting, even glamorous, with a more dashing uniform than the army or the air force, but from the inside he couldn't see much of that. All this 'Aye aye, sir' and saluting quarterdecks and talking about taking a boat ashore when you were in a hutted camp and taking a bus into town. He had had six months ciphering in Portsmouth, a leisurely voyage in a troopship round the Cape and here he was, doing a job that was only fit for a Wren. And at twenty-four he still had to mess in the gunroom with a lot of kids and that jumped-up so-and-so Hastings who treated anyone who hadn't come through Dartmouth like dirt. At least he didn't have to bunk with Hastings, or sling a hammock like the midshipmen. Captain's secretary. There was that way the Captain had, of lifting only his left eyebrow, the unscarred one, and saying 'Mr Jenner' with the slightest stress of the 'Mr', which meant trouble was coming, and there had been a lot of that lately.

Captain's Requestmen and Defaulters at 1100 hours. Three men wishing to discontinue shaving, one to resume shaving; 'Telegraphist Meadows, to see the Captain in private, sir.' 'All right, I'll see you afterwards.' Stokers Brown and Wallace, absent over leave fifteen days, four hours and seventeen minutes and missing the ship on two occasions. 'Anything to say?' 'No sir.' A few words in mitigation from the Senior Engineer. 'Do you accept my award or do you elect trial by court martial? . . . Remanded.' Brown and Wallace would get ninety days, subject to confirmation by Beecham, and Brown would lose his good conduct

55

badge in addition. Thurston had spent several minutes with his head under the cold tap and after breakfasting on the black coffee and dry toast was more or less capable of facing the day, but the escorting Marines would insist on stamping their big boots on every possible occasion; the band was at practice, thumping out 'The Nelson Touch' with much drum-rolling and a trombonist who was ever-so-slightly out of time.

One other case, Boy First Class William Alexander MacGregor, Official Number P/JX 421011, absent over leave three hours and five minutes. 'Anything to say?' 'Stand up straight, MacGregor!' 'No sir.' The signals officer said a few words in mitigation. 'Six cuts.' 'Six cuts,' repeated the Master-At-Arms in ringing tones. 'On cap. Salute the Captain. About turn! Double *march*.'

So MacGregor would be marched below and the traditional ritual of punishment would take its course. He always found ordering a caning unsettling; he remembered too keenly the cold sickness in the stomach beforehand, the effort of will to keep silent.

He saw Telegraphist Meadows. It was the usual story: a friend had written from home to say that Meadow's wife had been going around with an American soldier 'and it looks like there's a kiddy on the way.' Meadows didn't look old enough to be married, let alone the father of one child already. 'Me mum looks after her while Violet's at work.' Nothing to be done except stopping his allotment, having proper enquiries made and trying to get him a posting nearer home.

A walk around the upper deck, telescope under arm, accompanied by his 'doggie', Midshipman Graham, Chief Yeoman of Signals O'Shaughnessy and messenger, Boy McCormick. The Instructor Lieutenant was taking a class of senior midshipmen in meteorology, the Gunnery Officer exercising his crews against the stopwatch, a lesson in aircraft recognition was going on for the lookouts.

Back to his cabin, a cup of coffee and a couple more aspirins. The mail had arrived and he read it while he drank the coffee. One from his wife. Mrs Crosby, the daily woman, had slipped on the stairs and sprained her ankle, the hens had stopped laying for two days but had now started again, and she was writing this at work between jobs. A duty letter from George, in his penultimate term at Dartmouth now, less than six months before he went to sea as a midshipman. He had hardly seen him since the war began; their leaves just didn't coincide. Once, just after he had taken her over, *Marathon* had been in Plymouth for four or five days and George had got permission to come down for a few hours, to be shown over the ship by one of the midshipmen, to be made a great fuss of by Spencer ('Young Mr Thurston, a real nice young gentleman, sir.') He had intended to have a serious talk with George about girls, but somehow it had never happened. It came to him then how little he really knew him. George was growing up, with his father mostly absent, though he tried to do things with him when he was at home. George had sat in that chair there, keen, mad keen, itching to get into the real war, with no conception of what it was really like, working his way through a massive slab of Spencer's fruit cake. Fourteen and a half then, his first-born and only son: 'Dad, you were a snotty when you were fifteen!' It wasn't all that long since George had been running around the garden with a toy rifle, shouting 'Bang, Kaiser Bill!' or falling in the River Dart and having to be fished out by his father. He had taught him to swim after that. Not all that long, even, since he had first seen him, the day after he was born. 'There, isn't he beautiful?' Not beautiful; George was brick-red, with clumps of dark hair, and screamed lustily when he was taken out of the cot and handed over. Better not tell George any of this; he'd think he was going soft in the head.

One other letter, from Arthur Hancock, who had

been his closest friend since Osborne. Hank was back in uniform now after wangling his way into a job in the Intelligence Division of the Admiralty as a civilian.

*I told them I was on my feet all day in court, and that I did all the things one might expect, and my wife would back me up on that, but the medicos wouldn't have it. Shore duties only. So I'm doing the same job but instead of 'Mr Hancock, would you mind . . .' it's 'Hancock, do this,' and 'Hancock, do that', the oldest Sub in the business, ten bob a day and no chance of a dock brief to supplement it . . .*

Hank was irrepressible. He had waltzed in to see him in hospital at Greenock after *Seydlitz*. 'Well, Bob, the Germans have done nothing for your looks!' 'Kate, I rushed all the way to Greenock to offer comfort to this fellow on his bed of pain and all the ungrateful blighter could do was give me filthy looks and tell me I was making him laugh too much!' 'Ever tried to laugh when your jawbone's held together with bits of piano wire?' He could have done with Hank here now. 'I always knew you were a head case. To lose one ship, Captain Thurston, may be regarded as a misfortune. To smash up the next one looks like carelessness.' Hank would no doubt wine and dine him, and fill him with absurd legal anecdotes to take his mind off all this.

The Surgeon Commander came up, on the pretext of discussing the VD figures. 'Going up again. I think it's time for another of my blue film shows. Keeps the men amused if nothing else.'

The PMO's VD lectures were regarded by most of the men as entertainment; Savage had even parodied one for a concert a few months earlier. 'This,' he would announce, holding a sheath inflated to gigantic proportions, 'could save your life. At least it will save you from this,' cue shots from various angles of syphilitic sores and pricks rotting away, to jeers and catcalls and shouts of 'Silence there. The next man is on a charge.'

'You'll soon know if you've picked up a dose of clap. It's like pissing broken glass. I've had it myself, so I know. Using one of these may be like wearing gum-boots in the bath but it's a damn sight less painful.'

Savage stood up and shut the door. 'Now we've both calmed down, let's talk about you.'

He was right. Savage was keeping an eye on him. The doctor produced a small bottle from his pocket. 'These should help you sleep. One to be taken when you turn in. No alcohol. But that's strictly a temporary measure. All they'll do is damp down the symptoms a bit, not deal with the cause. I had a chat with Spencer after I saw you yesterday.'

'You what?'

'One of his jabs was out of date and I took the opportunity to have a word with him off the record.'

'Dammit, what do you think you were doing?'

'Just filling in the picture. Don't take it out on Spencer. He's a very loyal man and I had a job to drag anything out of him. He's very worried about you.'

'Is he? That's very touching.'

'You can't go on like this, you know.'

Thurston gave a non-committal grunt.

'You're in a state of acute anxiety neurosis, brought on by overstrain, overwork, too little sleep, too much worry, and so on, which is hardly helped by your insistence on pressing on regardless. You're managing to do the job but you're tearing yourself apart in the process. The only real way to deal with this is to take away the source of the strain, which is why I advised you to take a couple of month's leave. Take away the cause, peace, quiet, fresh air and the rest, and it usually cures itself. Just taking pills won't do it. Hit the whisky last night, did you?'

'I suppose Spencer told you that as well.'

'No. Simple observation. There's hangover written all over you. That won't do you any good either. You've got to have a break, sooner rather than later.

A couple of months' leave and you must be due a shore job anyway. Obviously you'd prefer to stay where you are, but you can't flog on for ever. But, since you seem determined to stay, we'll have to try another task. It might help to talk about things. What's on your mind?'

'Nothing.'

'You're not a very convincing liar. Trouble at home?'

'No.'

'Missing your wife?'

'No more than usual. PMO, I would appreciate it if you would go and practise your Freudian ideas on someone else, and let me get on with my job.'

Savage stood up to leave. 'All right. I think you'll survive another convoy but that's the limit.'

Thurston looked up from the file he was pretending to study. 'Carry on, PMO.'

The Captain inspected the midshipmen's journals, saw the padre about Sunday's hymns. A Damage Control exercise went ahead. Lieutenant Harker came in with a signal; the parents and sister of Boy Gibbons had been killed in an air raid two days earlier.

Boy Gibbons was small and painfully scrubbed, with a shock of carroty red hair and a mass of freckles.

'Sit down, Gibbons.' Gibbons looked startled and sat. 'I'm afraid this is bad news.' Gibbons knew. It couldn't be anything else. ('Mr Thurston, your brother has been posted missing.') Gibbons sat very straight, his hands resting on his knees. His face gave nothing away. Trot out the usual platitudes. 'A direct hit. They wouldn't have known anything about it.' ('He may well be a prisoner of war.') But there was no certainty about that, nothing in the signal, just as he had known with absolute clarity that George was dead.

'Yes, sir.'

'Have you any other family, Gibbons?'

'My brother's in the army, sir, the RHA, and my other sister's married and lives in Basingstoke.'

Until now Gibbons had been little more than a name and a face, one of forty-odd boy ratings aboard *Marathon*. ('Go home and comfort your mother.' 'My mother's dead, sir, and I'd rather not.')

'Had we been nearer home I would have sent you on compassionate leave. I'm sorry it's not possible.'

'I know, sir. That's all right, sir. I'd rather stay with the ship.' Gibbons was starting to fidget, holding himself in with an effort. 'I don't get on with my married sister anyway.' His voice hadn't finished breaking yet.

'If there's anything you need, you can see me at any time. There's your divisional officer, and the padre, if you want to see him.'

'I'm a Catholic, sir.'

'That doesn't make any difference, but we can get hold of a Catholic padre if you'd prefer.'

'I'll be okay, sir.'

He had Spencer make Gibbons a cup of tea, had a quiet word with Boy McCormick, who was in the same mess as Gibbons. Lieutenant Taylor, Gibbons's divisional officer, said he would keep an eye on him and make sure he was kept busy. Thurston went on deck to see the results of the Damage Control exercise and discussed it afterwards with Bradshaw. Another signal arrived, scheduling a convoy conference for 1600 hours.

# — Chapter Five —

The Admiral's day cabin was packed, officers clumped in groups; the Fourteenth and Eighteenth destroyer flotillas, lieutenant-commanders for the most part, the majority under thirty. The Commodore, a retired vice-admiral at the other end of the age scale at over sixty, with his staff, four Merchant Navy captains. The Fifteenth Cruiser Squadron, Philip Woodruffe of *Ariadne*, Charles Dowding of *Bellerophon* and Bill Broadhurst of *Persephone*. Stewards took coats and caps and circulated with tea and coffee, briefcases snapped open. The air was heavy with tobacco smoke. All had been on at least one Malta convoy; several had had other ships sunk under them. Dowding's hair was quite white, though he was only forty-five; Thurston knew for a fact that Broadhurst drank too much, the last few weeks at Malta he had been practically living on gin. Not that he had any reason for complacency, not after last night.

'. . . so I said, "Good God, woman. I said I wanted to hire it, not buy it." '

'Hello, Bob. Bill has just been reminding us of the charms of Massawa.'

'Did you actually find something to do there?'

'That was the only thing and it wasn't very good. Like fucking a sack of potatoes. I used to think Scapa was the arsehole of the universe until I discovered Massawa.'

'Scapa has its compensations, don't you think?' said

Woodruffe. 'The light effects can be quite marvellous.' He was not being entirely serious.

'Yes I know. You've said all this before. Scapa has something for everyone. You can paint. Bob can go for bracing walks with a sketch pad and fall off horses, and Charles can go chasing off in pursuit of the greater-crested blue tit!'

'The trouble with you, Bill,' sighed Dowding, 'is that you're such a *philistine*.'

'Is it true, Charles, that you're training your lookouts in bird recognition?'

'I'm afraid not, though I've a couple of snotties who are quite keen. I must say,' he glanced around, 'this is an improvement on the last charade.'

Beecham had decided before the last operation to hold the Captain's conference ashore in civilian clothes, in the interests of security.

'I know you're supposed to be able to tell an N.O. by the cut of his jib,' Dowding continued, 'but that was ridiculous. It wasn't only the clothes, though your cavalry twills were a give-away, Bob. All those beards on the destroyer chaps, and not a moustache or pair of spectacles between us.'

'They might have given us more than an hour's notice,' said Broadhurst. 'I was halfway round the golf course. Someone had to rush out and get me.'

'Good thing you weren't somewhere else.'

'If you're referring to Marjorie Fleming, we're just good friends.'

'Ah, things are starting to move.'

Chairs scraped as the Admiral came in with his flag lieutenant.

'Good afternoon. I expect you all know why you're here. Stonehenge is on. Put those cigarettes out, please. We've already lost Lieutenant-Commander Haley, and having you all dead of tobacco poisoning will not get us to Malta.'

'Perforated ulcer,' muttered someone behind Thurston. 'Blew up just after lunch. They'll be cutting him up about now. His Number One's taken over.'

'Too much corn dog,' said Broadhurst.

'As you all know the Malta situation is critical. Once again stocks of aviation fuel and all types of ammunition are down to emergency levels and unless replenishment is achieved Malta cannot hold out for very much longer. A matter of days rather than weeks, gentlemen. This is where our merchant ships come in. We have a tanker, *Nebraska Star*, carrying aviation spirit. *Berwickshire* carries ammunition and torpedoes for the submarines. *Empire Wave* and *Empire Liberator* have cargoes of ammunition, defence stores and some food. For the Royal Navy the task is quite simple. We must get Stonehenge to Malta.'

Two and a half years the island had held out, bombed around the clock from the Sicilian airfields sixty miles away, the people taking refuge in rock shelters and surviving, not living, on a diet of bread and tomato sauce.

'We will break straight for Malta, to economise on time and fuel. Standard zig-zag pattern, not the steps *Jellicoe* indulges in!' Beecham was rewarded by a ripple of laughter and a furious glower from one of the destroyer captains. On a previous convoy *Jellicoe* had gone to port instead of starboard on one leg of the zigzag and almost collided with one of the merchant ships. 'The close escort will be *Jade, Jewel, Pangbourne* and *Parkhurst*, under Commander Gibbs in *Jade*. The cruisers will take station astern. The Eighteenth Flotilla and the starboard division of the Fourteenth will form the anti-submarine screen under Captain Blackwood in *Pathan*. The merchantmen will form two columns, two cables between ships; *Empire Wave* and *Nebraska Star* ahead, *Berwickshire* and *Empire Liberator* astern. Commodore Paget will fly his broad pennant in *Empire Wave*, and no doubt you Merchant Navy chaps have heard all this before, but do pay attention to the

Commodore's signals and try to keep in station. We're trying a new tactic this time. One cruiser and the close escort only will go into Grand Harbour. The lucky cruiser is *Marathon* and command of the escort will then devolve upon Captain Thurston.'

So Beecham still trusted him.

'Bad luck, Bob, but it saves the rest of us from the Dog,' said Broadhurst.

'And keeps you out of the Gut.'

Charts were issued, zig-zag diagrams and signals instructions.

'Now you all know the standing orders. Wireless silence is to be maintained and signalling kept to a minimum. Once again I emphasise to the merchant ships, be alert. We don't want the Commodore to waste time with endless repetitions.'

One of the merchant captains frowned.

'Heard it all before. Three years of convoys and they can read morse by now,' Thurston said to Dowding.

'Stop that whispering,' said Broadhurst. 'Pay attention to the headmaster, like good little boys.'

'Blackout regulations will be strictly adhered to. As you all know a man smoking on deck could give away the entire convoy, and if I see a raised deadlight I shall take the greatest pleasure in using that captain's balls for a necktie.' Beecham coughed and continued. 'Escorts cannot be spared for lame ducks. Our numbers are minimal already. Therefore, anyone who should be damaged will have to fend for himself. This applies mainly to the escorts. Your responsibility is to get the merchant ships through. Neither will there be any stopping for survivors. I'm sorry, gentlemen, but the safety of the convoy must come first. In any case,' he glanced out of the scuttle, 'I doubt very much whether it would be of any use.'

The Admiral handed over to his staff officer (Operations), who went through the detail of the plan.

'Well, gentlemen, that's the lot. Any questions? Yes, Bill?'

'Will the drinks be on you, sir?'

'When Stonehenge gets through, old boy, I'll have you all to dinner at the Cecil and send the bill to Lord Gort!'

'It's gonna be one hell of a party, Admiral,' said an American voice, the Master of the *Nebraska Star*.

'It's gonna be one hell of a party all round,' said Dowding. 'Well, if that's all? You may inform your ships' companies of the situation at once. We sail at 2200. And the very best of British luck to you all. And that includes *Nebraska Star*. Stonehenge must get through!'


'Everything all right, Bob?' Beecham said to Thurston as he was leaving.

He set his teeth, lied through them. 'Yes sir.' There was nothing else to be said.

The captains went up on deck.

'Well, I daresay the local Funf is busy with his morse key by now,' said Dowding. 'A sudden concentration of boat traffic around the flagship.'

'Not to mention all the packing cases waiting on the dockside for the past fortnight.' Dowding turned aside to greet a bearded commander. 'Malcolm Nicholls. He was at Dartmouth with my young brother. Just taken over *Leonidas*. Can I hitch a lift, Bob? I sent my coxswain back.'

Petty Officer Stephenson had been lying off. Now he brought the boat to the gangway. The swell was rising; it was becoming a grey, miserable evening.

'A rule of this vessel, sir, if you're sick you clean up your own mess,' said Stephenson to Dowding. He was a Geordie, and direct.

'I'll bear that in mind.'

'Bear off forrard! Bear off aft! Slow ahead.'

The boat slid away from the gangway and began to

roll as she left the shelter of the flagship's side. In the bows Macleod was already soaked. Dowding settled his raincoat more closely around him.

'A little of Bill goes a long way, doesn't it? Heard from Kate recently?'

'Keeping the Min of I on their toes. How's Dorothy?'

'She claims to look like the side of a house.'

Dowding had only married fairly recently, creating a minor scandal because his wife had divorced her first husband in order to marry him, and the first little Dowding was due imminently.

Conversation flagged, Thurston looked out again at the weather.

'Pretty grim prospect,' said Dowding. 'With any luck the U-boats might stay down.'

*U-boats.* For a moment Thurston saw the flames again, and then a raft on an empty sea, a grey heaving sea like this one, a high Welsh voice babbling in delirium, a face white and cold like sculpted marble.

'Bob, are you feeling all right?'

*Pull yourself together, you bloody fool!* 'Yes, Charles, I'm all right. Just a bit tired.'

'Are you sure? You've gone a bit white.'

'Had a drop over the odds last night.' First Spencer and now Charles Dowding, in front of his boat's crew. He pushed a hand that shook slightly into his coat pocket, glanced out through the scuttle. 'This is you.'

'Boat ahoy?'

'*Bellerophon!*'

Dowding stood up, straddled his legs against the motion. 'Thanks for the lift.'

'See you when it's all over.'

Dowding faced him for a moment. 'Look after yourself, Bob. You're a rotten liar.'

Salutes were exchanged. 'Thank you, Stephenson.' Dowding stepped on to his gangway, judging the best moment in the roll; his legs disappeared upwards.

'Home, sir?'

'Carry on, Stephenson.'

*Marathon* made ready for sea. The engine room was raising steam. Libertymen returned from shore leave. The Surgeon Commander despatched a couple of patients who would not be fit for duty within forty-eight hours to hospital ashore. The padre held a communion service and a few men went to him for confessions. The Captain held a briefing for heads of department, broadcast to the ship's company and found time to write to his wife before the mail went ashore.

He had been the navigator of a small cruiser then. The Torpedo Officer had been invited to play tennis one Saturday at 'old General Wingfield's' and to bring a friend. It started inauspiciously enough. Thurston's motorbike had one of its periodic attacks of temperament and he arrived hot, dusty and covered in oil after pushing it the last two miles. Kate always claimed that the first words he ever said to her were, 'Can you show me where I can wash my hands?' Kate was the General's second daughter; her fair hair had reddish lights in it; she had green eyes and distracting ankles, and was an unexpectedly vigorous tennis player, quite different from any other girl he had ever met. 'Then he knocked me down.' 'I did say it was my ball.' 'You weren't leaving me anything to play. I was getting bored. And it meant you had to help me up.' 'I suppose that was what you wanted all along.' On the Monday he threw caution to the winds, obtained two tickets for a performance of *The Rivals* that night and rang up to ask her to accompany him.

The marriage of junior officers was discouraged; the Navy paid no marriage allowance and considered that they should devote their energies to their profession. Until he met Kate he had no intention of marrying before he was a commander. However, six weeks later he proposed, out (walking) on Dartmoor with their feet in a stream; and she told him, laughing, to get down on his knees and do it properly, and then accepted.

'Of course I'll marry you. I'll marry you tomorrow if you like.'

He had been almost surprised at that; there seemed to be dozens of eligible young men around Kate and her sisters, and he was an obscure lieutenant aged twenty-four, with uncertain prospects and no money beyond his pay. His father advised him to wait; his captain, a bachelor, declared that 'an officer married is an officer marred', and that he would be, 'no damn use for the first two years, if ever'. The General interrogated him on his war record and his prospects – what grounds had he for considering himself a fit husband for his daughter? He would be a lieutenant-commander by automatic promotion on 20th January 1928; beyond that he preferred not to speculate, but he was a first-class navigator, which meant he was qualified to pilot ships of any size and draught, and an interpreter in Hindustani and Urdu, and intended to sit for the Staff College exam once he was senior enough. The General pronounced himself satisfied, warned him that Kate was a head-strong girl – she insisted on riding astride – and she was still very young, but if both were of the same mind in a year's time he would not stand in their way.

It had not been easy at first. They began their married life in two rooms; nine months and four days later there was a child, and a year after that, another, by which time he was doing a two-year commission on the China Station and Kate was living with her parents once more. Helen had already been walking when he first saw her and, of course, George hadn't known him. But it had all worked out in the end. George was at Dartmouth; Helen had taken her School Certificate a year early and passed with credits in all subjects. On the outbreak of war Kate had declared herself unwilling to sit around waiting for her husband's infrequent spells in port, in dingy hotels with other naval wives, and taken a job with the Ministry of Information in Portsmouth. Thirteen months now since he had seen any of them. Letters arrived via the Cape, a minimum of six weeks out of date. He hadn't known until two months later that they had been bombed while *Marathon* was at Malta; only death or serious injury merited an official signal, and Kate made light of it all.

*The drawing-room windows are still missing, but the gas and electricity are back on and the water wasn't affected. Everything is ALL RIGHT.*

He finished the letter, blotted it, put away his pen. It was flat again, but he couldn't tell Kate that everything had gone wrong; she was too far away to be able to do anything, and it would only worry her.

*Is everything all right? Your last couple of letters seem a bit low. There's a limit to what you can say about the weather where you are.*

Two hours to sailing, everything ticking over with the ease of established routine, out of his hands until sailing time. He could go through the written orders again, but he knew them already. A straight course to Malta, zig-zag in accordance with the diagram provided, speed fourteen knots. Three days out, oil in Grand Harbour, perhaps get ashore to stretch his legs, and three days back.

Spencer was moving about, taking things up to the sea cabin. 'I put some more dubbin on your seaboots, sir. Do you feel like anything more to eat?'

'No, thank you, Spencer.' He never felt like eating much before sailing these days.

'Sure, sir? You didn't 'ave much breakfast or lunch.'

'Spencer, stop fussing!'

He had trusted Spencer, and Spencer had blabbed to Savage about him. Spencer recognised the tone, and the lift of one eyebrow which meant that the Captain wished to be left to himself. The Old Man had been very correct with him for most of the day, which was a bad sign. He must know.

Spencer went out. Thurston took out his pen again and started a letter to George. Not a great deal he could say; the things which would most interest him would not get past the censor.

*'Look after yourself, Bob. You're a rotten liar.'*

The advice was laughable in the circumstances. He had to put all this out of his mind and concentrate on the job in hand. He had locked away Savage's pills; they were worse than no use at sea. A double knock on the outer door. That would be the post corporal, about to go ashore with the mail. He finished the letter, addressed it. Just get through this convoy.

# — Chapter Six —

*Marathon* slipped her moorings, topped up with oil and followed *Ariadne* out through the boom. Pearson shivered and glanced uneasily at the bucket bracketed in the corner near the chart table, hoping desperately that he was not going to be sick already.

'Turn that light down.'

Already turning green as the ship rolled into the swell of the open sea, he took off a glove and fumbled for the dimmer switch on the binnacle light, turned it down until the figures on the compass card were barely discernible, and was promptly told to turn it up again.

'Midships . Meet her.'

'Midships, sir. Meet her.'

'Steer two-eight-eight.'

'Steer two-eight-eight, sir.'

The dialogue between the Captain and the Chief Quartermaster on the wheel, unseen several decks below, as *Marathon* negotiated the swept channel. Pearson wished he had not had that second cup of coffee after dinner. Would he be allowed to go to the heads below, or would he have to use the bucket? He shivered again, despite the layers of clothing Norris had advised him to put on: long johns, two pairs of socks, a sweater knitted by his mother, a scarf to fill the gaps, his brand-new duffel coat and seaboots.

'Starboard twenty.'

'Starboard twenty, sir.'

The ship heeled as the helm went over, putting him off balance for a moment and increasing the discomfort in his throat and stomach. The First Lieutenant had put him on this watch, for the experience. 'You'll see more of what's going on from the bridge. Keep your ears pinned back and things will soon start to fall into place.' He wished the First Lieutenant was here now, or someone else that he knew, even Nairne.

'Midships. Steer three-one-seven.'

'Midships, sir. Steer three-one-seven.'

'Nothing to port.'

'Course three-one-seven, sir. Nothing to port.'

Nothing to port? But there was one of the destroyers just over there. Surely someone must have seen it?

Someone noticed his puzzlement. 'Confused? "Nothing to port" simply means that the quartermaster mustn't drift to port of the course he's been given. If he wavers at all, it must be to starboard.'

The Navigator straightened from the binnacle, called out a bearing. The Captain glanced over to port, watching the destroyer begin his turn.

'Port twenty.'

'Port twenty, sir.'

'Notice we didn't begin our turn until *Pathan* was out of the way? That's because she's much handier than we are,' said Pearson's informant, whom he recognised as O'Shaughnessy, the Chief Yeoman of Signals. 'Mind, I think the Captain sometimes forgets that she isn't a destroyer. Took her into Sliema Creek once. Stern first at fifteen knots. No wonder I've got grey hairs.'

'Midships. Steer three-oh-two.'

'Midships, sir. Steer three-oh-two.'

'Any questions, Mr Pearson, just ask away.'

He had more questions, but the discomfort was growing worse. It was no good, but what was he supposed to say. 'Sir?'

The Torpedo Officer turned towards him. 'What is it?'

'Permission to go below, sir?'

'What for?'

'Call of nature, sir.' He could feel himself blushing, hoped no one would see it.

'Oh, very well, but be sharp about it.'

It was going to be a close call. He stumbled down the ladder, nearly fell from it as the ship rolled again, seemed to fumble for ever before he got through the layers to his trouser buttons, got them unfastened. Just in time.

Midnight, the merchantmen settled in their two columns, close escort and cruiser escort deployed around them, more destroyers just visible further off. Dull grey forms on a dull grey sea flecked with soapy foam. The wind had got up; *Marathon* buried her long nose in a head sea as she held to her westerly course. The lower messdecks were already awash. Two hours out from Alexandria, but already the land was far behind; only the sea and Malta were ahead.

'Bloody cold, innit?'

'That's the *gregale* for you. Thought the Med was sunny? Come out here for the sun.'

The First Lieutenant took over the watch from Lieutenant Taylor, with Sub-Lieutenant Cowper-Coles under instruction. Able Seaman Courtney relieved Petty Officer Hicks on the wheel. Pearson, relieved by the Polish Midshipman Zurokowski, headed for his hammock, chilled to the marrow and deadly sick.

'You lot are the cream of England. All the clots. The rich and the thick. Mr 'Ancock, you march like a pregnant camel, sir! A what, Mr 'Ancock? Louder, Mr 'Ancock! Wipe that grin off your face, Mr Thurston. You march with the camel between your bloody knees!'

The first term at Osborne was the worst, the second very nearly as bad. The naval cadet worked harder, played harder, was disciplined more fiercely and beaten more frequently than any public school-boy. He was roused by a bugle call at seven o'clock in winter, six thirty in summer, knelt for prayers as 'one gong' sounded; left knee down, right knee down, left hand up, right hand up; dashed naked to the plunge bath and dropped into cold seawater, right under, then doubled back with five minutes to be dried, dressed and fallen in outside for inspection. At the double, always at the double. His sea chest and bedspace were inspected nightly as he lay in bed in the position of attention, pyjamas buttoned to the neck, the point of the chin a precise one inch from the top of the sheet, four inches of sheet showing, four inches of white counterpane, his initials on the blue rug over his legs exactly centred, clothes folded in the prescribed manner, all windows opened to the same distance, deck beneath cleaned by hand. Any defect meant a tick, and three ticks accumulated meant he was doubled outside into the gangway and beaten. He received six cuts from the cadet captain of his term should he wear his lanyard too low or his cap at an angle greater than that prescribed for his seniority, place his hands on his hips, speak to a cadet senior to himself, fail to leap nimbly out of the way of a cadet senior to himself even if that cadet tried to walk through him, fail to pass a senior gunroom at the double. He was forbidden to have pockets in his trousers or side pockets in his jackets; he was paid one shilling a week, provided by his parents, and expected to display his marks to his fellows after a beating at a penny a peep. He wrote a duty letter home once a week, but there was one he could never post, if he was there of his own choice: *Dear Father, I hate it here.*

But there were compensations. The curriculum concentrated on practical matters; seamanship, navigation and engineering, instead of the Latin and Greek of the public schools. A cadet was addressed by officers and masters as Mr – ' his parents wrote their letters to –

Esquire, Royal Navy. He played games six days a week, but not only rugby and cricket; he sailed, fenced, boxed, played squash and hockey and spent long afternoons pulling on the river. And friendships were made. 'God, not you two again, the Unholy Alliance, Mr Hancock and Mr Thurston!' He and Hank had got into a fight on the first day, while waiting for the ferry at Portsmouth, been awarded three cuts apiece and been told off for boxing instruction. 'On a charge before you even get to the College. I'm goin' to remember you two!'

And you went home on leave at the end of the term, not as a schoolboy but as a member of the mightiest navy the world had ever seen, toughened, hardened, able to take whatever was thrown at you, and lorded it a little over elder brothers who had yet to get into uniform. Some had fallen by the wayside. One boy did not survive the first day; after refusing to climb a ship's mast with the rest, he tearfully demanded to go home to his mother. Another disappeared on a visit to the mainland and was found by the police two days later wandering in the New Forest. Found guilty of desertion, he was doubled into the gym under escort, manacled to a vaulting horse and twelve cuts were laid upon him. It was a disturbing and awe-inspiring spectacle.

He had been nine years old, going on ten, when his vague thoughts of a life in the Navy had become compacted into something concrete. It was the end of the summer term, the beginning of eight weeks of freedom; he was sitting on his trunk at Newcastle Station, having come off a train from Morpeth and waiting for another to Wooler, reading a forbidden comic and slowly eating an equally forbidden sausage roll. The boy was three or four years older, walking nonchalantly up and down the platform, hands on hips, in all the glory of brass buttons, a strip of twisted braid on either side of the collar, white lanyard looped round his neck and passing into his top pocket, cap set well

76

back, with the great crest of the Royal Navy in bright gold wire. He walked past, and got on another train, oblivious to the impact he had made. His grandfather told him that night that the boy must have been a cadet of one of the naval colleges, and it became gradually accepted that just as Edmund was going to Oxford and George to Sandhurst and then into the Guides, he was going into the Navy. So it was that on a soft spring evening when he was twelve his father had taken him to Wooler, in uniform for the first time, shook his hand, gruffly told him to work hard and remember he was a Thurston, issued him with tickets, money and instructions. Get on the sleeper at Newcastle, have breakfast at King's Cross the next morning, take a cab to the Science Museum (tip the driver sixpence), where he was to occupy himself profitably until twelve, when he was to take a cab to Victoria and catch the 1233 to Portsmouth, where he would be met by staff of the Royal Naval College. There was no question of his father or anyone else going with him. It was time to put away childish things.

The Instructor-Lieutenant came up from the plot with a met forecast and a long face. *Nebraska Star* went out of station and provoked an irate signal from the flagship. The cocoa came round and a selection of bully beef sandwiches. Jenner sat in the cipher office, alternately reading and dozing. Pearson, lying nauseous in a bucking hammock, wondered for the hundredth time what on earth had possessed him to join the Navy.

'I'm going below, Number One.'

'Aye aye, sir. Goodnight.'

A glance at the radar screen, then at the plot two decks below, a word with Schooly. The Captain's sea cabin was a rectangular steel box at the rear of the bridge, eight feet by four and a half, lit now only by a dim red bulb to safeguard night vision. Room for a bunk, professionally made up by Spencer, with drawers underneath, a minute washbasin, a writing surface, a chair bolted to the deck, buzzer from the Officer of the Watch, voicepipe and telephone. He placed his cap and binoculars on the rack above, took off duffel coat and seaboots and lay down.

At sea you spent between sixteen and twenty hours a day on the bridge and the rest three seconds from it, because when things happened, they usually happened fast. The first intimation of the presence of a U-boat was all too often a torpedo hit, on your own ship or on someone else's. You went to sleep praying that the Officer of the Watch would call you in time. There was always a reluctance on his part to risk the wrath of an inrascible superior and you guarded against it by setting out in writing all the circumstances in which the Captain was to be called. On sighting any enemy vessel, or vessel not positively identified as friendly, any aircraft not identified as friendly, on obtaining any radar or asdic contact, on sighting flares or starshell at night, on any change of course not part of the zig-zag pattern, any ship going out of station, any change in weather or visibility, *in any doubt or uncertainty*. But there was always the inexplicable. You developed a sixth sense, which got you up and out through the door without being fully awake, or knowing the reason why. But mostly you relied on the watchkeepers and spent time in here not engaged in sleeping or eating in reading, writing letters, dealing with the most urgent paperwork, drawing if in the mood, with one ear always cocked to the voicepipe. He read a few pages, then stowed the book away, listened for a moment to the usual noises, the regular ticking of the gyro, muffled voices, the never-ceasing low hum of machinery, wedged himself with feet and elbows against the motion.

'Captain, sir.'

He reached for the voicepipe. 'Captain.'

Lieutenant Harker's voice; the watch must have changed again. He listened to the story. *Empire Liberator* had engine trouble. Once he might have stayed where he was and seen how things developed, but not now. 'All right, I'm coming up.' He swung his legs over the side of the bunk, thrust his feet into the boots, grabbed coat, cap and binoculars in a series of practised movements.

*Empire Liberator* reported that she had a leak in her superheater, and requested a reduction in convoy speed.

'Reggie's not going to like this,' said Harker to the midshipman.

'Signal from Flag, sir,' reported the Yeoman. *'All units reduce to ten.'*

'Acknowledge.'

Lamps blinked, blue and heavily shaded.

'Signal from Flag, sir. *Execute.*'

'Two-one-oh revolutions.'

'Two-one-oh revolutions, sir.'

The telegraph clanged. In a moment the ship began to lose way, the intensity of her motion altered. The plot called up another change of course, the convoy went on to the port leg of the zig-zag. Thurston stayed where he was for a few moments, talking a little to Harker, then went back to the sea cabin.

The dream woke him once more. 0603, not worth trying to sleep again before First Light and the call to Dawn Action Stations. He turned over, drew his knees up, trying to get comfortable, trying not to remember the reality which lay beneath the dream.

There was blood in his eyes and he couldn't see. He ripped off his anti-flash hood, used it to wipe his eyes, his fingers slithering over the wet rent across his forehead. Then he spewed, all down his chest. Lieutenant York was dead, torn almost in two, guts damply glist-

79

ening in the dim light which filtered through the splinter holes. A severed head moved gently with the ship's motion. A shattered groin, pink and white where the bones of the pelvis showed through. He tried to move, but his feet were caught up under something. His mouth opened again in a soundless scream.

*Take a grip on yourself. Or you won't get out.*

Take a deep breath. Look around. Wipe the eyes. Take stock of the situation. Turret's crew all dead. A direct hit, or nearly so, the armour plate broken and crushed like an eggshell. The deck beneath was growing hot which meant . . . ? *Think you bloody little shyster!*

The magazine was on fire! He put his hand out to the voicepipe. Out of reach. The telephone? The cable was cut through. He wiped his eyes, rested his weight on his hands, tried to wrench his legs clear of the wreckage. The twisted metal tore at his ankles. He gritted his teeth, tried again, tears of rage and pain coming into his eyes. A bit further! Still out of reach. His left foot was moving. He took a grip behind the knee with both hands, pulled with all his strength. Pain shot up his leg. He cursed. The foot, at last, came clear. He twisted over onto his stomach, got a purchase on the deck, reached across York's body for the tube. Briefly, their eyes met. His mouth swam with saliva. *Oh God, don't let me be sick again!* He wrenched it from the bracket.

'Open magazine flood valves. Close flash doors.'

'Open magazine flood valves. Close flash doors, sir. Aye aye, sir,' the supply assistant in the magazine checked back. The voice was oddly steady.

The sound of water, and of men trapped by hatches which could only be opened from above. Dead men all around; the miasma of blood and cordite fumes and burnt flesh, and the sweet-sour reek of his own vomit. All of them dead, bits of them plastered all over the turret. York, Petty Officer Booth – 'If Mr York gets killed, you're in command of the turret, but if he gets it, you'll get it too.' He became aware of dampness inside his trousers, a rising wave of shame and disgust.

The ship seemed to be stopped. There had been other explosions, in the last seconds before the world blew up. The flagship had led them in to finish off the *Wiesbaden*; they had got off a couple of salvoes and then suddenly rounds were falling all around, the shadowy shapes of German battleships appearing in the periscopes. Was she sinking now, with him trapped like this?

*Get a grip, you bloody little coward!*

There was air coming through the splinter holes, not water, and light. His ears seemed to be all right – thank God for the cotton wool he'd stuffed in them just before they opened fire. He must have flung his hands up to protect his eyes; he had taken his antiflash gloves off to do something and the backs were scorched and beginning to blister, the palms cut in a couple of places from scrabbling at the wreckage around his legs. His head was still bleeding, eyes filling up again, and his right foot was still jammed, he couldn't shift whatever was on it. Firing was still going on, but far off, other ships. His handkerchief was against his head, clenched in his fist, growing sodden with blood. His ankle was swelling up inside his boot, hands beginning to smart. Was he going to die in here?

*Get a grip! You're a naval officer!*

He started to sing 'John Peel' in the hope of taking his mind off things, the sound echoing strangely around the broken turret.

'Who's there?' A staccato bark that sounded like the Commander.

'Midshipman Thurston, Sir!'

'Anyone with you?'

'Nossir.'

'Are you all right?'

81

'Yes sir.' Automatic. 'I can't get up, sir. My foot's stuck.'

'Sit tight. We'll get you out.'

It seemed to take an age, shoving and heaving with tommy bars to try to get the hatch open. His watch was smashed, the hands stopped at twenty-five minutes to six. They talked to him all through, news of the battle. The ship was badly damaged and had been taken in tow by the seaplane carrier *Engadine*. The squadron had taken the full fire of the German Fleet. The flagship had blown up; *Black Prince*, the next astern, was badly hit and limping away under her own power. The battle was moving away eastwards.

'Something to tell your grandchildren.'

He lay for several hours on a stretcher in the wardroom flat, among other less serious casualties, after they cut him free, woozy from the bang on the head and sick, and aching all over. The light was dim, men talked in sharp Cockney voices, smoked, moaned and occasionally howled in their own private agonies. A sick-berth attendant put stitches in his head with what felt like a marling spike ('Hold still unless you want your eye poked out.'), strapped his ankle and dressed the flash burns on his hands. Someone else brought round mugs of tea, which set him vomiting again.

After a long time there was movement and officers talking in hushed voices. The ship seemed to be stopped again.

'Can you walk?'

'I think so.'

More orders. A bearded seaman who he didn't know put an arm around his shoulders, got him to his feet and led him up a series of ladders to the deck.

'Coom on, sir. Oop yer coom. This is where we get off.'

It was early morning, *Engadine* lying alongside, stretchers being manhandled over the rails. Men were fallen in by divisions on *Warrior's* deck, incongruous yet fitting.

'Not long now. Once the crocks get off. You won't even get your feet wet.'

The last stretcher went across. The ache in his head had become pounding pain now that he was upright. His hair was stiff with blood, more squelched in his right boot. He was going to be sick again.

'Top Division, quick march!'

'Now when I says so, you jump for the net that *Engadine* 'as so kindly rigged for us and they'll 'aul you up. Think you can manage?'

Men were jumping the gap, squad by squad, all up and down the length of the ship. The seamen guided him to the rail. 'Sure you can do it? I can whistle up a stretcher easy.'

'I'm all right.'

He was rocky on his legs. He could hardly put his left foot to the deck. The burns were on fire again.

'Ready, sir?'

*Warrior* was very low in the water. The ships rolled slackly, black water gleaming between them. He was over the rails, holding on with one hand, finding places for his feet. Back together.

'Now!'

He jumped. Hemp cordage scraped his face. He was slipping, going down. Hands grabbed his clothes. 'Up yer come. Soon be back in Blighty.' His ankle gave way, he fell in a heap on the deck and threw up once more.

'Get rid of him before he ruins my planking!'

Someone steered him to one side, the bearded seaman again. He grinned, his teeth very white in the depths of the beard. Thurston managed a shaky grin back. *Warrior's* men were falling in once more, in perfect order. The last man, the Captain, made his jump; pipes shrilled, salutes were exchanged. A few minutes later the ship turned turtle and sank, the cheers of her men ringing out into the morning.

Two men half led, half carried him below, where someone pushed a needle into his arm and sweet relief flooded through him as the pain rolled away. He was concussed, so they kept him in bed for a week in the Dowager Countess of Somewhere's Military Hospital and made a great fuss of him because he was so young. Once, Lady Somewhere came on a tour of inspection and sent him blushing to the roots of his hair by loudly exclaiming 'Oh you poor baby boy!' He went home to Langdon on a month's leave, walking with a stick, the raw new scar over his eyes and cracking headaches. His stepmother fussed over him and tried to persuade him to sit quietly in the garden, instead of galloping Rocket bareback in search of the only relief he knew. George and Edmund were in France, Alice was nursing. His father, puzzled, asked, 'Anything wrong, old chap?' a couple of times, took him for a walk and attempted to draw him out, but the chasm between them was too wide. There was a row; he spent the last week of his leave with Hank, clanking about on a tin leg now, cramming for Cambridge and lodging with an uncle who was at the Admiralty. Then on to his next ship, his injuries healed, a slim gold wound stripe on one sleeve, but something had changed. Even in *Oudenarde's* fifteen-inch turrets with their thirteen-inch armour he was screaming inside all through. The Snotties' Nurse quietly shifted him to another action station and nothing was said, but he'd failed; in the extremity of fear he'd failed.

Jutland. Twenty-six years ago. He had tried to put it behind him, but the memory kept coming back, in the distorted form of his dream, or as part of the delirium which came with malaria. It had come when he and Kate were three weeks married; she had put her arms round him, asked him what it was; he had told her the bald facts, but the full horror was too deep.

He got up, shaved, changed his shirt. Spencer arrived with his breakfast. 'Mornin', sir. Lovely weather for the ducks.' Gradually he became bolder. 'Be nice to get back to Malta, sir, visit me old haunts.'

'Stay out of the Egyptian Queen this time.'

'At least I 'aven't an 'ook to lose now, sir.' Spencer said without malice. The Egyptian Queen in the Strada Stretta had been the scene of Spencer's most recent fall from grace. The charge sheet told a sorry tale. Leading Seaman Harold Thomas Spencer, Official Number P/JX 137421, had become intoxicated, disputed the price of wine, smashed three chairs and the proprietor's spectacles, worth a total of one pound, seven shillings and fourpence, and resisted arrest by the shore patrol, 'These bein' haggravated offences, sir, bein' committed when the ship was hunder sailin' horders.' The Master-At-Arms had difficulty with his aspirates. Despite a black eye and a night in the cells to sober up, Spencer had managed to appear a picture of innocence across the Defaulters' table. 'Anything to say?' 'Nossir.' Justice had to be done, and had to be seen to be done, but the whole business left a sour taste in the mouth. The loss of his leading rate and fine of fourteen days' pay would not stop Spencer from smashing up another bar the next time he went on a bender. And half an hour later he had been serving him lunch just as usual.

'Spencer, you're a damn fool.'

# — Chapter Seven —

There were five air attacks that first day. The destroyer *Jellicoe* lost a man from splinter wounds and *Berwick-shire* had pumps going from a near miss which holed her on the waterline. She was lucky; her cargo was ammunition. The westerly gale continued, the wind howled and occasionally shrieked around the open bridges. No man moved on the upper decks except when unavoidable; even so, *Persephone* lost two men overboard. Between raids the turrets were trained on the beam to prevent the crews from being flooded out: *Marathon*'s masthead lookout had to be brought down, soaked through and half frozen, and they never saw the sun. The sick bay began to fill up again; a stoker came off a ladder when going on watch and smashed his left kneecap into half a dozen fragments. Savage decided regretfully that all he could do was to immobilise it until he could get the man to an orthopaedic surgeon ashore. Lieutenant Harker was flung out of his bunk and broke three ribs, which meant that Mr Skinner, the Warrant Telegraphist, took over as Signals Officer, and Sub-Lieutenant Cowper-Coles got his watchkeeping certificate.

*Marathon* had been closed up at Action Stations or Second Degree Readiness all day, broken only by the occasional stand-down for a mug of tea, a cigarette and a plate of lukewarm stew or the eternal bully beef sandwiches – the fuel had been drained from the galley fires in case of battle damage. Commander Bradshaw waited in the Damage Control centre, everything and nothing until something went wrong, Paymaster Sub-Lieutenant Jenner sat in the cipher office with nothing to cipher, the telegraphists listened to atmospherics and swapped paperbacks among themselves. Midshipman Pearson threw up once more in the bridge bucket and wondered how long this could go on. He was not reassured when someone told him it was far from unknown for this sort of weather to go on for weeks on end. 'Thought the Med was sunny, didn't you? But wait till you see the Denmark Strait.' The ship pitched into the great green mountains, solid water came back and slammed against the superstructure; she rolled sickeningly, lay over on her beam ends for a heart-chilling instant of time, then flicked back upright, hung there for a second, and began to go over . . . 'Aye, she goes over easy, but she always comes back.'

'Sick?' the Captain had said. 'You get over it more quickly if you keep on deck and standing watches.'

He envied the captain, his voice icily calm as he issued his orders, cap at an angle which expressed everything. He envied everyone. Pearson had been soaked through within two minutes of beginning his watch on the bridge, the windiest place on earth with a ferocious eddy which cut through all his layers of clothes. Next it would be down a treacherous series of ladders and across the open deck to his action station in B Turret, under Sub-Lieutenant Hastings, and his stomach was going again.

'Cocoa, sir?'

'Thank you, Spencer.'

'Bit rough, sir.'

'Good for the liver,' said the First Lieutenant.

'Change of course coming up, sir.'

'Very well.'

A call from the plot, the eighteen ships turning in unison, here and there a change in engine revolutions to maintain station.

'How long to last light, Pilot?'

'About ten minutes, sir.'

'How *long*?'

'Er, eleven minutes and forty-one seconds, sir,' Hart said after some violent mental arithmetic.

'Thank you.' He paused. 'Mr Hart!'

'Sir!'

'*When* I ask for some information, I expect the precise figure. Not "about this", or "nearly that"!'

'Aye aye, sir,' Hart said defensively.

He shouldn't have shouted at the Navigator. There would be the usual warnings to 'watch out for the Old Man' after that. He took a pull at the cocoa, absently rubbed the scar on his jaw. He had had certain reservations about Lieutenant (N) The Honourable Henry Archibald Le Patourel Hart when he first arrived as the replacement for the navigator killed in the *Seydlitz* action. The cut of his uniforms was subtly different, he wore his hair too long and affected monogrammed silk handkerchiefs and expensive shaving lotion. But he had turned out to be highly competent; in spite of his airs and graces he had passed out third from the top of the Long 'N' course and proved since then that it wasn't a fluke.

'Pipe "Cruising Stations".'

Two-thirds of the ship's company off watch, the cooks getting busy. Anybody's guess how long the lull would last. They had been at sea less than twenty-four hours, but already they were settled into seagoing routine, two more days to Malta, a life of watch-keeping, eating and sleeping in snatched intervals, cold, wet and deafness from gunfire. Thurston's left shoulder had begun to ache, as it always did in this sort of weather, deep within where the splinter from *Seydlitz* had smashed through. *Empire Liberator* had repaired her superheater, and the convoy was once more making fourteen knots, but barely in the teeth of the head sea. The merchant ships, with less engine power, were finding it difficult, the escorts had raised their asdic domes to save them from damage; the U-boats would be dived, keeping below the weather, biding their time.

'Change of course coming up, sir.'

The commander came up from Damage Control. It had become a minor ritual to talk over the events of the day at this time, enemy permitting, and play a game of chess on a pocket set which belonged to Bradshaw.

Into the sea cabin, two mugs of cocoa produced by Spencer.

'I'll do some toast, sir. With Gentleman's Relish. I know the Commander likes Gentleman's Relish.'

'How's it looking below, Ted?'

'Par for the course. Wet.' Bradshaw grinned. 'Some of the lads are wishing they'd joined the army. Plenty of bumps and bruises, but only one real casualty since the forenoon. Assistant Cook Travis let a fanny slip and covered himself with boiling soup. The doc says there's no lasting damage, but supper will be a little delayed. How about you, sir?'

'Oh, I'm all right,' he said hastily. He didn't want any kind of sympathy from Bradshaw.

'I could take over for a couple of hours, so you can get your head down. I've done nothing all day.'

'Not now. Your move, Ted.'

Spencer returned with the toast. Bradshaw considered, and moved a bishop. 'I'd love to know just what my wife's doing at the moment. I've had another letter claiming that she can't manage on the housekeeping. It beats me what she finds to spend it on.'

Thurston moved a rook to take Bradshaw's king's pawn. 'Check.'

'Captain, sir,' from the voicepipe.

'Captain.'

'Radar's gone dead, sir.'

'All right, I'm coming up.' He stood up. Bradshaw was putting the chess set away.

'No radar, no asdic. Back to the Mark One eyeball.'

The familiar awful smell lingered in the radar cabinet. The radar mechanic was opening up his tool roll, selecting a screwdriver. 'Can't be certain what it is until I've opened the thing up and had a proper look, but it smells like something's burnt out. Probably one of the valves. Start with that anyway.' He picked up the screwdriver, a signal that he wished to be left to get on with the job.

Midshipman Pearson looked at his plate with distaste and decided against eating.

'Don't you feel like it?' said Nairne. 'I'll have it if you don't.'

'Gannet!' shouted Graham.

'You ought to have something,' Norris advised. 'Spewing up nothing is the worst of all.'

'Have some soup,' suggested Graham.

'What sort is it?'

'This is Action Stations Soup. No one knows what's in it; it is unique to *Marathon*. You can't even get it in Poland.'

'No,' said Krasnowicz.

'But it's good stuff. It'll put hair on your chest.'

'I knew someone who ate it and turned into a bear,' said Cowper-Coles.

'Yes, it's called Hastings,' said Norris.

The gunroom was crowded, a ceaseless traffic in and out, some off watch, others snatching something to take away with them, a powerful smell of wet wool and oilskins, puddles on the corticene deck. He started on the soup, gingerly. It was hot and tasted better than he expected. His appetite came back in a rush.

'Feeling better?' Norris asked.

'Yes, thanks.'

'You see now, it does wear off,' said Cowper-Coles. 'Just thank your lucky stars she isn't a corvette. They do everything except loop the loop.'

He was off watch now, could retire to his hammock.

90

That was another thing to get used to. 'Better than a bunk in weather like this,' someone had said. 'You don't get thrown out.' There had been little enough privacy at *King Alfred* but there was none at all for a midshipman in a cruiser. Pearson was an only child and his only previous experience of living in close proximity to other boys had been a Scout camp when he was eleven. The other midshipmen, particularly the regulars who had been through Dartmouth, seemed quite unselfconscious about stripping off in front of one another. They wandered through the chest flat with towels slung nonchalantly over one shoulder, and got together noisily in the bathroom, which had three baths but no partitions. He envied them their easy confidence, their ability to make a joke of anything, even if the humour was coarse and the talk returned again to sex. He climbed into his hammock; he was dead tired and dry now for the first time that day. And he hadn't expected it to be so noisy. Inside the turret it was absolutely deafening when the guns went off, and painful, until Hastings had produced some cotton wool and told him brusquely to 'put it in your fucking ears'. On the bridge it was just as bad, in a different way, when you got the 5.25s, the sharper crack of the four-inch directly in front and below, the rattle of the two-pounders, orders shouted above the din, all at the same time. He wasn't sure which was worse, to be out there among the enemy aircraft, seeing the bombs come down, the pluming water, or under cover, waiting for the hot steel to come through the armour plate which wasn't worth the name. The Gunner's Mate had told him that if Hastings was killed he was in command of the turret, 'but don't you worry, sir. If he gets it, you'll get it.' This was supposed to be reassuring.

Thurston stood on the bridge, getting the water out of his night binoculars, now half concealed inside his duffel coat. He polished the lenses with a handkerchief and took a long slow sweep around the convoy. Two days out from Malta. He had been over the chart with Lieutenant Hart, plotted positions by dead reckoning – no chance of a sight in this murk. The worst part still to come, with the convoy in range from Crete, Sicily and North Africa, in daylight because of the delays, where the last convoy had been forced to turn back. *Don't start thinking*! At least the weather was keeping the U-boats down, though the merchant ships must be shaking themselves to bits in this sea. Malta in forty-eight hours' time and all night in his bunk while the oiling went on. He bent to the voicepipe.

'Watch your steering, Quartermaster. You're four degrees off.'

'Aye aye, sir. Course three-oh-six, sir.'

He took a few paces, to keep the circulation going in his feet. There was a chair for the captain's use on the port side of the binnacle, but he rarely used it except when eating; he found it too easy to fall asleep. So three paces in each direction, talk for a moment to Lieutenant-Commander Barnett and the Yeoman of Signals, sweep round the horizon once more.


Surgeon Commander Savage had a look at the injured stoker, suspended in a sick-bay pipe cot, leg encased in box splints, his pupils reduced to pinpricks by morphine.

'Hello, Simmonds. How goes the leg?'

'Not too bad now, sir. Bloody silly thing to do. I just wish this rolling would stop.'

'As soon as it does, we'll get you fixed up. You'll be playing football before you know it.'

'Thanks, sir,' the man said wearily. 'That's only about the tenth time I've heard that. I don't play football anyway.'

Savage laid a hand on his arm. 'Petty Officer Sellars will give you some more dope. Try to relax and get some sleep.'

Savage went back up the sick bay, mentally ticking off his patients. Three men already prostrated by seasickness and having to be fed intravenously, one man with a broken wrist, the Signals Officer in his cabin, and Simmonds. Curse the weather. To set that leg was a job which would have required all a surgeon's skill even ashore with plenty of time at his disposal and an operating theatre which was not in continuous motion. Keep him going for another two days and ship him ashore to Bighi. Curse the bloody weather and the bloody war.

'Sir?' said the sick-bay petty officer.

'Nothing, Sellars. Just thinking aloud.'

# — Chapter Eight —

## Scapa Flow, March 1917

*Oudenarde* should have been a good ship. She was brand-new, one of the crack Fifth Battle Squadron of twenty-five-knot battleships, and she was oil-fired, which meant an end to the hard labour of coaling ship every week or ten days. But, when her sister ships had been in the thick of the fighting at Jutland, *Oudenarde* had been boiler cleaning, and frustration festered among her crew as the months dragged by in fruitless sweeps into the North Sea, and it became increasingly clear that the High Seas Fleet would not venture beyond the protection of its booms and minefields again.

Midshipman Thurston was restless. Already he was sick of battleships, of the endless waiting in Scapa for the enemy to come out. *Oudenarde* rarely put to sea for more than three days a month, and that only brought a different kind of monotony. For the rest her midshipmen ran boats, wrote their journals, did PT and rifle drill on the quarterdeck, played endless games of bridge, listened to the gramophone and discussed ways to get into destroyers, coastal motorboats, submarines, the RNAS, anything except stay in a battleship in the Grand Fleet.

Sub-Lieutenant Dauncey found an outlet for his frustrations in bullying the junior midshipmen. Tradition held that warts were to be 'chased' and gunroom evolutions had taken place in both *Hyperion* and *Warrior*, but Dauncey devised new ways to ensure the maximum numbers were spreadeagled across the table and beaten with a dirk scabbard, boasting that the marks he made remained for six months. He had selected midshipmen fight him bare-knuckled after dinner, with a dozen for any who failed to go three rounds. The senior Sub, a retiring soul, let him get on with it, the senior midshipmen were divided. Two or three sided with Dauncey and acted as his acolytes, two or three more thought he went too far and something ought to be done, the majority agreed that Dauncey was hard on the warts, but it was something that everybody went through.

Midshipman Thurston didn't like Dauncey, and it had become only too clear over the last eight months that Dauncey didn't like him. By tradition senior midshipmen were exempt from evolutions, but there were always means. He was given boat duties of the tedious sort which meant wakeful nights waiting at the gangway or landing stage, extra watches, ostensibly to show the juniors the ropes. Someone cut his hammock lashings one night and deposited him head first on the steel deck. Once Dauncey knocked an ink pot over a chart he was correcting, which meant a dozen, and paying for the chart and correcting a new one from scratch. None of it was important in itself, but it only added to the sickness of it all. Leave? He hadn't been home since the row with the old man. His grandfather and stepmother sent him news, and his stepmother sent him a fruit cake every week. In any case the vicarage would be just as dispiriting. George had been missing in France since August, and was now officially presumed killed. Edmund was out there again after being wounded, a captain with the MC now.

Then Dauncey found out about him and turrets – he didn't know how – and turned to new tactics, finding him duties that took him into the magazines and shellrooms, preferably by torchlight, taunted him with his cowardice, even diverted his attention away from his main target among the warts, a pimply youth with the unfortunate name of Eustace de Courcy. He had tried to conquer turrets; he used to take a book and sit inside. A turret on make-and-mends, but even in the quiet of Scapa the terror was just below.

It all came to a head one night after returning from yet another bloody useless sweep. Dauncey drank steadily all through dinner, put the warts through all the evolutions and laid into them with a cricket bat, then started on the seniors, swearing he would 'flog you all!' One was made to eat pickled onions until he was sick, then beaten for wasting rations. The Paymaster Midshipman, blind as a bat without his spectacles, was boxed until virtually senseless. Dauncey stopped, swallowed a gin, called to the steward to bring him another, swished the cane against his trouser leg, considering his next victim.

For Thurston there was a glorious instant of red rage, as he grabbed Dauncey by the shoulder, pulled him round to face him, and slammed his fist full into his chin. No science, only raw anger, until his nose broke crunchingly when he walked into Dauncey's right cross, and heard again the quiet voice of PO PTI Kelly from Osborne, 'Keep your head and you can lick anybody.' The other midshipmen had drawn back and shoved the furniture aside; it was between him and Dauncey. They were well matched: he had the advantage of height and reach, but Dauncey was three years older and at least a stone heavier.

'Who's the coward now?' Triumph surged up as he broke through Dauncey's guard and his fists slammed into Dauncey's rotten lousy gut. It might have lasted a little longer, had not Dauncey hit his head on the table edge going down for the second time. Then the triumph evaporated. He was trying to get his breath, blood from his nose settling in a clammy patch on his shirt front. 'Doc' Orde, the Surgeon-Probationer, pushed through and took charge, sent someone for the Duty Lieutenant-Commander. Dauncey was removed to the sick bay with a suspected fractured skull, and

Midshipman Thurston, after the PMO had dealt with his broken nose and told him robustly that not even Harley Street could restore his Grecian profile, was confined to his quarters under close arrest.

He was standing in the First Lieutenant's cabin, cap under arm, escort withdrawn to the flat outside, the Snotties' Nurse pacing up and down, stabbing the air with an empty pipe.

'Well?'

'Nothing to say, sir.'

'You do appreciate that you're in very serious trouble?'

'Yes, sir.'

'You are fortunate that Sub-Lieutenant Dauncey seems to have a hard skull. Otherwise you could have been facing a murder charge. As it is, I am informed by the PMO that he will be recovered in a week or two.'

It seemed to call for some sort of answer. 'Yes, sir.'

'For God's sake stop saying "Yes, sir"! Mr Thurston, I am going to get to the bottom of this business.' He stopped his pacing, his voice softened. 'How can I prepare your defence if I don't know what actually caused all this? Robert, you're the brightest one of the lot. I refuse to believe that you got up after dinner last night and took it into your head to half kill Sub-Lieutenant Dauncey.'

Since it was impossible to both confine a midshipman to his quarters and isolate him from his fellows – a snotty possessed no more space than was sufficient to sling his hammock – they put him in Dauncey's cabin, with a sentry with a fixed bayonet outside and the scuttle boarded over in case the prisoner decided to wriggle through it and attempt to swim the four miles to the shore. He was relieved of all duties, meals were brought to him, and he could put his feet up on Dauncey's bunk and work his way through a pile of books

97

undisturbed, a privacy that was as rare as gold dust to a midshipman.

What would the old man say? Probably have apoplexy, his son striking a superior officer, ruining a promising career before it had properly begun etcetera etcetera, and wasting all the money spent on his education etcetera etcetera, showing a total want of responsibility and self-discipline. A marked man, forbidden direct communication with the other midshipmen, dependent for news on notes passed by the stewards, and morse messages tapped on the bulkhead from Doc Orde's cabin next door. He moved outside the cabin only under escort, took his exercise separately with one of the Gunnery Instructors, rifle over his head, twenty-five pounds of sand on his back, eighteen-inch bayonet banging against his left buttock.

'Pick your knees up! Up! Up! I can see your elbows bending! Geddit up! Fifty press-ups, on your knuckles, *Go!*'

Thurston dropped to the deck, obediently pumped out fifty, plus one extra just to show him. Up again, pick up the rifle, double mark time.

Sweat trickling into his eyes, thigh muscles turning to jelly, an ache in the balls where Dauncey had kneed him, push up against the rifle.

'Are you tired, Mr Thurston? Are your little arms hurtin' you?'

'No, GI!'

'Then you bloody soon will be. I've broken better men than you, Mr Thurston.'

Up all the ladders to the bridge, down again the other side, double mark time again, reflect with satisfaction that the Petty Officer was puce-coloured from the exertion of shouting at him.

'What are you grinning for? Are you enjoying this?'

'Yes, GI!'

And he was, because they were playing a game, and

he could take anything the bastards threw at him. Then half an hour's arms drill to wind down.

'Oh, Mr Thurston, you are 'orrible. This time I want to see some snap! I'm going to teach you what happens to silly boys who strike their superior officers!'

Back below, the cabin door locked behind him, flake out on the bunk, every fibre in his body stretched and stiff, the weariness flooding over him.

The Snotties' Nurse walked round behind him. He concentrated his eyes on a patch of bulkhead directly in front. So it went on, alternately hard and soft, part of the game, part of the Navy he loved and now he hated.

'I take it you're prepared for this to go on indefinitely, Mr Thurston. It doesn't do anybody any good, you least of all.'

'Yes, I hit him,' he had told the Duty Lieutenant-Commander. 'And I hope the bastard dies.'

'Sit down.'

'Rather stand, sir.'

'Sit down!' Rear Admiral Sir Cecil Wyatt faced him across his desk.

'Sir, I request a court martial.'

'Request denied.'

'Sir, I am entitled to a court martial.'

'You young fool! It's not your head that's on the block any more. Can you imagine what the gutter press would make of this? Next time, do it with the gloves on. I suppose you think you're being made a scapegoat.'

'Yes, sir!' he said hotly.

'That, Mr Thurston, is not the case, however it may appear. I have no doubt that a court martial would be inclined to take a lenient view of your offence. You're only seventeen, you were clearly subjected to considerable provocation, and the contest could hardly be said to have been one-sided. However, I have no doubt that, though the court martial would award you only a nominal punishment, Their Lordships would dispense with your services at the earliest opportunity. Seems a bit of a waste.'

The Admiral settled his forearms on the desk, leant forward slightly. 'You've done pretty well so far; people seem to think pretty highly of you. Pity to spoil all that, just for a brief notoriety and your name in all the newspapers.' The Admiral's eyes seemed to bore into him. 'Mr Thurston, I am now going ashore for a round of golf. On my return I shall expect a full written account of everything that has taken place in the gun-room since you joined this ship.' The voice was quiet, but incisive. 'There won't be a court martial. Interests of the service and all that. But rest assured that the service has no more use for Sub-Lieutenant Dauncey. My secretary will provide you with writing materials.'

It all came out eventually. Dauncey disappeared, the Snotties' Nurse returned from an interview with the Captain a much-chastened man. Rumour had it that the Captain had had his knuckles soundly rapped by the Admiral, even, some claimed, the Commander-in-Chief. Midshipman Thurston received twelve official cuts, and three months' stoppage of leave, to encourage the others, and a fortnight after, when the fuss was beginning to die down, was promoted Acting Sub-Lieutenant and posted to the destroyer *Ostorius* at an hour's notice. Months later, he ran into Dauncey at some railway station, a private soldier in the Middlesex Regiment. He had been ordered to resign his commission, on grounds of ill-health, and been called up into the army almost immediately. Dauncey was killed in France before the year was out. And this was why, twenty-five years on, Thurston had made it clear to Hastings and others before him that he would not tolerate any form of chasing of midshipmen and that all punishments were to be logged and reported to him.

0345 hours. Pearson felt a hand on his shoulder, a torch in the face.

'Up you get. On watch in fifteen minutes.'

He slid out of his hammock, his feet landing in a puddle on the deck, fumbled for his seaboots. They were not only new and stiff and the source of some large blisters, but also wet through.

'Stick a light bulb in them,' said Graham, 'a light bulb, on a long bit of cable, inside. It doesn't actually dry them out, but at least they're warm and wet instead of cold and wet,' he explained patiently. 'And take the laces out,' he added as an afterthought. 'Makes it easier to kick 'em off.'

Pearson thought for a moment. 'Oh, I see.'

Where was it this time? Oh God, the bridge again! At least B turret was out of the wind. Where was his duffel coat? His cap?

'Come on, Pearson! You'll be adrift if you don't get your act together!'

'Shut up and let a man sleep,' groaned one of the hammocks.

'Sorry, Angus, you lucky toad.'

'God, it's cold. Is it still pissing down?'

'How should I know? Wake up Schooly yourself and find out!'

'For God's sake, pipe down!' said Angus.

Krasnowicz slipped and cursed loudly.

'Oh go back to Poland!'

'Pearson, where's your tin hat?'

Oh God, where had he left it? He reached for the light switch.

'Don't do that, you stupid bugger! Night vision!'

'Are you trying to waken the dead?'

Curses came from the other hammocks. Someone produced a shaded torch, thrust Pearson's tin hat and respirator haversack at him. 'Come on. If you can't take a joke you shouldn't have joined.'

101

0355 hours. Nothing seemed to have changed on the bridge, except that it was colder and wetter than ever.

'It's been pretty quiet,' said Norris. 'The Yanks still can't keep in station. Just keep your eyes skinned and stay awake. Bloody cold. I hope you've got your long johns on. 'Night.'

Sub-Lieutenant Cowper-Coles was keeping his first watch at night. He was twenty-six, a stockbroker in civilian life, in the Navy less than a year. Three months in a corvette on convoy duty, *King Alfred*, then *Marathon*. A bit of stage fright, but he kept telling himself there was nothing much to worry about; he had done it all before with the First Lieutenant there. Anyway the Captain and Navigator were on the bridge, and the radar was working again after the radar mechanics had had the set in pieces all over the deck. For all that, he would be grateful if nothing happened before 0800.

'Dirty night, isn't it, Sub?'

'Yes sir. She's a lot steadier than *Hyacinth* all the same.'

Convoy spread out to port; *Nebraska Star, Empire Wave*, a destroyer that must be *Jade, Ariadne, Jewel, Persephone, Bellerophon, Berwickshire, Empire Liberator, Pangbourne, Parkhurst*. Port leg of the zig-zag, course two-seven-eight degrees.

'Hold on to your hats.'

*Marathon* pitched into another great swell, seemed to go far under, then her bows began to rise. Pearson wobbled, grabbed a convenient stanchion, held on as the spray hit him once more. It was so unfair, he was soaked through already, with all but a few minutes of his four-hour watch to go, and the cap he'd picked up definitely wasn't his, and was unlikely to stay on much longer.

'God help sailors on a night like this,' shouted the Chief Yeoman.

'Not quite what you expected, Mr Pearson.' The Captain's deep voice and clipped Dartmouth accent.

'No, sir.'

'You get used to it. Watch *Nebraska Star*, Sub. She's losing way again.'

The First Lieutenant appeared from below. 'Just come to check on my protégé. Everything all right, Mr Cowper-Coles?'

ffrench moved over to the binnacle, talking to Cowper-Coles.

'Mr Pearson, I didn't know you'd transferred to the Polish Navy,' said the Captain drily.

He whipped off the oversize cap, noted with a sinking feeling the Polish badge and, peering inside, the words WLADYSLAW ZURAKOWSKI stamped on the browband.

'Sorry, sir. I couldn't find mine. I must have picked up the wrong one.' This must be worth a dozen at least.

'Easy to do, but don't assume. Check.'

The First Lieutenant butted in. 'What size do you take?'

'Er, seven and an eighth, sir.'

'Bridge messenger, take this back to its rightful owner – don't wake him – then go to my cabin and get my Sunday best.' He turned to Pearson. 'That'll do you for the rest of this watch.'

Pearson thanked him and, remembering that it was time to write up the log, retired to the chart table. Why hadn't he joined the army? At least a battlefield didn't behave like a bucking bronco, and surely it couldn't be any wetter. What was he doing here? He was an art student. He had never been further from home than Torquay, not even across the channel. Perhaps if he had he would have known how beastly it was to be seasick.

In an effort to distract himself from his stomach he went back over the things he was supposed to know about. No point thinking of home; it just made him feel even more wretched.

'Director Firing's really dead simple,' Nairne had told him, unable to resist the temptation to retrace ground which had already been covered at *King Alfred*. 'All the spotting is done from the Director Tower, which is well above all the spray and rubbish which gets chucked up, and equidistant between all the turrets. In the Director Tower they observe the range, bearing and estimated course and speed of the target. That gets passed down to the Transmitting Station, where the band feed everything into their boxes of tricks, plus our course and speed, and things like the met, winds, temperatures and so on.'

He could see why the winds should be a factor, but why temperature?

'The higher the temperature, the hotter the charge. The hotter the charge, the faster it burns, and the further the round goes. You also have to allow for our roll and their roll. The band do all kinds of mathematical wizardry with all that stuff, and out come bearings and elevations for the guns. That gets passed to the turrets and appears on the layer's dials. He lines up on the data from the TS, the Officer of Quarters presses a button when that's done and the gun ready lamp lights up in the Director Tower. When all four turrets show ready, the Director Layer fires them all at the same moment. In case anything goes wrong, the layer and rangefinder in each turret are making their own observations, and if necessary we can go straight into local control and do without the Director. But that means we're all firing at different times and on different data, the observations are made from much nearer the waterline, so it's not nearly as efficient. Once we've opened fire the Director adjusts the fall of shot until we've bracketed the target, one salvo over, one under, then halves the bracket until we've got her straddled, and then with any luck we've got her. Of course, if she's a Jerry warship she's doing the same thing, so it gets quite exciting, and if more than one ship is firing at the same target, you've got to be careful to adjust your own fall of shot, not someone else's.

'Mr Pearson, keep your eyes on your sector.'

Here he was, Midshipman of the Watch, maker of cocoa, runner of messages, a medium of abuse between officers of differing seniority, as Nairne had told him; wet to the skin, hopelessly, miserably seasick. Even when this watch was over, it would be Action Stations again, and another day spent in the reverberating steel drum called B turret.

Someone told him to make the cocoa. He went below to the galley, glad to be out of the weather, but sicker than ever under cover, in company with the Captain's messenger, a maddeningly cheerful boy seaman named McCormick. Cocoa. You heated up the water in a large pot known for some reasons as a fanny, took shavings from a large block of plain chocolate with a clasp knife, and dropped them into the water, added quantities of sugar and condensed milk, strung a sufficient number of mugs on a piece of wire and attempted to negotiate the ladder back to the bridge without spilling the cocoa or losing the mugs or throwing up.

'Give us that,' said McCormick cheerfully, whistling tunelessly through his teeth and taking the fanny from him.

Pearson followed with the mugs, turned aside to be sick again. Even sergeant-majors would be better than this.

'I think I'll stay for a cup,' said the First Lieutenant.

'That's all you came up for, Number One.'

The arrival of the cocoa brought a slight but perceptible relaxation. The Captain told a story.

'. . . The Admiral retired for the night, saying. "Call me if it comes on to blow." Half an hour later it did come on to blow and I went to shake him. "Call me if it blows any harder." It did, so I went aft again. "Call me if it blows any harder." Once again, it blew harder.

"Call me if it blows any harder." By this time it was blowing pretty hard, and I was fresh out of Dartmouth and very green, green about the gills too, as a matter of fact. "But sir, it *can't* blow any harder!" I was still singing treble then. Of course it did, and I shook the Admiral yet again. He sat bolt upright in his bunk. Actually it was a large brass bed with knobs on, and he was wearing a nightcap, which was something I'd never seen before. "Midshipman of the Watch, you assured me it *couldn't* blow any harder!" '

Pearson sipped his cocoa, wondered if the story might be mainly directed towards him.

'The Yanks are going out of station again.'

'Call them up, Yeoman.'

'Where is Nebraska?' enquired the Navigator.

'Somewhere a long way inland.'

An hour to First Light.

'I'm going below for a shave and something to eat, Sub. Don't hesitate to call me. Pass the word for my steward.'

'Aye aye, sir.'

Cowper-Coles was all right. He needed to be left alone for a while, without the Captain breathing down his neck. The Hon. Henry Hart was prowling around the chart table if he needed any advice. Pearson; he was less sure about him. Thurston made a mental note to have a word with ffrench, though more than likely it was nothing more than seasickness. ffrench was a damn good officer; the only reason he wasn't wearing a brass hat now was that he had been in the wrong place at the wrong time, or the wrong side of someone at a critical moment. He rubbed his eyes. A shave, a proper wash, and breakfast.

There was a basin in the sea cabin, a mirror and just enough space to turn round. Spencer had left some dry clothes out; shirt, trousers, socks, a vast and somewhat shapeless sweater knitted by his daughter. He pulled his shirt over his head. There was always the necessity to hurry. Once, very early in the war, in *Connaught* on the Northern Patrol, he had decided to take a bath while things were quiet; there had been a call and he'd caused both amusement and embarrassment by arriving on the bridge barefoot and in a towel in the midst of a sudden snowstorm, hotly pursued by Spencer with his clothes. He had a good scrub, in sections, with several changes of water, lathered his chin and began to shave.

Pearson. In at the deep end. He wondered how he had survived *King Alfred* with all his innocence intact. Most of the snotties, regular or not, came to their ships with nothing wrong except inexperience. Pearson would probably shake down all right, it might just take a bit longer. It reminded him of George; he would be seventeen in March and join his first ship in April. But he would do all right. George was one of those boys who sailed through prep school and Dartmouth. He was in the college or house teams for rugby, cricket, boxing and swimming, though he seemed to concentrate on sport to the detriment of his academic work; he was a cadet captain, and seemed set to become an equally happy and successful midshipman. But seventeen, and in wartime.

Thurston steadied himself against the bulkhead, tilted his head back to get at the awkward bit beneath the angle of the jaw where he tended to cut himself. Yet he had been much the same, and even younger when, mad keen, he went into the war, and mad keen to stay in it. He, Hank and a couple of others had hatched a scheme to desert and join the army if the Navy decided to yield to public pressure and send them and their fellows back to Dartmouth. There was a photograph his father had taken at about that time, of his three sons in uniform in the front steps of the vicarage. Two second lieutenants of the Northumberland Fusiliers, with walking sticks and half-grown moustaches, and the tough young seaman, with a voice that could still reach Top D, grinning, a bit cocky, cap rakishly tilted.

Better get a move on. Spencer would have his breakfast ready in a minute. He finished dressing, coated his itching feet with gentian violet, brushed his teeth, combed his hair. Spencer came in, removed a lid with a flourish. A tempting smell of bacon met his nostrils.

'Sorry, sir. *The Times* wasn't delivered this mornin'. Don't know what the paper boy's playin' at. Dirty weather innit. Regular potmess below. All the sprogs are wishin' they were at 'ome with their mummies. Coffee, sir? Now drink it while it's 'ot.'

He ate, wrote a few lines to Kate at the same time (must remember Helen was due a letter), listened with one ear to Spencer.

Sub-Lieutenant Cowper-Coles was pacing the bridge as to the manner born. 'Thirty-six minutes to first light, sir. Starboard leg of the zig-zag. Course three-one-four degrees.'

'Anything to report?'

'No, sir.' Cowper-Coles grinned, the pride showing in his face.

'Nothing at all?'

'No, sir.'

'Carry on, Sub.'

'Pipe "Dawn Action Stations".'

The light slowly strengthened, the outline of the ship became clearer, sharp and solid, instead of vague blocks of deeper darkness. B-turret, the upper deck, A-turret, the triangle of the bows and the anchors and cables, the cold grey sea.

Pearson began to feel more cheerful. He stamped his feet, brief pain as the circulation returned. Not much longer now. He looked around him, mentally sketching the scene. The lookouts, binoculars to their eyes, slowly sweeping their sectors, a little knot of signalmen on the starboard side, Boy McCormick, face sunk into the collar of his greatcoat. Lieutenant Hart, coming out from behind the oilskin-hooded chart table. The Captain, eyes narrowed in his bony, hawk-nosed face, followed the destroyer up ahead. Sub-Lieutenant Cowper-Coles . . .

'Radar . . . Bridge.'

'Bridge.'

'No peace for the wicked.'

The alarm went off.

# — Chapter Nine —

There were seven attacks the second day. Soon after 1100 *Berwickshire* was straddled by a stick of bombs from a Junkers 88. A dull red glow appeared on her fo'c'sle, shifted slowly aft.

'She's hit,' someone said unnecessarily.

'Floating fucking bomb,' mouthed one of the signalmen.

Pearson turned towards the chart table, felt for his propelling pencil to record the event in the log.

'Christ, will you look at that!'

White fire rose into the sky, wreathed in smoke. Successive explosions thudded into Pearson's eardrums. *Berwickshire*'s bows floated, separated from the rest, for a moment, then disappeared, steam rising to combine with the smoke. The after section, still driven by the engines, ploughed on crazily.

'The poor sods. The poor fucking sods.'

There was another explosion. Debris scattered over the deck. Pearson bent to pick up a shell fragment. 'Careful!' someone told him, too late. He yelped as he made contact with the red-hot metal, shoved his fingertips in his mouth.

Thurston, binoculars to eyes, saw a man leap into the sea, arms upraised, clothes and hair on fire. He looked away, saw a couple of heads in the water.

'Pipe Away Seaboat's Crew. Tell the engine room to stand by.'

The remains of *Berwickshire* stood vertical, and disappeared, so that only white water and a few patches of burning oil remained. Even the aircraft, their bomb loads expended, had disappeared. Thurston bent to the voicepipe, ready to issue further orders.

'*Parkhurst*'s going in!'

*Parkhurst* heeled out of station, the bow wave creaming back as she worked up towards her maximum speed. Thurston straightened up, snapped the voicepipe cover shut.

'Flag to *Parkhurst*, sir. *Resume station forthwith*.'

*Parkhurst* skidded neatly round a patch of burning oil, a scrambling net appearing on her port side.

'He's got his answering pennant at the dip,' said the First Lieutenant.

'What does that mean?' hissed Pearson.

'It means *Your signal not understood*,' ffrench grinned. 'The Admiral's loving it. Take a look.'

He handed Pearson his binoculars. The Admiral was thumping his fist on *Ariadne's* bridge screen, mouthing what Pearson presumed to be curses.

Two of *Parkhurst*'s men were halfway down the net, hauling a sagging form out of the water, getting the man's arms over their shoulders and beginning their slow climb upwards. Thurston made a slow sweep over the scene. That seemed to be all, scattered patches of oil still burning, a few fragments of wreckage, one man.

'Couple of months' ammo gone west,' someone said.

'Tell the seaboat's crew to stand down,' Thurston told ffrench.

*Parkhurst*, her answering pennant now hoisted impudently close up, to indicate receipt of the signal, resumed her station. The Commander of the close escort issued a dressing-down by lamp, a matter of form only. The Commodore signalled the merchant ships to watch their station-keeping.

'*Parkhurst* signalling Flag, sir. *Survivor dead*.

*Marathon* was closed up at Dusk Action Stations. Gun-layers peered into their sights, foreheads pressed to their rubber eyepieces. Below decks men waited in the fug, in shellrooms, Damage Control parties, engine rooms, boiler rooms. The loneliest man aboard waited in the shaft tunnel, connected to the outer world only by a slippery tube seventy feet long and too low to stand upright, watching the shaft bearings with an oil can to hand.

'Radar . . . Bridge.'

'Bridge.'

'Aircraft bearing green one-oh. Fourteen miles.'

'Sound the alarm.'

Thurston snatched the binoculars off his chest, swung his head round on to the bearing and lifted them to his eyes, peering into the murk. The familiar three-engined shape of Italian SM79 bombers, some with torpedoes slung beneath their bellies, fighter escort weaving above.

The four twin turrets trained, the barrels elevated.

'Number One pom-pom on target and tracking.'

'Director Layer sees target.'

Rounds slammed into the breeches of the twin four-inch in front of the bridge. Cotton wool was stuffed into ears, minute adjustments were made to tin hats.

'Number Two pom-pom on target and tracking.'

'Open fire.'

'Open fire, sir.'

Flares burst over the sea, blinding bars of magnesium, casting their cold white light over the convoy.

'Shoot!'

'Alarm starboard. Commence, Commence, Commence!'

The ship shuddered as every gun opened up, heeled over to port as the main armament went off, but even the full weight of the convoy's armament, 5.25s, the destroyers' 4.7s, the antique six-inches aboard the merchant ships, four-inch, eight-barrelled pom-poms, left the flares still burning, suspended mockingly from their parachutes.

It was always the same, however many times he faced it. The knot in the stomach, the knowledge of what steel and high explosive could do to a man, the sheer naked vulnerability. Thurston rapped out his orders in flat clipped tones, half his mind concentrated on the avoiding action, listening to the information coming through the voicepipes, watching the aircraft, the other ships, analysing, calculating. The rest floating free, in excitement and heightened awareness, of the clatter of cartridge cases from the four-inch, sharp amid the roar from the 5.25s, the clean curves and straight edges of the binnacle, the points of fair stubble outlined on Boy McCormick's chin. The shouts from the Officer of Quarters on the four-inch, Paymaster Lieutenant Rigby, 'Down a hundred . . . Shoot!' 'Load!', the practised movements at the breeches. 'No correction, Shoot!' He heard Jenner's voice far off, the usual action commentary for the men below decks.

'One, two, three, four, about two dozen of the bastards. We're turning to port. One's going down. Oh, well done, boys. Let's get a few more.'

The bombers swept in low over the sea. All around there was noise, the 5.25s, the higher crack of the four-inch, guns thudding back on their recoil cylinders. The bombers held their course. *Marathon* jinked from port to starboard, unable to take really effective evasive action, for there were the merchantmen to protect, unable to surge ahead with her sixty thousand horsepower. Noise and pounding concussion in the ears, cordite in the nostrils, pluming water alongside, a sense of oneness with Petty Officer Hicks, handling the wheel far below.

'We've got another! Tail knocked right off!'

'Cease fire.'

The main armament cut out abruptly. Firing on the bearings and elevations necessary would endanger the merchant ships. Only the close-range weapons were still firing. Watch *Bellerophon*, turning to port and getting a bit close. Watch her, shading his eyes from the flare above her.

'Torpedo tracks to starboard!'

'Hard a-starboard. Full ahead port. Full astern starboard.' Cold, disciplined, emotionless voice which did not seem a part of him. Pray the helm didn't jam. Pray *Bellerophon* was clear.

Even with the helm hard over and the engines racing against each other, it was an age before the bows began to come round.

*It's happening again.*

'Turn, you bitch!' Cowper-Coles.

*Come on, girl. Turn!*

The ship shuddered, then lurched violently to starboard, the sound of the explosion reached them.

'Midships. Slow ahead both.'

'She won't answer the helm, sir.'

*Marathon* slewed out of line, the way falling off her, the list increasing. Somewhere amidships she was badly holed, the chill sea pouring in. The air filled with escaping steam from the boiler release valves, the roar of water came from the engine-room voicepipe, shouts of men struggling to escape.

*It's happened again.*

The binnacle light had gone out. The ship lay dead in the water, ready for the Italians to finish her off.

Pearson had been knocked off his feet by the lurch. He was scrabbling for footholds on the wet deck, pulling himself back upright.

'What's happening?'

No one seemed to notice him.

'What's happening? Are we sinking?'

'Don't ask such bloody silly questions!'

*Connaught* had gone down in three minutes. But she had been at Cruising Stations, watertight doors open, and the torpedoes had broken her in two. Thurston

114

was applying his mind to the problem. One engine room gone; she wouldn't make more than two or three knots on two shafts, if the bulkheads held. If the bulkheads held . . . When was he going to get some damage reports!

Someone else stood up, one of the signalmen. 'Who was the great fat lump who landed on me?' In the circumstances it seemed terribly funny.

The convoy was moving on past them. Firing had ceased. The enemy had used up their bombs. The attack was suddenly over.

'From Flag, sir. *What is your situation?*'

It would come to a tow, at best, assuming she stayed afloat. That all depended on the level of damage, and Ted Bradshaw and Damage Control. *Ariadne* closed. Beecham's voice, distorted, floated across the gap.

'Muster your men on deck. We'll take you off.'

'McCormick!'

'Sir!'

'Loudhailer.'

The boy passed him the instrument. Not that. They'd fight for her first. 'No! Detach a destroyer to tow us and we'll get her back!'

He could guess what Beecham was thinking. *The insubordinate bugger*. And after *Parkhurst* earlier in the day. It was a long moment before the flagship's lamp began to blink.

'*Will detach* Leonidas. *God speed and good luck.*'

Lamps flashed again, the flagship and the destroyer. One engine room gone, and God alone knew what was going on around it. Come on, Ted; what are you doing down there? Another signal, *Ariadne* to *Marathon*, personal for Captain; *Good luck. See you in the Cecil.* Thank you, Philip.

It had all been practised so often, the procedures laid down. Bradshaw would assess the damage, set his men to dealing with it, send reports to the bridge by messenger. Every officer and man aboard was trained in basic first aid, at least one man in every position designated a First Aider and trained and equipped as such. Damage Control and fire parties had been exercised *ad nauseam*.

*Leonidas* closed, flashed a brief signal, began to circle. The asdic set pinged reassuringly. One thing that was working. God help them all if there was a U-boat out there, or if the bombers came back. Six minutes had passed since the torpedoing.

'Half the fucking ship flooded, and no water where we fucking need it! Right, blankets, hammocks, anything. Get on with it!'

Chief Petty Officer Alfred Burgess dug his hands into the nearest hammock rack, lifted out a lashed bundle, shoved it at the man behind him. 'Get the rest out, and get on!'

The lighting was off, but the Marine barracks was lit up well enough, flame licking away the thin film of paint on the bulkheads, the electrical wiring overhead, all the furnishings, the kit and personal possessions of the ships' sixty Royal Marines.

Burgess ripped away the hammock lashing, the canvas billowed out. Smoke caught in his throat.

'Cover your faces up. Use your nose-wipes. Wet 'em first.'

'What with, Chief?'

'Pee on 'em dunderhead!' Burgess pulled out a handkerchief, opened his trousers and waited for the water to come. 'Don't think about it! Do it!' He tied the sodden cloth over his mouth and nose, felt the urine running over his chin, first hot, then cold.

Burgess was shouting at his fire party, marshalling them into a line and moving them forward, flailing at the flames with the hammocks. There was heat, playing over their exposed faces, an airlessness created by the fire and the acrid smoke over everything, fumes of burning paint. Burgess fumbled with one hand at the toggles of his duffel coat, flapped the hammock at the fire with the other, sweated heavily inside his clothes, began to work the coat off, swapping the hammock from hand to hand.

'Get on!' he yelled at a man who seemed to be hanging back. 'That's not a pen! Do it as if you meant it!' *Bloody bunch of no-hopers*, he said to himself. Supply assistants, stewards and writers, not a real seaman among them. The coat fell away at last, he kicked it behind him. The smoke was thicker here. He found himself choking, jerked forward almost double until he began to breathe again.

Flap, flap with the hammock, smoke in his eyes and mucus streaming from them, heat all around. The end of the hammock began to burn; he stamped on it, leaving a ragged semi-circular edge, charred at the fringes.

The ship rolled drunkenly. The man next to him overbalanced, tried to save himself, arms upraised, then toppled over a burning kitbag. A scream. The man was scrabbling to his feet, patches of yellow flame appearing across his chest and upper thighs. He was staggering back towards the door, his upper body surrounded by fire.

Burgess jerked round, grabbed the man by the shoulders and sent him sprawling to the deck. He was still screaming, a thin high wailing. Burgess rolled him over, on a patch of deck now mercifully free from flame, beat on his back with the hammock. Other men came crowding in.

'Don't just stand there! Get on and fight the fucking fire!' He turned back, smelt the burnt flesh smell rising from the man's body. 'It's all right, Morton. It's all right.'

'Chief . . .'

'It's all right.'

'Chief . . .'

'You're just a bit singed, that's all.' He raised his

head. 'Cowan, get the first aid party up here, at the double.'

'I want to get up.'

'Just stay where you are.'

'Chief . . .' Morton lifted his shoulders from the deck. Burgess pushed him back. Morton coughed. A blackish dribble came from his mouth. In the light of the still-burning fire his chest looked like the crackling on roast pork, charred black in raised strips. The field dressing they all carried wouldn't go near that. Burgess turned aside, praying that he wouldn't be sick. Morton shivered; Burgess thought he should cover him up, took off his jacket. He was talking to Morton again, telling him that the doctor would be there in a minute, and he would be tucked up in the sick bay before he knew it, breaking off to shout at the men who were still fighting the fire. He should be back with them, but he could not tear himself away; he had a son not much younger than Morton himself. He found he was gripping Morton's hand. 'Not much longer now, son.' *Oh my Ker-ist.*

Then the first aid party was there, putting a white sheet over Morton's chest and taking him away on a stretcher. Morton looked back at him almost beseechingly; the sick-bay Petty Officer jerked a thumb downwards. Burgess turned back, suddenly desolated and alone, then remembered that he had a job to get on with.

A lone figure appeared from below. His hair had gone, his features burned into unrecognisability. 'Forrard engine room.' The voice was cracked and hoarse. There was a Leading Stoker's badge on the charred sleeve of his overalls. 'On fire. After boiler room flooding.'

'Casualties?'

'Dunno, sir.'

'Get down to the sick bay. Well done.'

118

The stoker swayed. Someone grabbed him and began to lead him away. The smell of his scorched flesh was sickening.

'Chief Yeoman. Signal *Leonidas* to that effect.'

O'Shaughnessy seemed steady enough. Thurston told Cowper-Coles to muster the Confidential Books. Just in case.

The ship was stopped now, broached to, water breaking over her decks; without engines there was no hope of keeping her bows-on to the sea. The Commander's messenger, Boy Secombe, appeared from the ladder.

'Commander's compliments, sir. The forrard engine room's gone . . .' Secombe was out of breath, his boy's voice rising an octave or more.

'All right, Secombe, get your breath.'

Secombe put his head down, breathing hard, then straightened up and completed his message. 'The forrard engine room's gone and B boiler room's flooding, but the after engine-room bulkhead's bein' shored up and it's holding. We're on fire in some of the fuel tanks and . . . well, all over the place, sir. Can't get near enough to check it out properly. The fire parties are all at it . . . That's all, sir.'

'Thank you, Secombe. Give the Commander my compliments.' An incongruous touch of formality. 'Would he find out the casualty figures, draught fore and aft, increasing or decreasing, the fire situation, fuel and ammunition states, and send up a full estimate of damage as soon as he is able.'

'Aye aye, sir.' Secombe gulped, checked back the message, mouthed some private joke at his friend McCormick, and dashed away again.

More reports came through. Bulkheads were being shored up, with doors, lashed hammocks, mess stools, tables. The Commander(E) was working on the emergency power supply. But the fire was raging between decks, burning uncontrolled in the Marine barracks amidships. Thurston could taste its heat, the heavy oiliness of its smoke.

The Surgeon Commander was receiving casualties in the sick bay. A first aid party under Surgeon Lieutenant Bradley was working under orders from Damage Control. Loose fittings and depth charges were being jettisoned, and the torpedoes fired set to sink. 'Fuckin' waste,' one of the lookouts muttered. 'Three thousand quids' worth each.' *Leonidas* prowled a few cables off. The rest of the convoy had disappeared westwards.

Commander Bradshaw came up to the bridge, mopping his brow with a large khaki handkerchief. 'We've lost about fifty feet of bottom, as far as I can see. I can't do much about that. There isn't a collision mat that'll go near it. The Chief's got the pumps going now, the ones we can get at, that is. The emergency lighting is on, but we're only just starting to get the fire under control.' He grinned. 'There isn't a pair of eyebrows left in the fire party. I suppose I look like a nigger minstrel.'

McCormick and Secombe were whispering surreptitiously in a corner, giggling.

'Go and make some cocoa, McCormick. You go with him, Mr Pearson.' Give the poor little devil something to do. He lowered his voice. 'What are our casualties?'

'Not good, sir.' Bradshaw's face was blackened, there was dried blood beneath one eye. 'Fourteen dead and accounted for, and it's likely to be a lot more. Twenty-six missing, including Senior and young Buchan I'm afraid. At least forty seriously wounded or burned.'

'Thanks, Ted.' Suddenly he felt very tired.

'Permission to carry on?'

Bradshaw disappeared, Secombe at his heels.

'Cocoa, sir?'

Unnoticed, Spencer had appeared at his elbow, bearing a steaming jugful, made very hot and strong, thick with condensed milk and melted chocolate, enough to stand the spoon in. 'I figured you could do with something, sir. Long time since lunch.'

He sipped it, burned his mouth, felt the warmth of the brew steal down into his stomach. 'Spencer, there's rum in this.'

'Is there, sir?' Spencer was all innocence. 'S'pose a rum jar must have got smashed up.'

'Do you expect me to believe that?'

'Nossir!'

There was a shout of laughter from all those within earshot. Spencer was good for morale.

'Now drink it while it's 'ot, sir.'

It occurred to him that this was one of the times when training simply took over. Something switched off and he could stand here drinking cocoa and swapping bad jokes with Spencer. He glanced over the bridge screen, taking in the men already at work on the upper deck, making preparations for the tow. He noticed a man standing by himself on the boat deck, hands in the pockets of his jacket – he wasn't wearing a duffel. He caught a faint glimmer of light off the oak leaves of a brass hat, wondered who it could be. Not Bradshaw, nor the Commander(E). The head shifted a little; he recognised the spectacles. What was the Paymaster Commander doing there? He'd probably been forced out of his action station in the ship's office by the fire, but he didn't look as though he had been near the fire, and in any case he should be in the galley organising action messing, not standing on the boat deck admiring the view.

'Another cup, sir. And I done you some wedges.'

'Spencer, how did I manage all those years without you?'

'Dunno, sir,' Spencer said cheerfully. 'I'll nip below and give the young gentleman an 'elping 'and. Don't seem to 've got the hang of kai yet.'

When he looked back, the Paymaster Commander had gone. He had probably just been getting a

121

moment's air anyway. Thurston put it out of his mind. There were more important things to deal with.

The Commissioned Gunner came up from the Transmitting Station with an ammunition state. Spencer and Midshipman Pearson brought round cocoa and sandwiches. Surgeon Lieutenant Bradley, a bespectacled young man known for the usual obscure reasons as The Deadly Virus, arrived with a casualty report.

'We've about twenty bad cases, sir. Mostly burns but some splinter wounds, and there are a couple of men with broken ankles from the blast wave. The worst cases are in the sick bay itself and we're clearing one of the messdecks for the others. We haven't been able to shift to the wardroom because of the fire, but we're managing. There have been quite a lot of minor burns and injuries among the fire party and Damage Control parties, but nothing serious.'

'Numbers?'

The doctor consulted a notebook. 'All told there are fifty-seven wounded at the last count. Seventeen dead that we know about. We may not be able to identify them all.' He shuddered, then collected himself. 'The burials should take place as soon as possible, for reasons of hygiene.'

'Don't try to teach me to suck eggs!'

The Deadly Virus jumped to attention.

'Sorry, Doctor. Go on.'

'Yes, sir. The padre won't be fit to do it, sir.'

'What happened to him?'

The Deadly Virus looked pale and strained. A muscle jumped in one cheek. Thurston remembered that he had only been qualified about a year, and this must be his first real experience of battle casualties. 'He and I went to the paint stores with a first aid party just after we were hit. He just attached himself to us. One of the men – Ordinary Seaman Wilmott – was overcome by the fumes and the padre dashed in to get him out. His hands . . . he tried to put the fire out

122

with his bare hands.' He paused, screwed his eyes up. 'Sorry, sir. Wilmott's dead. He went about ten minutes ago.'

The padre was on the face of it an unlikely hero, a gentle scholarly man with his mind on the finer nuances of theology, far from the traditional pipe-smoking, rugger-playing naval chaplain.

'Let me have a complete list as soon as you can.' He didn't trust himself to say any more. *Marathon* had been a lucky ship recently; no fatal casualties since *Seydlitz*. 'Pilot!'

'Sir?' Hart emerged from the chart table.

'Let's take a look at the chart.'

The main chartroom was two decks below, dimly lit by emergency lighting, but luxuriously dry and out of the wind. Thurston leant over the table, resting on both hands, water dripping off his cap on to the glass which covered the large chart of the Mediterranean basin. A neat pencilled cross marked *Marathon's* approximate position, about as far from a friendly harbour as it was possible to be.

Where to make for? Malta was out of the question in this sea, even reckoning without the air attacks. Alexandria? The wind and sea would be astern, but it was even further off. Was there anywhere else? He picked up a pair of dividers, twiddled them reflectively.

'Pilot, am I correct in thinking that the Eighth Army has just recaptured Tobruk?'

'Yes, sir. Only just. It was in today's intelligence summary.'

'Dig out the large-scale chart.'

Hart rummaged for a moment, unfurled a chart and weighted down the corners. They studied it in silence.

'Not so good.'

'No, sir. The harbour's full of wrecks and all the approaches are mined.'

'Chart up to date?'

'Yes, sir. Of course, those are only the things that have actually been reported.'

'And if I were the German commander I'd have mined the whole harbour before I pulled out.'

It was tantalising. Tobruk was, relatively speaking, so close, but the chart was cluttered with wreck symbols, minesweeping would not even have begun and the dockyard facilities were basic.

Thurston straightened up. 'Course for Alexandria, Pilot.'

'Aye aye, sir.'

He picked up a rag and mopped the water off the glass. 'And be sure to get a haircut when we get in.'

'Of course, sir.' Hart grinned. This was an old controversy between them. 'I could not trust my tresses to the barbers of Tobruk.'

Nothing to do now but wait, wait while the cable party got the three-inch wire out of its stowage and flaked out in long bights on the fo'c'sle, while a signal was composed, ciphered and transmitted, while men fought the fires between decks. Midshipman Pearson also waited, suspecting that he was deliberately being kept busy, and grateful for the occupation.

At last Commander Bradshaw came up to report that all was ready. *Leonidas* closed the cruiser, her stern beneath the flare of the bows, so near that it seemed they must collide. The line fell short. Bradshaw swore under his breath. Another great swell, the destroyer heeled to one side, away from the plunging bow.

'Nicholls is bloody good,' Thurston breathed.

In a lull in the wind the second line flew true. A party in *Leonidas's* stern, bucking in the wind and sea, hauled it in. The destroyer drew away a little. First the grass line, floating on the black water, then the hawser itself, paid out slowly, bit by bit. The wind howled, the sea broke in great crests, now the only enemy.

'From *Leonidas*, sir. *Tow fast.*'

Thurston heard himself say. 'To *Leonidas. Lead on, Macduff.*'

*Leonidas* began to inch forward, the wire tightening, then straining to overcome the inertia of five and a half thousand tons' deadweight, and untold thousands more of seawater. For long-drawn-out minutes the agony continued, all ears straining for the crack of the tow parting, all hoping against hope that it would not. Another lurching roll, then the bows dropping into a trough, all on the bridge grabbing for supports.

Almost imperceptibly *Marathon* began to move, then gathered speed as the destroyer's engines gained the upper hand, the motion smoothing out. Lamps flashed. Make or break. They had to turn *Marathon*, bring her round on to the proper heading, risk all the gains.

'From *Leonidas. Turning to port on to one-one-two. Ten of port wheel.*'

'Acknowledge, Chief Yeoman.'

The destroyer began her turn, Thurston bent to the voicepipe, the tow scraping across the fo'c'sle. 'Port ten.'

'Port ten, sir . . . Ten of port wheel on, sir.' Petty Officer Hicks, his voice as steady as ever.

*Marathon* began to come round, buffeted by the sea, wallowing slackly. No one spoke. The figures moved on the compass card, with agonising slowness. The bows dropped into another trough, the wire tautened. Thurston's hands tightened. He glanced at the compass, then back. His teeth clenched. Just a bit longer. Another gout of spray; he was soaked through, had been for hours, but he didn't care. The destroyer began to straighten up.

'Ease to five.'

'Ease to five, sir.'

'Midships . . . Meet her.'

'Midships, sir. Meet her . . . Wheel amidships, sir.'

'Done it!' exclaimed Bradshaw, smashing a fist into his palm.

'Steer one-one-two.'

'Steer one-one-two, sir.'

# — Chapter Ten —

The burials took place on the quarterdeck shortly after dawn, attended by all who could be spared from other duties, only a couple of dozen of them, soaked through and filthy, dead tired after the night's labour. Some had tried to spruce themselves up; their efforts seemed somehow more poignant.

Nineteen shrouded bundles at his feet; two more had died before morning.

'Off caps.'

The wind cut in, spray lashed the open deck.

*'I am the resurrection and the life, saith the Lord; he that believeth in me, though he were dead, yet shall he live, and whosoever liveth and believeth in me shall never die.'*

No Polish ensign for Midshipman Krasnowicz, dead for a country that was not his, and buried in a faith that was not his either. But he had seen Zurakowski dart out, and place something on the white ensign, a Polish naval cap ribbon.

*'I know that my Redeemer liveth and that He shall stand at the latter day upon the earth, and though after my skin worms destroy this body, yet in my flesh shall I see God . . .'*

Nineteen dead, twenty-six more somewhere in the water and oil below decks.

*'The Lord gave, and the Lord hath taken away. Blessed be the name of the Lord.'*

He had done a funeral aboard *Sirdar*, two days out from Shanghai in 1931, an able seaman killed by a falling block, a harsh bright morning in the China Sea. He tried to remember the man's name, and found he had forgotten it. He went on, more quietly now, the book forgotten, the remembered words coming steadily, the nineteen canvas bundles draped in their ensigns before him, cap beneath his arm, wet hair plastered to his head.

Midshipman Krasnowicz, Petty Officer Crawley, Able Seaman Horrocks, a regular on Captain's Defaulters, Stoker Selby, who played football for Preston North End, Able Seaman Craig, who would never be an officer now. Two bodies burnt beyond any identification, the sickening sweetish stench of charred flesh reaching his nostrils, ('No dog tags, sir. Two-badge Stoker First Class, possibly Miller D.A.')

*'Forasmuch as it hath pleased Almighty God of His great mercy to take unto Himself the souls of our dear brothers here departed, we therefore commit their bodies to the deep, to be turned into corruption, looking to the resurrection of the body, when the sea shall give up her dead . . .'*

The nineteen corpses slid one by one into the sea, the firebars sewn into the shrouds carrying them swiftly from sight. The sad and lovely cadences of the Last Post hanging for a moment, before being carried away on the wind; the three volleys, cartridge cases clattering on the deck, before the brazen jauntiness of Reveille broke through the sadness with promise of resurrection.

*Charlie, Charlie, show us a leg,*
*Charlie, Charlie, lash up and stow.*

*'Stir up Thy strength, O God, and come and help us, for Thou givest not always the battle to the strong, but canst save by many or few. O let not our sins cry against us for vengeance, but hear us Thy poor servants begging mercy, and imploring Thy help, and that Thou wouldst be a defence unto us against the face of the enemy. Make it appear that Thou art our Saviour and mighty Deliverer; through Jesus Christ Our Lord, Amen.'*

Thurston returned to the bridge and entered the nineteen names in the log, each with the time-honoured suffix 'DD' – 'Discharged Dead'. And the missing – Lt(E) W. R. Stead RN, Sub-Lt(E) H. M. Buchan RN, Mr C. H. Sutcliffe RN, Commissioned Engineer . . . Turner A. W., Stoker Petty Officer, Crombie J. T., E.R.A . . . Meade R., Leading Stoker . . . Dawson P., Stoker 1st Class . . . Hodgson G. W., Stoker 1st Class . . . Bell E., Marine, Hawkins J. M., Marine, Watts G., Musician . . . *This bloody bloody war* . . .

It was not until he noticed the date that he realised it was Sunday.

# — Chapter Eleven —

'D'you hear there? This is the Captain speaking. Good morning.'

'What's good about it?' said Angus.

'Pray silence for Father's pep talk,' said Nairne.

'Firstly, thank you all for your magnificent efforts during the night, which made it possible for our ship to remain afloat. We are now making for Alexandria under tow. However, none of us can relax and think the job is done until we reach port. All I can promise you is hard work and short commons . . .'

'Corned beef!'

'. . . But, God willing, we shall win through. This morning we buried nineteen of our shipmates . . .'

'Poor old Kras,' said Graham. 'How's Zura taking it?'

'All right, I suppose. He mutters a bit. In Polish.'

'Since he *is* Polish.'

'Pipe down, you two. I'm trying to listen,' Cowper-Coles broke in.

'That is all.' The tannoy clicked off.

'Well, that was short and sweet.'

Pearson sat at the gunroom table, wearily spreading blackcurrant jam on a slice of bread; there wasn't much else to eat, with only emergency power on. He couldn't remember ever being so tired before; he had been on his feet all night, wet through and still seasick. He had come below, searched for his cap and finally found it, fallen from the rack and half crushed behind his sea chest. Graham had lent him another, so he could send the First Lieutenant his back. The ship had gone to Defence Stations now, except for the Damage Control and fire parties which were still at work. The talk around him was of Krasnowicz.

'At least we won't have to put up with his bloody violin-playing any longer.'

'Does anybody want a violin?'

'Did Kras have any relations? I suppose we ought to send them his gear.'

'He didn't get any letters.'

'It may have escaped your notice, Alec,' said Angus heavily, 'but the postal service to Poland has been somewhat disrupted of late. Anyway, Zura'll know. We'll have to do the same for Buchan as well. Or have you got your eyes on some of his stuff?'

'I think we should have a wake,' said Nairne, 'What is it they drink in Poland?'

'Vodka,' said Cowper-Coles. 'Terrible stuff.'

'And Graham can play the Polonaise until it's coming out of our ears,' went on Angus.

Nairne picked up his cocoa mug and began to sing, gradually joined by the others.

> So stand to your glasses, steady,
> They are all we have left to prize,
> Drink a cup to the dead already,
> And one to the next man to die!'

Pearson pushed away his plate. He didn't feel hungry any more.

'What's up? That's all you'll get, you know. You heard our distinguished leader.'

> Now a truce to this mournful story,
> For death is a distant friend,
> So here's to the life of glory,
> And the laurels to crown each end.
>
> So stand to your glasses, steady . . .

131

He jumped up, swung a punch at Nairne, who was doing an imitation of sobbing violins. Nairne ducked. Someone grabbed Pearson from behind.

'I've never heard such a lot of heartless brutes as you! Krasnowicz is dead and no one's a bit bothered! Let go!'

'If you'll stop being such a bloody fool,' said Norris, who had him by the arms. Released, Pearson made for the door.

''Ark at 'im,' said Nairne, helping himself to more bread.

Pearson went out into the chest flat, pulled his lashed hammock from the rack and began to struggle with it. He'd never slung one before; there had been beds at *King Alfred* and until now there had always been Marines to do it. The lashing came undone, the ship rolled and the canvas unfolded itself over him. The return roll sent him off balance, pitching him against the bulkhead. Almost in tears with misery and frustration, he struggled upright and tried to fight his way out, the ship continuing disinterestedly to roll. Footsteps behind him as the canvas at last dropped to the deck. He turned and recognised Cowper-Coles, bulky with duffel coat in the dim light.

'What's up?'

'Nothing, sir.'

'Don't say that. Here, give that to me. I was an OD for six months, after all.' Cowper-Coles picked up the hammock and began to sling it with practised efficiency.

'Thank you, sir,' Pearson said uncertainly.

'You don't have to call me sir, except on watch. CC, or Gerald if you must. Look, Pearson, don't think the rest aren't bothered about Krasnowicz. All that banter doesn't mean anything.'

'Doesn't it? None of them seem the slightest bit bothered. All they talk about is violins and what to do with kit.'

'Pearson, there's a war on and people get killed. Most of us have seen it happen before now. In my last ship we used to pick up survivors and see half of them die afterwards. If you were to get upset about all of them you'd go mad, and you'd never be able to keep on doing the job. All of us knew Kras much better than you. Do you know how he and Zurakowski got here? They were cadets at the Polish Naval Academy when this lot started. Zurakowski's brother was a pilot in the Polish Air Force and crammed them both into a single-seater fighter to get out to Rumania, with German tanks rolling on to the airfield as they were taking off. Then they worked a passage through the Black Sea to Greece, then Italy, went through Italy when the Italians were still neutral, got to France and joined the French Navy. When France threw in the towel they got to England and joined up again. The brother was killed flying in the Battle of Britain. Ask Zura about it some time.' Cowper-Coles finished with the hammock. 'There you are.'

'Thanks.'

'I've not finished yet. You've got to stop feeling sorry for yourself. You'll get used to this if you let yourself. You might even stop being seasick. And we have it pretty soft compared with the men. Some of the messdecks are under six inches of water and they still have to live in them. They don't have stewards and drinks and tablecloths and all the rest like we do. Come on, if you can't take a joke you shouldn't have joined.'

Thurston's world was the bridge, and the sea, and the tow. *Marathon* limped along at three knots, barely making steerage way, towards the distant refuge of Alexandria. The new course had taken them towards the North African coast; they crept forward thirty miles from the land, *Leonidas* rolled lightly over the waves, the cruiser wallowing ponderously through them. It was wet; his trousers clung in sodden slabs to his legs,

133

the towel around his neck was soaked, his collar was a limp grey rag, his shirt a cold compress.

The tow filled every hour, every minute. *Marathon*'s lifeline began in her bows, extended across a hundred yards of sea to the bucketing stern of the destroyer. The bows would slew to one side, the quartermaster on the wheel would fail to hold her, the steel hawser would strain towards breaking point.

'Port ten,'

'Port ten, sir. Ten of port wheel on.'

It would take a long time to move back into line, the rudders barely bit at this slow speed. But you couldn't hurry it, had to resist the temptation to put the helm hard over and get the thing over with. Agonisingly slowly, *Marathon* would begin to drift back, the strain would come off the wire, almost imperceptibly.

'Midships. Meet her.'

'Midships, sir. Meet her.'

You had to catch her, otherwise slack would build up and the next heavy sea would yank the wire taut and place a breaking strain on it all over again. It was something they had exercised often enough before, towing and being towed, but never in a sea like this. And this was only the first day.

He had been over the chart with Hart.

'A hundred and forty hours, sir, at this speed.'

They tried for five knots, but in this sea the motion and strain on the tow were too much. Back to three knots, the sickening wallowing. He was very tired. Apart from the burials he had not been off the bridge since first light the previous day, but he could not drag himself away from the tow, not while this sea was running. There was the bucket in the corner by the chart table, and every couple of hours Spencer would appear.

'Starboard ten.'

'Starboard ten, sir.'

Able Seaman Courtney on the wheel. There were

two quartermasters on watch at a time now, doing thirty minutes apiece, turn about; it took too much concentration to handle the wheel any longer.

'Cocoa, sir.'

'Thank you, Spencer. Midships. Meet her.'

'Midships, sir. Meet her.'

Spencer looked tired, bundled up in his duffel coat, unshaven.

'Go and get your head down for a bit, Spencer.'

'I'm all right, sir.'

'Go on.' He lowered his voice. 'That's an order, Spencer.'

Spencer straightened. 'Aye aye, sir.'

It was afternoon when the enemy found them, halfway through the First Dog Watch. *Marathon* and *Leonidas* had plodded along in their own private world since before dawn. They had begun to think that the respite might last, and that the bombers would concentrate on the convoy.

Thurston had left the Commander on the bridge and gone to the sick bay to see the wounded. It was not a task he relished, but it had to be done. There was so little he could say. 'Hello, so-and-so, how are you feeling? You did a good job,' come out with the odd bit of banter, move on to the next man.

*Well, young Thurston, feeling better? You must have a hard skull, what? You did a damn good job.*

But he couldn't think then what he was supposed to have done and he was too tired and aching to care much.

'Hello, Wardle, feeling better?'

'Yes, sir. Thank you, sir.'

'The PMO tells me you'll be back on your feet in a couple of days.'

'Yes, sir. Be glad to get out of here. Place stinks of disinfectant.'

That was on the messdeck, where there was joking

135

and laughter, and the smell of tobacco smoke. In the crowded sick bay were the more serious cases; a man with both his heels shattered by the shock wave from the explosion and a probable broken spine, men who had swallowed fuel oil, two with lungs scorched, tubes and drips and plasma. Stoker Simmonds, still waiting for his leg to be set. The padre, unconscious, grey-faced, his hands burned to the bone.

'I don't think he'll make it,' Savage was saying. 'Shock mainly. That's always the problem with burns, shock and dehydration. If he'd been younger he'd have a better chance, but . . .' He shrugged. 'Really we're just filling him up with morphine and praying. And that's quite serious.'

Midshipman Pearson had kept the Afternoon Watch on the bridge. When it was over he retired to his hammock, forsaking the opportunity of more corned beef sandwiches. He was deadly tired, had hardly managed to drag himself awake to go up; he seemed to have spent the whole of his watch in a stupor of exhaustion and seasickness, being shooed about by Lieutenant Taylor. At one stage he had roused himself enough to enquire whether this happened every time the ship put to sea. This was considered hilarious, but the laughter was brittle and no one gave him a satisfactory answer. If he had only been a bit older, he would have passed out of *King Alfred* as a sub-lieutenant and then he would have been eligible for shore jobs, all the kudos of naval uniform, without the sheer misery of service at sea. Why anyone should actively desire this he would never know. He lay in his hammock, lifebelt round his middle, tin hat and gas mask to hand, the ship's motion rattling the chains in the rifle racks, bumping him against his neighbour, Midshipman Norris RNR.

He wasn't the only one. Coming below he had picked his way over rows of men sleeping on camp beds and mattresses, lifebelts half inflated as pillows, doubled over and tied with string, as near to the outer air as they could get. He wondered whether he could make it through all those watertight doors, each with six clips to be shifted to get them open. Norris had survived a sinking, in his last ship, and two days in an open boat off Freetown. Pearson shuddered. Tired as he was he couldn't sleep. Thoughts kept crowding in, of more torpedoes tearing through the half-inch steel plate, of the closed doors, the rising sea. He wasn't much of a swimmer, two lengths in a boiler suit in training had nearly defeated him. Norris seemed friendly enough, he had chatted for a while before turning over and going to sleep.

'You don't want to take every word Smart Alec Nairne says as gospel. He thinks he's going to be the next First Sea Lord, but he's all wind and piss.'

Timidly, Pearson had asked about the 'Dozens'. Norris roared with laughter.

'That's typical. He's just trying to put the wind up you. All that went out with Jellicoe. The Captain does give cuts, but you have to pass a dud cheque, or make a real idiot of yourself. It's never happened in my time. The officers just stop your leave or give you extra watches, which is more of a bind if you ask me.'

The alarm went off, buglers sounded through the loudspeaker on the bulkhead above him. He grabbed the steel pipe and swung himself out of the hammock, groped for seaboots.

'Come on! Action Stations!'

Oh no, not again! He gathered up his things, shrugged into his duffel.

'Get a move on, Pearson!'

He started to run, almost fell over the coaming.

'Shut that bloody door!'

Up the ladders to the deck. Why, oh why, was his action station right at the other end of the ship, with a hundred yards of lurching open deck in between?

Thurston had seen all the wounded. He was drinking a mug of tea and talking to the Surgeon Commander, taking the opportunity to dry off a bit before going back up. The sick bay was tidy after the labours of the night, only a bucket of blood swabs to bear mute witness.

The telephone shrilled.

'Captain, sir.'

'Tell them I'm coming up.'

He put down the mug, half finished. The bugles sounded. Up the ladders in a sprinting long-legged run, cursing inwardly all the time for letting himself be caught below.

'Radar reports large formation of aircraft, sir. Ten miles and closing.' Sitting ducks. There was no chance of taking evasive action, nor any for *Leonidas* unless she slipped the tow. He had kept that to himself, as he had to remain silent on what it was like to spend four days on a Carley float, watching other men die from cold and exhaustion of the spirit.

'I'll get back to Damage Control,' said Bradshaw.

'No, stay here.' He wasn't sure what made him say it.

He glanced around him. Midshipman Zurakowski was white-faced, silent, unnaturally so since Krasnowicz's death. His lips moved now, in Latin. Hood was trying to look unconcerned, and failing.

*For what we are about to receive . . .*

A dozen Italian bombers, coming in low, fighter escort weaving above.

'Where's the fucking air force?' cursed a signalman.

'Shut up, Keenan!' The Chief Yeoman.

A familiar reassurance from the voicepipe. 'Chief QM on the wheel, sir.'

Thurston picked up the telephone to the Director Tower. 'Open fire.'

'Open fire, sir.'

The main armament opened up, followed a moment

138

later by every other weapon on board. Noise and pounding concussion, more from *Leonidas*. Thurston's mind was taken up with the tow, keeping the ship moving on and the wire taut while the shock of firing shoved her continually off course, *Leonidas* jinking out of time under the weight of her own barrage.

'Praise the Lord and pass the ammunition, Praise the Lord and pass the ammunition,' mouthed Keenan.

Fear, fear which knotted up the stomach, that made you want to run and hide, anywhere, or pray for a hit, just to get it over with.

'Starboard ten.'

'Starboard ten, sir.'


Pearson was in B turret, hunched in his seat beside Sub-Lieutenant Hastings, opposite the gunlayer and rangefinder on their saddles; the loading numbers at their breeches, the turret communications number, Boy Gibbons, headset clamped over one ear, jaws working unconcernedly on a lump of toffee.

'Load.'

The 5.25-inch shells came up through the floor in their cages, were rammed home into the breeches. Up came the silk-bagged cordite charges, innocuous-seeming; the breech blocks slammed shut. The layer and trainer were at work, the barrels elevating into high angle.

'Gibbons, get rid of that!'

Gibbons shifted the toffee to the other side of his mouth, out of Hastings's line of vision.

'Ready!'

Hastings pressed the indicator switch which would activate the gun ready lamps in the Director Tower.

'Shoot!'

The guns slammed back on their recoil cylinders as the Director Layer pressed his trigger; the breeches crashed open before they had stopped moving.

'Sponge out! . . . Load!'

Noise, and waves of acrid cordite fumes each time the guns went off. Pearson was excited in spite of himself, but what was happening outside?

'Shoot!'

They couldn't take evasive action! What would it be like? And he couldn't swim much.

The explosion came, the ship bucked and lurched, as she had last night. Was it another torpedo? He felt a thump on the back of his thigh, coming from underneath.

*Oh God, this is it!*

Then there was Hastings's voice, shouting down the tube. 'What's happening down there?'

'Fire in the handling room, sir!'

'Can you put it out?'

'Trying to, sir.'

'Keep me informed.' He reached for another tube. 'Magazine . . . Wake up, you dozy bastards.'

'Getting a bit hot sir,' said one of the loading numbers.

'Not bloody surprising!'

'Reckon the Director Tower's got it, nothin' comin' through on the dials,' said the gunlayer.

'May just be a cable cut.'

'Gibbons, get through to the Director Tower!'

Gibbons did not move.

'Wake up, you dozy little so-and-so!'

'Think 'e's 'it, sir.'

'Pearson, see if he's all right.'

He got up, felt his leg give way, remembered the thump it had had. He staggered the few paces, put a hand on Gibbons's shoulder.

'Gibbons, are you okay?' His voice lacked Hastings's Dartmouth authority.

No answer. He pulled him round, saw the blood, white and splintered bone, bits of broken headphone. 'Gibbons, oh God, Gibbons.' He fell forward on to his knees and threw up.

'Shut up, Pearson!' Hastings shouted into the voicepipe. 'All right! Open magazine flood valves. Close flash doors. Clear the turret.'

*Gibbons!*

'Shut up! The magazine's on fire. Clear the turret!' Hastings was on his feet, holding his forearm, blood coming out from between his fingers. 'Everybody out!' He sounded furious.

Someone opened the hatch. Fresh air poured in, breaking through the cordite miasma.

'Careful with Gibbo. Steady.'

'Come on, Pearson. Don't just stand there! Give them a hand!'

The gunlayer had gone through the hatch and pulled Gibbons's inert body after him, another man pushing his legs from beneath. He grabbed a foot and shoved.

'Ah, just leave it to me, sir. Nearly there, Jim.' The feet disappeared.

'Get on, the rest of you!'

Ten more went. What was happening outside? Was the ship sinking?

'Go on, Pearson! If you can't take a joke you shouldn't have joined!'

He hated Hastings in this moment. He put his hands up, grasped the sides of the hatch, felt someone grab an arm, kicked out with his legs. His head came out into the fresh air, cold damp bracing air.

'Out you come, chum.'

He landed face down on the turret roof, feeling the blood trickle down the back of his leg. No pain, for some reason.

*Gibbons!* He was sick again, turning aside at the last second, all the bread and corned beef and cocoa he had had for lunch.

'Stretcher party coming!'

Hastings appeared from the hatch, white-faced and swearing. Pearson sat up.

'You're 'it, sir.' Someone started to wrap a bandage

round his thigh. 'Cushy one that. Straight in and straight out. You're lucky. Six inches higher and you'd 'ave been singing soprano in the choir.'

They loaded Gibbons on to a stretcher and took him away, the Surgeon Lieutenant walking beside him. The Commander was also there, loudly telling Hastings to go below and get his arm seen to.

'I'm all right, sir, really I am.'

'Go below and get yourself fixed up, Mr Hastings! You're putting blood all over the fo'c'sle!'

The man finished his bandaging. 'Can you walk?'

'I don't think so.'

'Not to worry.' Two men put him on a stretcher, started strapping him to it.

'What's that for?'

'So you don't fall off on the ladders and smash something else up. Now, as Confucius would say, lie back and enjoy it!'


Incredibly, only that one bomb had hit them.

'From *Leonidas*, sir. *Are you still there, Big Sister?*'

The tow must have parted, but there had been no high-pitched crack, no broken end flailing across the fo'c'sle. It was still there, hanging slackly over the waterline.

'Wops must have sent their learners in.'

Watch the tow, watch *Leonidas* as she brought the wire taut. They began to move. Thurston unclenched his hands. There were bloody furrows in the palms where the nails had gouged in.

The damage reports came through. The bomb had set off a cordite fire in B turret's handling room; the turret was out of action. Twenty-three men had been killed or wounded, the main switchboard smashed, the galley wrecked. A fighter had raked the Director Tower with cannon fire, killing the Gunnery Officer and Director Layer, and badly wounding every other man there.

142

'Here we go, picking up the pieces again!'

Concentrate on the tow. Ted Bradshaw was clearing up the mess, a first-aid party beginning the difficult task of bringing the dead and wounded down from the Director Tower for Savage to deal with. He had the ship.

*Leonidas* had come through unscathed and shot down four enemy aircraft. No further damage to the hull below the waterline. The bulkheads seemed to be holding. But only three turrets, no Director Control unless something could be patched up, sixty-one men dead and missing and more wounded. It was as bad as *Seydlitz*. He wondered from time to time about his motives for attacking the *Seydlitz*. Had there been a proper appraisal of the situation, that to try to shadow her in that visibility without radar was to risk losing her altogether, or was there only a primitive lust for glory?

Paymaster Sub-Lieutenant Jenner appeared from the cipher office. 'Signal, sir!' He was breathless with excitement. 'From CinC Med repeated Admiralty. They're sending us fighter cover!'

'Nice timing,' Thurston said drily.

'They'll be with us tomorrow morning.'

'Bit bloody late,' muttered Keenan.

'Log it, Jenner.'

# — Chapter Twelve —

Long after dark Savage came up to the bridge. He had
spent over an hour operating on Boy Gibbons, time
which might have been more profitably spent on some
of the other wounded, another hour on Midshipman
Norris. He came to make a report to the Captain,
to get some fresh air, to get away from the sick-bay
atmosphere of blood and ether and other men's pain.

'We're getting a bit crowded now. I've taken over
another messdeck. Another dozen cases, but only two
of them critical, thank God. One more amputation –
Leading Steward Green from B turret, left hand off.
He should come through it all right. Young Hastings
had a compound fracture; he wanted to go straight
back as soon as I'd set it, but the shock's got to him
now.'

'Cocoa, sir?' Spencer had appeared at Savage's
elbow.

'Bless you, Spencer.'

'Have you all the men you need, Doc?'

'Yes, sir. I've co-opted a few unemployed stokers
and some of the band, and they're doing a grand job.
I must say this makes up for the times we spend waiting
for patients to turn up.'

There was a persistent rumour that in normal times
the sick-berth attendants spent all their time washing
and starching the Surgeon Commander's white coats,
and playing cards.

'Starboard ten.'

'Starboard ten.'

'Quite an eyestrain job.'

'You get used to it. You watch her stern light. The blue one.'

'Ah yes.' Savage took a pull at the cocoa. 'To think I had the chance of Harley Street. Must have been mad.' He looked the Captain up and down, decided against saying anything for the time being. 'Anyway, I'll to my cabin. I've left young Bradley holding the fort and I'm going to get my head down, which is what I would advise you to do.'

'Later, Doc. Midships.'

'Midships, sir.'

'Goodnight, Doc.'

Pearson was on a mattress on one of the seamen's messdecks, his leg stretched out in front of him. The Surgeon Commander had glanced at it.

'Gone right through, which saves all the bother of having me dig around to find the bits. You'll be playing football again in no time.'

The wound had been rebandaged, they had given him anti-tetanus and morphine, which put him into a comfortable state of apathy. He was out of it, honourably wounded and out of it, warm and comfortable under blankets and not even seasick now. The sick-berth attendants were friendly and one of them even brought him a pile of *Reader's Digests* to look through. He had forgotten all about Gibbons, suffused with a warm sense of well-being.

Most of the wounded were asleep, or in varying degrees of stupor from morphine, but some talked in low voices. Marine bandsmen moved among them with cigarettes and mugs of tea.

'What happened to you, youngster?' asked the elderly three-badger next to him. Pearson told him, disjointedly. He didn't like to think of what had brought him here, to remember Gibbons's broken head, and Hastings swearing at him with hate in his voice.

145

'Don't you fret. Beaky'll get us back.'

'Who?'

'Beaky. Hardover Bob. The skipper, the Old Man, the Captain.'

Pearson sat up in surprise.

'Want a tickler?' The man dug into his pockets, without waiting for an answer, brought out a flat tin and expertly rolled a couple of cigarettes. 'Quite a boy is our Beaky. I remember 'im in *Sirdar*, when 'e was a two-and-a-half. Did you 'ear about the *Seydlitz* business?' The man settled himself comfortably to tell his story. 'Well, I was with the Commander when we got hit – good bloke, old Bradshaw, but he can't hold a candle to Beaky – and he says, "Connor, you come with me," and we doubles away to the bridge to see what's happened. Proper potmess. Bodies all over the shop.' Connor paused for dramatic effect. 'And there's Beaky standin' in the middle of it all, cool as you please, carryin' on as usual, drippin' blood all over the shop. Schooly was complainin' there was gore coming down the tube and ruinin' his plot. And Beaky just stays there right through, wouldn't 'ave the doctor or nothing – told old Savage to get below and deal with the wounded!' Connor paused again. 'Gotta light? Me matches are wet. Couldn't talk proper on account of 'aving 'is teeth smashed up, so 'e was just writing things down for Jimmy ffrench – turn two points to starboard, go into the smoke, all that sort of thing. And old Bradshaw was jumping up and down, saying he oughter take over, and Beaky wouldn't let him, not until it's all over and Jerry's sunk and then he tells old Bradshaw to take over now and walks off to the sick bay, cool as you please. Hell of a bloke is our Beaky.'

Connor puffed appreciatively. 'Course I shouldn't really be here. Only had three months to go for my pension when this lot started. Twenty-nine years I been in the Andrew. Started at *Ganges*, 1913 it was. You've never seen anything till you've seen *Ganges*. Mind, it's gone soft now.'

Pearson lay back, listening to Connor ramble on, about ships and strange places and a hundred brushes with authority.

'All right, put him down here,' came the tired voice of the sick-bay Petty Officer, 'And pipe down, Connor, you're a corrupting influence on the young.'

Pearson saw Norris's ashen face, a mass of blankets. The eyes opened.

'Hello, Pearson.'

'Hello, Norris.' He didn't know Norris's Christian name. 'How are you?' He didn't know he had been hit. *Oh my God*.

'The doc's stuffed my guts back in. He told me not to laugh or I'd bust the stitches.' Norris tried to grin. 'In the Director Tower. Gunnery Officer's dead. Got it right in the chest.' Tired grey face and tired grey voice. 'Dying for a drink.'

'I've got some tea.' He leant over towards Norris, brought the mug up to his face.

Before Norris could take a drop someone leapt over a couple of mattresses, jerked the mug out of Pearson's hand. 'Don't give him that, you stupid fucker, not with a gut wound!'

'Sorry,' he mumbled, flushing.

The Petty Officer looked weary. 'Just remember in future, sir.'

Norris drifted off. Pearson fell asleep. When he awoke Norris had gone.

'Died in the night,' one of the bandsmen told him. 'The doc got to work on him again, but it didn't do any good.'

Another funeral at dawn, the ensigns lowered to half-mast. Fifteen men. Lieutenant-Commander Barnett, who had been *Marathon's* Gunnery Officer throughout the commission, Chief Petty Officer Sloan, the Director Layer, who had been a leading seaman in *Sirdar* when Thurston was a lieutenant-commander in his first command. Midshipman Norris had started as a *Conway* cadet, been an apprentice with Elders and Fyffes and then transferred to the RNR because, 'I got sick of waiting to be shot at, sir.' And there were the others, the funerals of yesterday. Months ago, when they were at Massawa bottom-scraping, he had had a dinner party for some of the officers and midshipmen. Krasnowicz had been there, so had Guns and the padre. He asked Krasnowicz to bring his violin and the lad had played for them after dinner, a Bach concerto, with an expression of rapt concentration on his face, the precise notes echoing round the cabin in the sudden stillness, the suffocating Red Sea heat. Someone, ffrench probably, had ragged Krasnowicz mildly for choosing a work by a German composer; the midshipman had leapt to attention. 'Zir, music is international!'

It made him think of music, the last evening he had spent with Philip Woodruffe. Philip had a good record collection and a source of excellent brandy which he refused to divulge; it had been a civilised time of mess kit and good food and gentle debate on the merits of various composers. He didn't envy Philip his job, with Beecham breathing down his neck all the time. Beecham liked to pass himself off as the bluff and simple sailor, but had taken care to provide himself with a flag-captain who possessed one of the most brilliant minds in the service.

No news of the convoy, no signals, nothing. They should have reached Malta by now. Perhaps *Empire Liberator* had had more trouble with her engines.

'Radar . . . Bridge.'

'Bridge.'

'Small formation of aircraft, bearing green six-oh,'

'I think this could be our fighter cover.'

'Beaufighters, sir,' said Midshipman Graham, who

148

made a hobby of aircraft recognition. 'The Mark two version with . . .'

'Thank you, Mr Graham,' said Lieutenant Taylor, who was Officer of the Watch. 'Make *Nice to see you*.'

Lamps blinked.

'Reply, sir. *Sorry to miss the fun. Glad to see you're still afloat.*'

'Better late than never,' said Taylor.

'Don't think much of their morse,' said the Yeoman.

'Breakfast, sir,' announced Spencer.

'What is it?'

'Cheese on toast, sir. Best I could manage right now. Thought you'd like somethin' 'ot. D'ye want it 'ere or in the dog kennel?'

'Here please, Spencer.'

He sat on the bridge chair, eating with slow relish, Spencer supplying him with black coffee. He was at the stage when he needed something to keep awake.

Able Seaman Dawson on the wheel, working turn-about with Courtney. The Navigator had a streaming cold and seemed to spend most of his time trying to unblock his nose, while swearing it was better on deck in the fresh air than in the fug below. Lieutenant Harker had come up from the sick bay a little earlier, heavily strapped up beneath his clothes, and insisted on resuming his duties. 'It only hurts when I laugh now, and since there isn't much to laugh about . . .'

But some were finding things. The PO telegraphist who edited the ship's weekly newsletter had put together a few copies of a 'Special Disaster Edition' which were now in circulation, consisting largely of a spread of his own cartoons on the theme of 'What did you say when the Big Bang happened?' The wardroom Chief Steward was depicted emerging from a serving hatch and saying 'You rang, sir?' The Surgeon Commander rubbed his hands and announced 'More victims!' to a jackal-like Deadly Virus and a lugubrious Petty Officer Sellars. Mr Knott, the Commissioned

149

Gunner, whose deafness was notorious, asked plaintively, hand to ear, 'Did I hear something?' Thurston was shown on his bridge chair with a copy of *The Times*, pondering 'Flood in six letters?' The Naafi manager exclaimed furiously, 'They can't do this to me. I'm a civilian!' The Paymaster Commander saw an opportunity to write off all his deficits and the Bandmaster tapped a music stand with his baton and told the band, 'I suppose we'd better practise "Nearer, My God, To Thee".'

Down to the sick bay. The padre – no change. Sub-Lieutenant Hastings, protesting that he could manage perfectly well with one hand.

'You're staying where you are, Sub.'

'But sir . . .'

'Don't argue with me. We need you fit.'

Boy Gibbons.

'Difficult to predict anything with a bad head wound, sir. Quite honestly, he'd only have about an even chance ashore with a first-class neurosurgeon and all the facilities. All this motion doesn't help either. But,' Savage studied his fingernails. 'He's young, and a trier. He'll put up a fight.'

Gibbons's face was waxen and composed, oddly beautiful below the bandages. He was – had been – one of those cheerful, cheeky sort of boys who were popular with the men and tended to be a bit spoilt by them. McCormick was very quiet today. Sixteen, George's age.

He had been over to Dartmouth when he was on leave after *Seydlitz*. George had asked him to come and watch him play in the first match of the season, though he recognised a certain element of showing off. After all, in the Dartmouth cadet's scale of values, a father who was a cruiser captain ranked pretty high, and a recently wounded cruiser captain higher still.

'I really don't want to miss this, Dad. I'd be really

sick if I'd been through all this and then missed it by a few months.'

There was a timelessness about Dartmouth, the cadets in white trousers doubling from place to place, cadets under punishment doubling up and down the hill, 'Pick your knees up, Mr Francis!', the slippery polish on the decks, the long corridors flanked with term photographs going back to the *Britannia*. They found Blake Term 1914 with Cadet R.H.M. Thurston third from left in the second row, between Cadet C.D. Wedderburn who had gone down with *Hogue* six months later, and Cadet A.H.St V. Hancock, whose cap had unaccountably fallen over his eyes. Fifteen years and ten yards further on there was Lieutenant-Commander Thurston with the Exmouth Term of 1929. George had been old enough then to start taking an interest in things outside, and perhaps it was because of that that he had never shown any interest in anything other than going to Dartmouth.

He saw George score a try against Exeter School, doubled up the King's Stairs with him just to show that he wasn't an old crock yet, watched him devour a plate of indifferent wartime cakes in Mrs Taylor's tearooms in the town.

'Don't forget I'm a growing lad and need the protein.'

'You get protein in red meat, not in cream buns.'

'I hope I go to a cruiser, they say all the battlewagons are just resting on the sardine tins that get thrown overboard. I'd really like to get into destroyers, but they don't seem to take RN snotties. Of course Mother would rather I stayed in Scapa all the time. Sure you don't want the last one, Dad?'

Yes, he had been much the same. He could have taken George up to the College chapel and told him something of what lay behind the brass plates on the walls. *Cecil Courtney Blake, Midshipman, HMS Hyperion*. Tich Blake, fifteen years old and four feet ten

151

inches tall when he was hit by a sniper below Achi Baba one dark night, 29 May 1915. A month earlier Tich had been proudly displaying his dirk belt after commanding the steam pinnace in the initial landings, the clasp stove into the shape of a spoonhead, an impressive and matching bruise on his midriff. *James Francis Tuck, Midshipman.* Tommy Tuck, who had slept in the next bed for two years, blown up with *Invincible* at Jutland. But George would know soon enough, leave him his shining pride a little longer.

Savage watched him go, his eyes bloodshot and red-rimmed with fatigue, the old scar standing out starkly white against the red of windburn. God alone knew what kind of private hell the Captain was going through, and what the long-term effects of so much strain would be. He sighed, and began giving instructions on dressings to his petty officer.

'Signal from CinC Med, sir,' announced Jenner. 'Rome Radio reports us sunk.'
   'Tell that to the Marines!'
   'That might give us a bit of peace,' said ffrench.
   'Don't speak too soon,' counselled Hart.
   'The Chianti will be flowing in Taranto tonight.'
   'Mama mia!'
   'This puts us level-pegging with the *Ark Royal*.'
   'But look what happened to her.'
   'I think our Damage Control is a bit more reliable.'
   The Beaufighters circled overhead.
   'I feel like telling them to fly round the other way. They're making me dizzy,' said ffrench.
   'At least they're here,' said Hart, reaching for his handkerchief once more.
   'Someone ought to put you to bed with a hot water bottle and a whisky toddy, Pilot.'
   'I might just take you up on that.'
   That was a good sign. ffrench was always ribbing

Hart and the Navigator usually replied in kind. They didn't have much in common otherwise; Hart elegant, aristocratic, deceptively languid; ffrench quite a bit older, fair, a bit craggy, rather like a Viking.

'Port ten.'

'Port ten, sir.'

Jenner appeared once more. 'They've made it, sir!' He waved a signal flimsy.

'Read it, please.'

'From CS15 to Admiralty, repeated CinC Med, *Marathon* and *Leonidas* . . .'

'Nice of them to remember us,' said ffrench.

*'Convoy MW14 reached objective 0300, 23rd. No further casualties. God save the King.'*

'Have that broadcast, Number One, and I suppose we should splice the mainbrace.'

'About time,' muttered a signalman.

'Pipe down!' ordered the Yeoman.

'I hope Their Lordships appreciate all we've done for them.'

'Whipping boys for the convoy.'

'Yeoman, signal that to the flyboys as well.'

'Something to tell your grandchildren, Pilot.'

'If I survive to see them,' Hart said drily.

'If you don't get yourself under cover with some dry socks, I don't suppose you will.'

'You sound just like my nanny.'

'I'm sure you were a lovely little boy, Pilot.'

'Midships.'

'Midships, sir.'

Stamp the feet, work the shoulder, unscrew the lenses of his binoculars to let the water out, go over the chart once more.

'It's going to be a hot night in Valletta tonight,' said Hart.

'Cheer up,' ffrench replied. 'If we miss the party we also miss the morning after.'

Something happened that afternoon, during Cowper-Coles's watch.

'Object bearing green two-oh, sir.'

Thurston swallowed a mouthful of the sandwich he was eating without taking time to chew it, felt it stick halfway before sliding down, swung into the direction the lookout indicated. He scanned the zone: nothing out there but heaving grey water, slashed with soapy foam.

'There it is again, sir.'

He still couldn't see anything, shut his eyes and screwed them up a couple of times, then tried again.

'It was very small, sir . . . I'm not sure, but I think it could be the top of a periscope.'

In the circumstances the lookouts were going to start seeing phantom periscopes sooner or later, but . . . There was something out there, suspended in the trough between two swells.

'Ah yes, I have it. Keep your eyes on the tow, Sub.'

He focused his binoculars. A squarish metallic-looking spot rising just above the water . . . It could be a periscope.

'Make to *Leonidas*. *Object twenty degrees off my starboard bow. Range . . .*' That was the difficult thing to estimate by eye; the radar would be no more reliable, and a periscope was too small to show up. '*Sixteen hundred yards*.'

'Acknowledged, sir.'

If there was a U-boat out there he would be getting himself into position for a shot, raising his periscope only for a few seconds at a time, to minimise the risk of being seen. He could make something over eight knots submerged, *Marathon* and *Leonidas* barely three.

'Starboard ten.'

'Starboard ten, sir.'

*Gently, Sub*. The object had gone again. If it was a U-boat it would reappear somewhere quite different.

154

He tried to put himself inside the U-boat captain's head. Get into position for a beam shot, fire a spread which would get both ships, but get a little closer to make sure. He had all the time in the world. Gunfire could force him down, but he was still in a position to fire. Asdic was all very well, but the attacking ship had to get on top of her, and plaster her with depth charges, to sink her or at least make her go deep. And *Leonidas* was hamstrung while *Marathon* was on tow.

'From *Leonidas*, sir. *I think it is a periscope.*'

But if he slipped the tow unnecessarily there would be all the difficulty and dangers of re-rigging it, and both ships would be at the mercy of any genuine U-boat during that time.

'Midships.'

'Midships, sir.'

'Object bearing green three-oh, sir.'

It hadn't moved as far as he would have expected, and the range had barely decreased. It looked exactly the same, a greyish square on top of the water. The lookout was rubbing the lenses of his binoculars before putting them back to his eyes. A periscope was usually taller than that, but . . .

'Make to *Leonidas*, *Prepare to slip tow*.'

The bridge had gone very quiet. He realised that the remains of the sandwich were balled in his hand, and threw them at the bucket.

'From *Leonidas*, *Your signal not understood*.'

'Keep on making it until he does understand,' he said curtly.

'Aye aye, sir.'

'Thinks he's fucking Nelson,' breathed the bridge messenger.

He stole a glance at Cowper-Coles. He seemed to be all right.

'You'd think he'd have his periscope up a bit higher,' the lookout mused. 'Can't see much from that level.'

The sound of engines reminded him of the Beaufighters circling overhead.

'Yeoman, tell the aircraft to investigate object thirty degrees from my starboard bow.'

'*Leonidas* still not acknowledged, sir.'

'Leave him for a minute.'

The leading Beaufighter's lamp winked. The aircraft banked into a turn to port the sound level rose as it flew low over them, dropping almost to wave height. The Beaufighter's 20-mm cannon were sufficient to breach a pressure hull, but the aircraft was not equipped to detect or deal with a submerged submarine. 'Hurry up!' someone said.

The Beaufighter began to climb away from the water, swung round into another turn. The lamp blinked once more. They waited tensely for the Yeoman's report. 'Sir.' His face creased into a broad smile. '*Object is a biscuit tin!*'

'Time someone cleaned up the ocean,' said the bridge messenger disgustedly, submerged in a wave of laughter from the rest, the slightly hysterical laughter of released tension.

Supper once again was cold corned beef.

'McCormick, tell the Paymaster Commander I wish to see him in my sea cabin at once.'

McCormick's grin relished what was to come.

In the few minutes he had to wait while McCormick found the Paymaster Commander and delivered his message, Thurston sat on his bunk and wondered what he was going to say, what indeed had happened. Paymaster Commander Wilkinson had spent much of his career as secretary to the man who had risen in that time to become Second Sea Lord, and had been appointed to his present post almost entirely because he was in the zone for promotion and needed sea time to be eligible for a fourth stripe. Until now he had been competent enough – there had been no complaints about his department – though he carried a vaguely superior air, as if the post was unworthy of his talents, and always managed to make Thurston feel that he was being sized up as a possible flag officer. But now he seemed to have given up; Thurston recalled seeing him on the boat deck the night they were torpedoed. He stretched his arms above his head and extended them behind. God, he was tired. It was the first time he had stopped all day.

He started awake at the knock on the door, massaged one eyelid with an index finger. 'Come.'

'You wished to see me, sir.'

Thurston did not invite him to sit down, but got to his feet, facing him in the narrow confines of the cabin. 'Paymaster Commander, in two days your department has yet to produce a single hot meal.'

'Yes, sir,' the Paymaster Commander said urbanely. He was rather sleek in appearance, a slight tendency to corpulence was concealed by his tailor, his teeth were excellent and shown to good effect when he smiled.

'What have you got to say about it? And what are you going to do about it? Since the ship was torpedoed your department has conspicuously failed in its main task. Do you honestly expect the men to work as they have been working and will continue to work on cold corned beef?' He had originally thought he would try to buck him up, remind him that he had a job to do and there were means which were not available in Whitehall, but he found he was laying into the Paymaster Commander, and enjoying it.

'Well, sir . . .'

'I'm not going to listen to excuses! The men are working their guts out, and you can't even be bothered to get off your backside and get them fed! I have put up with this for long enough!'

'Sir . . .'

'Hear me out! I am fully aware of the damage to the

157

galley, and that most of your men are on Damage Control. You'll just have to bloody well improvise, like the rest of us! And you can get rid of your damn superior Admiralty attitudes at the same time. You may be very good at pushing paper all day, but as soon as the going starts to get tough you give up!' He stopped, fixed the man with a penetrating stare. 'Either, Paymaster Commander, you stir your stumps and start to do your job, or I shall relieve you of your duties.' He paused to allow the words to register, then added, more quietly, 'Do you understand?'

'Yes, sir.' The Paymaster Commander sounded shaken. He probably hadn't been shouted at since he was a midshipman.

'You may go.'

2000 hours. In England it would be 1800. Kate would be arriving home from work, getting off the train at Portsmouth, walking up the lane from the station, dark now, perhaps raining. Helen would have her books spread over the dining table, finishing off her homework before supper. Inside, with a fire burning, insulated from the weather, the news on the wireless. Later on perhaps Kate would have one of her committees and Helen would go out to the pictures or something with some of her friends from school; Kate said that she was starting to take an interest in boys. Fifteen now, and outgrowing the tomboy stage of trying to keep up with her elder brother. He remembered that he still had to write to her.

'Course one-oh-six, sir. Able Seaman Grice on the wheel.'

2300 hours. Rain. Strained eyes peering at the blue light in *Leonidas's* stern. An oilskin never kept all the wet out; there were gaps and condensation and water ran off the hem and soaked his trouser legs above the knees. Thurston had shaved for the burials that morn-

158

ing and it had left him scraped and raw and bleeding in a couple of places. There would be another funeral in the morning watch. Twice Savage had come up to the bridge and conferred briefly with the Officer of the Watch. An exchange of salutes: 'Sir, Writer Morton died at 1932.' 'Sir, Marine Walsh died at 2007.' Walsh was one of the ship's boxing team, a welterweight if he remembered correctly, Morton he couldn't place.

God, he was tired, and dead inside. ffrench had the watch, he was conning the ship, but Thurston's eyes still followed the light, his brain registered the movement and made its calculations. Spencer had been up half an hour ago, with cocoa and sandwiches.

'Wouldn't you rather 'ave something 'ot, sir? I could rustle up something easy.'

His night glasses were half full of water again. He passed them to the Midshipman of the Watch – Nairne – who disappeared gratefully into the relative shelter of the chart table.

'Now how should I celebrate the Relief of Malta, which may yet attain the fame of the Relief of Mafeking?' mused the First Lieutenant to no one in particular – the Navigator was asleep on his mattress in the chartroom. 'Dinner at the Phoenicia, I think. I shall begin with soup, asparagus for preference. And then, I am rather partial to lobster.'

Nairne returned with the binoculars.

'You'll be lucky, Number One. When I was last in the Phoenicia all they could produce was a very scrawny chicken and that must have been on the black market.'

'One can dream, sir. Just now I'd settle for the civilised surroundings. Port ten.'

'Port ten, sir.'

'Aren't we going the wrong way for the Phoenicia?'

'Quite so, Mr Nairne. Have you any better suggestions?'

'Er, No, sir.'

'Thank you. Midships.'

'Midships, sir.'

Footsteps on the ladder. Ted Bradshaw. He was short, not more than five foot seven, but so broad-shouldered that dressed for the weather he looked almost square.

'Come up for air, Commander?'

Bradshaw grinned. 'That's my excuse. All quiet below, sir. I've just been round again. Men in good heart, the ones that are still awake, that is. They're all laying plans for leave and bets on where we're going for the repairs.' He lowered his voice. 'How about you? Time you got some rest.'

'Oh, I'm all right.'

'Sir, you look all in. If you go on like this you'll knock yourself up pretty thoroughly. Now, are you coming quietly?'

'What do you mean?' He was puzzled more than angry.

'Come on, Number One.'

ffrench left the binnacle. He and Bradshaw took the Captain by the arms and bundled him quietly but efficiently into his sea cabin.

'What's all this about, Commander?'

'I believe the technical term is mutiny, sir.' ffrench was clearly enjoying himself.

Bradshaw was more prosaic. 'You, sir, are going to get your head down, while the First Lieutenant and myself look after the ship. I gather your man Spencer is at the moment preparing something edible. Don't worry, we'll shake you for First Light. Goodnight, sir.'

The door shut. Spencer appeared a moment later with a tray. 'Corned beef hash, sir. Sponge pudden to follow.'

It was surprisingly hot, considering that Spencer had had to negotiate a long series of ladders and passages up from the wardroom. If Spencer could do it, why didn't the bloody Paymaster Commander stir his stumps? Hot soup had begun to appear in the First Watch, but that was all. But he was too weary to feel really hungry, and it was an effort to force the food down. Spencer rummaged in the drawers beneath the bunk, deposited a pile of dry clothes beside him.

'Now get these on, sir. Can't 'ave you catching your death.'

'Spencer, you sound like the Navigator's nanny.'

'Just doin' me job, sir. Don't like the sound of Mr 'Art's cough.' He went out, shaking his head.

Fed, dried and changed, Thurston lay back, braced his feet against the bulkhead and shut his eyes. But sleep would not come. There was the tow, he felt every movement of the helm, the waiting for the ship to come back on to her heading, the twanging tension of it. And images of men; Krasnowicz, Sloan, Craig, Norris. Barnett, who had a daughter a year old whom he had never seen. He had meant to check with Lieutenant Taylor about Boy Gibbons, snatch a word with Gibbons himself when they got to Malta.

*Dear Mrs So-and-So, I killed your son, your husband, your brother, just as surely as if I had taken his neck in my great prizefighter's hands and slowly slowly throttled the life out of him . . .*

Sixty-two men now, seventy-odd from *Seydlitz*, three hundred and eighty with *Connaught*.

*I should not be here. I should be dead with the rest of them.*

The door opened.

'Don't you every bloody knock? . . . Sorry, Doc.' He sat up, swung his legs over the side. 'Thought you were Spencer.'

'Don't get up.'

'What are you doing here, PMO?'

'Just keeping an eye on my patients.'

'And to tell me that I shouldn't bawl out the Paymaster Commander because he's a simple pen-pusher who shouldn't be exposed to things like this. That may be, but he is here, and he had better start pulling his weight.'

'I agree with your analysis, and a bawling-out is just what he needs to shake him up, but I haven't come to talk about the Paymaster Commander. How are you feeling, in yourself?'

'All right.'

'Don't give me that. It's another thing about you Dartmouth chaps. You're all either hypochondriacs, or you have to be just about dead before you'll admit to being the slightest bit off colour. Come on now, a little honesty.'

'All right, Doc. If it makes you happy, I feel like chewed-up string.'

'And strung up, and upset, I know. When did you last sleep?'

'Before this lot started.' God, it was nearly three days ago.

Savage sat down on the chair. 'I'm taking the liberty of prescribing for you.' He pulled out a bottle from his coat pocket.

'What's that?' His eyes had started to stream again.

'Bushmills, me bhoy.' The Surgeon Commander produced a very fair imitation of an Irish brogue. He sloshed some of the bottle's contents into a conveniently placed cocoa mug and passed it across.

'Since you're obviously in on this conspiracy,' Thurston smiled wearily, 'I suppose you'd better join me.'

'Thank you. I don't mind if I do.' Savage took a mouthful from the bottle.

'How's your department, doc?'

'Much the same. I'm getting away from all that for a couple of hours. I've just had another tussle with young Hastings. He's not badly hurt, but he's in no condition to rush back to watchkeeping, not after a general anaesthetic. And I don't want him falling on that arm after all the trouble I went to. In the end I

162

told him that if I had another squeak out of him I'd bonk him over the head with a bedpan.'

Thurston chuckled. 'Good lad, Hastings.'

'He is, but there are times when his zeal is a little misplaced. And you're just as bad. Get that stuff down you and don't start telling me you don't drink at sea. You made a dreadful patient. It was a damn good thing you couldn't talk.'

'I'm sure you strapped up my jaw on purpose.' Thurston's index finger rubbed the neat horizontal scar on the left side.

Savage thought with professional interest that someone had made a nice job of tidying that up. 'It was medically necessary, sir.'

'It must have been the pinnacle of Spencer's career. Me flat on my back and completely at his mercy.' The whiskey was doing its work, the blackness was lifting.

'He did a damn good job.'

'I know. I shouldn't joke about it.'

'I did tell him he was wasted as a captain's steward and should remuster as an SBA. Excellent bedside manner.'

He must be tired, the way this small glass of whiskey was affecting him. 'I suppose I shall see the funny side of this in a day or two. It's not every night that I get manhandled off my own bridge by my Commander and First Lieutenant.'

'At the instigation of the PMO,' Savage said smoothly. 'You're just about out on your feet. May I smoke?'

Thurston pulled out his cigarette case, lit one for Savage. The doctor noticed the design engraved on the back.

'May I have a look?'

An Indian cavalryman, his horse snorting and half rearing, leaning out of the saddle, a tiger turning at bay before the lance.

'What's the origin of this?'

163

'It's nothing very ancient. Something of my grandfather's. He was Indian Army, the Guides cavalry. He went through the Mutiny, lost an eye in the assault on Delhi, blew sepoys from the guns before breakfast. Yet with all that he spoke seven languages and became an authority on Persian poetry, of all things.'

'He sounds quite a character.' Savage's clinical curiosity was aroused.

'He was. He was the finest horseman I've ever met and he was still hunting two days a week when he was over eighty. He taught us all to ride, my brothers and me, and if we spoke to him between two and four in the afternoon it had to be in Urdu. He started to teach me Persian, but I forgot most of it when I went to sea. The Urdu's been useful though. I was named after him, as a matter of fact. There's even a story that he went spying in Afghanistan disguised as a Pathan horse trader. He would never say whether or not it was true, just "There are many blue eyes among the Pathans." It might well have been true. He spoke Pushtu like a native and with a beard and enough tan he could have passed as a Pathan – it's quite true about the blue eyes.' He noticed that Savage was still looking at the cigarette case. 'The wording on that is a Persian couplet of his, not one of his better ones. The exact nuance is lost in the translation, but the rough sense is *Where duty, or honour, may call, there will the faithful servants go*. Unfortunately the word for servants can also mean slaves, and it's dangerously close to the word for monkeys! *Banda* instead of *bander*.'

'As in *bander-log*?'

'That's it. God, here we are in the midst of all this, drinking whiskey and talking about grandfathers and Persian poetry!'

'Makes a pleasant distraction from tows.' Savage smoked in silence for a moment. 'I didn't know you had any brothers.'

'Not now. They were both killed in the last lot. One

on the Somme and the other in the Ypres Salient. And a sister. She's a doctor, oddly enough.'

'I suppose you'd make her a dreadful patient as well.'

'Unlikely. She's a paediatrician.'

Savage stubbed out his cigarette. 'It's a funny business, the way the human spirit reacts to extreme stress. The sickness figures always drop while we're at sea, and shoot up in harbour, whereas for purely practical reasons one would expect it to be the other way round.'

'I suppose in harbour they've time to feel ill.'

'And of course there's a powerful taboo on letting down your messmates, or anything that can be remotely construed as letting down your messmates. At the moment I'm only seeing injuries and most of those are clamouring to go back to duty as soon as we've patched them up. None of them can tell me why. It's not just training. I think it goes deeper than that. This is something I'm interested in. There's more to psychology than dreams and the Oedipus Complex!'

'Back on your hobby-horse, Doc,' Thurston said gently.

'In a way. You could say I'd been practising a little psychology on you just now. Drawing you out a bit. You know and I know that the men, and the officers too, have families at home, and they miss them, they feel afraid at the usual times and they feel grief when something happens to their mates. But we all expect them to carry on regardless and to put a brave face on it all. We train them to carry on with the job whatever happens. One gun number gets hit, another drags him out of the way and takes over. But things can't go on like that for ever.' Savage paused and looked at his watch. 'That's enough for tonight. I didn't come to lecture. Time you got some sleep.' He stood up to leave.

'Goodnight, Doc.' Thurston was lying back, feet against the bulkhead. Savage looked around the sea cabin. It was bare and functional, not even a family photograph, a bleak place for the Captain to spend his time when not on the bridge. Thurston's eyes were shut, his features gradually relaxing in sleep. He looked younger, even a little vulnerable. Savage smiled to himself.

'You've never learned to let go, have you?'

# — Chapter Thirteen —

## Denmark Strait, North Atlantic, 8 July 1941

Twilight, after a fine summer day, almost warm for these latitudes, the time when it never really got dark, but the light settled to a strange soft glow, reflected off the pack ice beyond the horizon. The heavy cruiser appeared out of a bank of mist ten miles away, a long grey silhouette. *Northumberland* was at the opposite end of the patrol beat, five hours' steaming away.

'To Admiralty, repeated *Northumberland* and CinC Home Fleet, *Hipper-class cruiser believed Seydlitz sighted in position 66° 32' North, 24° 05' West. Am engaging.*'

'Hoist battle ensigns.' He felt an obscure thrill. He had never thought he would issue that order on his own authority.

They fought for two hours, making use of patches of mist and dodging in and out of smoke screens, *Marathon* trying to get closer, into effective range for her smaller-calibre guns, damage her, slow her down; *Seydlitz* trying to break clear, evade the pursuit that was coming, escape from the confining strait and disappear into the vastness of the Atlantic. *Marathon* hit her aft early on, but her guns were firing, her speed unimpaired. *Northumberland* was on her way at best speed, *Renown* and *Prince of Wales* raising steam at Hvalfjord.

They came out of the screen, got off a couple of salvoes at fourteen thousand yards. Splashes and muzzle flash, binoculars to the eyes.

'Straddle!'

There was a searing wave of hot air, a savage punch in the left shoulder that flung him back against the binnacle, blood in his mouth. He seemed to see one of the four-inch lift bodily from its mountings, and the world slid away.

The gyro alarm cut through his fuddled eardrums, brought him back to dazed and blurry conciousness. He shook his head, trying to break clear of the fog. He got to his feet shakily, steadied himself against the binnacle. The alarm was still shrieking, cutting through his head. Lift the bar and break the circuit. He found it, pulled it up with a hand which did not seem to work properly. The ship was turning, in a wide flat circle. Oh yes, he thought dully, the last order he had given was a turn to starboard.

'Report ship's head.'

'Bearing one-nine-six, sir, ten of starboard wheel on, sir. Gyro compass gone dead, sir.' The quartermaster had changed. Who was this? He sounded young and very afraid.

'Midships. Steer by magnetic.'

'Midships, sir. Steer by magnetic, sir.' The man checked back the order very quickly, his voice rising up the scale.

'Who's that?'

'Campion, sir. The Chief QM's dead, I think. He's all broken into little bits.'

'All right, Campion. Just stay on the wheel until someone comes to relieve you.'

A near miss, tons of yellow water cascading over the decks. Where was *Seydlitz*? Out there to starboard, closing in for the kill. The ship reverberated as another salvo crashed out. Splashes, steer towards them.

'Port thirty.'

'Port thirty, sir.'

He looked around him as the ship heeled. All around were bloody heaps of blue serge, the Navigator, Officer of the Watch, Midshipman Anderson, the Chief Yeoman.

'Midships. Steer one-five-two.'

'Midships, sir. Steer one-five-two, sir.' Campion sounded steadier.

One of the lookouts was staring at his foot, which lay on the other side of the bridge, the boot still on, his eyes already beginning to glaze. Watch the splashes, take her back into the friendly bank of smoke.

'Are you all right, Campion?'

A frightened, brave 'Yes, sir. I think so.'

His mind was beginning to work, running over it all. The engines were untouched, pushing *Marathon* through the water at twenty-eight knots, with a couple of knots in reserve over *Seydlitz*, the turrets crashing out at regular intervals, Gunnery Control in full operation.

His shoulder was numb and his hand came away bloody, a hole high up beneath the collar bone. His speech was slurred and his face felt lopsided; there was something lodged in the lower jaw the same side, a back tooth knocked half out, blood coming out from another hole and running down his neck. Into the smoke, invisibility inside the acrid oiliness, drifting slowly eastwards. *Seydlitz's* radar was not precise enough for accurate gunnery. Time to draw breath, to find out what the damage was, to get something done about it. He felt cold and shivery and a little sick.

Then Ted Bradshaw was swaying in front of him. 'Are you all right, sir?'

A disembodied voice. 'Yes, I'm all right.'

He was sitting on the Captain's chair, with Petty Officer SBA Sellars cutting away his shirt and busy with bandages.

'You're lucky, sir,' Sellars said mournfully. ''Alf an inch from the lung. Not bleedin' that much. Must've missed the artery.' Sounds of cloth ripping against a

169

sheath knife. 'Gone right through, sir.' Sellars perked up noticeably. 'I could get three fingers in that.'

'Just get on with it.'

'Aye aye, sir. 'Old still.'

Sellars strapped his left arm to his side with practised efficiency, played around inside his mouth – 'Got any false teeth, sir!' – stuck something over the hole in his cheek. 'Anything in the face always bleeds like stink,' he said cheerfully. 'I'll just tie that up, sir.'

'No!'

'Got to do that with a broken jaw, sir.'

'No.'

Without thinking, Thurston rejected Bradshaw's suggestion that he go below, Sellars's offer of morphine. He settled himself on the chair, pulled his duffel coat more closely around him, turned to Bradshaw, told him to get back to Damage Control.

'Sir?'

'Get on with it! And send ffrench up here.'

Bradshaw disappeared, ffrench arrived a few minutes later. Thurston started giving him instructions, scribbling on the back of a signal pad because his jaw was stiffening and wouldn't work properly. The ship was coming back to life. The dead and wounded had been carried away below, a fire party was at work. *Marathon* burst out of the smoke screen and back into the fight.

The battle went on through the night hours, a weary slogging match. They hit *Seydlitz* again, she seemed to slow down, but all her turrets were firing.

Spencer brought a blanket and a mug of tea, 'fer the shock,' but his face was swelling up and he couldn't swallow. Savage came up, confirmed that his jaw was broken and advised him to go below. Thurston told him, through his teeth, to go away and see to his wounded. On, on, through the ghostly twilight, get off a couple of salvoes, keep changing course to confuse *Seydlitz's* gunnery control, keep firing.

Dawn came and went. The numbness turned to pain, spreading and intensifying, but it wasn't too bad as long as he kept still and didn't talk or take deep breaths. Strained weary faces all around; ffrench, Harker, Midshipman Hastings, signalmen and lookouts, ghostly in the blue light of the far north.

'Signal from *Northumberland*, sir. *Enemy in sight. What is your seniority?*'

He scribbled 'Oct '39' on the pad and passed it to the Yeoman. George Griffin, punctilious as always. It would only have taken a moment to have his Midshipman of the Watch look up the Navy List.

They closed on *Seydlitz*, forcing her to split her fire, hit her again, *Marathon's* 5.25s and *Northumberland's* eight-inch. Her mainmast and ensigns had gone; through binoculars Thurston could see a man nailing another to the stump. There were fires on her upper decks, two of her turrets were silent, the others firing raggedly in local control. *Northumberland* ordered *Marathon* to finish her off with torpedoes. At 0633 *Seydlitz* heeled over and sank, dozens of her men leaping from the decks into the sea which would kill them before anyone could reach them.

A long time after, he swam up into consciousness, drawn there by pain. He lay in his bunk, blankets tight around him, the deckhead moving gradually into focus. There was an unnatural quietness, the ship rolling on a beam sea, steadily, unhurried, not the steeper sharper motion of past days. He became aware of Spencer sitting on the chair, a shaft of sunlight from the scuttle falling on the pages of the comic he was reading. It must be evening or early morning. He wondered what he was doing here, instead of in his sea cabin, then slowly began to remember.

The Surgeon Commander had done his work in the stripped-down wardroom, under emergency lighting, a boy seaman holding a torch for him. Faces above him, one of the sick-berth attendants trying to quiet another man nearby, the polished dining table cold against his back, something clapped over his face and a sharp command to breathe in.

His right hand began to explore, seeking the sources of the pain. It seemed to take a long time and a surprising effort. Tight wrappings cased his chest, constricted more strongly at each breath. His left hand protruded from them, somewhere near the opposite shoulder, numb and foreign-feeling but unmistakably still there, intact. A rustle of paper as Spencer turned a page, unexpectedly loud in the silence of the cabin. His hand moved on upwards, met contrast in the unsullied flesh of neck and throat, then more bandages, passing under this chin and covering most of the left side of his face. It seemed grotesquely swollen. His tongue found the gap where the hanging tooth had been, spongy and blood-tasting. Another page turned, the rustle louder still. He let his hand fall back on to the sheet, clenched and unclenched the fingers, finding a reassurance in their smooth controlled working. He shifted his head to glance at the clock on the locker top. Spencer looked up. 'Sir?' Pain lanced through his shoulder, his mouth opened involuntarily, met resistance, another jolting pain, a strangled gasp. Spencer's bulk blotted out the light. 'You gotta keep quiet, sir. You can't talk for the moment, so don't bother tryin', but everythin's all right. The doc's got all the bits out, and we're on the way back to Scapa.' He fiddled with the pillows. 'It's about nine o'clock, still the same day. So just lie quiet and let me do the work.'

For several days he wandered through a haze of pain and fever and four-hourly morphine injections, a detached observer as his body fought back. From time to time he became aware of the outer world as it swirled into his consciousness. Savage, his shirt cuffs spotted with rusty colour. Ted Bradshaw, worn and anxious; 'Everything's under control. We're on the way to the Clyde. They've even given us a destroyer escort.'

Petty Officer Sellars. But mostly Spencer. Spencer put a pad and pencil next to his right hand, so he could write down anything he needed. Spencer would carefully prop him up and spoon milk and lime juice and sludgy brews of cocoa into the gap between his jaws. He read to him from P.G. Wodehouse and a succession of paperback thrillers to distract him from his pain, gossiped, and held his head while twice daily Sellars packed sterile tape into his shoulder wound with a long steel probe. There was a half-formed memory of being carried across the quarterdeck with rain on his face and a rush of men to put a hand to the stretcher. And a long time after, white walls and hospital smells and Kate holding his hand.

Of course, the press had gone to town over the *Seydlitz* business. The sinking of the *Bismarck* had been overshadowed by the loss of the *Hood*, but this was the finest David and Goliath confrontation since the *Jervis Bay*. By the time the newspapers had finished it was as if *Marathon* had sunk the *Tirpitz*, *Scharnhorst* and *Gneisenau*, with the *Hipper* and *Prinz Eugen* thrown in for good measure. Various newspapers had published photographs of *Marathon* with funnels like colanders and grinning sailors peering through splinter holes, and 'what it was really like' stories which ranged from the merely inaccurate to the wildly exaggerated. According to the *Daily Mirror, Northumberland* had only reached the scene in time to see *Seydlitz* sinking. Of course, the incident had everything for the imaginative reporter. It mattered not that a modern light cruiser was considerably more of a match for *Seydlitz* than a converted liner had been for the *Admiral Scheer*, that it had simply not occurred to her captain to do anything else and he hadn't been in that much pain anyway, and that in any case Ted Bradshaw and James ffrench had been doing most of the work by the latter stages – the *Daily Mail* forbore to mention either of them by name – that

*Marathon* had suffered seventy-two dead and ninety-four wounded.

# — Chapter Fourteen —

Dawn Action Stations. Wind south-westerly, Force Four. Sea moderate. Visibility moderate to poor. The Beaufighters prowled overhead; every two hours a new flight took over, flashed a recognition signal and a quick quip.

'Lucky buggers, goin' to be home for breakfast.'

'Port ten.'

'Port ten, sir.'

Still no sights. How long was it since they last saw the sun? The third dawn on tow. The rest of the squadron would be back in Alex tonight, his fellow captains dining at the Cecil, by courtesy of the Governor of Malta, Field Marshal Sir John Standish Surtees Prendergast Vereker, sixth Viscount Gort.

'Midships.'

'Midships, sir.'

'Did you sleep well, sir?' ffrench had asked with a grin.

The Honourable Henry's cold had gone down to his chest, he coughed continually and didn't look at all well.

'You sound like a case of galloping consumption,' declared ffrench.

'I hope you'll subscribe generously to my funeral expenses.'

'Don't remind me of funerals,' said Thurston.

'And I'll make sure Virginia doesn't get your *Esquire* nudes.'

'Thank you, Number One. That won't be necessary. I've just decided to survive after all.'

They tried five knots, there was more vibration, the yawing increased, but the tow seemed to take it.

Midshipman Pearson was starting to be bored. He had heard most of Connor's stories for the second time and some for the fourth. He rather hoped the sick-bay staff would move him alongside someone with different conversation. His leg didn't bother him that much, so long as he didn't try to move it, except when the dressings were changed. Midshipman Nairne had been in to see Hastings and spoken to him in passing. Graham had been in, so had Cowper-Coles, but neither could stay for more than a few minutes; they had watches to keep of course.

'Rough about Mike Norris, isn't it? And he thought he was safer here than in the banana boats.'

'Nasty way to go, shrapnel in the guts.'

'Better than getting it in the privates.'

'Not much difference, when you're dead.'

'I'd rather go intact, all the same.'

'You never know what you might find up there. If heaven's all it's cracked up to be.'

'How can you be sure that's where you're going?'

'Remember what the padre tells us, CC. God loves a sinner.'

'And the Lord chasteneth those whom He loveth, Jack, so watch out!'

They all laughed. Pearson listened to the banter and wished that he could be out of there. He was surprised to find himself missing the gunroom world.

'Is there anything you'd like us to get you?'

'Well,' the germ of an idea was forming, 'there's a sketch pad in my sea chest, near the top. Could you get me that?'

'Rembrandt strikes again! No problem, but it might

take a bit of time. I'll send it down to you as soon as I can.'

'Thanks . . . CC.'

The padre died shortly before three o'clock. He opened his eyes briefly, murmured something in Latin and drifted away before Savage or Bradley could get to him.

'Sir, Padre Whitehead died at 1455,' again the old sense of being dead inside. With hands charred to the bone it could only have been expected, and that gentle scholar was not the kind of man who would put up a fight for his own life. He had his faith, and death for him was not an end but a beginning.

*Greater love hath no man* . . . The padre had come from his Oxford college to minister to his fellow men, who largely failed to appreciate his quietness and asceticism, his academic air, but at the last he had in totally unexpected fashion dragged another man out of a fiery hell at the ultimate cost of his own life.

> *'Behold, I shew you a mystery. We shall not sleep, but we shall all be changed in a moment, in the twinkling of an eye, at the last trump; for the trumpet shall sound and the dead shall be raised incorruptible, and we shall be changed.'*

Thurston wondered whether this was for the padre, or was it more for his own comfort? He was getting sick of funerals, even of the sonorous beauty of Cranmer's prayer book.

The hammock-shrouded corpse slid into the sea. He shut the book with a snap. He used to invite the Padre up to his cabin on occasions to talk books over a glass of sherry. And he remembered Gibbons; a fractured skull, and the brain laid bare, the possibility of permanent brain damage if he lived, and Savage could not

177

be hopeful. Two more days, if they could keep to five knots.

*Oh God, Thurston, stop getting so bloody morbid.*

He turned away and went back up to the bridge, took over the con, since Cowper-Coles was on watch and lacked the fine judgement which only came with experience. He sent the Navigator to the sick bay; Savage promptly diagnosed bronchitis and packed him off to his cabin with his Marine servant to look after him. Bradshaw came up from below. Spencer produced a plate of nameless stew and found him some dry socks. He was very tired again, as if the night's sleep had never been.

'Coffee, sir?'

'Black.'

'Comin' up, sir.'


The tow parted just after midnight. Maybe Harker's ribs were paining him, perhaps he fell asleep for a moment. There was a crack like a thunderclap, the broken end lashed viciously across the fo'c'sle, hit a man from A turret who had been on his way to the heads, smashed both his legs to bloody pulp. His screams echoed around the bridge.

'Who the hell is that?'

'What's the silly bugger doing there?'

'Pipe for a stretcher party, and warn the Surgeon Commander.' It took an effort to stop himself running to the man's side, but that wasn't his job.

The man was roughly splinted, stupefied with morphine and carried to the sick bay, where Savage amputated both his legs above the knee.

It took a long time to pass another tow. *Leonidas* floated the grass line across on a cask. The hawser had to be hauled in by hand, there was no steam on the capstan.

'McCormick, ask the Bandmaster to bring his men

up and make some noise. Mr Harker, you have the ship. Mr Zurakowski, come with me.'

The First Lieutenant was organising a much-expanded cable party on the fo'c'sle. 'We'll pull facing aft. Nobody is to walk backwards. Someone heavy at the end. Where's Benson?'

'Here, sir.'

Unseen grins. Marine Benson stood six foot three and boxed at sixteen and a half stone.

ffrench marshalled the men into a single line with the rope at their feet. 'Now we want the tall ones at the end and the short arses in the bows, no humps in the middle, and there's a quick way of doing that . . . Tallest on the right, shortest on the left, in single line, *size!*'

The men arranged themselves, a dozen bandsmen and their instruments squashed into a vacant space by the rails.

'Pick up the rope! Bandmaster, some hauling music. Ready, *heave!*'

The band striking up 'In a Persian Market', lengths of grass line passing soddenly through his hands, a change to the heavier rope.

'Where's the dancing girls?'

'Keep it moving. Come on, Benson! The eyes of the Corps are upon you!'

A change of music, the humorists taking up 'The Volga Boatmen'. The three-inch wire, its weight bearing down on his shoulder, blunt points of wire sticking through the greasy surface into his palms.

> *Yo-heave-ho, yo-heave-ho,*
> *Pull together, yo-heave-ho . . .*

God, he was proud of them! Four days and four nights of being almost constantly on the go, dealing with all the damage and fires on top of the usual watches and periods at Action Stations, short-handed because of casualties. And unremitting tension and cold food and lack of sleep. And being continuously wet and all too frequently seasick. Yet hardly a man had gone sick without an injury, and those who had were mostly too sick to stand.

'Heave!' ffrench had his shoulder to the hawser, Midshipman Graham there behind him. The Bandmaster was conducting for all he was worth, rising up on his toes. They began to move forward.

'Heave! It's the Fleet Sports and we're pulling against the flagship!'

A ragged cheer went up. They stumbled a few more paces, Benson's broad back and bull neck filling the space ahead, hands slipping on the wire. Inertia, the weight pulling him back, off balance.

'Two-six, Heave!'

'Heave!'

> Hauling, Hauling, Hauling
> Always bloody well hauling!

Another pace. 'Come on, Benson,' he hissed.

'One more effort! *Heave*!'

A last effort, the towing eye was hammered home over its anchorage. The men staggered out to the sides, white teeth grinning in dirty faces, covered in water and grease. Benson turned and slapped him hard on the back. 'Thanks, mate . . . Sorry, sir. Didn't recognise you in the dark,' he said woodenly, snapped to attention.

'That's all right, Benson.'

The band triumphantly struck up the Radetsky March. Toes tapped, faces were wreathed in smiles. God, he was proud!

'Tow secure,' reported ffrench.

Once more the nerve-jangling wait as *Leonidas* began to move forward, taking up the slack, the appalling hiatus between the wire coming taut and the cruiser beginning to move.

'From *Leonidas*, sir. *Cinderella shall go to the ball.*'

Well, if the brash young Commander Nicholls could still do it . . .

'Make, *You may go dancing, but I'll call the tune.*'

'Sir?'

'Mozart. *Marriage of Figaro.*'

*Leonidas's* lamp began to flash once more.

'Tell him to shut up!' Nicholls's bounce became a little wearing at this hour.

'Take the con, Mr Harker.'

Savage came up, blood-smeared. 'He'll live, if the shock doesn't get him.' He sounded beaten, unutterably weary. There was brandy on his breath.

Ordinary Seaman Garrard, a plumpish, rather bumbling former post-office clerk, older than most and married with several children. It was pointless to say that he should not have been there.

'Course one-oh-nine, sir. Able Seaman Dawson on the wheel.'

Midshipman Zurakowski made a mistake in the log. The bridge bucket overflowed.

# — Chapter Fifteen —

'Sandwiches, sir.'

'Corn dog *again*?'

'Sorry, sir,' Spencer said dolefully. 'You've 'ad the last of the cheese.'

ffrench studied his cocoa. 'When one sees the state of the mugs, one wonders what this stuff does to the stomach,' he mused.

'Clogs you up, sir,' said Spencer.

'I shall remember that, Spencer. Now I need cheering up. Does anyone know any jokes?'

'Why can't a blind sailor tickle nine Wrens?' asked Midshipman Nairne.

Silence.

'Because he can only gesticulate!'

'That, Mr Nairne, is one of the worst jokes I've ever heard.'

'It's on a level with the one about the dog with no nose,' said ffrench.

Nairne explained the joke to the bridge messenger and ffrench told a long story which seemed to involve him in a rickshaw journey through Kowloon without his trousers.

'Port ten.'

'Port ten, sir.'

Watch the light, swinging slowly back to starboard. Don't let her drift too far, Number One. He glanced at ffrench, standing next to the binnacle, chin sunk into his collar, Nairne alongside him.

'Midships.'

'Midships, sir.'

Thurston thought about Kate for a moment. Safely home and asleep in bed at this hour, in ignorance of all this. Or perhaps not. On survivors' leave after *Connaught* she had told him that she already knew before he rang her; she had woken up suddenly, piercingly aware that something had happened to him. He was sceptical, but comparing notes it seemed that it had happened at the same time as the torpedo hit, as he was being sucked down with the ship.

'Course one-oh-six, sir. Able Seaman Gaunt on the wheel.'

ffrench was talking to Nairne of bathrooms. '. . . Pink-veined marble with hot and cold plunges, and a steam room of course.'

'You mean a Turkish bath, sir?'

'Exactly that. With Circassian dancing girls for the massage. Not for you, Mr Nairne, you'll have to make do with the usual retired all-in wrestlers.' He sighed. 'Ah, what wouldn't I give to be in a Turkish bath now.'

'The cold plunge can easily be arranged, Number One, and wasn't it Agamemnon who was murdered in his bath?'

'I believe so, sir. Or perhaps the steam baths they have in Finland?' he continued after a pause.

'The sort where they hit you with birch twigs?'

'*Very* stimulating, Mr Nairne. Good for the circulation of old men like me, but those of your tender years can get the same effect from an hour's brisk PT and a cold tub.'

Thurston pulled himself up on to his bridge chair, tipped his cap over his eyes. He would not sleep; it was a matter of resting the eyes and taking the weight off the feet. He wondered how Nicholls was doing.

0815 hours. Gunroom breakfast.

'God, I'm bored,' said Jenner.

'Bored?' said Cowper-Coles. 'Count yourself lucky

183

to have the time to be bored. Why don't you get down to some admin?'

'I could, but since most of the stuff has got to go through the Captain . . . I don't think it's the right time to tell HM that the Signals Officer's confidential report is due.'

'You'd probably come out without a head! Tell you what, why don't you find some mail to censor?'

'Do you honestly think the men are writing letters now?'

'You never know. And it would give you something else to get bored with.'

'Well, CC,' Jenner helped himself to toast. 'How goes the war?'

'Much as before. I must say I'm damn glad they've made Mr Knott acting Gunnery Officer instead of me. Being Officer of the Watch is quite as much responsibility as I need at the moment.'

'Were you in contention?'

'Well, with Hastings out of it, it was Mr Knott or me, so they've hauled him out of the TS and I'm staying in my turret.'

'I suppose the Bandmaster's running the TS?'

'He is, but I'm not sure that gunnery is his strong point.'

'I sometimes wonder whether music is, when you hear the band going through 'On the Quarterdeck' right over my head thirty-six times in one morning!'

'Ah, JJ,' Cowper-Coles cut into his lukewarm scrambled egg, 'you fail to appreciate the Royal Navy's true glory. What better than to hear the dulcet strains of 'On the Quarterdeck' thirty-six times in one morning, inspiring you to greater efforts as you bash away at your glorious typewriter?'

'I'm going to throw my glorious typewriter at you in a minute. Why didn't I join the bloody army?'

'Because you thought navy blue would go with your

eyes.' Cowper-Coles disposed of the last of his egg and reached for his toast rack. 'Pass that jam, Zura.'

'And there's another thing. We've got mildew in the cabin. I opened my wardrobe to get something out and my best shoes are covered in the stuff.'

'It's the same all over the ship. The Honourable Henry's got mildew on the lungs. Just be thankful we're not ankle-deep in the stuff.'

'Don't start on about when you were in corvettes, for God's sake,' said Angus.

'What is mildew?' enquired Zurakowski.

'All this is more than enough for me.' Jenner took another piece of toast.

'What did you do in the Great Malta Convoy, Daddy? Oh my son, I censored letters while others fought the war around me. Tell me, JJ, what sort of insurance premiums would you give us now?'

'I don't think my old insurance company would insure any of us. When I was on leave last, before I came out here, I had a drink with a chap I started with. He was safe all right – flat feet! Apparently some chap from submarines asked him for a quotation for a thousand pounds worth of cover. It worked out at five hundred a year. The chap said thank you very much, but that was more than his pay for the year.'

'Anything else to eat?' called Angus.

'Guess!'

Pearson had asked the Surgeon Commander, when he came on his rounds, whether he could get up.

'You're obviously feeling better, aren't you?' Savage smiled. 'But you won't be putting any weight on that leg for a day or two yet, and this isn't the best time to try to get the hang of crutches.'

He had a pencil, and Cowper-Coles had sent his sketch pad down. He scribbled idly, trying to get back into the way of drawing. It was three, no, four months since he had left art school, and Enfield, and he had done very little since then, even aboard the *Mauretania* coming out. He was propped up on one elbow, pad held in the same hand. There was Petty Officer Sellars crouched beside a mattress on the other side of the compartment, dealing with a dressing, half in shadow, materials laid out beside him. Pearson sketched the scene in outline, gradually filling in the detail, wishing he had something better than a propelling pencil, praying that Sellars would not move before he was finished. It was coming, he added another line. He paused; this was the point where he had to be careful not to put in too much. The hesitation made him aware of an audience. He turned to the left, took in with a growing blush the large square hand which held a brass hat.

'Sorry, sir.' He was supposed to lie to attention, wasn't he?

'That's all right. I shouldn't be looking over your shoulder.' The Captain dropped into a crouch. 'Keep going.'

'I'm just about finished now, sir.' He shaded in a patch of shadow, then put the pencil down as Sellars, oblivious, stood up.

'You were at art school, weren't you, Mr Pearson?'

'Yes, sir. Well, it wasn't the Slade or anything like that.' He was embarrassed again, thinking of the drawings in the Captain's cabin.

'May I have a look at that?' The Captain took the pad from him, twisted round for a better light. He seemed genuinely interested, asked a few questions, listened as Pearson talked about art school, haltingly at first but gradually growing in confidence. 'Thank-you,' he said at length, handed the sketch back. His eyes met Pearson's, an intense gaze that made Pearson realise how tired he must be. Strain had carved deep lines on either side of his broken nose and his face had taken on a hollowed-out look. But he had moved on and was exchanging a word with a stoker with a broken leg.

1400 hours.

'The flyboys' reliefs are a bit late.'

'Probably got lost.'

Stamp the feet, work the shoulder, scan the murky horizon with binoculars, drink another mug of black coffee. Savage had just been up. A case of suspected appendicitis had turned out to be suffering from constipation and severe indigestion – 'corned beef poisoning,' said ffrench – and the sick-bay staff were greatly exercised by the discovery of a dead rat in the dispensary. The Paymaster Commander was stirring his stumps at last and the wardroom galley was producing hot meals in shifts for all the men, though most of the food had gone cold by the time it reached the messdecks. He would have to do something about the Paymaster Commander once they got in, he hadn't been much use to start with and had now proved himself a liability in an emergency. He smiled to himself; it was the first time in days that he had thought beyond the immediate future.

'Flight Commander signalling, sir,' announced the Yeoman. '*Sorry to leave you, but tanks running low*.'

'Acknowledge.'

'Bloody Brylcreem boys, couldn't cross a road,' muttered someone.

It wasn't all that surprising. Finding two ships without ASV radar in this murk by dead reckoning from a dead reckoning position was like looking for a needle in a very large haystack.

The minutes ticked by.

'See anything?' ffrench kept saying.

Thurston felt restless and edgy. Too much black coffee and too little exercise.

The signalmen were whispering to each other.

'Pipe down!' shouted the Yeoman.

'Lookouts! Watch your sectors!' ffrench said sharply.

Still no sign of them. 'Time, Mr Nairne?'

'1412, sir.'

Only twelve minutes since the scheduled change. But what was keeping them? The new flight should have been in radio contact with the old lot, picked them up on radar once they were within range.

'See anything?'

'Nossir.'

He was pacing again, his restless legs propelling him through the four paces the confines of the bridge permitted, hands thrust deep into pockets, jaw set.

'Anything you want, sir?'

'Not now, Spencer!' Spencer turned and scuttled away down the ladder. 'Time, Mr Nairne?'

Nairne extracted his wrist from beneath his duffel coat and a bright red sweater. '1418, sir.'

Thurston consulted the chart, trying to put thoughts of aircraft out of his head for a moment. Another thirty hours' steaming. Back to the binnacle, another sweep with binoculars.

'Yeoman, ask *Leonidas* if they're picking anything up on radar.'

*Leonidas*'s radar was a later mark. Lamps flashed.

'Nothing, sir.'

It was just as bad for Nicholls and his men. They had the same vigilance all through, the constant varying of engine revolutions to keep the wire taut, the same vulnerability.

'See anything?'

He wished ffrench would stop saying it.

'Starboard ten.'

'Starboard ten, sir.'

1423.

'Radar . . . Bridge.'

'Bridge.'

'Aircraft bearing green one-two-five. Ten miles.'

Funny direction for them to be coming from.

'Who's on the radar, Number One?'

'Holmes, sir.'

Holmes was a good man, knew what he was doing.

'Midships.'

'Midships, sir.'

'What does it look like, Holmes?'

'Hard to say, sir. About five or six. They're not coming for us. They seem to be circling.'

'Set working properly?'

'Yes sir.'

'Keep me informed.'

Lift the binoculars, screw the eyes up, look out into the murk. Muttering behind him, a too-loud laugh.

'Pipe down, Mr Nairne!'

'Radar . . . Bridge.'

'Bridge.'

'Coming closer, sir. Still circling, but shifting over this way.'

'Range?'

'Seven miles, sir. Closing.'

'Number One, sound Action Stations.' Better play safe.

ffrench pressed the switches. The alarms shrieked, bugles began sounding, omitting the final 'G' which meant a routine call. Feet clattered on the ladders. Tin hats went on.

'Course one-one-two, sir. Chief QM on the wheel.'

Reports came through.

'Closed up, sir,' reported ffrench. He brought out a stopwatch from his pocket. 'Bit slow.'

'Thank you, Number One.'

It was difficult to keep still, to play the part of the nerveless commander.

'Radar . . . Bridge. Aircraft closing.'

Couldn't see them yet, not with the cloud base almost at sea level.

'We're not going to make it! They'll kill us all!'

Thurston whipped round. One of the lookouts, an ordinary seaman named . . . Roberts? Richards, that was it. 'Watch your sector, Richards.'

'We haven't a hope! They'll kill us all!'

'Shut up, Taff,' said his neighbour.

'Radar . . . Bridge. Aircraft bearing green two-five. Three miles.'

Richards was shouting, almost incoherently now. 'They're going to kill us all!! '

'Get him off my bridge!'

Nobody moved. All seemed to be transfixed. Richards's voice rose higher. A Welsh voice, on a raft, calling for his mother. Thurston stepped forward. Richards was screaming now, his white eyes huge in his face. The raft, and Morgan. His fist slammed into Richards's jaw, with all his weight behind it, the same blow that had felled Sub-Lieutenant Dauncey all those years before. But this wasn't Dauncey, but a terrified boy from some Welsh valley. The moment of red rage passed, he looked down at his hand, and at Richards lying crumpled on the steel plates, sobbing, holding his chin.

'Sir!' He jerked back one more. It was the Yeoman. 'Aircraft in sight, sir. Signalling. It's BK, sir! They're ours!'

'Acknowledge. Number One, tell the Gunnery Officer he is on no account to open fire.'

'Flight Commander signalling, sir. *Sorry we're late. Difficult to find you in this murk.*'

Watch the yaw! 'Port ten.'

'Port ten, sir.'

'Secure from Action Stations, Number One.'

'Aye aye, sir.' Relief had flooded into ffrench's face. 'Midships.'

'Midships, sir.'

'I can manage without another half-hour like that,' said ffrench.

One of the signalmen was bent over Richards, murmuring to him. 'Steady, Taff. It's all right now,' patting his shoulder. Richards sobbed on.

'Bridge messenger.'

'Sir?'

'Get Ordinary Seaman Richards to the sick bay.'

The signalman and Boy Secombe got Richards to his feet, guided him to the ladder.

'Come on, Taff, easy now.'

Thurston turned, pushed to the bucket and threw up.

# — Chapter Sixteen —

1700 hours.

'You know what I could just do with,' said Connor. 'A bacon buttie.'

'Here we go again.'

'Lovely thick bacon done so's the rind is nice and crisp but it's still soft in the middle. Done on toast of course, with lots of butter and bacon grease comin' through, so it's soft in the middle but still crisp outside. Bit of mustard spread on the bacon, and pepper too. And about a pint of really hot strong tea with lashings of sugar, not the gnat's piss we've been getting.'

'Knock it off, Stripey. Don't start us all off.'

''Course you know what we'll get. Bully beef! And the same old horse-piss soup.'

'If I have to eat any more bully, I shall scream.'

'Will someone please stop talking about food,' pleaded another man.

'Let's talk about something else then,' said Connor. He turned to Pearson. 'You got a girl?'

Pearson felt himself turning red. What could he say? 'Not a steady girl.'

'That's what you need, kid. A nice bit of skirt. Despite what Mummy says, it's not just for pissing through. 'Course you ain't a real sailor till you've had a nap hand.'

Pearson felt worried.

'Know what that is? The pox and the clap, kid. Twice!'

Pearson went redder still. This was worse than

school, the comparison of parts which went on in the changing room after games. He thought of Enfield. It would have been nice to go home a wounded hero, but he had been assured that all would be taken care of in Alexandria. He wondered what his mother would say when she got the telegram. Had one already been sent? Probably not. He'd better write and say he was all right, but a letter would take at least six weeks.

'There was this bint in Shanghai . . .'

'Sorry, Stripey, I'm going to sleep.'

Pearson thought again of Enfield. Perhaps he could send a telegram himself? His parents had been proud of him when he was on leave after *King Alfred*. His father had taken him to the golf club for a drink a couple of times; his mother had invited various of her friends and their daughters to tea. They had all admired his uniform, and his proud new midshipman's patches, but it was shaming to have to admit that he had yet to join a ship and had not actually spent a day at sea. Girls? There had been a couple at art school with whom he had been quite friendly, and one had even asked for an address to write to; he had written importantly *Midshipman D. A. Pearson RNVR, HMS Marathon, c/o GPO London*. But so far there had been no letters. He had been back to his old school, had a cup of tea with the headmaster, said that, yes, he was very happy in the Navy, and was looking forward to getting to grips with the Germans. And he had gone back to art school, walking along the corridors in uniform, finding it strange that only weeks before he had been a student here himself, wondering what the GIs at *King Alfred* would make of the ones who remained.

Someone else had seen him drawing during the morning and asked rather shyly if he would draw him 'for my girl'. He had done him head and shoulders, grinning, cap on the back of his head. 'Are you a real painter?' 'No, just a student.' But the idea had caught on, he had done half a dozen since, and promised others when he could get hold of more paper.

Footsteps. Someone else with yet another cup of tea? But no, it was Cowper-Coles, and with him Nairne.

'Hello, Pearson, how's things?'

'Oh, not too bad.'

'Smile and be happy, behold, things could get worse.'

'How?' said Cowper-Coles. 'And before you say anything, it was already raining when I came off watch!'

They all laughed.

'Situation normal,' said Cowper-Coles.

'You'll never guess what happened on the bridge just now. You remember that call to Action Stations we had about 1430?'

Pearson remembered. There had been sudden movement in the sick bay, attempts by the more mobile to gather up their possessions, to find lifebelts and surreptitiously move nearer to the door and the ladders, an awful tension as the minutes ticked by with no sounds of firing, no news. Could he climb all the ladders with his leg? He would need help, but would he get it? No talking, a sudden silence, each man locked in his own fear. And then the bugles had sounded again, the First Lieutenant broadcast that the unidentified aircraft were British. For a moment the silence continued, then they all started to laugh, a sudden release of pent-up tension.

Nairne continued. 'One of the look-outs had hysterics, started screaming and all sorts. Some Taff.'

'What happened then?' said Cowper-Coles.

'You may well ask. The Old Man hit him. Finest right uppercut I've seen since Joe Louis.'

'What happened to him?'

'Richards, you mean? Oh, he's in here somewhere. They've probably got him in a strait-jacket, stupid little squirt. See you, Pearson, I'm going to have a word with Hastings.'

'Personally,' Cowper-Coles said drily, 'I've had enough excitement for one day. You've been doing your artistic bit again, I see.'

'Yes, something to do. Er, CC, do you think you could get my drawing box – it's got all my pencils and stuff – and some more paper. It's in my sea chest.'

'Going to get yourself into the Royal Academy?'

Pearson grinned. 'I'm not all that good really.'

'Oh I don't know. I can't draw to save my life. See you again, Rembrandt.'

Thurston sat on the bunk in his sea cabin, back against the bulkhead, facing the Surgeon Commander, as he had done nearly forty-eight hours before. He was blind weary, more so than at any time since the initial attack, perhaps more tired than at any time in his life. It was difficult to concentrate on Savage.

'Richards will be all right. I've got him under sedation and I'll talk to him in the morning. You gave him quite a wallop but you don't seem to have done him any permanent damage. What happened exactly?'

Thurston told him, baldly, sticking to the facts. He despised himself for his action. It was an absolute rule, both written and unwritten, that an officer should never in any circumstances strike a rating. It was an abuse of authority and destroyed his credibility in the eyes of his men. He wanted more than anything to lie down and forget the whole stupid business.

'As I thought. He was pretty upset.'

'I don't make a habit of hitting ratings.'

'Of course not. And I don't suppose you're going to put yourself under arrest and have Jenner prepare the papers for a court martial. In the circumstances you were probably quite justified. Quite justified,' he repeated. 'A man has hysterics at his post, panics at Action Stations. Panic is infectious and all that. So you hit him. But think about it for a moment. Who's Richards? He comes from Port Talbot or somewhere like that, and probably never went more than a few miles from there before he was called up. I expect he chose the Navy because he fancied being Jack Me Hearty with all the old ladies touching his collar for luck. He comes out here, into all this, and suddenly it's too much for him. In normal circumstances he might never have left Port Talbot and certainly never have had to face anything like this, and plodded through life quite happily without ever approaching his limits. There are a lot of men like him aboard, uneducated, inarticulate, and quite possibly not very bright, missing mum and dad, wife or girlfriend. But you expect, we all expect them to carry on and keep smiling. Most of them do, all too often at a price. But the odd one can't, for whatever reason, and we shouldn't condemn him for it.'

'Who am I to talk about guts?' Thurston said finally.

'Now don't start on that. You're human as well and you also have limits. But you've got it into your head that you have to be perfect. You mustn't show your feelings, you mustn't even have any feelings because they get in the way of efficiency and decision-making.'

*Here we go again.* He felt too weary to listen to one of Savage's lectures. The doctor looked tired too; he must have lost a lot of weight in the past week.

'Don't switch off, sir. What I'm trying to tell you is that you mustn't condemn yourself for having your own limit, and because you've reached it. You're an intelligent, feeling sort of chap and all this hurts you. But, of course, you're a ship's captain and it's seen as unacceptable to show your quite normal and natural feelings of fear and doubt and sorrow and everything else. Add to that the general pressures of the job, the lack of sleep and the rest, and it's hardly surprising that your particular safety valve has lifted a bit. Once we're back in Alex I'll guarantee that I'll be seeing chaps by the dozen, officers as well as men, with stomach trouble, headaches, and difficulty in sleeping, just for starters, all because they've been driven too far. Richards will be all right, he's got rid of it all. But you just bottle everything up, and it festers. You're in a much worse state than he was. I'm sorry, sir, but when this is over I'm going to put my foot down.'

Thurston didn't answer.

'For God's sake, man, you're not a coward. Dammit, you're a VC!'

'Oh leave that out, Doc.'

'Come on, sir. Having four rings and a brass hat doesn't stop you from being human. You're in this mess precisely because you've done your job too well, and you insist, as you were trained to, on treating your natural feelings as signs of weakness. I know it flies in the face of all your training, but you've got to loosen up a bit, let things out more.'

He glanced at his watch. 'Is that all, Doc?' Time he got back to the bridge.

'I hope some of that has sunk in. I'd better take a look at that hand before you go. What devotees of Hollywood films fail to realise is that when punching an opponent on the jaw with the unprotected hand one is quite likely to suffer the greater damage.'

Thurston had been flexing the fingers of his right hand while Savage was speaking. The knuckles were stiff and blackened. Savage manipulated the fingers one by one; his touch was cool.

'That hurt, didn't it? Still, I don't think there's anything to worry about. You'd have hit the deckhead if there had been. The stiffness is just bruising. It'll wear off in a couple of days.'

'Captain, sir,' came Taylor's voice.

'Captain.'

'Dusk Action Stations in five minutes, sir.'

'I'm coming up.'

Savage got up. 'Think about what I've said, sir, when you've a moment, and come and talk to me some time.'

197

He opened the door, turned back to Savage. 'Thanks, Doc.'

'Pity we never got to Malta,' said Connor. 'I could've shown you The Gut. Never 'eard of The Gut, kid? You've missed a treat. Bars, girls, all a man could want ashore. 'Course, it's not the same since this lot started, beer's like bloody dishwater now. But the girls . . . You've got to catch them young. Malt women go like sacks once they start 'avin' babies, an' always dress in black sacks 'cos they're always in mourning for some-one. But the young ones, ah, lovely. I've 'ad some of my best nights with Malt bints.' He grinned lewdly, rolled himself another cigarette. 'I could've introduced you to a couple I know. 'Course, you bein' an officer you'd 'ave your pick. There's plenty that only get their knickers down for a bit of gold lace. Best bar to start in is the Blue Grotto, that's about 'alfway up. The top end of The Gut's real respectable, all fents shops. You start near the top and work down. The filthiest bars are right down the harbour end, strippers, dancin', the works. If you want anything real . . . exotic, that's where you go. I'm a straight up-and-down man meself, but some men like other things. If it's boys you're after . . .'

Connor grinned. Pearson flinched. He wished he could get up, get back to the gunroom, where, if the subject was the same, the content was at least a little more refined.

'Wonder if they've solved the Great Rat Mystery yet?'

'Know what it died of? Corned beef!'

'Quickest way out of the Andrew, bein' allergic to corned dog. Quicker even than TB. You'd be back in civvy street before your feet touched the ground.'

'Why don't you try it, Stripey, then the rest of us might get some peace.'

Someone tried to change the subject. 'Wouldn't it be great if they sent us home for the repairs.'

'They never will,' Connor said scornfully. 'You'll 'ave to wait a bit longer to get inside your Mabel's knickers.'

'She's called Mary,' the younger man said sullenly. 'And it's not like that.'

''Ark at 'im. Pure young love. Nothin' so sordid as givin' 'er a quick poke. I s'pose you even write 'er poems. But if you're not pokin' 'er, I bet there's some Yank who is.'

'Stow it, Stripey!'

'Anyway,' Connor went on, 'we'll be goin' to America so you'll get your chance with the Yankee bints.'

'How do you know?'

Connor tapped his nose. 'Usual thing these days. Smashin' place New York. I 'ad two weeks there in the old *Kent*. 'Course it was Prohibition time, but real easy to get a drink, if you knew where to look. Bloody strong stuff, meths 'ad nothing on it. And the bints . . . we used to save our tots, and take it ashore. They couldn't get enough.'

'As long as they don't send us to fuckin' Massawa.'

'They won't. The dry dock's not big enough. Last time we 'ad to go in stern first, scrape that end, then go out, turn around an' do the bows. Felt like you was walkin' uphill. I could take a refit in Durban though. We 'ad a week there comin' out 'ere. Bloody good it was. The South Africans couldn't do enough for us. Me an' Wiggy Bennett got taken back to this 'ouse, real classy place . . .'

# — Chapter Seventeen —

0200 hours. Wind south-westerly. Force Three. Sea moderate. Lieutenant Harker had the watch. In the dim light coming from the binnacle he looked about forty instead of twenty-four. Midshipman Angus was no better, pallid, strained and utterly weary.

*The poor condemned English,*
*Like sacrifices before their watchful fires,*
*Sit patiently and inly ruminate the morning's danger.*
*Their gesture sad, investing lank lean cheek and*
*war-torn coat,*
*Presenting them unto the gazing moon,*
*So many horrid ghosts.*

The blue light in *Leonidas*'s stern seemed to be dancing before Thurston's eyes; there seemed to be more than one, swinging about, popping up at odd angles, disappearing, flickering, emerging elsewhere a moment later. He had had a couple of hours below, but it had gone beyond the stage when that made much difference. In any case he woke up every time the helm went over.

'Course one-oh-nine, sir. Able Seaman Dawson on the wheel.'

The sixth night since the torpedo hit. A curious equilibrium and sense of permanence had developed. The damaged bulkhead was bulging and strained, leaking water, but it was holding and the pumps were dealing with the flooding from it. The list was stabilised, the decks tilted over at fourteen degrees; legs now compensated for it automatically. They had got used to the grinding routine of four hours on and four hours off, the indifferent meals which turned up at strange times because the wardroom galley, designed to feed thirty or so, now had to cope with four hundred and more. There was the floodwater, swirling about between decks, the smell from the burnt-out area amidships. Nobody went through it willingly, preferring the wind and spray and the slippery upper deck. Fresh water was strictly rationed. Men preferred drinking to washing and developed boils and rashes and irritating salt sores. The food continued monotonous; men relived the great gastronomic experiences of their lives, or conjured up visions of pinkly roasted joints of pork, of crusty bread and strong cheese, of fruit cake, steak and kidney pie and jam roly-poly, and brought howls of protest from their fellows. Thurston found himself obsessed by oranges. He had had the loan of a horse from the army when the ship was at Haifa, and the groves on the hillsides had been heavy with fruit, ripening from green to golden in the hot sun of Palestine.

There had been a sight at last, three hours ago when the sky had unexpectedly cleared, placing them ninety-seven miles off Alexandria. Call it twenty hours. But there was no elation in being so close to home, no real recognition that all this could soon be at an end. It had taken him at least twice as long as usual to work out the three separate star sights, and he had made a first-term cadet's mistake with one of them and had to start again. But there it was, a neat cocked hat pencilled on the chart, ninety-seven miles off Alexandria, a latitude and longitude in the log.

'Starboard ten.'

'Starboard ten, sir.'

Harker had let her go too far that time. She took a long time to come back. Mustn't relax. Watch the light, watch the light.

Twenty more hours, if the bulkhead held, if the

weather did not worsen, if nothing else went wrong. *Leonidas*'s fuel was running low, her engines had been running at full stretch all through, but there should be enough to get home. He didn't know Commander Nicholls, who had only been in command of *Leonidas* about four weeks. They had spoken a few times through a loudhailer, but that was all.

'Midships.'

'Midships, sir.'

The lights still flickered. He ought to go below, sleep again, but he could not tear himself away. He told himself that Harker needed watching at the moment, his ribs gave him more trouble than he admitted. So did Cowper-Coles – Good God, he had only signed his watchkeeping certificate the day this happened. Ted Bradshaw was fully occupied with Damage Control, which was the sort of thing he did best, the feeding and water-rationing, and the hundred-and-one odd things which had to be dealt with. That left Taylor, and ffrench, who was proving a tower of strength, there was no other way to describe him.

0225 hours. Stamp the feet, fresh feeling coming to the raw surfaces. They were going to be a mess when he took his boots off. Poor old *Marathon*. The second time she had limped damaged out of battle in little more than a year. He had signed for her from her builders on the Tyne, taken her through the bleak months of the Northern Patrol, the action with the *Seydlitz*, Force K, everything. She was not his first command; that was *Sirdar*, the oldest and slowest destroyer on the China Station, nor his first post captain's command, that was *Connaught*, but she was special for reasons which he did not quite understand. *Thurston, you're a sentimental fool.*

'Port ten.'

'Port ten, sir.'

'Coffee, sir?'

'Black.'

Spencer had missed the sinking by the accident of being sent on compassionate leave the day before *Connaught* sailed on that Gibraltar convoy, because his mother had been bombed out. The man who had taken his place had gone down with her. He had followed him to *Marathon* at his own request; 'Someone's got to look after you, sir. Look what 'appened when I wasn't there.' But he had never once mentioned the sinking directly.

Thurston had been wretchedly ill the second night after he was hit. Morphine had smoothed the ragged edges of pain, but left the bright core untouched. He drifted in and out of reality, from fevered dreaming into a lucidity in which the slow fires burned on and on in his body and the only thing which mattered was the next injection. Spencer was there throughout the night, his voice telling of the inconsequential doings of Bertie Wooster, Aunt Dahlia, Stilton Cheesewright and the rest, sponging him down, spooning liquids down his arid throat, 'Come on, sir, you won't get better if you don't 'ave some more juice,' and gripping his hand through the darkest hours when the pain was at its worst, the ship rolling heavily, and the fever touched with madness. Much later there was the spatter of rain on the scuttle and sounds of Spencer bustling about in his usual fashion. 'Mornin', sir. Feelin' a bit more lively? You looked proper rough last night. Goin' up the Clyde now. Commander's takin' no chances, got the King's Harbourmaster on board!' Spencer sounded disgusted. 'Couple more hours an' you'll be tucked up ashore with a few pretty nurses. 'Ow about a cuppa tea?' Spencer grinned and he tried to grin back, but it hurt too much. He went back to sleep.

'Midships.'

'Midships, sir.'

The war had come at a critical time in his professional life. He was two years inside the zone for promotion; he was conscious of having done a good job as commander of a battleship. But nothing was ever certain; so much depended on being in the right place at the right time, saying the right things to the right people, and on having the right wife. It had been clear for months that a war was coming, the only questions were, what would set it off, and when.

A time of limbo, the last weeks before the war. He was back in England and waiting for his next appointment after four years in the Mediterranean, first as Fleet Navigator (Master of the Fleet had a better ring to it) and then in *Retribution*. There was no point in looking for a house or a school for Helen – Kate had set her face firmly against boarding school for her – until they knew where he was going, so they had gone up to Langdon for his leave. His father had finally given up his living the year before and moved out of the vicarage into a smaller and much less inconvenient house at the other end of the village. Langdon had a timeless quality; little seemed to have changed there since he was a boy; there were only two or three cars in the entire place and not a tractor to be seen. His father's only concessions to progress were a telephone, which Alice had persuaded him to have put in and a wireless set, which George spent the evenings tinkering with. So it was a time of waiting, and wandering, through a seemingly endless succession of hot bright days, and the green hills and emptiness of Northumberland. Walking, sketching, taking George out with a gun after rabbits, riding – the old man still kept two horses, and took not the slightest notice of his doctor's advice to give up hunting. He went to London with George for his Dartmouth entrance, parted from him on the steps of the Admiralty and spent the morning wondering how he was getting on before he met him again at lunchtime.

The telegram had ended it all, an acting fourth stripe and a ship, more than he had dared hope for. *Connaught* was an old, slow and unfashionable ship, but what did that matter? A hurried leave-taking, a dash south with George for navigation, and because he probably would not see him again before he went to Dartmouth, and into the business of preparing an old ship manned by reservists and new recruits for war service. Since she was a Portsmouth ship, and presumably would be there on occasions, Kate had got busy, found a house to rent a few miles out, and installed Helen in a local day school by the time war was declared.

0300 hours.

'Course one-oh-six, sir. Able Seaman Jones on the wheel.'

Another hour and ffrench would take over the watch, and then he could get his head down until Dawn Action Stations. The sixth night, and no one had been dry in that time. They were nourished on soup and corned beef and endless relays of cocoa and overstrong tea, unwashed, unshaven and fuddled with sleep. Some of them had never breathed fresh air since the torpedoing. Yet they worked on, and groused, cracked wry, self-deprecating jokes and cursed the corned beef, the weather, and whatever agency had brought them out of civilian life.

'Port ten.'

'Port ten, sir.'

The wind and sea pushed her over to starboard, the helm clawed her back, held her for a time, then the drift would begin again. Harker's shoulders were hunched, his hands in his pockets, feet stamping at intervals. The yawing had worsened again, not because of any worsening in the conditions but because the Officer of the Watch was tired and the Quartermaster was tired and their reactions slowed.

'Midships.'

A mad kind of normality. There were times in which he did feel he was going mad, the black moments when it would have been better if he had died in the turret with the rest, or gone down with *Connaught*, when there was an obscure comfort in knowing the revolver and ammunition were there.

'Watch your steering, Quartermaster.'

Three hundred and eighty-two men had died in *Connaught* or in the sea afterwards. The Board of Enquiry had absolved him of all blame for the loss, even commended him for his conduct in the water, but he was alive now and his men were dead.

There was one part of him which said that he had his full complement of eyes, arms and legs, that command was what he was trained for, that command of a ship in the most active sphere of war was the pinnacle he had been striving for since Osborne, that to back out now meant cowardice and disgrace. And there was another part, which said that if his efficiency was going he would be a menace to his ship's company, and in that case it was his duty to give up his command, no matter what the personal cost.

*The Paybob went to market* . . . Men huddled together on the Carley float, black with fuel oil, the wind knifing through their sodden garments, most of them seasick where they lay. Keep awake, keep them all awake, because sleep meant loss of resistance, an inexorable slide into death. He shouted at them, shook them, threatened them. Morgan had given up, lying with vacant eyes, muttering to himself in Welsh. Two dozen left out of four hundred, the rest gone when *Connaught* sank in three minutes. 'Are you all right, Townsend? Are you all right, Macrae? Are you all right, Jeffries?' A competition for the dirtiest story provoked slight interest, the change of lookouts a little more. He had been trained as a boy to pray, 'God bless Father, and the soul of my mother, God bless Grandfather, God bless Edmund, God bless Alice, God bless George, and make me a good boy,' and twenty-eight years of daily prayers and Divisions in the Navy, but was it hypocrisy to pray now? When it came to it, could he honestly stand up and say he believed in the God to whom he had paid lip-service all his life? And what God worth following could allow this? Another man went quiet. A surge of pure clean hate as he was ripped off into the sea and floated away. The sea, the cold indifferent sea, and the war, the useless bloody waste of it all.

The eighteen survivors limped ashore at Liverpool, a Liverpool of civilians, women, children, going about their normal ordinary lives. A combination of petrol and scouring powder got the oil off; the ladies of the Red Cross and WVS descended on them, provided clothes and telegraph forms and limitless hot strong tea. A representative of Gieves ran a tape measure over him and supplied a uniform, delivered by messenger in time for the Board of Enquiry the next day. He rang Kate at work and had the usual struggle with a pea-brained switchboard operator. 'Don't 'ave a Mrs Thornton 'ere. Sure you got the right number?' 'Mrs Thurston, T-H-U-R-S-T-O-N.' 'Oh yes. Sorry, didn't 'ear you properly.' It was strange to be speaking to Kate. 'Bit of a mishap. I can't say anything more now. I'll be home in a couple of days.' He had got through the Board of Enquiry, shaken hands with the men and they had all mumbled farewells, eighteen gaunt-eyed skeletons in the free-masonry of shared suffering.

The reaction came later. Something hit him when he had got on the train and glanced up out of habit at the luggage rack to make sure the porter had stowed his bags. Three or four of the men were on the same train; there was a row with the guard over their warrants; there was no way that anyone, serviceman or otherwise, could travel in the first-class on third-class warrants, no matter whether the third class was already full to overflowing. He had been quite disproportionately angry, made it clear to the guard just where the men had been while he was sitting on his fat backside in safety, reduced the man to grovelling and embarrassing apologies by the time he had finished. That seemed to exhaust something; he spent the rest of the journey in a kind of mad fascination with the winter landscape, looking out of the window, numbly drinking in the greenness of it all.

Kate was at the station, unexpectedly. 'I left work early. I've been here since three. I didn't know which train you'd be on . . . Sorry, I told myself I wouldn't cry, but . . . oh love.' 'Come on, I'm here now.' But that night and for the rest of his leave it was she who looked after him. As soon as his eyes closed in bed he was seeing his dead men, the raft, the empty sea, Galbraith with his head lolling over the lifebelt. 'Are you all right, Pierce? Are you all right, West?' – all the inexpressible agony of it. Kate drew his head down to her breast, stroked his hair, made shushing noises as if to a child. He was drowning in tenderness, warm and growing sleepy and safe at last. Gradually her caresses changed their meaning, her hands moved shiveringly the length of his spine, exploring, arousing, and she began very gently to make love to him. He came in groaning, gasping spasms, finally lost himself inside her, in love and rage and grief and expiation. She wrapped him in her arms, kissed the top of his head, mother to mistress and back to mother.

A week later his appointment to *Marathon* came through. The telephone rang when he was in the garden chopping wood: Jim Morton, a fellow cadet of Blake Term and fellow midshipman in *Hyperion*, now Naval Assistant to the First Sea Lord and dealing with captains' appointments. 'Sorry to hear about your wetting. Are you interested in a pierhead jump? . . . Can't tell you over the blower, old man, but it's a good one. Can you come in here tomorrow forenoon? And bring your gear, we'll be sending you straight up.'

He took Kate out that evening, for the only time that leave, but they came back quite early, and made love again, then lay awake looking at each other in the half-light. She had taken the news philosophically, with the wry comment that she sometimes wished she had married a man who came home every night; she had been bred to service life and it had happened before. But she had hoped, without saying so, that he would be home a little longer, perhaps get a shore job this time.

'*Marathon*, old boy. One of the Didos. Completing at Wallsend and due for trials next week. Arthur Penfold had her, but the silly bugger's gone and burst his appendix. He's going to be out of it for quite a while and we need someone in a hurry. Still keen? Wish it was me, but I've another six months to do in this bloody place.'

He saw *Marathon* for the first time early the next morning, after a slow overnight wartime train journey. Even dockyard debris could not disguise her purity of line, she handled like the thoroughbred she was. At first it had been much like *Connaught*: two weeks to work up and then the endless routine of patrolling, high seas and heavy weather; four or five days at a time in a Scapa which had changed little in twenty years, a bigger canteen for the men, more football pitches, a large balloon barrage and a greater proportion of khaki and light blue uniforms. Unless you were interested in walking, or things which involved walking, such as fishing or birdwatching, there was little to do ashore. He used to get ashore in the afternoons, before the light went, and put in six or seven miles at seven minutes a mile, alone with the wind and Scapa's sleety rain. Running had been his escape from *Oudenarde* in the other war; as a member of the ship's cross-country team, he had to get ashore to train. *Oudenarde* was still there, with one funnel where there had been two, swinging round her buoy, occasionally venturing forth with a very large destroyer escort.

'Course one-oh-six, sir. Able Seaman Courtney on the wheel.'

Two bodies had floated to the surface during the forenoon, blanched and swollen with seawater. They kept pace with the ship for a moment, then fell away astern, to be scavenged by sea birds, their eyes to be pecked out, their skulls made white and bare and smooth like huge billiard balls.

'Wake up, Mr Angus!'

Angus started, rubbed his eyes, peered afresh into the darkness. Harker was cleaning his binoculars, rubbing industriously at the lenses with his handkerchief. Angus stamped his feet, swung his arms across his chest; the signalmen were whispering together, sharing a dirty joke.

'Port ten.'

'Port ten, sir.'

'Time, Mr Angus?'

Angus started once more, fumbled for his watch. 'Oh-three-three-nine, sir.'

'Thank you, Mr Angus. Stay awake.'

'Aye aye, sir.'

Work the shoulder again. Bloody thing! He might ask Spencer to give his back a rub once they got in. That made him think of ffrench and his fantastic bathrooms. Nothing so exotic. Just limitless hot water, fresh towels, a whisky and some music, one of the Brandenburg Concertos or some Mozart; it would be an agonising self-indulgence to choose.

'Midships.'

'Midships, sir.'

One of the lookouts begun to suck his teeth.

'Stop that noise!'

'Sorry, sir. 'Ollow tooth.'

'Stop it!'

Angus sneezed violently, brought out a large and crumpled handkerchief. Another one. Hart was well out of it, half delirious with a high temperature. Gibbons was holding on, so was the man with no legs. Oh God, it was a hell of a price.

Feet on the ladder, the First Lieutenant, Midshipman Nairne, the Chief Yeoman, relief signalmen and lookouts. ffrench and Harker conferred in low voices, Nairne chaffed Angus.

'Watch relieved, sir.'

'Thank you, Number One.'

'Quiet night, sir?'

'So far. I'll be in my sea cabin. Shake me for First Light.'

Into the familiar red-lit steel box. Cap off, boots off, binoculars in the rack. Stretch out, listen to the noises through the door: ffrench talking to Nairne, the ping-ping from the asdic cabinet, the wind hissing through the ventilator.

# — Chapter Eighteen —

0800 hours. The Red Watch at their stations, the White and Blue Watches at breakfast below. Lieutenant Taylor was Officer of the Watch, Midshipman Zurakowski beside him, Able Seaman Grice on the wheel. A bright morning signal from *Leonidas* – how did Nicholls keep it up? A shave in half a mugful of water, a hasty splashy wash. Breakfast. *Real* eggs.

'Where'd you find these, Spencer?'

Spencer tapped his nose. 'Them as asks no questions, sir.'

'One of these days they'll catch up with you.'

'I can look after meself, sir.' Spencer flashed his conspiratorial grin. 'Got some Dundee marmalade this mornin'.'

'I won't ask where that came from.'

Real marmalade was one of the casualties of the war. Most of what reached the Mediterranean Fleet was stringy stuff in tins from South Africa or Canada. But Spencer seemed to be able to find the odd jar of the real thing.

'More coffee, sir?'

'Enjoying it, Spencer?'

'Roll on my twenty-two, sir.'

Spencer brought the latest news and gossip. One of the ship's cats had produced three ginger kittens in the Commissioned Gunner's bunk. Mr Knott was reported as saying that he hadn't the heart to turn them out, had borrowed a sleeping bag and turned in on the carpet. Ted Bradshaw came up, then the Commander

(E). Little had been seen of Burnley since the torpedoing; he had been continuously occupied in tending the auxiliary machinery and keeping watch on the damaged bulkhead. He was a good man; the plain facts that he was the son of a Bradford railwayman, had begun his naval career as a boy artificer and worked his way first to a commission and then to a brass hat by sheer ability and application proved it. He was not a great talker; he accepted a cup of coffee, filled and lit his pipe, gave a bald statement of facts between puffs, and returned to the depths.

'Won't be long now,' said Connor. 'Just think of all those little nurses. When I was 'avin' my rupture done . . . They used to make us lie to attention when the doctor came round. This little nurse came along. Ooh, she was lovely. I got an 'ard-on straight away. She looked me right in the eye and said, "Connor, put your knees down," "Sorry Nurse," says I. "Sister," says she. "It's not my knees, it's my . . ."'

Back to the bridge, watch the tow, the sky, broken grey cloud scudding across the blue. The wind blew cold, cutting through the damp blue cloth of his trousers. Sixty miles to go, sixty miles to go.

Another twelve hours' steaming. It was difficult to believe that they could be back in harbour tonight, that the long struggle to bring the ship home could be over. Exhaustion had brought a curious numb state of lethargy in which mind and body carried out their functions automatically, without thought or feeling. Men stopped work, and instantly fell asleep. They slept while raising a mug to their lips, while sitting on the heads, while waiting in the gangways.

'Port ten.'

'Port ten, sir.'

Nobody talked much now. They stood silent, each locked in his own struggle against sleep, their white

213

eyes staring red-rimmed from their taut strained faces. The Captain's secretary came up with a signal, saluted, gave it to Thurston. He tried to decipher it, to follow the scrawled capitals on the pink flimsy, but his eyes wouldn't focus any longer.

'Read it, please, Jenner.'

Jenner read it, a routine signal about nothing in particular, a strange thing in the midst of all this, but perhaps a reminder that they would soon be returning to the fold, to harbour routine and bull, an end to the limbo.

'Midships.'

'Midships, sir.'

Poor old *Marathon*, poor old ship. She wallowed heavily beneath his feet, drawing twenty-two feet as against her normal fourteen. There was the smell of death over her, sweetish, unmistakable. Twenty-four dead men on board, thirty-seven already buried, two others drifting in the sea astern. Garrard down in the sick bay with no legs. He had screamed for five solid minutes before the morphine put him out, until those on the bridge hated him, a desire to put a revolver to his head and squeeze the trigger if only it would stop him screaming. Hank had screamed when the splinter hit him, left his kneecap dangling by a couple of ligaments, swinging obscenely as the leg moved, jerkily, in time with the screams. Hank screamed on, the sound cutting through his brain.

'*Shut up!*'

He got his lanyard off, lashed it round Hank's thigh, on his knees on the dusty ground, in Hank's blood, took out his revolver, used the barrel to twist the cord tight, until it bit deep into the flesh.

'Shut up! For God's sake.'

Hank tried to sit up, to see his leg. He pushed him back. Hank looked up at him, quiet suddenly, his eyes pleading.

'Beak, don't leave me.'

214

The stretcher-bearers took a long time to come. It may not have been more than five minutes. He sat with Hank on that bare dusty beach, on that bright glaring Gallipoli morning, and talked of bridge. They had been ashore overnight and played a rubber with two sapper officers in a dugout, on a packing case, by the light of a guttering candle. Now he grasped at that, something to hold on to, to cut himself off from the blood and pain and horror.

'Beak, stay with me!'

Hank whimpered, he gripped his hand, talked of diamonds and spades and no trumps. The stretcher-bearers came at last, two bare-chested, slouch-hatted Australians.

'Poor little bugger. You his mate?'

The man passed him a waterbottle, casually. He choked on it. Neat rum.

'Don't like it, kid? I thought you sailors lived on the stuff.'

He followed them to the dressing station, walking alongside Hank, with the same dull numb feeling that had come over him when Ayah came out on the verandah and told him the Memsahib was dead. His trouser legs were plastered with blood and sand, Hank's blood, scarlet on white.

Two days later he talked his way into seeing Hank aboard the hospital ship. He couldn't think of anything to say to him, but left him the penknife his grandfather had given him for passing into Osborne. The same night they took his leg off six inches above the knee. He saw him again six months after, unfamiliar in civilian clothes, defiantly wearing a Royal Navy tie, breaking in an artificial leg. His naval career was over, but he had picked up the threads of life, gone to Cambridge and made a success of himself as a barrister, married, and cajoled the Navy into taking him back when another war came. Hank had remained irrepressible; Thurston had attended one of his first court actions while Hank was a struggling junior, a claim for damages arising from an industrial accident. 'Mr Hancock,' the judge declared, 'I must remind you that you are in a court of law, not an amusement hall.' 'As your Lordship pleases,' intoned Hank, with the faintest suggestion of his mischievous grin. There was an occasion when he and his family had visited them at Dartmouth, and George had announced in a loud voice, 'Uncle Hank, why have you got a funny walk?' Hank had taken him upstairs, removed his trousers and shown a fascinated four-year-old exactly how his tin leg worked. He liked children and had a habit of persuading them to kick him 'to see which is the tin one.'

The shoulder nagged. He didn't like to think about his feet. The ship rolled, he crooked a leg round one of the supports of his bridge chair. No point in sitting down. He had got to the point where it was less painful to keep going than to sleep and have to force himself into alertness. Spencer came up, another tired man. He seemed to have used up the last of his bounce at breakfast.

'Coffee, sir.'

'Thank you, Spencer. Go and get your head down. I shan't be needing you for a while.'

Spencer trudged away, eyes downcast.

'Port ten.'

'Port ten, sir.'

'I don't like the look of that bulkhead, sir.'

'All right, Ted. I'll take a look.'

The bulkhead was bulging ominously, leaking water down the centre, to join the three inches of dirty liquid which already slopped over the deck plates. A white-faced stoker stood to one side, eyes fixed upon it.

'Hall, sir, Stoker Second Class.' He answered the question without turning his head.

'How long have you been here, Hall?'

'Watch and watch since this lot started, sir.' His

voice was nervously high, with an awareness that if the bulkhead went there was no hope for him, mesmerised by the slow-dripping water. The Warrant Shipwright gave his verdict: going ahead in this sea was placing too much strain on the damaged members.

'All right. We'll try going stern first.' He turned to the Commander (E) as they moved away. 'Find a relief for young Hall if you can, Chief.'

Back up to the bridge, a weary effort to set one foot in front of the other. How much longer could this go on? How much longer could he go on? A signal to *Leonidas*, a simple acknowledgement in reply. Nicholls must be tired too. Draft a signal to CinC Med, pass it to Jenner for ciphering.

*Marathon* slipped the tow, *Leonidas* hauled it in. Once again the sickening wallow as the ship broached to, the sense of nakedness and insecurity at being parted from the destroyer. Again the gnawing wait for the line to be passed, the back-breaking labour of hauling it in.

> *Hauling, Hauling, Hauling,*
> *Always bloody well hauling!*

But the bounce, the defiance, had gone, weary men working with unresponsive metal, resigned to going through it all again.

'Come on, stir your stumps! Look lively there! A bit of effort this time!'

'Zombies,' muttered Bradshaw.

Again the drawn-out agony of the turn downwind, the unequal rolling of the two ships which brought the wire closer to breaking point. ffrench's left foot beat a tattoo on the steel plates, Chief Yeoman O'Shaughnessy muttered under his breath, 'Hail Mary, full of grace. The Lord is with thee. Blessed art thou among women . . .', over and over again, a rosary bunched in his fist. A pale Ordinary Seaman Richards watched his sector, a black smudge of bruising across his chin.

Thurston fixed his eyes on the destroyer, listening to the Chief Quartermaster's incantation from the voice-pipe.

'Three-six-oh . . . oh-one-oh . . . oh-two-oh . . .'

Still holding. Just a little more. Another lurching roll. He clamped his teeth together. Can't you stop that, Number One?

'Oh-six-oh . . . oh-seven-oh . . .'

'Holy Mary Mother of God. Pray for us sinners now . . .'

'Ease to five.'

'Ease to five, sir.'

A glance at the compass, as the destroyer began to come out of her turn.

'Midships. Meet her.'

'Midships, sir . . . Meet her, sir.'

'Hail Mary, full of grace. The Lord is with thee. Blessed art thou among women.'

'Steer one-oh-seven.'

'Steer one-oh-seven, sir.'

'Thank you, Hicks. Well done.'


After *Marathon* had settled to her new course, Thurston handed over the con to ffrench. As he turned away towards the heads he began to shake as if in an attack of malaria, so much that he had to sit down for several minutes until the worst of it had passed, and then steel himself to go back on deck. Savage was probably right: he couldn't trust his body any more. 'I'm sorry, sir, but when this is over I'm going to put my foot down.' . . . *Oh God, don't think about that until this is over!*

# — Chapter Nineteen —

It was long after dark when they came into Alexandria. *Leonidas* slipped the tow a few miles offshore, outside the minefields; two harbour tugs took over. Thurston signalled his thanks, Nicholls replied in his usual manner.

*'My fee is a case of whisky. Habbakuk 3.2 refers.'*

Midshipman Nairne brought out the Bible from the chart table. *'Revive thy work in the midst of the years. In the midst of the years make it known. In wrath remember mercy.'*

He tried to think of a suitable rejoinder, but there was nothing which could convey the unutterable, nothing which would not demean.

'Hands clean into the rig of the day.'

Men went below to clean up in buckets of cold sea-water and to shift into Number Threes. Thurston sent Boy McCormick for his best cap and changed his shirt. A party went round tightening the rails. The band formed up on the quarterdeck.

There was a sense of unreality as *Marathon* came into harbour, ratings lining the rails, the band marching and counter-marching to the strains of 'The Road to the Isles', which had become, over the last two years, for no obvious reason except that the Bandmaster liked it, a sort of signature tune. Back in the fold, after six days of being keyed up to screaming point, days of doubt and hope and fear and unstinting effort. It should have been one of the greatest moments of his life, but he could feel no elation, only a strange emptiness. The band changed to the slow march, 'The Flowers of the Forest', and measured drumbeats, then once more into quick time. The Bugler sounded the Alert, respects were paid to the flagship and to the ships whose captains were senior.

'Signal from Flag, sir. *Manoeuvre well executed.*'

And then the cheering started, from *Ariadne, Bellerophon* and *Persephone*, echoing across the dark water. He felt numb, unable to take it all in. His eyes stung and started to stream; no, it wasn't that. He groped for a handkerchief. *Oh what the devil.* He was standing at attention, the officers had drawn away from him, tears streaming down his face, numbly taking in the scene, the noise, the music, the cheering flung back from *Marathon*'s own decks.

Bradshaw pumped his hand. 'You did it, sir!'

'No, Ted,' he said slowly. 'We all did it.'

Bradshaw, ffrench, O'Shaughnessy, Hicks and all the quartermasters, Savage and his sick-bay team, the Chief, Stoker Hall fearfully watching the bulkhead, all of them.

Midshipman Pearson was loaded on a stretcher and carried up to the fo'c'sle deck. So it was all over. *Then shall he strip his sleeve and show his scars, and say, 'These wounds I had on Crispin's Day.'* He felt strangely proud and happy. Silly really, all he'd done was to get a fairly silly wound and be seasick. But he'd been there, in something that was greater then himself. He propped himself up on his elbows, looking about him, saw Cowper-Coles detach himself from the cable party and approach him, followed by Graham.

'So long, Pearson. Give those nurses a hard time.'

'See if you can fix me up with one.'

'Better warn them that Jack Graham is on the prowl!'

'Er, CC, could you give me a hand up. I'm sick of lying down.'

'Come on Jack!'

They got him upright, one on either side. He rested his weight on his good leg, leant gratefully on them. *We few, we happy few, we band of brothers, for he today who sheds his blood with me shall be my brother* . . . Even Hastings, in that moment. Hastings went past, arm in a sling, duffel coat over his shoulders, smiling.

'So long, Rembrandt. Keep the pictures coming.' Cowper-Coles disentangled himself, slapped him on the back.

'Boat ahoy?'

'Flag!'

'Barge approaching, sir.'

The ship was secure. The last of the wounded had gone down the gangway, the walking cases smiling, grimacing, laughing now it was all over. A long line of stretchers, swung over the side in cargo hoists; Ordinary Seaman Garrard, blearily conscious under morphine, not yet aware of his loss, Lieutenant Hart, Boy Gibbons, a still effigy beneath the blankets.

The barge reached the gangway. Beecham puffed up the accommodation ladder, the band played the prescribed excerpt from *Iolanthe*, salutes were exchanged.

'Well, Bob, it's good to see you back. We did wonder if you'd make it.'

They drew to one side, the Admiral went on. Thurston wasn't really listening, thinking of all the things that had still to be done. Most of it could wait until tomorrow – today, he thought, it was after midnight – he had told Bradshaw to fall out everybody except a skeleton watch.

'You had a lot of casualties?'

'Yes sir. We did.' It came out flatly.

'But we got the convoy through. That's worth everything.'

He wondered whether he hated Beecham. The Admiral's future was secure. He could look forward to further promotion, he would probably get a knighthood for this. He had looked around him, seen the damage, the long line of stretchers, smelt the death smell hanging over them. But it hadn't sunk in.

*They make a desolation and call it peace. Silentium faciunt, pacem appellant.*

Beecham was spruce and smart, smelling of soap and shaving lotion. Thurston was aware of his worn gold lace and eight days' grime.

'Well, Bob, I'll leave you to it. You'll be wanting to get your head down, what? Once again, you've done a damn good job.'

'Goodnight, sir.'

'Goodnight, Bob.'

More salutes. More *Iolanthe*. Beecham's feet rattled the ladder. With a change of engine note the barge pulled away.

Sudden quiet, a deeper sense of emptiness. The Marine sentry outside the Captain's quarters presented arms, his face expressionless. 'Goodnight, Leishman.' The cabin was unchanged, quiet, carpeted, everything in its place.

'Done your bath, sir.'

Another of Spencer's miracles. He must have lugged half a dozen buckets up from below, heated the water in pans on the stove.

'Sorry it's salt water, sir.'

'Doesn't matter. Bang on the door in about fifteen minutes in case I nod off.'

Spencer deposited a glass on the enamel surround and marched out.

He would dispense with Bach tonight and concentrate on the sheer sensual pleasure of getting clean. It was always the best time after getting in from sea, to lie in the hot water and scrub, wash the hair that had festered inside his cap for the last week. It needed cutting again, he noted. It was always slightly unexpected to see the same body emerge again from beneath the sodden garments, unchanged except for the usual marks of time at sea, salt sores on his shins, chafed patches on the sides of the neck from constantly turning his head. He was thinner than he used to be, the bottom ribs hadn't stuck out like that before sailing. Or had they? Hardly to be wondered at in any case. He sipped the whisky, sharp and astringent in his mouth. He shut his eyes, momentary shock as his shoulders made contact with cold enamel.

'Captain, sir!'

He started, called out to Spencer, stood up and poured a final bucket of fresh water over his head to wash the salt off, glowing and gloriously clean as he towelled himself. The next stage, the anointing of one's hurts. His feet were a mess again, puffy white skin coming away in strips, raw areas of pink which oozed fluid like broken blisters. He finished the whisky, rested his left foot on his pyjama-clad knee, waggled the toes comfortably, rubbed the purple fluid into the raw spaces between, the skin contracting stingingly as the stuff did its work, another part of the sleepy post-operation ritual.

'Will you be needin' anything else, sir?'

'No thank you, Spencer.'

''Night, sir.'

In five minutes Spencer would have slung his hammock, be undressed, in it, and asleep, one of the few ratings aboard with any degree of privacy. Through to the sleeping cabin, take Kate's photograph from a drawer and prop it up in its usual place. She gazed at him serenely from the frame; in another photograph George stood beside him in a garden, grinning rather cockily; Helen sat on some steps with a sheepdog puppy, at Langdon the last fortnight before the war. Everything was just as usual, strange that it should be so after the last eight days, bunk made up, sheets ironed into knife-edge creases, the book he had been reading on the locker top, the page marked, clock showing five minutes to one, the destroyer sketch hanging on the bulkhead opposite, product of a foray from Scapa when *Marathon* was still with the Home Fleet, one of the odd occasions when he indulged himself by sketching from the bridge. An H-class destroyer going into a head sea, ensigns streaming in the wind. He had been pleased with it, the way it captured the motion of sea and ship, the scudding fragments of cloud.

*Dear Mrs So-and-So, I killed your son, your husband, your father, your brother . . .*

# — Chapter Twenty —

'Good morning, sir. It is oh-six-'undred hours. Ze wind is Force Two, sous-westerly. Ze baromeetric pressure is twenty-nine-point-seven.'

Midshipman Zurakowski, with a flashing smile of the kind guaranteed to turn the head of any gullible female, young or not so young. Ah, the resilience of youth.

The sense of unreality continued. It was a fine bright morning, sun lighting on the water. Sub-Lieutenant Cowper-Coles paced slowly back and forth as Officer of the Watch, sword at his left side – squadron standing orders – telescope under arm, studiously ignoring his captain as Thurston stepped on to the quarterdeck and began his morning circuit. Twelve hours ago they were still at sea, fighting to bring the ship home; before the day was out *Marathon* would be dry-docked, the repairs beginning. Below decks the pumps were still going, a man still watched the damaged bulkhead. Somewhere below were twenty-four dead men, who would be brought out through the gash in the bottom once the dock was pumped out. Fifty press-ups, on his knuckles, jump up, double round the upper deck. The voice of a PTI floated across from the *Bellerophon*: 'Mr Grant! Get your bloody knees up!' *Marathon*'s snotties had been granted an extra hour in their hammocks. Stretch the stride an extra six inches to clear a ring-bolt, the breeze cool on his bare arms and back. He would be busy today. The remaining ammunition to be unloaded, a sweating, nerve-jangling job, in which it would only take one spark, one man made clumsy by fatigue, to set off a cordite fire or an explosion. Then the dry-docking, manoeuvring into the narrow confines with tugs and bare steerage way, inch by precise inch. There would be the dockyard people to see about the repairs, a visit to the hospital to see the wounded, a session with the Admiral, almost certainly another funeral. There were letters to write, sixty-seven of them, in his own hand. *Dear Mrs So-and-So, I am sorry to inform you . . .*

His sleep had been uneasy. He had woken several times, giving helm orders and unable to comprehend the absence of the tow. Once he had got up and started for the bridge before coming fully awake. It was only then that he remembered Savage's pills, but it was too late by then, because he had to be able to wake up and be alert this morning of all mornings. 'Mr Grant! I want to see you put some effort into it this time!'

It was going to be a perfectly bloody day.

The ammunition had been landed. The ship was in the dry dock. An interested swarm of staff officers gathered as the water went down and the hole was revealed. One by one the bodies were coming out, unrecognisable, bloated with seawater, black with fuel oil and decomposition, carried away on stretchers for the work of identification to begin. Men worked with scarves over their faces, fortified with rum, the visitors had melted away. Except one, a stocky black-bearded commander, who watched by himself, a little way off.

'I'm Nicholls, sir.'

They shook hands, in silence. There was nothing that could be said.

'Can we be ready for a funeral at 1600?'

'Yes sir,' Bradshaw said simply. He made a note on his pad.

'You and I to go. I'm getting sick of funerals, Ted.'

226

The sense of unreality remained. He savoured the mail over lunch, putting aside a bank statement and a bill from Gieves. Three letters from Kate, one from George, detailing another triumph on the rugby field. Helen had been to a church dance the previous Saturday and come back at nearly midnight escorted by a young Royal Marine officer cadet. 'He seemed a very nice boy, but she is rather young to be staying out so late, even on a Saturday.' The Min of I were producing a new series of posters about salvage and a tree had blown down in the garden next door, 'in one of your equinoctial gales on Monday night'. Helen had been to the pictures with the Marine, who was apparently on leave from OCTU, twice in the past three days, but he had brought her back by ten on both occasions. Kate and Mrs Crosby had been very busy making jam from an enormous crop of blackberries on a bramble clump near the railway line. George had written from Dartmouth to announce that he had grown out of all his shirts, though they had fitted him at the beginning of term. 'It must be all this rugby training. I told him to get what he needed and put it on your account' – that explained the Gieves bill. The Marine had gone back to OCTU, leaving Helen his photograph and promising faithfully to write. One letter in his father's immaculate copperplate, beginning as always, 'My dear Robert', and ending, 'Your Affectionate Father, Henry Maitland Thurston'. The weather had been wet and windy; he had taken a couple of services for the present vicar who was laid up with sciatica again. 'Another of Armstrong's land girls is pregnant. The culprit has not yet been found, but there is reason to believe he is one of a Polish gunner battery stationed at Rothbury. I have been reading the *Anabasis* once more after a good many years; it is instructive to see the relevance to our present situation. Maud sends her regards and we are hoping to see Alice again at the end of the week.' He had been receiving letters in that vein all his life. Spencer laying out his best uniform for the funeral. Sword, medals, gold cufflinks, shoes boned to glassy perfection. 'You'll be needin' your greatcoat, sir.' Spencer proceeded to attack the garment with a clothes brush and considerable vigour. 'Bad business, sir.' Ted Bradshaw confirmed that the barracks could provide accommodation for twenty-six officers and three hundred and ninety men for the duration of the repairs.

A session on the Report of Proceedings, logs spread on his desk, slowly pacing the carpet, Jenner with propelling pencil poised and shorthand pad on knees. It was difficult to keep the thread going; once the world turned grey, and he had to reach out to a chairback and thought for a moment that he was going to faint.

'Are you all right, sir?' Jenner asked solicitously.

'Just felt a bit dizzy. I'll sit down for a moment.'

'Couldn't this wait until tomorrow, sir? You don't look too good.'

'It's got to be done. Where were we, Scratch?'

He was glad it wasn't Spencer, who would have bustled about making cups of tea and suggesting what he called 'a nice lie down'. Just get today over with.

Once more there was a line of white ensigns and shrouded bundles, the destroyer stopped, rolling with the sea. *I am the resurrection and the life*. Her captain read slowly, painstakingly, a young lieutenant-commander in his first command. *Man that is born of a woman hath but a short time to live*. A desolation about burial at sea, the corpses disappearing into the vastness of the ocean, bringing each of the witnesses a little closer to his own mortality. *The trumpet shall sound and the dead shall be raised incorruptible, and we shall be changed*. Bowed cropped heads and flapping blue-jean collars, the bo'sun's call sounding the Still. It was all over in twenty minutes. Revolutions for twenty-five knots, back into Alexandria. He kept out of the destroyer captain's way, it was his ship, sat in the captain's cabin with Bradshaw; neither of them had much to say.

Then the hospital. The familiar smell compounded of disinfectant and floor polish, doctors talking in low voices, a slow progress through the wards filled with burned and broken men, his men. Boy Gibbons was dead, an hour ago, without regaining consciousness. After all that, to die after reaching home. Or was it home, a service hospital full of strangers? There would be another letter to write, to the married sister he supposed, and she would have to be traced, because Gibbons wouldn't have had time to alter his next-of-kin card. It struck him that he didn't even know Gibbons's Christian name.

Jenner brought the Report of Proceedings. He must have had the typewriter running red-hot. It was all there, fresh black type standing out from crisp sheets.

*From: Commanding Officer,* Marathon
*To: Flag Officer Commanding Fifteenth Cruiser Squadron.*

*Sir,*
*I have the honour to submit this my Report of Proceedings on the operations of His Majesty's Ship* Marathon *under my command, from 17–25 November 1942 . . .*

The words on the white sheets, the terse official phrases that represented all that had happened in the past days, the appendix listing the dead and wounded.

*I have the honour to remain,*
*Sir,*
*Your obedient servant*

and the space for his signature, Jenner added another name to the list.

*Died of Wounds 26 November:*

'What was his Christian name?'

Jenner consulted another list. 'Robert, sir.'

Thurston uncapped his pen, signed, five copies, blotted it, put the pen away.


'Boat ahoy?'

*'Marathon!'*

Petty Officer Stephenson and his crew had been at work; the boat was shipshape once more, paint scrubbed down, brightwork polished, miniature ensign flying, pennant to signify the Captain himself was on board, a demonstration of their personal pride.

'Sit down, Bob.' The Admiral was in an expansive mood. 'Help yourself to sherry. Or would you rather have gin?'

'I'll stick to sherry, sir.'

'A naval officer who doesn't drink gin?' Beecham poured himself gin, added water and bitters. 'That was a bloody good show. You could drive a couple of buses through that hole, what?' Bloody excellent piece of seamanship, you and young Nicholls. I'm putting him in for a DSO by the way. I expect you have some recommendations yourself.'

He hadn't thought about it. 'Yes, sir.'

'Anybody in particular?'

If one man deserved something they all did, but . . . 'My Commander, Ted Bradshaw, for one, and my First Lieutenant.' He would get ffrench his brass hat if it was the last thing he did. There was the padre, but would he have wanted such a thing? Burnley? Hicks? Savage?

'A DSO for Bradshaw? Oh, he's already got one. For the *Seydlitz*, wasn't it? I'll put him in for a bar. And your First Lieutenant, what's his name – German?'

'ffrench, sir. With two fs.'

'Ah yes, of course. You think pretty highly of him,

don't you? A DSC, unless *he's* already got one. Let me have a complete list as soon as you can. Drink that stuff up and have yourself another. I've been talking to the CinC. Once *Marathon*'s seaworthy you can take her to Boston or New York for a full refit. Might even get that condenser sorted out. Meanwhile, you can get off to the fleshpots of Cairo for a couple of weeks. Cheer up, man, you're a bit quiet.'

'Sorry, sir. Another of my boys died this afternoon.'

'Rotten luck. Which one was it?'

'Gibbons. The lad with the head wound.'

'Ah yes,' Beecham said, not very convincingly. 'A bad business, but it happens.' He poured himself another gin. 'And now we'd all like to hear what happened to you. I'll look at this bumph later.'

Thurston was aware that he told the story badly, but the warmth of the cabin and the drinks were making him sleepy. The whole story, from the torpedo hit through the air attack, the parting of the tow. He left out Ordinary Seaman Richards; that was a private thing, for *Marathon* alone. They listened, Beecham, Philip Woodruffe, the SO (Ops), the Admiral's Flag Lieutenant and Secretary. When he had finished, the Admiral turned to talk of the convoy.

'Actually, things seemed to go quiet after you were hit. The Wops must have gone home to celebrate. Pity about *Berwickshire*, and your chaps of course. Still, we can't let losses deflect us from our purpose, and after the last one . . .' Beecham must be thinking of his K. Thurston listened, and did not listen, accepted another glass of sherry. He was too weary to get steamed up about Beecham; he settled his head back, and let him ramble on.

'Wakey-wakey, Bob,' Beecham said genially. 'Have you eaten?'

He hadn't, but he declined. He wasn't hungry.

'Off you go and catch up on your sleep.'

Philip Woodruffe stood up. 'I'll see you over the side.'

Woodruffe's handshake was warm, his pleasure genuine. 'It's good to see you back. I honestly didn't think you'd make it. Sorry about Reggie. Sometimes just nothing gets through to him.'

> *Therefore I see no reason in the world,*
> *Why my heart grows not dark, when I consider*
> *The lives of warriors, how they suddenly have left their hall,*
> *The bold and noble thanes . . .*

He tried to remember where that came from, where he had read it. It might have been on that short course at Cambridge in 1919, a long time ago now. Salutes, clatter down the accommodation ladder.

'Home, sir?'

Petty Officer Stephenson came from Newcastle, and the second word came out as 'Sor'. Thurston felt light-headed from drinking on an empty stomach, a sense of the mind being no longer entirely connected to the body. Go back aboard, pick up the kit which Spencer would have packed, get ashore to the barracks.

In his day cabin the lights were on, but Spencer was elsewhere. Jenner had completed the list, left it on his desk. He had done his job efficiently enough, the names, ranks or rates, and Christian names of the dead, the names and addresses of next-of-kin. He wondered where Spencer was. Probably gone on deck for some air. He looked at his watch, decided to make a start on the letters before he went ashore. He pulled out a writing pad, good pre-war-quality paper with the ship's crest, and started with the first name on the list. *Dear Mrs Barnett*. He had never met the Gunnery Officer's Wife. *Mrs E. Barnett, The Old Vicarage, North Cerney, Gloucestershire. I am sorry to inform you that your husband, Lieutenant-Commander J. D. Barnett, DSC RN, was killed on . . .* What was the

232

date? Look it up, *22 November*. Next sentence. Don't mention that Guns had been hit through both lungs and taken five solid minutes to drown in his own blood, that next to him Midshipman Norris's belly had been ripped open and the Director Layer's head blown off. Tell her he was killed instantly, the usual platitudes.

> *Therefore I see no reason in the world,*
> *Why my heart grows not dark, when I consider*
> *The lives of warriors, how they suddenly have left*
> *their hall,*
> *The bold and noble thanes . . .*

But we can't let losses deflect us from our purpose. He stood up, walked across the the scuttle, stood still for a moment, clenched his hands. *I hate this bloody war!* He turned round, shouted it twice at the King's portrait on the bulkhead. The King gazed back impassively. Calm down, sit down again, start a new paragraph. Tell her the truth, that Jack Barnett had been a good reliable fellow and it had been a privilege to have him as his Gunnery Officer, and make it sound sincere instead of simply a letter of condolence. It didn't look too bad. *Yours sincerely*, sign, *R. H. M. Thurston, Captain*. His head had been aching steadily for the last hour, the disconnection remained. *We can't let losses deflect us from our purpose*. Read it through again, black on white, the light and the dark, blurring, dissolving, his eyes filling with scalding tears. *No you can't.* He hadn't blubbed since he was eight. *The bloody war*. He looked up once more at the King, serene in unknowing majesty. He picked up a paperweight and hurled it at the photograph. The glass shattered, he let his head fall forward on to his arms and wept as though his heart would break.

Spencer came in a few minutes later, found him collapsed across his desk, sobbing to himself like an exhausted child.

'Sir? . . . Sir?' He moved forward, treading very

233

softly, skirted the broken glass. 'Been drinking, sir?' Thurston was aware of Spencer moving round behind him, placing a hand on his shoulder. 'Sir, what's wrong?' He sounded confused and hurt at the same time.

Thurston's shoulders shook and heaved, he was unable to prevent himself from dissolving into a fresh paroxysm of crying. He lifted his head. 'Go away, Spencer. For God's sake.'

Spencer drew back, hesitated for a moment. 'I'll come back later, sir.' His footsteps retreated. The door closed.

After a time he heard the door open again, another voice, talking to Spencer. 'You were lucky to catch me aboard. I was just finishing something off.'

Savage felt his wrist, put an arm round him. He pushed him away. 'Go away. For God's sake.'

'That's not being very constructive. Let's get you next door.'

They were walking him through to the sleeping cabin, one on either side. His eyes met the King's once more, out of the broken frame. *Oh you gutless bastard.* Spencer lifted his legs up on to the bunk and began to take off his shoes. He rolled over on to his face. Spencer turned him back. 'It's all right, sir.' What was all right? Spencer fumbled with his tie and collar stud, bitten nails against his neck. He was trying to tell them something, but the words wouldn't form. He turned over again, shame buried in the pillow, the sobbing stifled. Spencer turned his back again. 'Just keep quiet, sir. It's all right. I'm sorry, sir.'

Savage was standing over him, a syringe in his hand. He was trying to form the words again, that he didn't want any of his bloody dope. 'This is just something to make you sleep. Let's have that sleeve up, Spencer . . . A bit further . . . That's it. Nothing to fret about. You're going to feel much better when you wake up.' The needle went in. He was talking again, aware that it wasn't what he was trying to say. He was being pulled away from them, their faces blurring and disappearing.

Savage straightened up. 'Good. That should keep him out for at least twenty-four hours. You were right to call me, Spencer.'

Spencer looked at the Captain in dumb misery. The Surgeon Commander must have seen the worry and puzzlement in his face.

'Strain and overwork. And driving himself too hard. He's had enough. More than enough. This has been coming on for months.'

'Will the Captain be all right, sir? I mean . . . I'm supposed to look after 'im.' His voice trailed away. Savage patted him on the shoulder. He wondered whether he should have asked.

'You think a lot of him, don't you?'

'Yes sir,' he said dejectedly.

'You get off and enjoy your leave and don't worry about the Captain. He's going to hospital where he'll be properly looked after.'

'Hospital, sir?' The Old Man hated hospitals.

'Best thing, in the circumstances. It's what he needs. He's got to have a proper rest, and be away from ships for a while. And a change of attitude, I'm afraid. He's too hard on himself. That's partly the system of course. Damn the war.'

'But will he be all right, sir?'

'The prognosis is pretty good in most of these cases, but he won't be commanding ships again for a while . . . I'd better stop talking and ring the hospital. There'll be a stretcher party coming up as soon as I can organise one.'

When Savage had gone Spencer pulled a blanket over the Captain, picked the glass fragments out of the photograph frame and straightened the King up. He packed the kit the Captain would need, pyjamas, washing and shaving tackle, books – the Old Man would go

235

mad with boredom stuck in hospital if he didn't have nothing to read – then sat down on the chair and reached for his tobacco tin. The only sound in the cabin was the Captain's breathing. He looked an awful colour; his head had fallen sideways against the pillow and his face glistened damply in the light from the deckhead.

'Blimey, sir, what 'ave you been doin' to yourself?'

# — Chapter Twenty-One —

## Alexandria, December 1942

'He'll live, if that's what you mean. Beyond that it's too early to make any predictions.'

'Did he really mean it?' Beecham asked incredulously; the news was only beginning to sink in.

'He meant it all right! It could hardly have been accidental. For what it's worth, it looks as though it was done on impulse, but it was in no sense a gesture. A pretty determined effort.'

Beecham did not reply immediately. All this had come as a complete surprise. He had been finishing his lunch, looking forward to getting ashore for a round of golf with the Chief of Staff, when the Surgeon Rear Admiral had telephoned, insisted on speaking to him personally. No, his Flag Lieutenant would not do. No, he wouldn't tell him what it was about over the telephone, he had better come over as soon as he could.

'Very fortunate really. The sister who looked in on him found him gone, and decided to check up. The bathroom door was locked, she got no reply, so she was suspicious. Then she saw blood coming from underneath and climbed straight over the top. Athletic girl, fortunately.'

'What I can't understand is why? What had he got to be so miserable about anyway? If anything he was too bloody perfect.'

'I note your use of the past tense.' The Surgeon Rear Admiral leant forward across his desk. 'Dammit, Reggie, don't you have any insight! He's not just miserable. He's ill. He damn nearly lost his ship and he did lose a lot of good men. Bound to be upsetting. And he's been living on his nerves for months. I can't go into details and in any case I haven't got them yet, but I'll hazard a guess that a whole lot of things have caught up with him at once and this Stonehenge business was just the final straw.'

'I should have thought of that. Terrible thing to happen to a good man. Can I see him?'

'No, you certainly cannot! He's still under a general anaesthetic and he'll be in no condition to see anyone when he does come to.' He sighed. 'Perhaps in a few days, all other things being equal, but he's going to need some psychiatric help and it might be better if you kept out of the way.'

An enamel basin against his chin, he was heaving into it, again and again, someone holding his head and murmuring reassurances. 'Spencer . . . ?' 'I'm Parry, sir.' The voice was Welsh, soft and young. A cup was held to his mouth; he shifted at the wrong moment and most of the water went down his neck. Pain; pain and strange dreams and something weighing him down, sucking him deeper into the sea of sludge through which he was trying to swim. He grew frightened and tried to break away, struck out for the surface. Someone was pressing him back into the sludge; he tried to fight him, shouted and thrashed. 'Steady, sir . . . Captain Thurston, can you hear me?' He realised he had been speaking Urdu. 'Now you've pulled the drip out . . . Steady. I'm just going to get someone to put it back in . . .' Footsteps, going away, and returning, and quiet voices. A needle went in, the pain receded for a time in a morphine haze.

'Where's this?'

'Rosyth. Keep quiet, there's a good boy. You mustn't talk.'

A long ward, with drawn curtains and a polished wooden floor off which boots echoed all day.

'Good, you're awake. Your mother's here to see you.'

'Stepmother,' he corrected automatically.

'We had a telegram. I came straight up.'

'Where's Father?'

'He had to take a wedding, and tomorrow's Sunday, but he's coming on Monday.'

'You're not very like your mother.'

'She's my stepmother.'

He surfaced, saw that both his arms were outside the bedclothes, one in plaster to the elbow, the other lashed to a board, tubes going in. A sick-berth attendant sat at a table, head bent over a book. Another needle. He slept, wakened. Daylight, another SBA, reading a newspaper, pale green paint, bars on the window.

'Today's Thursday. The operation was on Monday.' He set his teeth against the pain, turned his face to the wall.

Time passed. He lay in bed and let the SBAs deal with him. *Couldn't even manage that* . . . One of them shaved him, carefully but a little clumsily, then spoon-fed him chicken soup and tried to make conversation. Pills appeared and someone tried to persuade him to swallow them. 'It's just a painkiller, sir.' But that didn't matter, pain was something he knew, something he understood. A doctor came, spoke to the SBA and took the tubes out. A padre came, talked a little, sat beside him in silence for a time. The Surgeon Rear Admiral came, he pretended to be asleep. The SBAs changed over, with a rustle of newspapers and muted conversation. 'Any problems?' 'Not a squeak.' So this was it. He was to be deprived of anything with which he might injure himself again, watched, guarded, locked away.

Lunch came. The SBA tried to persuade him to

eat it, and then from time to time tried to start a conversation, but it was all one-sided. He had fair hair and a cheerful smile.

Some time in the late afternoon the door opened again, a voice told the SBA to wait outside.

'I'm under orders to stay until relieved, sir.'

'Wait outside.'

'Aye aye, sir.'

'I'll call you when I need you.' The man went out. 'Hello, sir.'

Thurston turned his head and opened his eyes, in a mixture of shame, relief and astonishment. 'Hello, Doc. Aren't you supposed to be in Cairo?'

'Came back early. There's not much to do in Cairo these days except fornicate, and even then there are limits to endurance. It's a good thing I did come back. You seem to have caused an A1 flap around here. There's a nice little investigation going on as to how you were left with a cut-throat razor, of all things, and both Reggie Beecham and the Surgeon Rear Admiral are doing their best to clear their respective yardarms.' He glanced at the plastered arm. 'Dear me, you've made quite a job of that.'

'Damn you.' His eyelids began to prickle, he buried his face in the pillow and then to his horror and shame he was crying again, in great tearing sobs. He felt Savage's hand on his shoulder, stiffened. 'Leave me alone, damn you.'

Savage sat down on the bed with a creaking of springs. 'Good, that's exactly what I wanted. About time, too. Go on now, get it out of your system.'

'I haven't blubbed since prep school. I don't know what's happening to me!'

Savage pushed a handkerchief into his free hand, called out to the SBA to bring two cups of tea. 'Now suppose you sit yourself up and tell me about it.'

He swore at Savage, the words half stifled in the pillow.

'Come on, you've hit rock-bottom and the only way out is up.' Savage's hands manoeuvred him, a fresh jolt of pain as something pulled on his arm. 'You've got to let it out some time.'

He hesitated, choked and blew his nose.

'In your own time.'

He hesitated again, for a long moment, then the words started to come, jerkily, disjointedly, the whole foul story; how he should have gone down with *Connaught* and had not, the long days and nights on the raft and the men, his men, who had died all around him, that he had killed five hundred of his own men and God alone knew how many more who were, through no fault of their own, the enemies of his country, that he had failed his men, failed in his duty, that he was an utter disgrace to his service and his uniform.

'I peed myself . . . blue funk all through . . . I don't know how long it was before they got me out.' He tapped the scar on his forehead. 'That's where I got this . . . And all the time York was looking at me . . . Dead, but staring at me . . . I don't know why . . . The rest all in bits and I was hardly touched.'

Savage stubbed out his cigarette, selected another. 'Drink that tea before it gets cold.'

'You sound just like Spencer.'

'Keep going, you're doing fine.'

'Then the Sub found out . . . that I couldn't take turrets any more . . . I don't know . . . I'd just shake . . . Couldn't breathe . . . just wanted to get out . . . no damn use . . . And I knew it was stupid . . . that it had happened before and would never happen again . . . but it was always like that.'

He took a pull at the tea, set the cup down on the locker top, blew his nose again.

'And whatever I did they kept on dying . . . just went quiet and that was that . . . And don't you see, Doc, if I'd been . . . doing my job properly . . . instead

241

of having a kip below . . . I'm not going to make excuses . . . All those chaps . . . just going quiet, no fuss . . . Why them, and not me?'

Savage interjected, probing at the raw wound. 'How did you get away from the ship?'

'I was blown to the surface . . . when the boilers burst, I think . . . I remember thinking that the books had got it all wrong . . . that drowning hurts like hell . . .'

'That wasn't drowning as such,' Savage said objectively. 'Your lungs were being crushed.'

Savage listened as he rambled and blubbered on through it. Jutland, Hank's leg, Dauncey, coming round again and again to the sinking. A torrent of words and dammed-up tears, the pain in his arm and pain inside.

'All right, that's enough for today,' Savage said eventually. 'You're still pretty shocked. This is going to take time. You didn't get into this state in five minutes and it'll take you more than five minutes to get out of it. But we've made a start. You've finally realised you need a bit of help with this and you're talking. Pity it took something like this to get things moving. That arm will be all right. Some of the tendons are cut through, that's why you've got that plaster on. Gives them a chance to heal, in the same way as a broken bone.'

Thurston had vaguely assumed it was there to stop him from getting at the stitches. Savage produced some pills from his pocket. 'Take these and get some sleep. I'll be back tomorrow . . . Being the difficult patient again? Do I have to fetch the Surgeon Rear Admiral to give you an order?'

Savage left, the SBA came in.

'What's your name?'

'Medley, sir. The next thing people usually ask is what I'm doing here.'

'Why is that?'

'I'm a Quaker, sir. They all expect me to be a Bible-punching conscientious objector, and tend to be a bit surprised because I'm not.'

The pills were starting to work. He was drifting off again, the pain ebbing. He turned on to his side, burrowed deeper into the blankets. Medley turned the main light off.

It might have been shock, or the lingering effects of a general anaesthetic, but for the first time in several weeks he slept the night through, without dreaming, then found himself coming half-awake the following morning and thinking of his wife. Waking up at home with Kate still asleep behind him, the desire which was only partly lust, leading on to slow early-morning love to make up for all the mornings when he was at sea. There was a small pink birthmark on one of her breasts, below the nipple; was it on the right or the left? He shifted slightly, bent his knees, his eyes still shut, unwilling to lose the mood yet. Kate. He ran his hand across her stomach, the warm smooth surface of her thighs. Her head was on his chest, hand caressing the nape of his neck. *Kate, I love you.* But there was only the coldness of stiff linen sheets. Kate. Oh God, why couldn't she be here now? He wanted her with him, to be held and comforted and kissed, to lay his head on those superb breasts of hers. And full wakefulness, and shame, bars on the window, the sick-berth attendant reading a book – Parry, the Welshman – and the pain which had brought him awake. He got up to go to the heads, Parry escorting him. 'Sorry, sir. I have to come with you.' Someone brought the newspaper and an assortment of magazines.

Savage arrived soon after breakfast. 'Feel better now you've got that lot off your chest? Good, you see it does help. Spencer sends his regards, by the way, and apologises for not coming in person, but he's on fourteen days' 10A.'

'What was it this time?'

'Took on two Argylls in an out-of-bounds brothel. He never learns, does he?'

Thurston raised a smile, the first in a long time, it seemed.

'Now let's get down to business. I've had a word with the people here and they're going to take you in hand. They've developed a system for dealing with this sort of problem. There's a chap called Campbell here; he'll be coming in for a chat later on. He's made a speciality of this sort of thing, whereas I'm just a GP who dabbles in it. I imagine they'll let you up tomorrow and move you on to the main ward. And don't look so shocked! You've got to appreciate that you're not the first commanding officer, or even the first post captain, to have a crack-up, and it's most unlikely that you'll be the last. Like you, they've simply been pushed too far.'

He thought of Morgan and his blank unseeing eyes. Savage patted his good arm. He wondered why on earth everybody was being so decent to him.

Time passed. The mail arrived, a letter from his father. *My dear Robert* . . . Bars at the window, the door locked from outside, a metal cage around the light bulb, everything which could be made into a noose or broken into sharp edges taken away, the SBA to watch any move he made.

'Do you play chess, sir?'

'A bit.'

They had two games. He suspected Medley let him win.

The nerve expert arrived before lunch.

'Captain Thurston? My name's John Campbell. I'm the trick cyclist here. Feeling a bit more human? Good, you'll be up tomorrow. No sense in keeping you in bed when you don't need to be.'

Campbell had spectacles and rather wavy fair hair. He looked a few years younger than Thurston. The straight rings were unexpected.

'I'm a dugout. I did ten years in the Navy before the war, then resigned because I got interested in psychiatry and there were no openings in the service at the time. Surprised? No goatee beard and Viennese accent?

'You seem to have had a bad time recently. Can you tell me something about it?'

He could get all that from Savage. 'No, I'd rather hear it from you personally.'

Thurston told him about the tow, baldly, aware that it was still too close.

'And before that? You obviously haven't been yourself for quite a while.'

'No.'

'Do you dream a lot?'

'Yes.' He could get all this from Savage.

'Bad dreams?'

'Yes.'

What else? Stomach pains? Headaches? Bad temper for no reason? Drinking? – not that much. But more than usual? – More than usual. Did he think it was affecting his efficiency? He told him about the steering jam. And how long had this been going on? Months, now; it had started insidiously, and gradually got worse. Did he think there was anything in particular which had set it off? No, he couldn't think of anything obvious, but things had been worse after the steering jam. Campbell looked up from his notes. 'Have you had anything like this before?'

There was the bad time after Jutland, home at Langdon on survivors' leave. One night he had been driven by the dream to walking the landing, up and down, up and down. A testy 'Robert, is that you?' from his father's room. 'Yes, Father' – they were expected to say 'Yes, Father' and 'No, Father', he and George and Edmund. 'Are you ill?' 'No, Father.' 'Then go back to bed before you waken the entire household.' He turned away and instead went down the stairs and into the garden, his bare toes sloshing through the grass, soaked now with dew, then gone to the field gate and whistled to Rocket and rubbed his nose, and gone back inside, dressed and taken him for a gallop, full pelt across the high moorland in the dark, Rocket's sweating sides between his thighs, the rough ground flying by beneath. His father had taken him aside the next morning and asked him if there was anything the matter; he had looked him in the eye and told him he was all right, that he was going to spend the rest of his leave with Hank and would his father have his sea chest sent on to *Oudenarde*.

Campbell was watching him. 'Yes.'

'When?'

'After Jutland . . . I got blown up and my ship sank.' Why don't you leave me alone? I've been through this lot with Savage.

'How long did it last?'

'I pulled myself together after I joined my next ship.' Campbell did not look satisfied.

'Did you confide in anyone?'

'No.'

'Why not?'

Because there wasn't anybody. George and Edmund were in France and Alice was a VAD. George was killed a couple of months later; at any rate he was posted missing and never heard of again. Nineteen and two weeks. 'See you in Berlin, Admiral.' His grandfather? His stepmother? His father? 'It just seemed like letting the side down.'

Oh God, he was going to start blubbering again. He was reminded once more of his father. He was nine and had come off and broken his collar bone. 'Don't you dare blubber, boy. I'll not have it.' And he had got back on and ridden home and the old man had been proud of him for not making a noise while Dr Harrison set it.

Campbell went on, asking a series of questions which

seemed to bear little relation to one another. 'What about your parents?' He came out with the usual answers, that his father had been in the Indian Army and resigned his commission to go into the Church, that his mother had died when he was six and his father had later remarried. Had his mother breast-fed him? He had no idea.

'How many women have you slept with?'

'About eight.' Five or six, between Kate and Mrs Bennett.

'That's not many for a man your age'

'I'm not a pansy if that's what you mean!'

'Just wanted to see how you would react. We'll leave it there for today. You've taken the first step and in some ways that's the most difficult part, and now you've got to try to look at things objectively. At the moment your perception of reality has got a bit distorted. You see yourself and everything you do or have ever done in the worst possible light. You're hung up with guilt, which is part of the syndrome, but torturing yourself with guilt won't bring any of them back. You might get some sort of backhanded satisfaction from making yourself suffer, but it won't do you or anyone else the slightest bit of good, especially since it damn nearly killed you. And you've got to get used to the idea that you're a human being with all the usual emotions, and there's nothing wrong with expressing them at the appropriate times. Sounds strange after all that training. Big Boys Don't Cry, and all the rest.' Campbell smiled. 'Are you more confused than ever now?'

Spencer came in the afternoon, unexpectedly, lugging a kitbag.

'I thought you were on fourteen days' 10A.'

'I'm 'ere on duty, sir. Got some of your things with me.' Red badges. Of course. 'I 'ad to talk my way in, sir. 'Ad to flutter me eyelashes at some of them nurses.'

He demonstrated, then turned to Medley. ''Ope you're lookin' after my boss properly.'

Medley grinned. 'I'll be outside, sir.'

The key turned in the lock. The watching had become a little less obtrusive. Medley had let him go to the heads by himself earlier – 'But if you're not back in three minutes, sir, I'm coming after you' – and had once gone out to boil a kettle, locking the door behind him, of course. Progress, yet only a fortnight ago he had been responsible for five hundred men and one and a half million pounds' worth of ship. The thought made him feel gloomy again, and he tried to distract himself.

'How was Cairo, Spencer?'

'All right. Funny bein' away from the ship. Usual sort of leave really, goin' round the bars. Not your style, sir. 'Ad a bit of a dust-up, expect you 'eard about it. Me and Dusty Rhodes – you know 'im – went off to this cat house, lookin' for a bit of skirt.' Spencer grinned lewdly. 'There were these two Pongoes in there – Jocks, Argylls they were – chuckin' their weight about like they was Rommel himself, and one of them starts sayin' the Navy 'as it soft. So what can Dusty and me do? We was just gettin' properly stuck in when in comes the Monkeys – Military Police – arrested me, Dusty, the Jocks and every bloke in the place. Turned out they was lookin' for Pongo deserters,' he said disgustedly. 'So me and Dusty get packed off back 'ere under escort, fourteen days' 10A and that's us. Lucky really, with you it would've been fourteen days' cells!'

'You won't get your hook back at this rate.'

'No, sir. Three badge AB, me, the aristocracy of the Andrew.'

Spencer went on in his usual fashion, rolling cigarettes and smoking them one after another. It sounded like a fairly riotous leave.

'Remember Hooky Sanderson, in *Connaught*, sir?'

'Leading signalman with the big nose?'

'Listen to 'oo's talkin', sir. Ran into 'im in Cairo – 'e's in a shore job in Port Said now, real cushy. 'E sends 'is regards and said to say that 'e wouldn't be 'ere now if it wasn't for you. Kept sayin' that every time 'e started driftin' off towards the pearly gates you kicked 'im and made 'im do *Eskimo Nell*. Never thought it of you, sir!'

It was good to see Spencer again, surprisingly so, stretching his blue jumper to bursting point in places, showing the yellowing remains of a black eye. 'Ah, it was a good leave, sir. 'Ave to get back now. Got to do my stint.'

'Work some of that beer gut off you.' Another half-hour and Spencer would be doubling round a parade ground with a rifle over his head and twenty-five pounds of sand on his back.

'Only thing that keeps me fit, sir, pack drill. I'll take your dhobi back with me. Don't think I can do much with that shirt you was wearing. 'Ave to do for polishing rags.' He picked up Thurston's shoes from the floor and cast a professional eye over them. 'Take these as well. Just starting to crack so I'll paraffin them an' start again. I brought you another pair in there. Is there anything I can get you?'

He had to think for a moment. 'Some toothpaste, if you can get it.'

''Course, sir.'

For a moment Thurston thought he was going to break down again.

'I'm really sorry about this, sir.' Spencer said awkwardly. His face reddened slightly as he picked up his cap and left.

# — Chapter Twenty-Two —

The face that stared back out of the shaving mirror had changed, all bones and angles now, the ruddy patches over the cheekbones disappeared, the nose more prominent than ever. His hair had grown too long, starting to sprout over the tops of his ears. Have to get something done about it. Parry was standing next to him – get on with it. The razor was in his hand, shearing into the lather on his cheek. Let it go a bit lower, when he was doing under the chin, half an inch in the right place. But Parry was there, visible in the mirror. He glanced down at his arm, the smooth off-white plaster which covered the wound. Both arteries and sundry nerves and tendons. Had he really done that? 'Three or four weeks in plaster. The ligatures'll just dissolve.' Parry was dispassionate, avoiding the real issue. He flexed the fingers, feeling the familiar shock of pain. Parry was a quiet, rather earnest Welsh boy; the accent was unsettling, putting him in mind of Morgan and Richards. Not much education, he had been working as a clerk in the Co-op in Abergavenny before he was called up. Medley had spent a year reading English at Cambridge; they had played another game of chess and talked books for a time yesterday before Medley went off duty.

After breakfast, down to the ward. It felt strange again to be in uniform, walking along the corridors, carrying his cap awkwardly in his left hand, Medley walking ahead with his kitbag. The four rings were an embarrassment; at least the red ribbon was hidden by the sling.

'You'll find it all a bit different here, sir. Only two rules. No booze and you make your own bed. It's all very informal. This is where you sleep.'

The room was similar to the one he had come from, except there were no bars on the window. 'If you'll follow me, sir.'

An assortment of chairs, a wireless set tinnily playing dance music, newspapers, a billiards table, men in various combinations of uniform and civilian clothes. 'Keep going, sir,' hissed Medley. He walked on, his shoes sounding unnaturally loud. His legs still felt shaky, his arm ached, he was hyperconscious of the sling and plaster. The sense of apartness, like the seconds of walking to the vaulting horse for a beating, stripped to the waist, the Sub rapping the cane on his palm.

'Another one for the nuthouse!' He tried to work out who the speaker was. The voice changed, he continued in sepulchral tones. 'This is the domain of Sigmund Campbell, the King of Combat Fatigue. Abandon rank all ye who enter here . . .' The voice came from a lieutenant-commander with a DSO and a continuous head-jerking twitch. 'Speak, stranger . . . What do you call yourself?'

They were all looking at him; even the noise from the wireless was far away.

'It's all very informal, sir.' 'Abandon rank all ye who enter here.' He swallowed hard. 'Bob,' he said at last, almost inaudibly.

'They call me Twitch. You can see why.' The man went into a particularly violent succession of twitches. 'Nineteen hours depth-charging on my last patrol. Haven't stopped twitching since. Sit yourself down, Bob.' He sat. Twitch made introductions. '. . . He was Number One of a destroyer, till they hit a mine. The old boy over there is a convoy commodore, Rear Admiral, Retired List. What happened to you?'

He said something about six days on tow.

'I heard about that.' Twitch looked at the sling. 'Razor was it? The revolvers and ropes don't usually get this far.'

Twitch went on. The ranks and ages seemed to range from the Commodore, who was about sixty, to a nineteen-year-old midshipman observer of the Fleet Air Arm. The destroyer Number One was trying to make himself understood through an impenetrable stammer, someone else staring ahead with vacant eyes. Unseeing eyes.

*Morgan.*

'. . . You should have seen Eddie when he first came in. He was absolutely rigid. He'd got into his bunk and just stayed there for two days. This isn't a bad place to land up in. An hour's chat with Sigmund every day and a spot of rug-making to keep us occupied. They let us have the prettiest sisters, and you can get ashore for a drink if you're a good boy and toe the line. Tell Sigmund that your mother didn't love you, or something. He's not a bad bloke, but sometimes I think he's the biggest head case here. He told the Commodore last week that he had repressed homosexual tendencies – wasn't that it, Commodore? The poor old Commodore was absolutely livid, told Sigmund in no uncertain terms that he'd been married thirty years and had five children, and stormed out looking as though he was about to have apoplexy! And he's got this great idea that we can all help each other. He gets everybody to give a lecture to the rest every day. Ten minutes on any non-service subject. That's all very well, but I've run out of subjects and poor old Jim takes so long to get anything out. Otherwise, it's really not too bad.'

The Commodore looked up from his book. 'Is anybody listening to that bloody racket?' He turned the wireless off, to howls of protest from someone, then stalked away.

'It's all a bit experimental, but the principles are sound enough,' Savage said later that morning. 'It's all geared to getting you back on your feet and back to some kind of duty as soon as possible.'

Some kind of duty. Not much left for him now. Why had they bothered to revive him? He drifted about, aware of the SBA's eyes constantly upon him, one of them following him wherever he went, struggled for a time with *The Times* crossword, exchanged a few words with Twitch.

'Sit down. Smoke if you want to.'

'I don't.'

'How are you today?'

'I'm going to discharge myself,' he said with as much dignity as he could muster. Had he really meant that? He didn't know.

'Why?' Campbell looked at him quizzically over his spectacles.

'Because I'm sick of this bloody place.'

'Already? you've hardly been here five minutes.'

'This whole bloody hospital.' He swallowed hard. 'And being followed around as though I was the latest exhibit at the zoo!'

'Really? And I suppose you think this place isn't doing you any good?'

He nodded.

'Well, you've hardly given it a chance. And if you discharge yourself, where would you go? Your ship is under major repairs, to begin with, and really you're in no fit state to go anywhere. I need hardly remind you that you damn nearly bled to death only a couple of days ago.'

Oh God, he was going to start blubbering again. 'Damn you,' he said fiercely, screwed his eyes shut for a second. *You're not going to give the bastard the satisfaction.*

'Now you're getting angry with me. That's an improvement on a few days ago when you weren't talking to anyone.'

Oh God, this was unnerving.

'It seems a pity to go back to square one, especially when you were doing quite well.' Campbell continued in measured tones. 'In your present state you're clearly a danger to yourself, but I'd prefer not to keep you here against your will, as I have the power to do. I'm not going to stop you from discharging yourself, but if you do, I'll guarantee you'll be knocking on this door again by tomorrow.'

He swallowed again.

'Now listen to me for a moment. You want to get back to sea, don't you?'

'Of course.'

'No "of course" about it, but I'll accept that for the time being. Later on we might go into that. Their Lordships have invested a fair amount of time and trouble in training you, and it seems that you're pretty good at the job.'

'I couldn't even bloody well kill myself!'

'On the contrary,' Campbell continued in even tones, 'it's entirely because Sister Clark found you when she did that you didn't succeed. That and blood transfusions. I hope that makes you feel better. As I was saying, you seem to be pretty good at the job, whatever your abilities as a suicide. Don't you think it would be a waste if you let yourself be shunted off to the sidelines just because you were too proud to accept a bit of help?'

Thurston was studying the pattern on the carpet, the colours swirling and merging, then pulling apart.

'It seems to me that you don't have much choice, but I'm going to give you the choice. I expect that left to yourself you'd sort yourself out eventually, but it would be a matter of months or even years, and I'd rate your chances of getting back to sea pretty low. The aim here is to speed up the process. *We* don't wave a magic wand. I can talk at you until I'm blue in the face, but ultimately it's got to come from inside. *You* do the work. Don't you think that a fellow who's survived four days on a Carley float in midwinter is tough enough to beat a bit of combat fatigue?'

Campbell placed his fingertips together, just like Savage, and sat back in his chair, waiting for an answer.

Thurston stared at a patch of carpet in one corner; green and brown swirls merging, pulling apart, making his eyes ache. Perhaps Campbell had a point; he didn't feel too good. The last person who had given him a choice like this was Beecham; it seemed like a hundred years ago. He was being pulled in every direction; one way the black pit still yawned beneath him, into which he had fallen earlier, on another course was something he didn't understand. If he understood anything any more . . . *You've hit rock-bottom and the only way out is up.*

'All right,' he found himself saying. ('I'll carry on, sir.')

'Good. Give it a fair trial anyway. Now there's nothing very special or peculiar about this place. We're not going to blame all your present troubles on an unresolved Oedipus Complex or your being taken from the breast too early. You'll find I approach things a bit differently from Jim Savage, but it's the same end that's in view. You've got to try to see things in perspective, and since there's a war on and we haven't the time for full-scale psychoanalysis, which you don't need anyway, we have to take some short cuts. But you won't be here any longer than is absolutely necessary, and what happens afterwards is between you and Their Lordships.

'There's nothing particularly odd, unusual or disgraceful about combat fatigue. All those other chaps outside have got some manifestation of it, the precise nature varies with the individual. At the moment you've been completely thrown, you don't know what the hell has happened to the intelligent rational self-sufficient fellow you're supposed to be. Those other chaps are just the same. You all need to find yourselves again, sort out your own particular problems. You do the job, we just help you along. Are you prepared to give it a go?'

There was less hesitation this time.

'Come back tomorrow at ten. That'll be your regular time from now on. Did Twitch put on his usual welcoming act?'

'That business? He did.'

'Bit unnerving, isn't it? He does that with everyone. There's a very good reason for putting you all in together, or rather, several related reasons. Firstly, you all come here thinking that only you has ever got the twitch, gone doolally tap, flak-happy or whatever the current idiom is, and seeing other chaps with the same trouble might actually convince you that this isn't the case. Secondly, you all need to get used to other people again, and this is especially true of a ship's captain. Obviously you're quite aware that in command you tend to get very isolated, and the bigger the ship, the worse it is. Finally, you can each help the others, both directly and indirectly. You're none of you cowards or inadequates and you all have the highest motivation to get out of here and back to duty. Any questions?'

Thurston hesitated. 'How long is this watching going on?'

'I thought that's what you'd say. Well, that depends on you. Will you give me your word that if you feel like killing yourself again you'll tell someone?'

'All right.'

'Will you give me your word?'

'I give you my word.'

'All right. Anything at all, just tell someone, one of the SBAs or any of the other chaps. Tomorrow at ten; and could you ask Frank Gillam to come in next.' Frank Gillam turned out to be a Fleet Air Arm lieutenant with burn marks round his eyes and a tic almost as bad as Twitch's.

That night the dream came again; it was back to the corridor, up and down, up and down. He wondered drearily how much mileage he had put in since the dream started. The night sister poked her head out, then went back to her table. After a time he heard footsteps, matching his own. One of the SBAs, come to watch him, to chase him back to bed and make sure he didn't try anything. In a moment he would approach, the usual 'What are you doing out of bed, sir?'

But it was the Commodore, similarly clad in pyjamas and unbuttoned greatcoat, head down, hands deep in the pockets, treading the same length of dimly lit corridor. Up and down, up and down, cold striking up through his bare soles – that would be another thing for the SBA to create about – pain nagging at his wrist, pain of a different quality in the older wound in his shoulder – not being able to use that arm was making it stiffen. Forty-four paces, turn on the left foot, forty-four paces, turn, seeking the numbness of exhaustion, the Commodore passing at the same point on each leg. After a time the incongruity made him smile, he about-turned, found himself falling in alongside, adjusting his stride to match. Up and down, up and down.

The Commodore spoke suddenly. 'What's yours?'
'Jutland.'
'Sinking.' Hesitation, then he expanded. 'Forty children on board being evacuated to Canada. I just keep on hearing them.'

'There you are,' Campbell said the next morning. 'It's

257

not just you. And I expect the Commodore is feeling surprised that this seems to happen to virile young captains as well.'

Campbell was different from Savage, more detached, more cerebral. Where Savage went for the gut, Campbell circled about, raising apparent irrelevancies, then darted in with a disconcerting thrust to the core.

'Let's start at the beginning. Where were you born?'

Osborne and Dartmouth? – yes. Was he married? – Yes. For how long? – seventeen years. Any children? – two. How old? – sixteen and fifteen. 'Quick work!' Any serious illnesses in childhood? – no. Anything since? – only malaria.

'Tell me about your parents.'

Where did he start? The Reverend Henry Maitland Thurston DSO, lately Major H. M. Thurston DSO, The Guides Cavalry. Mary Alice Thurston, third daughter of Sir Charles Crozier, tenth Baronet, of County Roscommon, died 16 July 1906.

Campbell was prodding. 'What sort of man was your father?'

'Is. He's still alive.' What could he say? How could he describe his father? That at the age of eighty-three he still hunted two days a week, though he complained he could no longer mount without a mounting block, that he read Homer in the original Greek, and believed in beginning his day with ten minutes of breathing exercises in front of an open window, followed by a cold bath. Did that convey the essence of the man? And his mother? 'All I can remember is that she could sit on her hair and was always ill.'

Campbell noted his struggles. 'How did you get on with your stepmother?'

'All right.'

'I'll rephrase that. How did you feel when your father remarried?'

'Surprised.'

'Shocked?'

'Surprised,' he said firmly.

'Why?'

'Well, it just came out of the blue to start with. I had a letter from him at Osborne to say that he and Mrs Forsythe were getting married during Easter leave.'

'Had he known her long?'

'He knew her from India. Her first husband was in the same regiment. She used to come and stay for the hunting. We all thought it was a bit of a joke, that he was only interested in her seat on a horse!'

'Why were you surprised?'

'Well, he was old, or at any rate he seemed old. He was over fifty, and she wasn't much younger. It just seemed a bit ridiculous.' More boldly. 'If you knew my father you'd know what I mean.'

Campbell laughed. 'How old were you?'

'Thirteen.'

'Ridiculous, and to a thirteen-year-old, probably indecent as well. Were there any more children?'

'No. My stepmother hadn't any from her first husband either.'

He sat facing Campbell, with his four rings and red ribbon, sunlight outside. Campbell made notes on large sheets of paper. He wondered what they were.

'What's all this got to do with me now, anyway?'

Campbell took a moment to marshal his thoughts. 'You need to understand yourself, to come to terms with the facets of your character which up to now you've considered unacceptable and tried to blot out. Otherwise, in a year or two when you're back at sea and come up against the same sorts of stress, this will happen again and there may not be anyone around to pick up the bits. We're all a product of our backgrounds, parentage, education, upbringing and everything else, even the ways in which we rebel against it. Today's session is simply taking a history, going over what's happened to you up to now, the factors which have influenced you. Your stepmother may seem irrelevant, but she must have had some influence on you, even only indirectly. Let's come up to date for a moment. What would you do if one of your officers came to you and said he couldn't go on?'

'It would depend who it was,' Thurston said after a pause.

'But would you take him seriously?'

'Yes . . . if he was any good.'

'Let us say . . . your First Lieutenant?'

'ffrench? He'd never.'

'Hypothetically.'

He had the feeling that Campbell was enjoying himself. 'Well, I'd send him on leave and I'd be sorry to lose him.'

'Anything else?'

'I'd be surprised.'

'Why?'

'He's not the type.'

'In other words he's not soft. Would you hold it against him?'

Another pause. 'No . . . because he's a good fellow and he'd have to have a good reason to do anything like that.'

'You would send him on leave, you'd be surprised, and you'd be sorry to lose him. Well,' Campbell was grinning broadly now, 'hasn't it occurred to you that people might be saying exactly the same thing about you?'

Thurston went to the library and looked Campbell up in the Medical Directory and the Navy List. Spencer came in the afternoon, ostensibly to pick up his washing.

'Well, sir. I got orders to cheer you up. From the PMO. But that don't make no difference . . . Gawd, sir, you look a mess, and you that's always telling the lads to get their hair cut. Hey, Doc,' he shouted at the SBA, 'give us a lend of your scissors.'

Parry grinned. 'If you hang on a moment, I know where there are some clippers.'

Without further ado, Spencer had sat him down, draped a towel round his neck and was snipping away at his head, 'Keep your nut still, sir, unless you want to finish up with no lugs.'

Spencer didn't change. He treated him in exactly the same way, even when he was flat on his back after *Seydlitz* with Spencer doing everything for him. Spencer was irrepressible; he would fall into a midden and come out still grinning. He would have been just the same with that German colonel, they had picked up in Force K days. 'Better get those wet things off you, sir, before you catch your death. Got you some of the Captain's things. Be a bit big for you, sir, but you and the Old Man is different shapes. Cuppa tea, sir? Now drink it while it's 'ot.'

'Nice to see you smilin', sir. Shift yer 'ead a bit to port. You looked proper rough a couple of days ago.' Spencer went on in his inconsequential way, shearing at the bristly nape of his neck. 'Not much news, sir; most of the lads are still on leave. Bit more off the top? Yeah, you was startin' to look a bit shaggy. Mind,' he said conspiratorially, 'I did 'ear that Mr ffrench 'as been goin' round with a young lady from Gezira. Very fetchin', they say.'

'Spencer!'

'Sorry, sir. Only tellin' you what I 'eard. There, that's a bit more like it.' Spencer removed the towel with a professional flourish, found a mirror and handed it over. 'Could take this up once this lot's over.'

He was sitting outside, a couple of days later, rereading *The Adventures of Brigadier Gerard*, culled from the hospital library, or rather, trying to, when a shadow fell across him.

'Hello, Bob, what's that you're reading?' He looked up, then jumped up.

'Sit down, for heaven's sake. You're supposed to be sick,' Beecham said heartily.

'Not that sick, sir.'

'Are you up to taking a turn around the place?'

'Nothing wrong with my legs.'

Beecham's good humour seemed to evaporate. 'I don't know what I'm supposed to say to you.' His eyes strayed to the sling, and then away. 'I came earlier, but they wouldn't let me see you, and I'm under orders not to upset you . . . I expected to find you in bed today . . . I'm sorry, Bob, I had no idea how bad things were.' His eyes strayed again. 'How's that arm?' he said at last.

'Coming on.' Avoiding the issue, that he had tried to kill himself and failed. Beecham was being decent, everybody was for some reason, but the fact remained. He moved the fingers as far as they would go, the usual pain.

Beecham skirted a flower bed. 'I should have known. You wouldn't have come to me otherwise. Dammit, I should have sent you straight home and hang Stonehenge!'

Thurston heard himself saying, 'That's all right. I don't think I twigged either.'

Beecham stopped, turned towards him. 'Thank you, but I shouldn't have let you carry on. I didn't give you much choice, did I? You did bloody well, but I shouldn't have made you . . . I've been talking to the CinC . . . That's not true, the CinC has had words with me. Get yourself fit, and there'll be something for you. He'll make sure of that . . . You did damn well . . . I shouldn't tell you, but you're in for another DSO. Not just for Stonehenge, but after that I'd say you're almost certain to get it. Of course, I shouldn't tell you.'

He said the appropriate things, shook Beecham's proffered hand. The Admiral looked tired; he seemed to have aged since he last saw him, bowed, greyer-faced. *Get yourself fit, and there'll be something for you.* But did he really deserve anything after this?

Another bad night, the dream, then up and down the corridor, forty-four paces and back the other way. He felt worse than at any time since arriving on the ward. Finished, whatever Beecham said when he was trying to be kind. Turn, step off again, his arm aching savagely. If he had done it at all he should have made a proper job of it.

'Excuse me, sir. I've just put a brew on.' A head appeared from the duty room.

Uncertainty, as always these days. 'All right. Thank you, Medley.'

'I thought you might have had enough of the Lady Macbeth routine.'

He accepted the proffered mug of tea, helped himself to milk and sugar. A book lay opened on the table; he wondered what it was.

'*The Warden*, sir. Have you read it?'

'Yes, but not recently.'

'I like the way everyone in Trollope gets so steamed-up over things that are completely trivial. It's very refreshing these days.' Medley poured himself a mugful and sat down. 'I always bring a book when I'm on nights. It can be pretty quiet.'

'I'm not disturbing you, am I?'

'No, sir. It gets a bit boring, and it's what I'm here for. Most of the officers come in here sooner or later.'

Thurston was warming his hands against the mug, looking around the room. Orders, timetables, a couple of filing cabinets, an electric kettle on one of the shelves, a framed photograph of *Warspite*, the former Fleet flagship. Medley indicated the book.

'I'm going back to Cambridge when this lot's over, so I try to keep my hand in. They know me very well at the Garrison Library. They don't always have the books I want, that's the problem, but my parents send stuff out.'

He found himself telling Medley about a commission he had done in the East Indies as a lieutenant, when long periods on passage had alternated with heat-enervated, drink-sodden spells in harbour. 'I could see myself ending up like something out of Somerset Maugham unless I did something about it.' Long afternoons off watch, lying naked on his bunk in a pool of sweat, wet towel across his stomach, the deckhead fan barely stirring the overheated air, wandering half lost through the other worlds of books.

He had wasted the time at Cambridge, like everybody else, letting off steam now that the war was over and they were free from discipline and routine for the first time in their lives. 'Just when you're finally starting to be some use, Their Lordships send you to Cambridge to read poetry!' He had done some rowing, played some rugby, bought his first motorbike and landed up in front of the magistrates for speeding, and tried to emulate his eldest brother by writing self-consciously bad verses to a young lady from Girton who took not the slightest notice of him.

'I've been meaning to ask you, sir. Are you any relation to Edmund Thurston, the poet? I got quite keen on First World War poets while I was at school and found some of his stuff in an anthology there.'

'Not *The War Babies*?'

'That was one of them.'

'He dedicated it to me, and I've never been so embarrassed in my life.' Medley looked puzzled. He explained. 'That's what the press called us, when we went to sea, or "midshipmites", which was almost as bad. Then this gooey poem of Edmund's appeared in the paper, and the Sub in *Hyperion* made me read it aloud in the gunroom one night. Took me months to live it down. Some of his later poems are a bit more realistic, once he got out there and had some of his illusions blown away.'

His spirits rising, Thurston accepted another mug of tea and listened comfortably as Medley talked about university. His experience of life had been totally different: his family were Quakers and therefore pacifists; he had been educated by Quakers and in any other circumstances there would have been no question of his going into any of the services.

'So, what are you doing in the Navy?'

'Ah, the burning question! Well, sir, I believe that Nazism is evil and should be resisted. Peaceful means have failed. This war is as much a just war as any war could be and though it should not have been necessary, I cannot condemn it as such. But I personally could not shed blood. It's a personal thing. However, I can make a contribution in a way which satisfies my faith and my conscience by doing this. I tried to get into the Friends' Ambulance Unit, but they were full at the time, the Navy wanted SBAs, and here I am. Does that satisfy you, sir?' Medley paused as a succession of yells came from down the corridor. 'That'll be Mr Gillam, I think. I'll just go and take a look.'

'It was,' Medley said when he returned a few minutes later. 'Mr Gillam can be quite entertaining. He dreams he's giving a flying lesson and it's all "left a bit, right a bit, watch your artificial horizon, don't let the nose come up." Then as far as I can see, the pupil crashes and he wakes up a bit upset. Finished your tea, sir?'

'Bit unsettling seeing your admiral, wasn't it? But if I didn't think you were ready for it yet, I'd have sent him away again. He's very concerned about you, been ringing up every day asking for news.'

'I don't know why everybody's bothering about me.' Thurston was on his feet, treading the carpet next to the window.

'For the purely practical reason that you're a highly

265

trained and experienced naval officer. It's taken the best part of thirty years to produce you, and you can't be replaced at the drop of a hat. Much less wasteful of time and resources to get you on your feet and back to duty. Even though you won't be going back to sea straight away, you're still a pretty valuable property as far as the service is concerned. You've done the staff course, haven't you?'

'Fat lot of good that is now!'

'What do you mean by that?'

*Here we go*. It was quite simple. He was hiding away in hospital when he should be out there getting on with the job he was trained to do. At sea, and meeting his responsibilities, not skulking in here.

'Not feeling so good today?' Campbell enquired when he had finished.

'Lousy.'

'And you think you're going back to square one?'

He nodded.

'That's really not the case. Remember last week when nothing and nobody could touch you? You've come a long way since then. You may be a bit down right now, but the basic course is up. It's never a continuous improvement, or hardly ever. More like a sine wave. You go up and down, but in this case the whole thing is on an incline upwards. You have a patch of the blues, but you get out of it given an appropriate stimuli. Part of the healing process is to find what works for you as an individual. You perked up when you were talking to Medley last night, for instance.'

He grunted in acknowledgement.

'Nice lad, Medley. You seem to get on with him, on a personal level, which is all to the good, and you're mixing with the other chaps.'

That was true. He was finding that he had things in common with most of them, beyond wearing the same uniform and being in the same nuthouse, especially with the Commodore, Twitch, and Frank Gillam.

'And still on the positive side, you're much less defensive with me and not kicking against the system as much, since there's less to kick against. Things are getting better, and paradoxically that makes the inevitable downs seem worse. And far from skulking in here, you could see this as making yourself ready to face your responsibilities again. If you'd broken a leg you'd hardly expect to go back to duty until it had healed. This is hardly a soft option, is it, having to strip off all that armour plate you've built up and take a long hard look at yourself, warts and all? It takes a fair amount of guts to face up to your problems and the various facets of your character, and to come to terms with them. In many ways it's much easier to do what you've been doing up to now, which is to run away from them, by bottling everything up and pretending to yourself and everyone else that they don't exist. Not surprising that you find it hard going.'

'Easier to take on the *Seydlitz* again.'

Campbell laughed and started off about his stepmother again. He found himself telling Campbell about his father's wedding, celebrated in a small church in Gloucestershire. Edmund was best man, and Mrs Forsythe was insistent that they all take part, so Alice had something to do, and he and George were ushers, though as it was a quiet wedding there weren't many guests to usher.

'That's interesting. Keep going.' Campbell was scraping at the edges again, the core of the thing was still intact, untouched. *Get yourself fit and there'll be something for you.* Beecham knew, and yet he was assuring him that all was not over. But was he speaking the truth, or just trying to cheer up the patient? *Get yourself fit*, get out of here and back to duty, whatever duty they were prepared to give him.

Campbell had moved on, made one of his stabs to the core. 'Tell me about your mother.'

'I've told you before; I can't remember her.'

'The fact that you can't remember her, or profess not to remember, is in itself highly significant, and something I would certainly go into in my peacetime practice.' He prodded. 'What can you remember about her?'

'Only that she was always ill . . . Being told to keep quiet, that sort of thing . . . I couldn't tell you what she looked like except from photographs . . . I just don't remember seeing her much.'

'What do you suppose was wrong with her?'

'I don't know . . . Women's trouble? . . . She had four children in five years, and I remember hearing somewhere – I couldn't tell you where – that she nearly died when she had me. I don't know how true that is . . . She used to stay in bed for days on end. I'm surprised the old man let her.'

Campbell pounced. 'What do you mean by that?'

Awkward question. 'He never let us lie in bed for no reason, and he never did himself. As soon as you were over the worst it was outside and plenty of fresh air. Didn't do me any harm.'

'You say "for no reason". What do you mean?'

'Just that you had to be pretty sick. He did practise what he preached. He put his shoulder out hunting once, just told my brother Edmund how to shove it back in, sent me to catch his horse, then remounted and carried on.'

'That's definitely the kill-or-cure principle! What did your mother actually die of?'

'I don't know.'

'Sure? Why not?'

He had been too young to know at the time, and his mother had rarely been mentioned afterwards, except by the Crozier aunts, who were always referring to 'poor, dear, Mary', but they had never mentioned what she died of.

'Have you never wondered?'

'Yes . . .' He was fumbling for words, wishing that he still smoked so as to have something to do with his hands. There were some things his father would never discuss, and his mother's death was one of them.

'What do you remember about it?'

They had gone to the hills for the hot weather, and she was ill, which was hardly unusual, then he was kicking a football on the verandah one afternoon and Ayah came out wailing and told him the Memsahib was dead, and his father came up from Peshawar a couple of days later, he thought, but by that time she was already buried.

'What happened to you then?'

He had gone to school in England and about the same time his father resigned his commission and been ordained. For a while the four of them had all spent the school holidays in Ireland with the Crozier aunts, now living in much reduced circumstances since Grandfather Crozier had broken his neck at the gallop in the finest hunt in living memory, leaving his baronetcy (created 1690, an ancestor had brought his regiment over to William of Orange at a critical point of the Battle of the Boyne, as the aunts were fond of telling), a thousand acres of mountain and bog and a pile of debts to a distant cousin. That lasted until he was about nine, when his father had got his living.

But what else could his father have done? Children whose parents were abroad went to school in England as a matter of course and were farmed out to relations in the holidays, otherwise they would get no education, they would be spoiled by the servants and pick up cheechee accents; anyway, the upheaval had only lasted a couple of years.

'All right, I'll stop you there. That's the grown man, the arch rationalist, speaking now. You've managed to rationalise what happened to you, even defend it, but it couldn't have been like that at the time. It must have been absolutely bewildering. When you were six your mother died, even now you don't know the cause, and your father sent you away. In a sense your mother abandoned you, and your father then punished you further by getting rid of you. That's how it would seem to a six-year-old. Yet you tell me there were sound practical reasons for it and claim that it didn't bother you. No doubt there were good reasons, and your father acted out of the best of motives. I expect he thought going to school would take your mind off your mother, but . . . You learned early on that if something hurts you, you shove it down and pretend it doesn't exist, put on a brave face and it's dealt with, all nice and tidy. But there comes a time when all the things which have been festering away quietly because you've never admitted, even to yourself, that they do matter, have to come out. And that, basically, is why you're here now. Inside this hard-case sailor there's a bewildered little boy who's just lost everything he knows. He'd like a bit of comfort, a bit of affection occasionally, but he's got to be a man and do without. If he breaks the rules he gets nothing, and if he happens to fall sick he's nothing more than a waste of rations. Does that sound familiar?'

'What do you mean?' he said quickly.

'Exactly what I said. Isn't that the way you treat yourself?'

Campbell put his hands together. Thurston shifted uncomfortably, waggled his toes inside his shoes. He stood up, walked to the window.

'Are you angry?'

It came out in a kind of icy calmness. 'I don't know.'

Campbell said nothing. Thurston was reminded uncomfortably of things in the past, seemingly forgotten, the utter apartness and isolation of the first days at prep school. He had hated that school, every stone of it, all through the five years he spent there, though in time the sense of apartness had lessened; being good at games and in teams brought a sense of belonging, and he knuckled down to work in time to pass into Osborne comfortably enough and to banish for once the unfavourable comparisons with Edmund, who had won the school's first Winchester scholarship, and George, who was Captain of both rugby and cricket. After that school he could take Osborne in his stride, his own man, no longer the dud younger brother who was never out of trouble.

'Are you angry?' Campbell said again.

He swung round, clenched his fist, thrust it into a side pocket. 'I've had enough of your bloody Freudian claptrap! What I think has nothing to do with you!'

'You see that this isn't a soft option,' Campbell said evenly. 'What are you angry about?'

He turned back to the window. *I hate this bloody war*. I hate this war and what the war has done to my men and what it will do to my son. I hate my father and despise my mother, and I hate and despise myself because . . . because . . .

'Could you send Jim Carpenter in, and I suggest you go and let off steam for a few minutes.'

He passed Twitch in the corridor. 'Has he decided you're a raving poofter as well? Bob, hey-hey, Bob . . .'

There was a punchbag set up in an empty storeroom. Thurston laid into it with his good hand, swearing in impotent fury, tears pouring down his face.

'Bob, are you all right?'

He stopped, the rage spent, out of breath.

'Campbell been giving you a hard time?' The Commodore pulled a hip flask out of his pocket. 'Feel like a stiffener?'

'Thanks.' He swallowed a couple of mouthfuls of the raw spirit. Brandy, and a good one. Suddenly he felt very tired, a vein hammering in his temples.

'You owe me one.' The Commodore put the flask away. 'He lulls one into a sense of false security and then goes in hard. Had me blubbering every time I saw

271

him for a couple of weeks, and insisted it was doing me good. We all feel like killing him sometimes. Something lingering with boiling oil.'

'Or spit-roast him over a slow fire.' He found his handkerchief and mopped his face, then straightened his tie and refastened his buttons. 'Thanks.'

In the afternoon he took a turn around the hospital grounds with the Commodore. It had become part of the routine, something which filled the long gaps when there was nothing organised which they were expected to do, but it was slowly becoming something more. The Commodore was twenty years his senior, had reached the top of the Captains' List in 1931 and, in accordance with the usual practice, been promoted Rear Admiral and retired the next day, to spend eight years sitting on benches and district councils and running boys' clubs, before Their Lordships had called him back. He had gone gladly enough, into a war he was really too old for, survived three years of slow convoys to and from Halifax, and even slower convoys to and from Sydney, Cape Breton. He had one son in submarines and one a sub-lieutenant in *Duke of York*; the third was still at school. He was a good person to be silent with; he was there, but did not intrude. Passing the main gate on each circuit, Thurston was tempted simply to walk through, to disappear into the anonymity of the city. He might have done, were it not for a vague sense that things had gone this far, and he had to see them through, and a glance the Commodore threw at him.

Philip Woodruffe came to see him. The conversation was kept firmly to safe subjects, music, painting, the weather. Here was another with instructions not to upset the patient. When Thurston mentioned the war, the squadron, the ship, the blow was parried and matters turned to trivialities. Woodruffe carefully avoided looking at his arm, or speaking of it. He knew, Beecham knew.

'Come on, Philip, I'm not made of glass.'

Woodruffe looked embarrassed, glanced at his watch. 'Sorry . . . Time I was going. I will say this. Reggie's gone very quiet since, and that's not at all like him.'

He sensed Woodruffe was relieved to go. They passed Twitch, who was talking to a new arrival. '. . . Poor old Bob, came steaming out as black as thunder, practically walked through me! That's Bob there, chap with the pot arm and the six-foot legs. Hello, Bob, what's that poor punchbag done to you?' To Woodruffe's obvious discomfiture, he laughed.

# — Chapter Twenty-Three —

Langdon, Northumberland, November 1917

Mortimer had read him the telegram, given him a glass of brandy, the first he had ever drunk. 'Your warrant's being made out. You should catch the nine-thirty train.' He was going to say something, but Mortimer cut him off. 'You are going on compassionate leave. You are going home and you are going to conduct yourself in a civilised manner towards that father of yours.'

At Newcastle he caught the last train to Wooler by dashing the length of the platform and over the bridge, getting the door open and jumping aboard as the train was pulling out, almost landing on top of a stout middle-aged lady. 'Really, young man. You should allow time to board in a seemly fashion.' He wondered yet again whether he should be doing this, whether the old man would condescend to have him in the house, thought of all the stubborn promises he had made himself, not to go home without an apology from his father. He could have turned aside and gone to Cambridge to spend the leave with Hank, blunted his sorrow at Edmund's death in alcohol and good company, but he had pressed on, and now there was nothing for it but to complete the journey.

It was a four-mile walk from the station and after eleven by the time he was walking up the vicarage drive. Most likely everyone would be in bed, but there was a light on in his father's study. He could still turn aside, curl up in the hayloft for the night and be gone before daylight. But he put aside the temptation, mounted the front steps, and reached for the bell-pull.

He was beginning to wonder if the light had been left on by mistake, but then the housemaid opened the door. 'Oh!' He stepped inside, put down his bag, automatically hung his cap on the hatstand and started to unbutton his greatcoat.

'Who's that, Ethel?'

She opened the study door a crack. 'It's Mr Robert, sir.'

He heard a chair scrape, the sound of shoes on carpet; his father emerged.

'How are you, my boy?'

Beyond the study door there was an oasis of yellow lamplight, contrasting with the dimness in the hall. 'Come in. Your stepmother's gone to bed. So has your grandfather. I was just going up myself. Have you eaten?' The vicar gave Ethel instructions, then when she had gone grasped him by the shoulders and steered him into the light. 'Let's have a proper look at you . . . You're looking well. Grown too.'

He was surprised to find he was looking at his father on the same level; he had grown by five inches and three stone since he had last been home, but there was the proof of it. His father seemed smaller than he remembered, and older; he had been iron-grey for as long as he could remember, but now his temples and moustache were whitened. The vicar moved to his chair, stretched one leg out on a footstool in front of him.

'I slipped on some ice coming back from the church the day before yesterday. Twisted my knee. It's nothing.'

He looked around the familiar room. There was the desk, the memory of all the times he had rested over it with his weight on his hands, fingers curled under the lip, studying the fine grain of the mahogany to distract himself from a beating. Edmund's photograph

275

turned face down, as if his father could not bear the likeness of his dead son; one of himself in *Hyperion* days; the vicar, slouch-hatted and ostrich-plumed astride a Basuto pony in South Africa. He didn't know what to say about Edmund, or whether to say anything at all. Ethel came in with a plate of cold meat, bread and cheese, and withdrew.

'How long are you here for?'

'I have ten days' leave,' he said carefully, then added, 'if you want me to stay.'

'I am very glad to see you,' the vicar said equally carefully. He picked up an envelope from the desk top. 'You had better read that. It came this morning.'

The letter was from Edmund's colonel. Lieutenant (Temporary Captain) E. C. C. Thurston MC had been hit in the stomach during a trench raid which, as adjutant, he need not have gone on, as the colonel was at pains to point out. After some delay another raiding party brought him in, but he died a few hours after in a dressing station behind the line. The colonel stressed that he had been unconscious for most of the time and would not have suffered, and went on to say that Edmund was a great loss to the battalion, and that he was most sorry to lose such a promising young man who had a great future ahead of him.

The vicar took the letter back. 'At least we know.' It was an indirect reference to George, who was still, after more than a year, listed as missing. He sensed that his father did not trust himself to say more.

Thurston finished the food, pushed the plate aside. The vicar reached for the decanter – 'You do drink this stuff?' – sloshed a couple of fingers into a glass, then poured a second. 'I am very glad to see you.'

'Could you take the mare out? This damn knee. I can't grip properly.'

Omega was his father's pride, a sixteen-hand half-thoroughbred he had bought as a green three-year-old and broken himself. He had been itching to ride her for years, but it had been pointless even to think about it, even before he fell out with the old man. The vicar walked out to the stables with him; he noticed that he was actually using the stick he had always carried; watched him tack up, lead her out, mount. Then he patted her neck, smiled and said, 'Watch her. She'll be very fresh.'

Omega, sensing a stranger on her back, bucked explosively down the drive, pranced daintily, side-stepping, in the lane beyond. He clamped his knees in, patted her with his free hand. 'Easy now, you silly girl.' He steered her into the side with his legs, 'You silly girl. Missing the old man?'

Girls. Thoughts of that night created pleasurable sensations even now. He thought he would not be thinking of such things when Edmund was dead, but the temptation, once again, was too strong.

The Grand Fleet was as celibate as any monastery, but now that *Ostorius* had transferred to the Dover Patrol it was possible to get to London on a free night, see a show and crawl around the Covent Garden pubs, or go to a party with people the Captain knew. It was one of those nights when it happened; it was still hard to believe. As people were leaving, Mortimer had called him over. 'Pilot, could you walk Mrs Bennett home.' It was an order, not a request. 'Barbara, my Sub-Lieutenant, Robert Thurston. Pilot, Mrs Bennett, an old friend of mine.'

Mrs Bennett preferred to walk, at least on a fine night. 'But slow down a bit, please, Robert. I haven't got such long legs as you. I may call you Robert?'

'Bob. Robert is what my father calls me.'

'What does your mother call you?'

'She doesn't. She's dead.'

'Oh, I'm so sorry.'

That was the usual sort of reaction. 'I can't remember her, so it doesn't matter.'

She invited him in for a few minutes, and he was sitting in her drawing room with a whisky before he had time to suggest he ought to be getting back. Mrs Bennett sat down next to him and he found himself telling her about some of the funny things which had happened in *Ostorius*.

'Is Jack really like that at sea?' She seemed to know the Captain pretty well. 'Good gracious, I've known Jack since we were children.'

It was difficult to imagine the Captain as a child; he had a momentary vision of a miniature version of the adult Lieutenant-Commander W. J. Mortimer DSC RN, complete with beard, dressed in an Eton suit, and burst out laughing.

'Does he give you a terrible time?'

Well, it was quite true that the Old Man's bark and bite were of roughly equal ferocity, and he threatened to get rid of him at least once a week, but he had lasted six months under him, which was at least twice as long as either of his predecessors.

'Oh, I promise you, he thinks a lot of you. He says you're the only Sub-Lieutenant who's ever stood up to him.'

He couldn't have been more surprised, not even when he realised that Mrs Bennett's hand had come to rest on his thigh and was starting to move in slow circles. He felt his face begin to colour.

'Come closer.' He moved, she reached up and kissed him gently on the lips. 'Put that glass down and kiss me properly.'

Her mouth opened to his, experimentally he put an arm round her. She took the other hand, moved it to her breast. He felt something harden beneath his fingers. Something inside was saying 'Go on, touch, feel,' something else holding him back. It struck him that this was the first time he could remember that he had been by himself with a woman, apart from his sister, stepmother or aunts, and they hardly counted. The internal voice was insistent. 'Go on, you might not get the chance again. You don't want to get killed before you've had a woman.' He wondered again where Mr Bennett was (or was he Commander Bennett or Major Bennett?). Mrs Bennett's tongue was stroking his lips; her hand moved upwards and inwards, settling on the bulge which was growing inside his trousers. He felt himself redden. '. . . so someone should show you the ropes.' He glanced at the hand, at the wedding and engagement rings. 'My husband was killed at Arras, in the spring.' ('Are you a virgin, Mr Thurston? . . . Soon sort that out.') He wondered whether Mortimer had done it to her, whether indeed he had put her up to this.

In her bedroom upstairs she got him out of his clothes. 'Aren't you beautiful? Like a Greek god.' The compliment surprised and embarrassed him; he wasn't weedy, but he was all arms and legs; Mortimer had christened him The Boy Sprout and claimed that he grew taller every time he turned round; 'Is it cold up there, Pilot?' The scar over his eyes had faded, but he was still self-conscious about it; so far Mrs Bennett hadn't mentioned it. 'Undress me.' The hooks and eyes were awkward; he broke a thumbnail in working down her back, but presently she was naked and alongside him in bed, and she proved a most understanding teacher as he explored the rich curves and contours of her body. She was old, thirty-one, but her body was beautiful and the last of his doubts were behind him. And for the first time in his life, a strange hand on his engorged flesh as she guided him inside. 'There, my young god, that's good, isn't it?' But it didn't last long, he was finished before he was properly started. 'It's all right. You're just a bit excited.' They talked and laughed again, about Mortimer as a boy and George and the things he used to get up to with him; presently he grew hard again and this time it was quite different. He never expected this, as Mrs Bennett moaned and bucked beneath him. 'Harder . . . oh my beautiful sailor boy.' Ladies were supposed to lie back and think of England.

Mrs Bennett woke him early; he reached for her and they did it again. 'I've enjoyed it,' she said at the door, 'but don't go away thinking I sleep with any man at all. You're the first one since my husband was killed. And if I didn't have some feeling for you, quite apart from the fact that you're far too young to be risking your life in this awful war, I'd never have let you touch me.'

'I told you to walk Mrs Bennett home, not screw her! Enjoy it? Since you're looking so darn pleased with yourself, there's a pile of chart corrections and correspondence to be dealt with by yesterday, and Able Seaman Hawkins from your division is in the police cells ashore, so you can go and sort that out before you do anything else.'

Mrs Bennett sent him a handsome pigskin wallet for his eighteenth birthday the following week, and a letter bidding him to come and see her the next time he was in London ('Scented writing paper, Pilot?'), but he hadn't yet. He wasn't sure why.

He transferred the reins to his right hand, thumped the cold-numbed left on his knee until the circulation returned. On up the track past Fenwick's farm, lean out to open the gate, manoeuvre Omega through, and shut it behind. He pushed her into a canter at the top, not that she needed any urging. 'Settled down now, girl?'

He had a sense that his father was trying to distract himself; this morning he had wanted to know all about *Ostorius* and how a destroyer compared with a battleship. He had given him an edited version, aware that he, like his father, was watching his flanks. The old man was interested, but he couldn't tell him what it meant to be away from *Oudenarde* and the howling boredom of the battle squadrons swinging around their buoys in Scapa and Rosyth; he didn't know about Dauncey, of course. *Oudenarde* was six hundred feet long and 32,000 tons; there were over a thousand men aboard her. *Ostorius* was 260 feet and a thousand tons, with eighty men. In *Ostorius* there were only five officers apart from the captain; they lived and worked on top of one another; there was something of the old oneness of *Hyperion* days, although the rest all ragged him and called him a dangerous Bolshevik intellectual since Number One found him reading *War and Peace* in the wardroom. The ragging had in fact slackened a bit since two midshipmen had joined them from *Queen Elizabeth* for training and he was no longer the youngest in the wardroom. 'Are they keeping you busy, Robert?' He was Navigator, Action Officer of the Watch under the Captain ('If you run me aground I'll have the balls off you!'), correspondence officer and general dogsbody, as befitted the junior commissioned officer on board, and more interestingly, Boarding Officer, though he had to admit that, while his boarding party practised enthusiastically and assiduously, smeared with burnt cork and hung about with revolvers and cutlasses, they had yet to board anything in anger.

'And what about this captain you seem to admire so much?'

'I'll give you a week,' he was told on joining. 'The Old Man eats subs. How long did the last one survive? Ten days?' 'I've no room for passengers. If you don't come up to *my* standards – I don't think much of Their Lordships' standards, the idiots they've sent me in the past! – I'll have you over the side before you know what's hit you! . . . Seventeen? And still with the cradle marks on your arse! Are you shaving yet? . . .

Struck a sub-lieutenant? Do you make a habit of assaulting your superior officers, Mr Thurston?' 'No, sir.' 'Now's your chance. I need someone to spar with. The First Lieutenant's getting a bit windy.'

Mortimer had his own methods of dealing with things, disposed of his three months' stoppage of leave by looking up the regulations and declaring that those under punishment must have sufficient opportunity for exercise, and ordering walks ashore under escort of an officer of at least lieutenant-commander's rank. But he had taught him a lot – 'Knocked off a few of your rough edges, Pilot.' 'Knocked' was the right word, those chill early mornings on the iron deck; 'Come on, Pilot! Hit me!' He found out after the first couple of sessions that Mortimer had been naval welterweight champion two years running before the war. Had it not been for Mortimer, and the intervention of Rear Admiral Wyatt from *Oudenarde* which had got him the appointment to *Ostorius* in the first place, he would still have been a midshipman in *Oudenarde*, under a cloud and reported upon to Their Lordships every quarter.

He slowed Omega to a walk for the steep bit, reined in. A vast vista of Northumberland laid out before him in the grey winter light. A greyish winter greenness now, stone walls and huddled farmsteads, further off the gaunter swell of the Cheviots. It was a view which always made him ache inside, even when he had not been away from it for a year and a half; he wished that he could draw properly and so capture it to take back to the ship. That was something they would rag him about. It was enough to be have a brother who wrote poetry. 'Poetry, Pilot? I will not have my officers reading poetry. Next thing they'll be writing it!' He had not really been close to Edmund, who was five years older and just about to leave prep school when he went there, and went on to Winchester and New College

282

while he went to Osborne and Dartmouth. He and George had always treated Edmund as a bit of a joke – 'He'll never *do* anything, he'll only write a poem about it' – it was difficult to think of him as a fighting soldier. Edmund usually retorted that it was the fool of the family who went to sea. George had only transferred from the Northumberland Hussars yeomanry to the Fusiliers on commissioning 'to wet-nurse Edmund' or so he claimed. Now any chance to get to know his eldest brother had gone. Both gone now; George missing, presumed killed; there had never been any firm news; Edmund died of wounds.

He neck-reined Omega round, dropped down to level pasture, white from the night's frost where it was shadowed by the drystone wall. He let the reins slacken, pushed Omega forward into a gallop, the muscles of her quarters bunching to drive her on, a sudden breeze fresh on his cheeks.

# — Chapter Twenty-Four —

'Calmed down now?'

'I apologise for my behaviour yesterday. It was uncalled for.'

'Don't apologise. On the contrary, we're getting somewhere. In my peacetime practice this would have taken six months, with you seeing me five days a week, and paying me three guineas a week for the privilege. Do you feel any different today?'

'I'm not sure . . . Refreshed perhaps? . . . It sounds silly . . . I've been thinking. I think the same thing must have happened to my father.'

'Go on.'

'I'm not sure of the exact details, but my grandmother died when my father was about three – cholera – and he was sent home, and it must have been worse than it was for me because he hardly saw my grandfather again until he went out to join the regiment. My grandfather used to say that he never went on furlough until the Canal was built.'

'And the only way to survive was not to feel. Rather unfortunate that your mother died young as well as your father's, and the pattern has repeated itself.'

Campbell made one of his abrupt changes of subject, yet he sensed it was not entirely a change. Had it been his own idea to join the Navy?

'Yes.'

'What did your father think?'

'That it was a good idea. He said the discipline would

be good for me, and I suppose he thought I would be provided for.'

'Why the Navy, since there was a strong army tradition in your family?'

'I'd always been interested in ships and sea things. I don't know why.'

'Anything else?'

Think. ('Why do you want to join the Navy, Thurston?' 'To serve my country, sir, and to make something of myself.' 'Thank you, Thurston. Would you ask the next candidate to come in.') 'I suppose I wanted to do something a bit different. My grandfather was Commandant of the Guides, my father was in the Guides, my brother George was going into the Guides. It was a bit . . . obvious? I must have wanted to plough my own furrow. Anyway, I didn't have to wait long. That was part of the attraction.'

'The Navy's catch-'em-young policy. How did your interview go? I always ask this, the answers can be quite amusing.'

('Hobbies . . . I see you live in the country, Thurston. Do you ride?' 'Yes sir.' 'So do I. Devilish good for the liver. Hunt?' 'Yes sir.' 'Got your own pony?' The Admiral had become conversational. 'Yes sir.' He thought he should say something more, so continued. 'He's five, fourteen-one, dark bay with a white fetlock near-hind, and he's called Rocket because he goes off like one sometimes.')

He had been rather lucky, because the Admiral at his interview had been a hunting man and he spent most of the time telling him how he had got Rocket unbroken last year and was breaking him on his father's instructions. ('My father tells me what to do, and my grandfather, but I do all the riding.') He thought he must have blown it, because none of the things they were supposed to ask came up; the number of the taxi he came in, the colour of the hall porter's hair, but to his utter amazement as he was going out he heard the

Admiral say to the rest of the board, 'Just the sort of bright lad we're looking for.'

Campbell grinned. 'Weren't you a bit young for bronco busting?'

'No, it wasn't like that at all. You take it all stage by stage. We'd been working on him for most of the summer holidays before I even got on his back.'

'Only joking, but it's not all that usual to give an eleven-year-old boy an unbroken pony. What do you think was behind that?'

Another of Campbell's open-ended questions. 'My father used to say that the best horse was the one you'd trained yourself, and there was . . . something special . . . in starting with a completely green horse and making something of him. Starting with him all over the place and finishing with him balanced, schooled, the lot. And you only had yourself to blame if he turned out to be no good!'

'Go on.'

He had to draw breath, and think again. 'I learned a lot from breaking Rocket. I couldn't just mess about on him or be slack. I had to be careful of his mouth all the time. The pony I had before him would take anything, but if I messed about with Rocket I'd ruin his legs or his temper. In the end he'd do anything for me. He'd go down a slope like that,' he indicated with his hand, 'without a bridle, and he'd do flying changes in a straight line when he was in the mood.'

'Obviously it taught you a lot about horses, but what else?'

Think. 'Having to discipline myself, and having to work for something important.'

'That was obviously something your father believed in. What else?'

'He expected us to stand on our own feet, and he was pretty strict.'

'High standards?'

'If you were going to do anything, you did it properly.'

'He expected a lot of you?'

'He did. What's so wrong with that?'

'Did he expect a lot of your brothers and sister as well, or just you?'

'All of us.'

'And what if you failed to do things properly?'

'We didn't. It was good training.'

'Hm. That's very interesting.' Campbell took off his spectacles. 'Let's just draw things together for a moment. Once again you had an early lesson in the value of self-discipline and hard work. Nothing wrong with that, of course, but in your case you tend to use them as a kind of defence mechanism. Keep everything under control, throw everything into your work. A useful sort of defence mechanism. You get personal satisfaction, approval and all the rest, all your awkward emotions are held down, and the world gets one of the willing horses without whom nothing could function. Basically, a good system. However, when things do go wrong and that little fellow inside starts demanding some attention, your reaction is to work even harder, be even stricter with yourself and trample the little demon down as hard as you can. Up to a point the system works well enough, but it can't go on for ever. Even starting at a disadvantage it's taken a tremendous emotional hammering to break you down, and without the war you might well have continued to function quite happily on those terms. Only now the whole system's become so overloaded that it can't take any more, but you're still reacting to yourself in the same fashion. To take a razor and slash yourself with it is, in a sense, a perfectly logical outcome. It's also one of the most angry things you could have done. If you're rotten right through, and have failed to meet your responsibilities, then self-destruction makes a logical conclusion. Actually, you're far from being a failure.

Your admiral can't understand what's happened to you because, and I quote, "He's too bloody perfect." You need to get used to the idea that you're not such a bad fellow really.' He paused.

'What sort of relationship do you have with your father now?'

'We got on all right. I don't see him much, but we get on.'

'Close?'

'No. I like to think I get on better with my son than my father did with me, but I don't know.'

'I'd be surprised if you were close.'

'. . . I don't hate him if that's what you're thinking. Maybe I feel sorry for him. I don't know. He must have had a pretty hard time of it. I . . . He joined the Guides when my grandfather was in command. I doubt if he was ever allowed to forget whose son he was. He must have been a good officer . . . When I was small he would take us around the horse lines, and even then it was obvious that the men thought a lot of him and he was good with them.'

Twitch left en route for England. 'Six weeks of telling Sigmund all my innermost secrets, and I'm still bloody well twitching!' he declared in exasperation. He would go on leave, then a shore job, and eventually back to sea, though not in submarines. 'I've had my fill of them. Some other poor bugger can take over. I'm going to get into escorts and do some depth-charging myself for a change.' He would miss Twitch, he made them all laugh. 'I took my patrol report to Captain S/m as usual, sat there twitching non-stop. Ended up bashing my nut against the bulkhead and knocking myself out cold. I came to with poor old Captain S/m bending over me and saying, "My dear boy, lie down quietly and wait for the ambulance." And here I am, still twitching.'

Thurston was inspired to do some drawing and produced a cartoon for Twitch to take with him, captioned, 'Solved, the problem of Perpetual Motion'. Campbell heard about it, and was provided with a representation of Thurston rising from a couch bolt upright with steam coming out of his ears, exclaiming, 'What I think is none of your business!' Beecham came again, warily, avoiding contentious issues and therefore with little to say. Commander Nicholls wrote, unexpectedly, saying he was sorry to hear he was still sick, and enclosing a bottle of brandy for medicinal purposes.

Thurston went to see the surgeon who had operated on him, who went over his hand with a needle and declared himself hopeful that the full use and sensation would return. 'The main thing is to keep using it, once you get the plaster off.' He got rid of the sling, though the plaster had to remain on another fortnight. Spencer came for his washing every other day, cleaned his shoes and good-naturedly agreed to do some pressing for the Commodore. He started running again, doubling round the hospital grounds first thing in the morning with Frank Gillam and the midshipman. A temporary hiatus in the mail was sorted out and he had three letters from Kate in one day.

'I think you're ready to tell me about the sinking.'

Just that. No preliminaries. 'Which one?' he said to buy time.

'You know very well which one. Though if you want to tell me about the other one as well?'

Stop that infernal grinning! He uncrossed and recrossed his legs, swallowed hard.

'Come on. When did it happen?'

3 November 1940, at approximately 2350, the time his watch had stopped, on passage from Gibraltar to the Clyde, hit by two torpedoes fired from an unidentified U-boat in a position some seven hundred miles south-west of Bantry Bay.

A panelled room in a requisitioned building in Liverpool, his swollen and aching feet shod in someone else's carpet slippers, sinking into a deep-pile carpet, a long polished table and arms heavy with gold lace in front, a gentlemanly inquisition.

'We were at Cruising Stations. I had handed over to the Officer of the Watch just after 2300.'

'Did you consider Lieutenant Galbraith to be a competent watchkeeper?'

A loaded question. 'He was a very experienced Merchant Service officer. I found him thoroughly reliable and highly competent.'

A muted exchange. The president of the enquiry looked at him quizzically. *De mortuis* and all that; he was on trial for Galbraith's reputation as well as his own, but it was true, Galbraith had an Extra Master's ticket and had commanded one of Brocklebanks' ships on the Calcutta run.

Until now only the enquiry had heard the full story, and even then it had been in a depersonalised form. Stumble on through it, with many hesitations, long pauses while he tried to find the words or fell back on terse formality, looking everywhere but at Campbell, at the burnished toecap of his left shoe. Spencer had been doing them, Spencer who had missed the sinking by being on compassionate leave. He was glad for Spencer, that he would never know the full horror. He was blubbering again, insisting to Campbell that he was all right, a throbbing ache in his plastered arm.

Campbell's calm voice interjecting. 'Relax . . .' He came out from behind the desk and sat next to him, put an arm around his shoulders. Thurston stiffened, looked away from him. 'I know talking about it is upsetting, but it will help in the long run. Relax . . . Don't try to fight it . . . Breathe in. Slowly . . . And out again . . . Slowly . . . Again . . . Deeper . . . Concentrate on doing that.' Campbell got him a glass of water.

'Feel better now? Let's take these things one by one.

You say you should have been on the bridge, but what could you have done which would have prevented it?'

Logically, nothing. The first intimation of the presence of a U-boat had been the first torpedo. Nothing on asdic; she must have been surfaced, trimmed down; it was a dark night and *Connaught* had no radar. 'But that's just making excuses. Dammit, I should have been there!'

Campbell again. 'This is a common enough reaction. Being a survivor is a heavy burden to carry. In spite of all logic, the survivor feels himself to be in some way to blame for the disaster, especially if he happens, like you, to be in a position of responsibility, and condemns himself for his survival when other people have died. But this is one of the things which happen in a war. Obviously it was a tragedy and a terrible waste of life, but realistically, there was nothing you could have done to prevent it. Don't forget that the Board of Enquiry cleared you, and that's hardly a foregone conclusion.'

Yes, but there were so few survivors that he was really the only material witness.

'But you told them the truth, didn't you? A chap like you wouldn't try to cover up for himself.'

'*Captain Thurston, I appreciate that this must be painful for you* . . . ' That panelled room, silence except for his own voice, going mechanically and almost inaudibly through its evidence, and the scratch of the shorthand writer's pen on his pad. '*Captain Thurston, I am sorry, but could you speak up a little* . . . '

'You told the absolute truth, and they found in your favour because there was no reason to blame you.'

Campbell went on, probing relentlessly at the hurt. Would he have achieved anything by going down with *Connaught*?

'No . . . I suppose not . . . but I keep thinking . . . that I should have had the . . . to die with them.'

291

'Guts? Decency? Perhaps that's the wrong concept? How did you get away from the ship anyway?'

'I suppose I was blown to the surface . . . when the boilers burst.' He had told Campbell that already, and Savage before him. 'I got sucked down, and then I was on the surface. I found something to hang on to . . . That's all I can remember . . . I'm all right.'

'What did you do then?'

'I swam around a bit, tried to find out how many had got away . . . Not many. Two Carley floats, about twenty chaps on each, some more in the water . . . Some of those were dead already . . .'

'Now, think carefully here. Isn't it possible that it might take more guts in those circumstances to stay alive and face whatever was coming to you? A Board of Enquiry cannot blame a dead man. They might, but in practice they very rarely do. *De mortuis nihil nisi bonum*. And for the rest of your life you have to live with the fact of that sinking, even though you were not at fault in any way. What do you think kept you going?'

He rearranged his legs, began a study of his right toecap. 'Well, I've always kept pretty fit, and I'm a good swimmer.' It was inadequate, and he knew it was.

'For an intelligent man you're remarkably good at missing things which are right under your nose. Think, there's a lot more to it than mere physical fitness. What were you doing while you were on that raft? What were your efforts directed towards?'

'Keeping the men going.'

'Say that again.'

'Keeping the men going.'

'Exactly. And that's what kept you going. In order to fulfil your responsibilities towards your men you had to stay alive. There are some contributory factors. You're a married man, so, whether you were consciously aware of it or not, you had your wife and family to keep going for. You're trained to cope in emergencies and to keep your head in a crisis. You

292

also have a strong constitution and you're a pretty determined fellow.' Campbell smiled. 'Not to say bloodyminded. You were doing what you could for your men, and that is the main thing which kept you alive. Most of them did die, but remember that some of them did survive.'

''E said to tell you that if it weren't for you 'e wouldn't be 'ere now. 'E said that every time 'e got near the pearly gates you kicked 'im and told 'im to do Eskimo Nell.'

'Do you understand? What have I just said?'

Hesitation, a fumbling for words. '. . . What you're saying is that I kept going because of the men.'

'Precisely. And since a commander is responsible for his men, isn't the idea that a captain should go down with his ship a contradiction?'

He was working his foot up and down, looking out of the window. Sunlight again, a couple of sisters walking past.

'Think about it. In some ways going down with the ship could be very convenient. It could also be seen as a means of evading a duty.' Campbell abruptly moved on. 'What happened after you got back?'

'I went on leave, and my wife looked after me. Then I went to *Marathon*.'

'Why?'

'Because that was the posting I got! . . . And . . . it was like getting back on the horse that's thrown you.'

'Straight back to duty and forget it ever happened. Get back to make sure your nerve is all right. Get back so you have less time to think about it. I've heard all the justifications before. But obviously you can't just forget about something like that and act as though it never happened. What you're showing now is survivor's guilt – you might call it that – like most of the chaps here in one way or another. Frank Gillam for instance. Do you know what happened to him? His aircraft was shot up over Catania; he flew back with

293

his observer badly hit, and managed to make a safe landing, though he was wounded himself. The observer died the next day, and Frank is still convinced that in some way he killed him. Just as you did, he went straight back as soon as his wound was healed, had two deck landing crashes, and then someone finally appreciated that something was wrong, grounded him and sent him here. Try talking things over with him some time. And the Commodore for that matter. It might help you all.' Campbell took off his spectacles and polished the lenses. 'It's not an easy thing to come to terms with, but bear in mind that the last thing your men would want is to have you torturing yourself over their deaths. Remember that when you start feeling badly about it all.'

He sensed that he was on the edge of something he didn't understand, some kind of crossroads. Campbell had put him on a course, but there was something more, something he had to do for himself. He wrote to Kate, finally; filled up twelve sheets of hospital writing paper and to hell with the censor! Campbell took him through the sinking twice more, then through Jutland and the whole stupid business with Dauncey, and falling out with his father. But the thing he did not understand was still there, within a confused mass of conflicting ideas, which was why, a day or two later, he found himself knocking on the door of the hospital's Catholic padre, the Reverend Father Thomas Fitzherbert OSB, according to his nameplate, hesitating and wondering whether to walk away again before the door opened.

'Come in,' and it was too late to turn away.

He had seen Father Fitzherbert before, around the hospital, but it took a moment to work out that he was the padre who had been sitting by his bed when he woke up properly that morning. He began to explain that he wasn't a Roman Catholic but would like a confession if that was possible.

'Father, I tried to kill myself.'

'I know. Tell me about it.' The priest was grey-haired and rather ascetic-looking, with a voice that was low and soft. He indicated a chair, sat down opposite, waited for him to begin.

He remembered now. *Come and see me when you're ready*, half-absorbed through all the despair and drugs. He had the odd sense that the priest had been expecting him. *Oh, rubbish.* Through the catalogue again, but this time there seemed to be a different quality to it, perhaps because this was of his own choice. Or was it simply that he was getting used to it? He wished once more that he still smoked, so as to have something to do with his hands, but you couldn't smoke in front of a priest in any case.

'And I was angry inside, Father, and I had to hurt myself, because of what I'd done. I was alive and . . . whole, and they were dead or crippled, and I had no right to be . . . I didn't deserve to be . . . I couldn't go on like that, knowing that I was responsible . . . and there was no way out of the mess and it was all my own fault.'

The last words came out in a rush. The priest sat on his chair, asking the occasional question to prompt him, but mostly silent. The room was bare, apart from a short shelf of religious books, some of which he recognised from his father's study, and a crucifix on one wall.

'Robert,' the priest said after he had finally dried up, 'Why have you come to see me?'

He was going to say he didn't know, but . . . 'Because I don't know where I'm going, or what is happening to me.'

'And you hope that God, through me, will sort it all out for you.'

'No, Father. Perhaps I shouldn't have come. I'm not

much of a churchgoer really. I just go through the motions.' He started to get up.

'Robert, I would be very surprised if any man was secure in his beliefs, religious or secular, a fortnight after he had tried to kill himself. And it is inevitable that you are confused and uncertain after learning that you are not quite the same man as you always thought you were. There are many who never find themselves. There are others who only do so after profound spiritual trials. You have only just begun, so try to be patient, and tolerant of your difficulties. If I may use my own experience; I decided to enter the priesthood when I was quite a young boy. I was ordained, served in a parish and then as a chaplain with the Irish Guards. The war made me question everything I had hitherto believed. What God worth following would allow that? While on leave I met the sister of one of the officers who had been killed, and for a time I seriously considered leaving my vows. I could no longer believe as I had been taught to believe, and I seriously questioned whether I should remain a priest. Yet I came to realise that there was more to God and to faith, and I must search for it, and I therefore became a Benedictine. I am still searching, and it is a search which will go on, but I know now that God is there. He is in every man, Robert including you. God desires your honest endeavours, but He does not expect man to reach perfection. He has mercy on the frailties of man and will forgive where there is true repentence, and a determination to keep on making the effort. Are you sorry for your sins?'

'I am.'

'You are sorry for a great deal for which you are not responsible. When you tried to kill yourself you believed that you were too wicked to be permitted to live, but in the end no man is so steeped in sin that he must be denied all mercy. You tried to destroy yourself, but at a time when you were in great spiritual torment. *Domine, non sum dignum . . . Lord, I am not worthy to receive you, but only say the word and I shall be healed*. You must realise that many things are outside your control, which you yourself cannot change. Would you have prevented that torpedo hit had you been able to do so?'

'Yes, Father. Of course.'

'You could not prevent the sinking, but afterwards you did what you could for your men. You cannot carry the whole world on your shoulders. That some of your men die despite your efforts to save them does not destroy the validity of those efforts. Do you not think that some of those who survived did so because of your efforts? That some of the men who died may have died at peace because of you? They did not die alone and uncared for, because you, and other men, were there? Survival is a strange thing. Why does one man live, and another die? You cannot condemn a man for the accident of his survival, that the blast wave which killed his comrade missed him, that there was something on the surface for him to grab hold of, and keep himself afloat, that he was the man whom some-one else saved. You, Robert, are alive today partly because of a series of chances; to a religious person, God did not intend you to die then; a secular person would say you had an extremely efficient guardian angel; and partly through your own inner strengths, both moral and physical. Those men of yours who died would not condemn you for your survival, nor can you be condemned because your efforts have not always been successful. God will forgive you those sins which you have committed, but in order for you to be healed you must forgive yourself.'

The priest finished speaking, watched him steadily. Campbell would have posed one of his awkward questions by now, but Father Fitzherbert seemed content with his silence.

'I cannot give you the Eucharist, since you are not

a Roman Catholic, but I will give you Absolution and then you must seek the blessing of your own church. *Dominus noster Iesus Christus te absolvat; et ego auctoritate ipsius te absolvo ab omni vinculo . . .*' The priest's hand on his head, sunlight streaming through the window and setting patterns on the books on the shelf and the floor tiles; a sense of certainty, however transient it proved to be. '*In Nomine Patris, et Filii, et Spiritu Sancti.*' He was reminded obscurely of one of his father's favourite maxims, *Nothing worthwhile is ever easy.*

# — Chapter Twenty-Five —

## Langdon, Northumberland, February 1943

'Well, Robert. I'm not sure quite what I'm supposed to say.'

Thurston stood up, put another log on the fire. Smoke billowed from the grate.

'Time that chimney was swept, but it's getting more and more difficult to find anyone to do it these days. The war, of course.'

The vicar's study was in half darkness, lit only by the lamp on the desk. His father sat opposite him, working his brown-spotted, blue-veined old man's hands. It was the sixth day of his leave. A remorse-stricken Beecham had got him a priority chit for transport home, which meant he had been back in England a fortnight after leaving Alexandria, after a succession of hard-arse flights across Africa to Freetown and then Gibraltar, and the final leg aboard a cruiser to the Clyde. *Merioneth*'s captain was a term mate who gave up his cabin, Spencer buzzed around him as usual and chatted cheerfully about the leave to come. His second DSO came through and Spencer sewed the small silver rosette on to the ribbon. 'Can't 'ave you goin' round improperly dressed, sir.' But the blackness of spirit descended again, the utter strangeness and uselessness of being a passenger aboard another man's ship. Sick at heart and sick in body too; he had come out in a rich crop of boils somewhere in transit, and then gone out with a recurrent attack of malaria the second night out from Gib, one of the bad ones which meant four days in bed on quinine, sweating it out beneath a pile of blankets. Three months' leave, and unfit for sea going duties for another six.

Campbell had told him cheerfully that he hoped he wouldn't see him as a patient again. 'The rest you can do without me, but don't be too proud to let people help you when you need it. Leave the armour plate off. Plenty of exercise and fresh air. That shouldn't be too much of a hardship. And let that luscious wife of yours look after you a bit.'

Campbell had put him on a course, but there was something more, something he had to do for himself. He had written to Kate from Alexandria, finally, filled up twelve pages of hospital writing paper. But the thing he did not understand remained, within a confused mass of conflicting ideas. It was Kate who had persuaded him to try to make his peace with his father.

The thing had hung over him all that day; last night they had arrived too late to do anything beyond eating supper and going to bed. Outwardly everything was the same as ever. The vicar met them off the train at Wooler, doffed his hat to the King's Commission, extended a hand, pecked Kate's cheek. Nothing was said; the thing remained hanging over him all that day; a walk with Kate, the familiar ritual of a bath, a second shave and dressing for dinner, the familiar trappings and inconsequential talk of the meal itself. Surprisingly, it was his father who had provided the opportunity, wittingly or otherwise, suggesting that they broach the bottle of whisky he had brought with him from Gibraltar.

The old man had listened in grave silence as he went through his tale, nodding here and there, a finger stroking the left side of his moustache in his habitual gesture of reflection. He was turning the glass in his hand, studying the clear tawny liquid within. A distinguished-looking man still, with steely blue eyes and the family nose, the hair white now but still plentiful, the moustache still carefully trimmed. He stood up, still poker straight, looking into the blackout curtain. The clock in the hall chimed half past ten. A gust rattled the window pane.

'North-easterly. Going to be a cold night.'

Thurston thought that in a minute he would excuse himself, go upstairs and tell Kate when she came to bed that he had achieved nothing and nothing had changed. He had been naive to believe that the old man could change his spots at his age, or that it could do any good to come clean with him; he should have let him go on thinking that he was due for long leave and a shore job in the normal course of events, and blame his gauntness on the malaria. The vicar was still facing the blackout curtain. He grimaced slightly, with the side of his face which was visible, one polished black shoe tapping on the carpet. Thurston stood up, reached for the door handle.

'No, just give me a moment . . . I'm not much good at this sort of thing.' He swallowed some whisky, turned abruptly to the opposite wall, looking at his own father as a subaltern in the full dress of the Bengal Horse Artillery before the Mutiny, ball buttons and Roman helmet with its mane of red horsehair, then much later in khaki and poshteen as Commandant of the Guides in Afghanistan. 'This is all a bit of a facer. Need time to collect my thoughts.' He managed a wry half smile. 'Much less difficult with a parishioner.' He walked the length of the room, returned to his chair. 'Could you top me up? . . . Thank you. Where did you manage to find this stuff? I haven't seen the Macallan since before the war . . .' The same half smile. 'You never confided in me much, and now that you have, I don't know what to say.'

Thurston recalled something he had overheard between his father and stepmother before they were married, when he was ten or eleven and had brought another bad report home from school, the old man saying despairingly, 'I'll never know what goes on in that boy's head.'

'I'm not really qualified to talk to you about the sinking . . . Nothing like that has happened to me, but . . . I hope . . . I would have done what you did in those circumstances. One can never know, until something like that happens. The other things . . .' The vicar took a deep breath, the words came suddenly. 'You see, Robert, in a way it happened to me. Not because of the war. I didn't see much active service when all's said and done . . . When your mother died . . . Should have told you about her properly years ago, but could never find the right moment, and you never showed much interest in your mother in any case.' He settled himself in the chair, paused to marshal his thoughts anew.

'Better begin at the beginning. I was thirty-four when I met your mother, with three years' seniority as a captain and, I suppose, well on the way to being a confirmed bachelor. It surprised the entire regiment when I went back to India a married man. She was nineteen, pretty, lively, and there was something about her that was a little vulnerable . . . Made me want to protect her. My furlough was drawing to an end; I had gone over to Ireland to catch the tail end of the hunting season, and if I was going to do anything I had to act quickly. Perhaps if there had not been that pressure of time things might have turned out differently. I suppose I was a bit lonely. Suddenly I had had enough of living in bachelor's quarters and spending my evenings in the mess. Anyway, I had known her three weeks when she accepted me, and we were married a month later. The Croziers had very little money after old Sir Charles broke his neck. Everything was bound up in entails and mortgages, and it all went to the heir to the title; your mother and her sisters got virtually none of it. I think they were all happy to see Mary provided for, and didn't stop to consider much else . . . Kate was a lovely girl and very suitable, but I didn't want you to rush things and perhaps make the same mistake. You're a bit like your mother around the eyes . . . Not much like her otherwise.'

The vicar broke off again, turned his glass between finger and thumb. 'I'm not really sure why it didn't work out . . . Let's say your mother and I weren't really suited. Nothing very dramatic. We simply had very little in common after the newness had worn off. My life was bound up with the regiment, your mother didn't really fit in with the other wives. Not sure why . . . Shyness perhaps. And she wasn't strong. Of course the climate didn't do her any good and she had problems with all of you.' He drank some more whisky. 'I'm not putting this very well . . . Narrow hips or something. That's why there were no more after you. You were born upside down and it took nearly two days. I remember vowing while it was going on that I would never subject her to that again. Never felt so useless in my life. They just shooed me out and told me to keep out of the way . . . Sorry, old chap, just one of those things. We had separate rooms after that. She was never really well again. She didn't seem to take any interest in you, and in the end we had to find you a wet nurse . . . You don't remember your mother?'

'Very little.'

'I don't know what it was, but she changed a lot. And as time went on and she didn't seem to get over it, I became very impatient with her. She had had a bad time with you, but she had time to find her feet again . . . I suppose we drifted further apart. I had no idea what to do for your mother, and nothing I did or suggested seemed to make any difference. I've been told since that some women do get like that after giving birth. I even took her to Srinagar, the two of us on our own, but she spent most of the time in bed. I don't know . . . It's a long time ago. When my furlough came round again I went to South Africa. Selfish of me, but it was the real war I had trained for and I wanted to be part of it. One of the happiest times of my life, up on the veldt with the Yeomanry. I started with a squadron, and by the end of my year out there I was commanding the regiment. I'll show you the diary I kept while you're here.'

There was a knock and the door opened. 'Maud and I are on the way up. We've locked up. Don't be too long.' The vicar stood up. 'I hope you're going to save some of that whisky for another night. I'm going to read for a while, so don't worry about waking me.'

'Goodnight, my dear,' the vicar said. Kate went out. 'Lovely girl, Kate. You're a lucky fellow.'

'I know.'

'I have to say that I've been much more happily married to Maud than I was to your mother.'

'I thought that.'

'She's a good woman. She and John Forsythe were good friends to me. Not that there was anything between us until your mother and John Forsythe were both dead. Your mother had remained in India while I was in South Africa. I had suggested that she take you all to Ireland, but she wasn't much interested even in that. When I returned to the Guides I'm afraid nothing had changed. I took to spending my evenings in the mess, being one of those crusty old majors we all joked about as subalterns. I engineered a posting to Quetta, thinking that the climate there would be better for your mother. It was at Quetta that I started to know Maud properly. I'd known her since she came out to marry, but only as the wife of a fellow officer. They were a great help to me, managed to keep me out of the mess on some nights at least, and Maud used to try to jolly your mother along a bit. I wish I knew what would have sorted her out.'

Thurston was standing up with his back to the fire, the whisky glass in his hand, warmth against his legs.

He ran an index finger between collar and neck. Months now since he had worn a wing collar, but the old man insisted on dressing, even when he and Maud were alone. He pushed his left hand into a pocket, found the squash ball that was in there, started squeezing it.

'Will you be able to manage a horse with that arm?'

'No reason why not.' In the event that was the one thing he had left out. He had glossed over the injury as a broken wrist sustained in falling from a ladder, aware that he had not told the whole truth, but it was too much a private thing, and the old man was eighty-four and had had enough shocks already.

'They could do with some more exercise. I'm not getting out so much now. Hunt's meeting at Milfield on Thursday. We could get a day then. Kate as well, if she wants to come out . . . Where was I? . . . It was pneumonia that got your mother in the end. It was a shock. I suppose I had got used to thinking there was nothing desperately wrong with her, that if she pulled herself together and stopped feeling sorry for herself she would be all right, that she was really making a fuss about nothing . . . After all, you were six and she should have been over that long before. You and your mother were in the hills for the hot weather. I was going to join you for my leave a couple of weeks later. There was a signal to say she was ill. By the time I got there she was dead and buried. All the time I had been thinking that it was nothing serious, a false alarm, and I should have stayed with the regiment. Nearly didn't go at all. There were no details. I didn't know how ill she was. But things were quiet and I decided simply to bring my leave forward.' He stopped, poured himself another whisky, pushed the decanter across.

'As I said, it happened to me, and with rather less reason perhaps . . . I don't know . . . I suppose I went to pieces a bit. I was second-in-command of the regiment by then, and . . . I don't know . . . I couldn't seem to do anything. I'd go into the lines and just sit in my office. Drinking quite a lot, as well. The regiment carried me. My babu dealt with the paperwork, so all I had to do was sign it . . . I can't remember how long that lasted. In the end the CO, George Parkhurst, simply told me to go on leave and not to come back until I had sorted myself out. Eventually I did pull myself together, but something had changed . . . I had to take stock of things, I suppose, and found that the army was not for me any longer, and I had been . . . going through the motions without believing it for some time before that. I had been telling myself it was just that particular job. Rotten job, second-in command . . . It must be the same in the Navy, one can't do the thing properly unless one believes it.'

The hall clock struck eleven. A dog barked down the road. The vicar stood up, facing the blackout curtain once again.

'I was getting on for fifty by then, still a major, and my chances of promotion were declining. I'd always hoped that one day I would command the regiment, like your grandfather, and when I was a subaltern I believed that if only I did the work I could go much further . . . It wasn't that which made me decide to resign. It wasn't a sudden thing, but I was able to take six months' half pay to consider my future . . . The regiment was very good . . . It was in that time that I decided to send in my papers and apply for ordination. And I've never regretted it.' He smiled. 'I loved the Guides. I did hope I would see one of you commissioned into the regiment. I thought George would, but, of course . . . It still does something for me when the newspaper reports Burma and the Guides are mentioned. But something had gone . . . I didn't want to spend the rest of my career presiding over boards of enquiry on Sowar Dost Mohammed's missing stirrup leathers . . .

'Eventually I married Maud, as you know, and took

orders, but there was a difficult period when I was making up my mind to resign, and wondering whether it was the right thing to do, when I had four children to think of, and whether I should have done more for your mother . . .' He drank some more whisky. 'I'm not making excuses. Obviously I could have done more for you children at the time . . . Too bound up with my own affairs . . . I remember seeing you off at Bombay, when you went to school, and you were a funny little fellow with fair hair and blue eyes, and you sent me a postcard from Port Said, full of spelling mistakes, saying that you had made "friends" with the men in the "enjin room" and the next time I saw you, your eyes had turned grey and your hair dark brown, and you behaved as though you hardly knew me.'

The stiff muscles of his arm were gradually loosening. Surprising that the old man had mentioned it. For him illness or injury were things to be ignored and fought through. The light from the lamp was reflected off the photographs of George and Edmund on the desk. Two smooth unformed faces, frozen for ever at the ages of nineteen and twenty-three, the grenade collar badges of the Northumberland Fusiliers. And himself, a bare three years ago, but before his world had broken apart. Was he still the same man as this square-jawed stranger who bore his name, standing on *Connaught*'s quarterdeck, telescope under arm, smiling, confident, in command of himself? Nothing could be the same again; he had lost his way and must find another. And the old man. ('I don't hate him, if that's what you think. Maybe I feel sorry for him. I don't know.')

'You and George were a couple of young rascals. Never had the slightest trouble with Edmund . . . Or Alice . . . Pity she doesn't seem interested in finding a husband. We'll have to get her up while you and Kate are here. Of course, she's very busy at the moment . . . Hospital's short-staffed at the moment . . . You were very independent, and there were times when nothing seemed to touch you. On the occasions when I disciplined you, you never moved, never flinched, simply walked away afterwards without a word, and as like as not did the same thing again.'

'Find out what Robert is doing and tell him to stop it!'

'Maud used to say you were Kipling's cat who walked by himself.'

The vicar had begun to ramble a little, perhaps from the whisky, perhaps from relief that he had got through his main disclosure. 'Have you seen anything of Arthur Hancock since you got back?'

'Briefly. Seems to be in good fettle. He hasn't changed since we were lads.'

The vicar poured himself another glass. 'This had better be my last . . . Shouldn't keep Maud and Kate awake . . . When you came back after Jutland . . . I didn't know what to do for you . . . You were obviously distressed, but you wouldn't let me near you . . . spiritually speaking. Or anybody else, not even your grandfather . . . You seemed to keep everyone at arm's length. The night you woke me up, and I told you to go away . . . Five minutes later I was cursing myself for a fool. I came to find you, but you were nowhere to be seen.'

'I took Rocket out. Over the fell bareback. Must have been trying to break my neck.' He let the squash ball drop.

'I knew there was more to it than you had told me, but . . . I could never talk to your grandfather either . . . I was furious with you when you went to Arthur Hancock's . . . and when you wouldn't come home when you had leave . . . and the way you would only write to Maud and your grandfather . . . How long did that last? . . . You must have been upset about George . . . Still miss him, and Edmund too, but not in the same way. I get his poems out every so often

308

'. . . I suppose I didn't handle it too well, not prepared to make the first move. Maud kept telling me to offer you an olive branch, so did your grandfather, but I wouldn't. I didn't know whether you would turn up when Edmund was killed . . . I was very glad to see you.'

'I don't know whether I would have done if I hadn't been ordered to, in effect. I thought you might throw me out, and I came walking up the drive thinking I might do better to kip down in the hayloft.'

They both laughed.

The vicar stretched his legs towards the fire. 'I'm very glad to see you now. I wish . . . that the circumstances had been otherwise, of course . . . I mean . . . that I'm sorry you've been ill, and you've had a bad time, but glad to see you all the same . . . Nothing like the air up here, and Mrs Armstrong's cooking will put some flesh on you . . . Great advantage living in the country. How young Arthur Hancock can bear to live in London . . . We'll get out for a proper ride tomorrow, go over to Bamburgh or somewhere, leave the ladies at home.'

He stood up, paused again, then said abruptly, 'You'll get this place when I'm dead, you and Alice. It goes to Maud for her life, then to you two in equal shares. Up to you what you do with it, of course, but I'd like to think of one of you living here. If anything happens to you, and you're not going to be ashore for ever, then your share goes to Young George, on trust until he's twenty-one. Calvert advised that.' Calvert was the vicar's solicitor. 'And there are some investments your grandfather left. Calvert has a copy of the will, and there's another in the desk. Maud knows about it . . . I think we had better get to bed. Maud fusses me these days. So does your sister. Keeps telling me I should slow down at my age.' He snorted through his nostrils.

An arm rested across his shoulders. He turned his

head, looked at his father's eyes, piercing blue beneath their bushy brows, marking the professional soldier of forty years ago. 'Goodnight, Robert, and thank you.' The hand squeezed, and then dropped.

'Goodnight, Father.'

'Kate did say she'd locked up? Memory's not so good.'

Kate was sitting up in bed, deep in a book, wearing a pyjama jacket of his over her nightdress. 'Langdon is just as I remembered. Arctic. How did you get on with your father?'

He was starting to undress, sitting on the edge of the bed to take his shoes off. 'Better than I thought . . . The odd thing was . . . that there was nothing really new. I knew already, or at any rate I had worked it out. I wasn't very surprised, in the end . . . Easier to face the *Seydlitz* again . . . But I'm glad I did . . . finally.' He was smiling, half to himself. 'I'll tell you properly in the morning, when I've had time to digest things a bit.' He unfastened his collar, laid it and the studs on top of the chest of drawers. 'How did you get on with Maud?'

'Oh, we had a pleasant evening on the church flowers, and what a dreadful child you used to be!' She laughed, and tossed the pyjama jacket to him.

In the first hours and days after his return there had been a tension between them, not just the usual shyness and strangeness which came from long separation. He was sleeping badly again, and waking up shouting from the dream, and there was a row his first night back, when he told Kate he would use the spare room so as not to keep her awake. He caught himself snarling at Helen, then heard her asking Kate, 'What on earth's happened to Dad?' It was easy for Campbell to say don't try to hide your feelings from your family. 'Let them accept you as you are. Your wife sounds a perceptive woman. She'll know more than you realise.' In a

310

way it was a relief that George was already back at Dartmouth after Christmas leave. The letter he had written Kate in Alexandria had remained in his pocket, unposted, once it was clear he was going to be invalided home. 'You'd better read that. I'm going for a walk.' He took the dog out, gave Kate half an hour, wondering how she would take the contents, how he was going to face her when he got back. 'Oh love,' was all she said, and put her arms around him and held him close.

He got into bed alongside her. 'Do you want the light off?'

'Not yet. I'm not really sleepy. Oof, your hands are cold!'

'Is that better?' He put an arm round her, pulled her against his chest.

'Your feet are cold too.'

'All right, Nanny, you can knit me some warm woolly bedsocks!'

Kate's body was warm, her breast soft to his chest. He kissed her, working his way round to the nape of her neck, one hand searching for the buttons of her nightdress.

'Oh love, I did miss you.'

'I missed you too. Yes sir, no sir, and when the Old Man laughs we all laugh. Do you know, the only man aboard who didn't treat me as God Incarnate was Spencer?'

'I like Spencer. He's sweet.'

'I must tell him that.'

'You take Spencer for granted.'

'I know, and I'm going to take you for granted in a minute.' Her hips moved to allow his knee between hers, so that she was half straddling his thigh. They kissed again, lingered over it. Kate's body was familiar, but he had been away from her a long time; there was all the sweetness of rediscovery. He stroked, then kissed her breasts, found with his fingers the differing

311

texture of the birthmark. She held his head to her, fingers in his hair.

She giggled. 'What would Spencer say if he saw us like this?'

'Spencer would be profoundly shocked at you. He thinks you're a real lady. And you're behaving in a most unladylike fashion just at the moment.'

'And who is the cause of that?'

'Now that's different.'

He ran his hands over her hair, loose now and long, so different from the close-cropped growth on his own head. Suddenly he could wait no longer to be inside her. 'Kate.' He slid slowly in and out, matching her movements, then quickening, becoming rough and hard, as detachment was lost and all sense of self. She moaned, clutched at him, whispered formless words of love into his ear. He wanted the climax to come, yet he wanted this to go on, not be ended, all life, all meaning, concentrated into the thrusts, the shuddering uncontrollable salvoes.

'Bob, are you awake?'

'Just about.'

'You look indecently comfortable.'

'I am indecently comfortable.' The breast was against his face, her fingers stroking the other cheek.

'I'm glad you're home,' she said after a pause.

'In spite of everything?'

'In spite of everything. Just don't get yourself into that sort of state again. I don't think I'll ever understand you men. What's so dreadful about a shore job? I never realised anybody could be as stupid and short-sighted as Rear Admiral Beecham! And sometimes you can be just as bad.' Her fingers touched the raised purple weal inside his wrist. 'There's something badly wrong with a system that lets that happen . . . But at least you're all right, more or less, and they're not going to make you go straight back. I might even see a bit of you now, unless they send you to Iceland or Freetown or somewhere.'

'Anywhere but the Admiralty!'

'Beast!' She shifted and came to rest with her head on his shoulder. 'And you're safe, and out of it for a while. Do you know, there have been times when I've wished you'd been a bit more badly wounded, so they would have to downgrade you permanently. It sounds awful, I know. Just damaged enough to be out of it for good.'

He was silent for a time, moved his arm across her back. 'Did you mean all that, what you said just now?'

'Of course I did, you great hairy sailor! Because I love you! I've loved you ever since I first saw you pushing that stupid motorbike!' She wriggled about inside his arm to get herself comfortable. 'I don't know about you, but I'm going to sleep. And so should you, if you're going to be traipsing over the fells with your father.'

'How did you guess?'

'Feminine intuition. Actually, Maud told me that your father has been saying that having you here would shake him out of his complacency and make him get out a bit more . . . Anyway, darling, I'm going to sleep.'

Left awake, he stared into the heavy darkness for a moment, relaxed and content, as if he had been on a long journey, which, though not yet over, was approaching its goal, coming down from the heights and looking across the plain spread beneath, the legs working with that long easy automatic swing, the body weary but knowing that the end was in sight. *Get yourself fit, and there'll be something for you.*

# — Historical Note —

Although all the characters who appear in *HMS Marathon* are products of my imagination, the events, and the roles of Thurston, Pearson, *Marathon* and the rest take place against a real historical background and are based on actual events.

The island of Malta was under virtual siege by sea and air from the entry of Italy into the war in June 1940 until the end of 1942; the gallantry of the garrison and civilian population being recognised by the unique award of the George Cross to the island by King George VI in April 1942. Great efforts were made to supply Malta by sea; at one stage supplies were brought from Gibraltar by submarine, and on several occasions the minelaying cruiser *Welshman* ran the blockade in the guise of a Vichy French destroyer. A number of convoys were despatched to Malta from both Alexandria and Gibraltar, most of which suffered heavy losses, particularly during the crucial summer months of 1942. The best known was Operation Pedestal, the survivors of which, including the tanker *Ohio*, reached Malta from Gibraltar on 15 August 1942. However, this was by no means the end of the siege, which was effectively broken in the last weeks of 1942 as a result of the Torch landing in Algeria and Tunisia on 8 November and the advance of the Eighth Army out of Egypt following the Battle of El Alamein.

Operation Stonehenge is based on a little-known convoy of four ships which reached Malta from Alexandria without loss on 20 November. *Marathon*'s role follows in broad outline that of the cruiser *Arethusa*, which was severely damaged by an aerial torpedo on the evening of 17 November and reached Alexandria by tow from the destroyer *Petard* five days later (see *Fighting Destroyer* by G. C. Connell for a *Petard*-eye view).

The cruiser escort for this convoy was formed by the 15th Cruiser Squadron, commanded by Rear Admiral A. J. Power and comprising HM Ships *Cleopatra, Arethusa* and *Euryalus*. Despite its beleaguered position – these were the only heavy ships left to the Mediterranean Fleet – the squadron had something of a reputation for 'bull': the Officer of the Watch did indeed wear a sword when in harbour. Rear Admiral Reginald Beecham is, however, a totally fictitious creation, as are all the ships.

*Marathon*'s earlier career also encompasses actual events. A number of German raiders, both conventional warships and armed merchantmen, attempted to break through the Denmark Straight into the Atlantic convoy lanes in the first two years of the war, and most succeeded, of which the *Bismarck* is much the most famous. All these were eventually either sunk or bottled up in harbour for the remainder of the war. Some very gallant 'single ship' actions took place against these raiders, notably the armed merchant cruiser *Rawalpindi* against the battlecruisers *Scharnhorst* and *Gneisenau* in November 1939 and the similar *Jervis Bay* against the pocket battleship *Admiral Scheer* on 5 November 1940. Force K, comprising the cruisers *Aurora* and *Penelope* and destroyers *Lance* and *Lively*, was based on Malta from November 1941-April 1942, under the command of Captain W. K. Agnew, and acted as a striking force against German and Italian shipping supplying the Afrika Korps, until air attacks on Malta eventually made its position untenable. I do not know whether the men of Force K suffered much from Malta Dog, but the disease, a form of dysentery, was epidemic among the garrison on land and proved difficult to eradicate.

Readers who feel the participation of Midshipmen Thurston and Hancock in the Gallipoli campaign at the age of fifteen to be unrealistic may not be aware that some four hundred cadets of the Royal Naval College, Dartmouth, were appointed to ships of the Reserve Fleet when the Royal Navy mobilised for the First World War on 31 July 1914. Their maximum age was under seventeen, and some members of the most junior term had yet to celebrate their fifteenth birthdays. It is sad to report that a disproportionate number were killed in the course of the war, some as early as 20 September when the old cruisers *Hogue, Cressy* and *Aboukir* were successively torpedoed in the North Sea by U–9, commanded by Kapitänleutnant Otto Weddigen, some 1,400 officers and men being lost. For the remainder of the war, the length of the course at Dartmouth was considerably reduced, and cadets went to sea as midshipmen at about the age of sixteen.

Gunroom bullying seems to have been a feature of a midshipman's life from Nelson's day and before, but appears to have been particularly rife in the period of the First World War after Jutland, when the Grand Fleet did indeed spend most of its time in harbour and there were insufficient legitimate outlets for youthful energies. Unfortunately, the Daunceys of this world seem to have been all too common at this time; Rear Admiral G. W. G. Simpson records in *A Periscope View* that each of the three ships he served in between September 1917 and the Armistice was as bad in this respect as the others. At times the midshipmen did take matters into their own hands; Simpson mentions that one midshipman, goaded beyond endurance, stabbed his tormentor repeatedly in the chest with a bayonet, and midshipmen from one of Simpson's ships set upon an offender and imprisoned him in his cabin, after which there was no further trouble.

The cruiser *Warrior* took part in the Battle of Jutland as described, though Midshipman Thurston's role is of course fictitious. Shortly after the Grand Fleet from Scapa Flow joined the battle cruisers from Rosyth in action with the German High Seas Fleet, Rear Admiral Sir Robert Arbuthnot led the 1st Cruiser Squadron in to finish off the German cruiser *Wiesbaden*, thereby drawing the fire of the entire German fleet. The flagship, *Defence*, blew up with all hands, including Arbuthnot, whose end was in keeping with his character – his principal interests in life were boxing and motorcycle racing, in which he participated enthusiastically, despite being in his fifties. Two other ships, *Black Prince* and *Duke of Edinburgh*, limped away damaged but sank during the night, in circumstances which are unclear because there were no survivors from either. *Warrior*, also damaged, may have been saved from the same fate by a fortuitous jamming of the helm of the battleship *Warspite*, which made one and a half circles around *Warrior* and drew the enemy's fire away from her at a crucial moment. *Warrior* was taken in tow by the seaplane carrier *Engadine* but foundered the following morning, although most of her crew were saved. Not mentioned in the novel is the unique award of the Albert Medal in gold to Flight Lieutenant F. J. Rutland of the Royal Naval Air Service, who went down a rope between the two ships to rescue a man who had fallen into the water while crossing between them.

Finally, readers who are as puzzled as Thurston by the source of the lines on p 232 may be interested to know that they come from the Old English poem *The Wanderer*, which may date from as early as the seventh or eighth century, as translated by Richard Hamer in *A Choice of Anglo-Saxon Verse*.